LETTING IN THE LIGHT

Cornwall, 1914. Edith Fairchild's good-for-nothing husband, Benedict, deserted her when their children were babies. Now the children are almost adult, Edith and Pascal, her faithful lover of two decades, are planning to leave their beloved Spindrift artists' community and finally be together.

But an explosive encounter between Benedict and Pascal forces old secrets into the light, causing rifts in the happiness and security of the community. Then an assassin's bullet fired in faraway Sarajevo sets in motion a chain of events that changes everything.

Under the shadow of war, the community struggles to eke out a living. The younger generation enlist or volunteer to support the war effort, facing dangers that seemed unimaginable in the golden summer of 1914.

When it's all over, will the Spindrift community survive an unexpected threat? And will Edith and Pascal ever be able to fulfil their dream?

CHARLOTTE BETTS

LETTING IN THE LIGHT

Complete and Unabridged

CHARNWOOD
Leicester

First published in Great Britain in 2022 by
Piatkus
An imprint of Little, Brown Book Group
London

First Charnwood Edition
published 2022
by arrangement with
Little, Brown Book Group
An Hachette UK Company
London

A catalogue record for this book is available
from the British Library.

ISBN 978–1–4448–4934–9

Published by
Ulverscroft Limited
Anstey, Leicestershire

Printed and bound in Great Britain by
TJ Books Ltd., Padstow, Cornwall

This book is printed on acid-free paper

To my grandfathers,
Tom Brand and Bill Spooner,
who both fought so bravely in the Great War

Chapter 1

May 1914

Cornwall

The afternoon was hot and breathlessly still, the only sound the humming of bees on the wildflowers in the high, mossy banks of the lane. The sun beat down upon his shoulders and he mopped his forehead, wondering if his journey would prove to be worthwhile.

He rounded a bend in the lane and saw a great copper beech, its purplish leaves silhouetted against the cobalt sky. Drawing closer, he glimpsed a substantial house behind a wall encrusted with lichens and fringed with ferns. He leaned on the gate to study the house and felt a stirring of interest. Built of stone, it was clad in Virginia creeper. There were two wings, set at right angles to the main façade to enclose a paved forecourt on three sides. Billowing lavender lined the central pathway to an elegant Georgian portico. So, Benedict Fairchild had been telling the truth this time. He'd said Spindrift House was very handsome.

A few yards down the lane was a sign pointing to the Spindrift Gallery and he walked between stone pillars into what had once been a cobbled farmyard surrounded by outbuildings. The doors of an ancient, slate-roofed barn stood wide open in welcome.

Inside the barn, the soaring roof was supported by hefty oak beams and clerestory windows illuminated the paintings, photographs and craftwork on display.

Clusters of visitors perused the exhibits, whispering to each other, as if they were in church.

A woman in her middle years was sitting at a desk, writing in a ledger. She stood up to greet him with a friendly smile. Her hour-glass figure was trim and her hair almost black, except for a streak of silver at the front. 'May I help you?' she asked.

'I'd like to browse.'

She inclined her head and returned to her desk.

He walked around the gallery, studying the structure of the barn. It seemed sound and might be put to any number of uses, a ballroom or a place to hold weddings perhaps. He paused before a group of small watercolours depicting Spindrift House. His eye was caught by the perfect rendering of the copper beech against the azure sky, exactly as he'd seen it, but in the picture, the Virginia creeper on the sunlit stone was ablaze with autumnal colour. Leaning forward, he deciphered the discreet signature. E. Fairchild. There was something so captivating about the painting, he knew he would have bought it even if the artist hadn't been Edith Fairchild, Benedict's wife.

'I'd like this one,' he called to the woman at the desk.

Her movements were graceful as she lifted the painting off the wall and wrapped it carefully in tissue and then brown paper.

'Can you tell me anything about the artist?' he asked.

She smiled. 'I am the artist. I live and work here in the Spindrift community.'

So this was Benedict Fairchild's wife! She was highly personable, with the unmistakable glint of intelligence in her green eyes — a beautiful woman still. Whatever could have made Benedict wish to live apart from her?

'If you'd care to wander around the courtyard,' she said, 'you'll see some of our craftsmen and women busy in their workshops.'

'Thank you,' he murmured.

As he was leaving, a young, dark-haired woman hurried through the door and he took a hasty sideways step to avoid a collision.

'Oh, I'm so sorry!' she said. She gave him a dimpled smile and lowered dark eyelashes over her hazel eyes.

He bowed his head and watched her as she made a beeline for Edith Fairchild.

'Mama!' she said. 'Have you seen my —'

'Pearl, shh!' Her mother put a warning finger to her lips and nodded at the other customers.

Outside, he strolled around the courtyard, where chickens pecked peaceably amongst the cobbles. He peered into a jewellery workshop, where a man and a woman were bent over a workbench, intent upon their craft. The door to a photographic studio stood open. Inside it a girl reclined on a chaise longue before a classical backdrop of Grecian pillars, while the photographer arranged his tripod.

A horse whickered at him over a stable door and he stopped to pat its velvety nose. The rest of the stable block had been converted into artists' studios with glazed doors. One bore a notice on which was written 'Studio to rent. Enquire in the gallery'. There was also an old dairy, a cart shed and a coach house. All looked to be in reasonable condition. Some of them might make suitable staff accommodation or could even be converted into annexes with extra bedrooms.

Excitement began to bubble through his veins.

Taking a furtive glance behind him, he tiptoed along a gravel path between two of the outbuildings. He passed a walled kitchen garden and, through an opening, saw a girl tending neat rows of vegetables. At the end of the path, he found the main garden. There was a terrace at the back of the house and a wide lawn, bordered with hydrangeas and rhododendrons. He slipped into the shrubbery and worked his way to the end of the property, where he unlatched a gate and went onto the headland. Seagulls circled overhead and a brisk sea breeze ruffled his hair.

As he walked across the clifftop, he recalled the day he'd finally threatened Benedict Fairchild with legal action for failing to settle his gambling debts. He'd been dubious when the man offered him a promissory note instead. Benedict was a slippery character, as others had learned to their cost. He had little ready money and nowadays lived on his expectation of inheriting his mother's house in Berkeley Square.

'It's quite simple,' Benedict had said. 'Think of the debt as an investment. If I come into my inheritance, I'll pay you, with an attractive rate of interest, the day probate is settled. But if Mother is still alive in, say, five years, my sixty percent ownership of Spindrift House will pass to you, in final settlement of the debt. You'll love the house and it's worth much more than the debt.'

The murmuring of the Atlantic drew him towards the edge of the cliffs. Catching his breath in delight, he stared at the shining sea, sparkling in the sunshine, and the cove of silvery sand below. His pulse raced. This place was absolutely perfect! He looked back at Spindrift House and, even without having seen the

4

inside, his mind was working out how to convert it into a superb small hotel. The station was nearby and the quaint fishing village of Port Isaac was already popular with summer visitors. Such a project, in this idyllic place, was sure to be a roaring success.

He chewed at his lip while he thought. Spindrift would be an excellent second hotel to add to his investment portfolio and he didn't want Benedict Fairchild's cash half as much as this jewel of a property. The first thing was to have their verbal agreement drawn up officially by his own lawyer, nice and tight, so Fairchild couldn't wriggle out of it. The only fly in the ointment was that, one way or the other, he'd have to persuade the current occupants to leave the house if the project were to succeed. A fleeting pang of regret pricked his conscience at the thought of Edith Fairchild and her enchanting pearl of a daughter being ousted from their home. But no matter what it took, he knew he simply had to have Spindrift House.

Chapter 2

June 1914

London

Edith and Pascal caught the train from Cornwall and arrived at her father's house in Bedford Gardens in the late afternoon. She'd left her childhood home as an eager bride twenty-two years before but her marriage to Benedict had foundered almost before it had begun.

The butler showed them into the drawing room, which looked exactly as she remembered it, with overstuffed sofas upholstered in crimson velvet, gold-embossed wallpaper, heavy damask curtains, dark furniture, and every flat surface smothered with ornaments.

Edith's father, silver-haired and substantially built, came forward eagerly to greet her. 'Did you have a good journey, my dear?'

She kissed his cheek. 'We did. Papa, may I introduce Pascal Joubert? Pascal, this is my father, Edward Hammond.' It was important to her that her sole surviving parent should warm to the man she'd loved for so long.

Pascal, darkly handsome in his new suit, limped forward and offered his hand. 'It is very good of you to invite me to stay, Mr Hammond.' His voice was only lightly accented nowadays.

'Delighted to meet any of Edith's friends, of course,

and young Jasper has told me how much you've supported him in his chosen career. He's delighted you'll be attending his graduation exhibition tomorrow.'

'We have anticipated the event with great pleasure,' said Pascal. 'Jasper is a gifted artist, like his mother.' He smiled at Edith.

'Can't deny I'd have preferred the boy to go into one of the professions,' said Mr Hammond, 'and I might have found him a position at the bank, but he displays a great passion for his art.' He frowned and smoothed his moustache. 'I hope he'll combine it with good commercial sense and make a decent living.'

'I'm sure he will, Papa,' said Edith. 'After all, he wouldn't have been awarded a studentship at the Slade if he hadn't shown promise.'

Mr Hammond waved them to sit down. 'Jasper's worked hard,' he said. 'Young Lucien's not work-shy either. Both your boys are a credit to you, Edith, and I've enjoyed having them lodging with me. It's done me good to have some young blood around the place. I'll miss Jasper a great deal when he returns to Cornwall. Still, Lucien will keep me company here until he qualifies.'

'I can't thank you enough for what you've done for them over the last few years,' said Edith.

'Think nothing of it. When that toad of a husband of yours left you in the lurch, I promised I'd pay all the boys' school fees and so forth, didn't I? Besides,' her father's voice was gruff, 'I'm fond of them.'

'And they're very fond of you.'

'Lucien will join us for dinner,' he said, 'but Jasper may be late. He has to finish setting up his exhibition for tomorrow. Tell me now, how are my granddaughters?'

7

'Pearl has been assisting Pascal's cousin Wilfred,' said Edith. 'Do you remember him? He was a student at the Slade with me, along with my friends Dora and Clarissa. Although Wilfred's best known as an illustrator, he has a thriving sideline in interior decoration. Pearl offered to help him place orders and deal with clients and she's showing an aptitude for the aesthetic side of the business too.'

'Can't she find a husband?'

Edith laughed. 'I'm not sure she wants that yet. And many young women are employed these days, Papa.'

'I suppose she'll be wanting the vote next?'

'And why not?' said Edith, lifting her chin.

'I suspect it might exhaust me, trying to argue with you about that,' said her father, a gleam of amusement in his eyes. 'The country's in a bad enough state with the workers' strikes, without the wretched suffragettes waging war on all men.'

'Any intelligent person, if they stop to consider it,' said Edith, 'must avow that there is great inequality between the sexes.'

'No doubt you're right, my dear, but do these women have to be so strident and unfeminine? I tell you, these continuing dark forces of unrest will bring about the decline of the Empire.'

'Really, Papa, you do exaggerate. If anyone brings the Empire crashing down, it will be the Kaiser.'

'You may well be right about that. Tell me about Nell. Lucien misses his twin very much.'

'Nell's a dear girl. Quiet and unassuming and, like Lucien, she shows great interest in the natural world.'

'Dora and Ursula, who usually manage the kitchen garden at Spindrift House, are holidaying in Germany for the summer,' said Pascal. 'Nell offered to take on

8

the responsibility while they are away.'

'I'm pleased my granddaughters are useful girls, not like some of the empty-headed creatures whose mothers keep inviting Jasper and Lucien to parties and balls.'

The carriage clock on the mantelpiece chimed.

'Good Lord!' said Mr Hammond. 'I haven't even offered you a cup of tea and now it's time to change for dinner.'

★ ★ ★

The following morning, Edith and Pascal took a cab to the Slade School of Fine Art in Bloomsbury. Edith's father intended to accompany Lucien to the exhibition later in the day, after his younger grandson had finished his lectures at the Royal Veterinary School.

The courtyard outside the Slade was milling with students and visitors. Edith looked up at the classical façade of the building with its semi-circular columned portico. 'It's been more than twenty years,' she said, 'and yet it's still so familiar to me. I was happy here. It pleases me a great deal that Jasper has followed in my footsteps.' She smiled up at Pascal, her eyes soft with love. 'Though it was always you he came to for artistic guidance.'

'I have been hoping for this day ever since he was a petit garçon who came to show me his first drawings.' Pascal took her arm and they went inside.

Already, the rooms were thronged with visitors and humming with their chatter. Edith paused in the doorway. 'After living in the country for so long, it's a little daunting. Thank heavens I bought a new hat.' She touched the brim of her rosé-pink straw.

'As always, you bring grace and elegance with your presence,' said Pascal, 'whether you are wearing a chic hat or an ancient painting smock.'

'Flatterer!' she murmured.

'Ah, there he is!' said Pascal.

Jasper was weaving through the crowd towards them. He looked very grown up in a dark suit with a jaunty red carnation in the buttonhole and a matching silk handkerchief in his top pocket. The last-minute nerves he'd displayed that morning over breakfast appeared to have dissipated and he greeted them with a beaming smile.

Edith's heart nearly burst with pride when he showed them his display. Over the years, he'd enjoyed painting seascapes under Pascal's tutelage but now the scope of his work had broadened and she was particularly struck by her son's portraits and life drawings.

'There's a new certainty and confidence in your work that will take you far,' she said. 'And I say that as a professional artist, not as a proud mother. Truly, Jasper, you have the potential to achieve great things.'

He flushed slightly. 'I always strive to reach the standards you and Uncle Pascal set.'

Pascal, his eyes glistening, gripped Jasper's wrist. 'I am so proud of what you have achieved. This portrait is truly remarkable,' he said. 'You are a worthy rival to John Singer Sargent.'

'I'd certainly like to be,' said Jasper. 'Come and tell me what you think of this one.' He drew Pascal towards another painting. 'It's such an interesting mix of media . . .'

Edith hung back, to allow them time together, and wandered around the room studying the other displays. There was real talent displayed here and it was inspiring to see the youthful ebullience of some of the work. Not all of it was successful but there was a willingness to experiment that was inspiring. She was studying an extraordinary canvas, an explosion of brightly hued geometric shapes forming the background to a more traditional oil portrait, trying to work out if she liked it or loathed it, when she felt a touch on her arm.

She glanced up and her stomach turned over.

A tall, broad-shouldered man stood beside her, a quizzical smile on his lips. 'I thought it was you,' he said, his gaze fixed on her face.

Her mouth was dust-dry. 'I didn't imagine you'd stir yourself to visit Jasper's exhibition.'

Benedict shrugged. 'He sent me an invitation and I had nothing better to do. I haven't seen Jasper since he was a boy. Besides, it's good to revisit the place where we were so happy together as students.'

'That was a long time ago,' she said.

'You're still as lovely as you were then.' His voice was low and seductive.

But he was no longer the god-like figure Edith had thought him when she fell in love with him, half her lifetime ago. Time and excesses hadn't treated Benedict Fairchild well. There were pouches of loose skin beneath his eyes and his waistcoat buttons strained over his stomach.

'I could easily fall in love with you, all over again.' He touched the back of his forefinger to her cheek.

Edith recoiled. 'Don't!'

'You haven't changed a bit and it's been . . .' he frowned '. . . how long?'

'Seven years. Seven years since you left me to bring up Roland, the son you and your mistress abandoned.'

11

All the old grievances she held against her husband seethed inside her again.

'It wasn't like that!' he protested. 'I know our marriage encountered a few small difficulties but —'

'Small difficulties?' hissed Edith. 'After deserting me and the children, you returned to Spindrift years later in the blithe assumption I'd welcome you back to my bed. And when I didn't, you installed your latest mistress in my household.'

Benedict rubbed the back of his neck. 'I thought you were having an affair with the Frenchman. Once he'd returned to France and Tamsyn had gone, I offered you and Roland a wonderful new future in Berkeley Square.'

'Wonderful for whom?' Edith challenged in a furious undertone. 'The price I'd have paid for that wonderful future would have been to give up my cherished career as an artist, in order to live with a husband I knew could only bring me further unhappiness. While I sat at home bringing up your mistress's son and being an unpaid companion to your elderly mother, you would have humiliated me by tomcatting around with every woman in town. How could you possibly have imagined I'd welcome that suggestion?'

'Harsh words don't become you, Edith!'

Her new hat felt as tight as an iron band around her head. She massaged her temples. 'I won't quarrel with you,' she said. 'I refuse to allow you to ruin the day when we're celebrating Jasper's success. Why don't you go and say a few words to him?'

'Where is he?'

She pointed to Jasper's display.

Benedict frowned. 'Surely that isn't Pascal with him? I thought he was in France, confined to a wheel-

12

chair after his accident?'

'He's still lame but, thankfully, able to walk again.'

'And he's back at Spindrift?'

Edith nodded.

Catching hold of her wrist, Benedict said, 'Are you still having an affair with him?'

'What affair? You never had any proof of that,' said Edith. She shook herself free of his grasp, her pulse racing.

Benedict stared at Jasper and Pascal's backs as they viewed a canvas together. Jasper had reached the same height as Pascal and they both had very dark hair, though Pascal's was flecked with silver now.

And then Pascal said something to Jasper and, laughing, they turned to face each other. They tipped their heads back in mirth, their aquiline profiles a perfect mirror image.

'My God,' whispered Benedict, 'how could I have been so stupid? There's my proof of your adultery! Jasper's the Frenchman's son, isn't he?'

Edith swallowed. Her heartbeat pounded in her ears.

Benedict laughed harshly. 'You treacherous bitch!' He turned on his heel and shouldered his way through the gathering towards the two men.

Chapter 3

Dizziness swept over Edith and she steadied herself against a wall. The fear that had haunted her for so long must now be faced. But not here, not now! She must stop her husband from ruining Jasper's special day.

She was too late.

Benedict grasped the lapels of Pascal's jacket and shook him.

Pascal dropped his silver-topped walking cane and it clattered to the ground.

'All this time,' shouted Benedict, shoving his face close to Pascal's, 'you and Edith have been laughing at me behind my back!'

The buzz of conversation ceased and a sea of faces turned to study the disturbance.

Edith pushed through the crowd, desperate to reach Jasper.

'Now I understand why that cuckoo in the nest has always been such a disappointment to me,' yelled Benedict. 'I should have realised Jasper wasn't my son . . . that it was your poxy French blood that ran through his veins!'

Jasper's mouth fell open. Transfixed, he stared at them both.

Edith let out a mew of distress and renewed her efforts to reach him. Benedict thumped Pascal's head against the wall. 'Stop it!' she cried.

Dragging Benedict's hands off his collar, Pascal glanced at Jasper's stunned expression. 'We shall discuss this outside,' he said.

'Not bloody likely! I'm going to give you the public thrashing you deserve!' Benedict made a fist and pulled back his elbow.

A woman screamed.

Pascal deflected Benedict's blow with his forearm and forced his fist into the air. Faces contorted and muscles trembling with effort, they struggled with each other. Benedict was by far the bigger man but Pascal had a wiry strength.

Edith thrust herself through the circle of onlookers and grabbed Benedict's sleeve.

He jabbed his elbow backwards into her chest, winding her, then aimed a kick at Pascal's knees. Pascal gasped. Seizing the advantage, Benedict continued to kick viciously at his legs until he sank to the ground.

Jasper shook his head as if waking from a nightmare and threw himself at Benedict. He received a blow to his cheek that sent him sprawling to the floor.

Pascal attempted to protect himself from Benedict's feet, lying curled up with his arms about his head.

Someone yelled, 'For shame! Don't kick a man when he's down!' Two students pulled Benedict away but he shook them off, his breathing laboured and a triumphant smile on his lips.

Edith fell to her knees beside Pascal.

Jasper, jaw clenched and blood trickling from his grazed cheekbone, stood before Benedict. 'You utter piece of shit!' he said. And then punched him, hard, on the nose.

Benedict staggered backwards, an expression of astonishment on his face.

Someone cheered.

Benedict touched a hand to his nose and stared disbelievingly at his bloodied fingers. 'You'll pay for that, you little bastard! And as for you . . .' he turned towards Edith and Pascal, huddled together on the floor '. . . at last you've given me grounds to evict you from Spindrift House. And, believe me, I will!' He turned to the bystanders. 'You all heard them admit to their adultery, didn't you?'

A man with a leonine head of grey hair stepped forward. Stony-faced, he said, 'What I saw, what we all saw, was a savage and unprovoked attack on a physically impaired man.' His voice was calm and authoritative. 'If evidence of such an assault were brought to my attention in my position as magistrate, I'd have no hesitation in sentencing you to face the full force of the law.'

'Take him down!' yelled one of the students.

There was a scuffle and then four men frog-marched Benedict from the room. His yells of protest were heard fading away down the corridor.

Jasper lifted Pascal up, tenderly supporting him. They remained locked together for so long, Edith wondered if they'd ever let each other go.

At last, Jasper drew back. His eyes were bright and his smile a little crooked. 'All my childhood,' he said to Pascal, 'I wished you were my father. And today, that dream has come true. I would rather, a thousand-fold, be your illegitimate son than Benedict's legitimate one.'

One of Jasper's friends helped him to conduct Pascal to the front of the building, while another ran ahead to hail a taxicab.

Outside, Edith tensed when she saw Benedict leaning against a lamp post, watching her with a baleful

16

stare.

'You've made a fool of me,' he said.

A shiver ran down her back at the threatening tone of his voice, but she knew she'd be lost if she allowed him to intimidate her. 'Oh, no, Benedict,' she said, 'you did that all on your own. There was no need to draw attention to yourself by shouting from the roof-tops that you'd been cuckolded.'

His cheeks flushed a deep, angry red. 'I'm going to make sure everyone knows what an adulterous vixen you are.'

'Thereby making even more people laugh at you.'

'A woman who betrays her husband is unfit to be a mother. I'll ensure you're denied access to my chil-dren. My legitimate children, that is. You can do what the hell you like with the frog spawn.'

She hoped he didn't hear the jagged edge of fear in the laugh she forced out. 'The only child now in my care is your mistress's son, the one you foisted upon me. And while we're pointing the finger at each oth-er's acts of adultery, I wonder what your mother will think when I tell her you have not one illegitimate child but two, by different mothers?'

His nostrils flared and he became very still. 'I can do no wrong in Mother's eyes.'

'Since you've been living in her house for the past seven years, I'll wager she'll have had enough of her wastrel son's ways by now. Your expectations of inher-iting her house in Berkeley Square are dependent upon her good opinion of you, I believe?'

Benedict hesitated just long enough for Edith to know she'd touched a nerve. He took a step closer, close enough for her to see a vein throbbing in his temple. 'I've already entered into negotiations to sell my share of Spindrift House and the purchaser will see you off, soon enough.'

His jubilant smile made her feel sick. Was this the truth or only another of his lies?

'And if you ever come anywhere near my mother,' he said, 'I'll make sure you never exhibit your work at the Royal Academy again.' He grasped her shoulder in a vice-like grip.

She wiped a fleck of his spittle from her cheek. 'Then I shall be obliged to discredit you by informing the Royal Academy that the canvas you exhibited there to such acclaim a few years ago was not your work, but mine.' His fingers dug painfully into her shoulder but she suppressed a cry of pain. 'I have all my preparatory sketches. And then there are the other paintings you took from me over a period of several years and signed with your name before you sold them. My friends will attest these are my work too.'

Jasper ran towards them and knocked Benedict's hand away from Edith's shoulder. 'Do you stoop so low as to bully a lady?' he said. 'Are you not content with beating a man who is lame?'

Benedict squared up to him, cracking his knuckles. 'Get out of my sight, you little bastard!'

Jasper sneered, 'Willingly. I hope never to see you again. And you may expect a constable to knock on your door and arrest you for assault.'

'Jasper!' said Edith. She caught hold of his arm. 'Come away now.'

He resisted for a moment but then allowed her to lead him towards the waiting taxi.

★ ★ ★

18

Later that afternoon, back at her father's house, Edith held a murmured conversation with the doctor who had been summoned.

'Mr Joubert should suffer no lasting damage,' he said, 'though the bruising is extensive and will cause him considerable discomfort over the next week or so.' He hesitated. 'The patient didn't care to discuss how he received his injuries but, should you require me to bear witness to the extent of them for any proceedings, please call upon me.'

After her father's butler had closed the front door behind the doctor, Edith paused outside the morning room. Her hands still trembled. It wasn't only Pascal's injuries that distressed her but also the hideous embarrassment caused to Jasper on his special day. She cringed at the recollection of the disdain in the onlookers' eyes. Several women had turned their backs on her, exactly as if she bore a scarlet A for adulteress branded on her forehead. She'd always known that, one day, she'd have to tell Jasper the truth and reveal she wasn't the paragon of virtue he imagined her to be, but she hadn't been prepared to be exposed so soon.

Straightening her back, she went into the morning room.

Jasper stood up. 'I think,' he said, 'you'd better tell me everything, Mama, don't you?'

Pascal, reclining on a day bed, attempted to ease himself into a sitting position.

Edith hurried to help him, fussing over plumping up the cushions and rearranging the rug over his knees to delay the moment when she had to explain herself.

'Edith?' said Pascal. He rested his hand gently on her wrist. His naturally olive-skinned complexion was ashen and his eyes hazed with pain.

'Yes,' she said. She hardly knew how to form the words for what had to be said. Jasper's gaze was fixed on her and she forced herself to meet his eyes. 'I apologise unreservedly for what happened today. Your wonderful exhibition . . .' Her throat closed up while she made every effort not to weep.

'It wasn't all bad,' said Jasper. He gave a snort of laughter. 'After all, no one will ever forget Jasper Fairchild's graduation exhibition, will they?'

'You shouldn't have discovered the truth like that,' said his mother. 'I intended to tell you when you returned home this summer.' She stared at her fingers, knotting them together in her lap. 'Benedict and I were on our honeymoon in Provence when I discovered him in the act of being unfaithful to me. The woman in question later bore him a daughter.'

Jasper's mouth twisted in revulsion. Absent-mindedly, he picked at his thumbnail. 'I ran into Gabrielle in Trafalgar Square a few weeks ago. She's visiting London, employed as a lady's companion. I already know she's Papa's . . .' he hesitated '. . . that is, Benedict's illegitimate daughter and Pascal's niece. She's two weeks older than me. So I assume it was Pascal's sister Delphine that you saw Benedict with?'

Edith bowed her head. 'I thought my world had ended.'

'All that summer I watched Benedict treat Edith with contempt,' said Pascal. 'He was jealous of your mother's artistic talent, which is so much greater than his own. Then, one day, I found her sobbing in the shrubbery. I had loved her from the first day we met and meant only to calm and comfort her. But,' he looked away, 'I took advantage of her. I accept full

20

responsibility for my wrongdoing.'

'I won't let you take all the blame,' said Edith. 'I clung to you, desperate to be comforted.'

'What happened this morning only reinforces my joy that Benedict is not my father,' said Jasper. 'Mama, why did you wait so long to tell me? You must have known I'd be happy to discover Pascal is my father?'

'I didn't even tell Pascal until eight years ago. It was heartbreaking, concealing the truth from you both,' said Edith, 'but you can't imagine my terror when I found I was expecting a child that wasn't my husband's. Benedict would have cast me out if he'd learned of it then. I felt I had no choice but to hide the truth and be a good wife to him.'

'You were the best wife,' said Pascal, 'but he treated you abominably.'

'By the time Benedict deserted me,' continued Edith, 'your brother and sisters had been born. For the past twenty-two years, I've lived in dread he'd discover he'd been cuckolded. He'd have ensured I was forced out of Spindrift and never saw my children again. I feared that, if I told you while you were young, the truth might slip out, bringing down his vengeance upon us all. And now he's told me he's already in negotiations to sell his share of Spindrift. Can you imagine what it'd be like if a stranger moved in? They might make life so difficult for the community that we'd have to leave.'

'I doubt Benedict would make you leave Spindrift,' said Jasper. 'At least, not when you're saving him the effort of bringing up Roland.'

'He would have sent his own child to an orphanage if I hadn't taken responsibility for Roland,' said Edith. 'And Benedict's so furious with me now, I'm

21

sure he'll seek revenge.' She dabbed her eyes with her handkerchief.

'He's unutterably vile,' said Jasper. 'Pascal, you must press charges against him.'

He shook his head. 'I will not allow him to cast a slur upon Edith's character in open court. It would be reported in all the newspapers.' He turned his palms up and gave a Gallic shrug. 'Perhaps I deserved to be beaten for my wrongdoing.'

'Never!' Jasper paced over to the window. 'But I do wish you'd told me the truth earlier.'

'We wanted to,' said Pascal.

'What your father isn't telling you,' said Edith, 'is that the shock of discovering I'd kept the truth from him was the cause of the accident that nearly killed him. It was all my fault.' She closed her eyes, reliving that terrible day. 'He'd longed for a son and felt utterly betrayed that I'd kept such a secret from him. He backed away from me,' her breath caught on a sob, 'and tripped at the edge of the cliff. He fell onto the rocks below.'

Jasper let out his breath. 'So that was why you returned to France, Pascal?'

'I believed I was completely crippled,' he said. 'No longer fit to be a proper, even if a secret, father to you, and I could not bear to be the object of Edith's pity.'

'That was the worst year of my life,' said Jasper. 'You didn't reply to our letters. The agony of being rejected by you was almost worse than if you'd died. When we were reconciled, my heart nearly burst with happiness.'

'I respected your mother's wishes not to tell you I was your natural father because I had to ensure her safety and that of your siblings,' said Pascal.

'I've known forever that you loved each other but I never did understand why you tried to hide it.'

Pascal glanced at Edith, an unspoken question in his eyes.

She nodded.

'We fell in love after Benedict left Spindrift,' he said. 'It has been our great sadness that we cannot marry or live together openly because of our fear of what he might do.'

'Soon he will no longer have the power to forbid me contact with my children,' said Edith, 'because in two years you'll all have reached your majority. Pascal and I have waited so long to live together openly as man and wife. In two years' time we intend to set up house together in France, so as not to disgrace any of you. You must make up your own minds as to whether or not you can accept that we're unable to sanctify our union with marriage.'

Jasper grinned. 'Why would that disgrace me? I'm beyond the pale myself now that everyone knows I'm illegitimate. But you can't leave the community!'

'We'd come to visit every year. The community still owns forty percent of Spindrift, so whatever revenge Benedict tries to wreak upon us, you'll still have a right to stay there.'

Jasper caught hold of his parents' hands. 'And I'll never have to owe him any sort of respect, ever again.'

'I have waited for so long to call you my son,' said Pascal, his eyes glistening, 'that I can hardly bear to have you out of my sight.'

'I'll come home immediately term ends,' said Jasper. 'We have so much time to make up and I must start earning a living. And I wanted to talk to you about the possibility of us setting up summer and Easter painting schools together, Pascal.'

Edith watched her lover and their son, dark heads close together as they made plans for the future. Now she'd laid down the burden of her painful secret and Jasper hadn't castigated her for it, she should have been elated but was still apprehensive about what Benedict might do next.

Chapter 4

June 1914

Cornwall

It was late afternoon but still very warm when Pearl pulled up the pony and trap outside Port Isaac Road station. After a short wait she saw the plume of steam that heralded the arrival of the train.

A few minutes later, Lily emerged, her slender figure laden with an assortment of travelling bags.

Pearl waved and jumped down from the trap to hug her and relieve her of a carpet bag, a tartan rug and a newspaper.

'I can't tell you how pleased I am to see you,' said Lily. 'I nearly suffocated between Bodmin and Wadebridge, trapped in a carriage with two elderly gentlemen smoking cigars.' She stowed her Gladstone bag under the bench seat and settled down next to Pearl with a sigh of relief.

Pearl smiled at her friend's lively chatter. The same age, the two girls had grown up together at Spindrift and Pearl had missed Lily while she was studying for her stenographer's diploma in Truro. 'Congratulations on passing your examination!'

'Thank you.'

Pearl flicked the reins and the trap rolled forwards. 'Did Adela write to you? She's returning home to Cliff House today.'

Lily clutched at the brim of her hat as a gust of

wind threatened to snatch it away. 'It's going to be just like the old times, isn't it? Look out, world! The Three Sisters will be together again!'

'Except we aren't quite sisters,' said Pearl.

'Close enough. Especially we two. It's not surprising really, when you think what devoted friends our mothers are.' Lily tucked a strand of flaxen hair under her hat and gave Pearl a sideways glance. 'I can hardly wait to see Noel again. It's been months, though he did write to me while I was away.'

Pearl knew Lily had a crush on Noel Penrose, the eldest of their friend and neighbour Adela's two brothers, but hadn't known they'd been writing to each other.

'We'll have a wonderful summer,' said Lily, 'but I have a feeling that afterwards nothing will ever be the same again. Once I'm working, there'll be no more long holidays or forbidden trysts playing pirates with the Penroses.'

Pearl laughed. 'We haven't played pirates for years!'

'But we still meet Adela, Noel and Tim in secret. It's ridiculous that, at our age, we can't be open about our friendship because of an ancient feud between our parents.'

'Adela's letter said they'd meet us in the cove after dinner,' said Pearl.

'Yes, Noel wrote to tell me,' said Lily.

Pearl navigated the trap along the narrow lanes, thinking about Adela's horrible father, Hugh Penrose. There'd been a terrific argument between him and Pearl's papa before she was born, over the disputed ownership of Spindrift House. Hugh had hated the Spindrift community ever since.

Lily stretched out her hand to snatch handfuls of

frothy umbels of Queen Anne's Lace from the hedge-row as they bowled along.

'I suppose you're right about nothing being the same again,' said Pearl. 'Adela's mother is intent on finding a husband for her. Once she's married, she'll have to live elsewhere.'

'What about you?' asked Lily.

'I'm not looking for a husband. At least, not yet,' said Pearl.

'I know that! I meant, will you stay at Spindrift?'

'For a while,' said Pearl. 'Working with Wilfred is interesting. He's been at Spindrift all my life, but it's different now I'm no longer a child. He's amusing if sharp-tongued sometimes, but he's taught me so much about interior decorating. Perhaps, one day, I'll have my own business.'

'Then take advantage of this chance by learning everything you can and make your mistakes at his expense,' said Lily.

'Home!' said Pearl, guiding the trap between the stone gateposts to Spindrift's courtyard.

The two elderly collie dogs, Blue and Star, rose to their feet and came to investigate.

The door to Clarissa and Augustus's jewellery workshop door opened and Clarissa hurried out to greet them.

Lily flew into her mother's arms. 'I've missed you so much!'

'Welcome home, sweetheart!' said Clarissa.

As always, Pearl couldn't help noticing how alike Lily and her mother were with their silver-blonde hair, blue eyes and willowy figures. They'd always been very close-knit.

Running footsteps and children's voices came from

behind them and Roland and Rose raced into the courtyard. At almost eleven and only a month apart in age, they'd become honorary siblings, just like Pearl and Lily.

'How's my favourite little sister?' said Lily.

Rose ran to hug her. 'I thought you were never coming home!'

'Is there any news from Will?' asked Lily. Her step-brother had married an American girl a few months previously and was now a lecturer in the University of Chicago's law school.

'I'll give you his latest letter to read,' said Clarissa. 'He sounds contented.'

'He always was happiest in an academic atmosphere.' Lily held out her carpetbag to Rose. 'Help me carry my things inside and I might find you some humbugs. There's one for Roland, too.'

Pearl ruffled her half-brother's hair. 'Roly, will you help me stable Teddy?'

Roland went to fetch the grooming brushes, while Pearl undid the buckles to release the pony from his traces. She put the trap away and watched him while he groomed Teddy and then, without being asked, fetched a bucket of water from the pump. He was a sturdy boy and Pearl thought it likely he'd have their father's stature when he was fully grown. His eyes were hazel, like Benedict's and her own, but he'd inherited his almost black hair from his birth mother. Fleetingly, she wondered where Tamsyn was now and if she ever had any regrets about deserting her son so as to take up a new life without the inconvenient baggage of her lovechild.

'You're very good at this, Roly,' said Pearl.

'Lucien said that Nell and I must be responsible for

28

Teddy while he's away.'

'Well done!' Pearl said and was rewarded with a broad smile. Over the years, the jealousy and then the pity she'd initially felt for her deserted little half-brother had grown into love.

★ ★ ★

Evening sun slanted through the dining-room windows and a warm breeze stirred the gauzy curtains. There were only seven places set for the community's dinner tonight instead of the full present complement of fourteen, since Edith and Pascal were with Jasper and Lucien in London and Dora and Ursula were visiting Ursula's German cousins in Baden-Baden.

Pearl was already seated when Nell arrived, still in her gardening skirt.

'You might have changed,' said Pearl, pulling a leaf from her sister's tangled hair.

'Mama comes to dinner in her painting pinafore,' said Nell indignantly. 'I thought it more important to water the lettuces than to waste time primping for family dinner.'

They heard Lily's voice in the hall, giving a lively account of her experiences at Miss Starke's Training Academy for Lady Stenographers. She entered the room arm-in-arm with her stepfather Julian and Clarissa, closely followed by Wilfred and Augustus.

'I was saying that Miss Starke is a fearful old harridan,' said Lily. 'She inspected our hands for cleanliness each morning, as if we were still in the nursery, before we were even allowed to touch the typewriters. There was no talking and she rapped our knuckles with a ruler if we transgressed. Honestly,' she said, her eyes wide, 'it was worse than being back at school.'

'But now you have your diploma,' said Julian, 'and the world is your oyster.'

'Are you seeking a situation, Lily?' asked Augustus. He sat facing the windows and the sun gleamed on his gold-rimmed pince-nez.

'I shall enjoy a Spindrift summer first.' Lily took a sip of water then added, 'But I'm determined to make my own way after that.'

'Our mothers made us see the importance of never relying on a man to keep us,' said Pearl.

'Not all men are like your father, Pearl,' said Clarissa. She smiled at Julian. 'You need to find the right one, that's all.'

'Plenty of time for that,' said Wilfred. 'Now tell me, Lily, have you spotted yet what's changed in here?'

Pearl held her breath.

Lily looked about her. 'Oh!' she said. 'I was talking too much to notice. It's lovely!'

'I gave Pearl free rein,' said Wilfred. 'I thought she should experiment at home before I let her loose on my clients.' He brushed a tiny speck of fluff off his immaculately tailored jacket. 'She's done well, hasn't she?'

'I chose eau-de-Nil for the walls,' said Pearl. 'Water of the Nile. Isn't that romantic? I wanted the room to reflect the light from the sea. Do you like the frieze?' She was pleased with the sinuous seaweed, cockle-shells and stylised waves winding their way around the room above the picture rail. 'I designed it and Wilfred painted it.'

'It's beautiful!' said Lily. 'It feels as if we're dining in a rock pool.' She smiled at Pearl.

Daisy the maid carried in the tureen of soup then

and everyone turned their attention to their dinner.

Later, after the plates had been cleared, Clarissa and Julian retired to the drawing-room for coffee with Augustus and Wilfred.

'Let's go down to the sea,' said Lily. 'We'll meet the others and watch the sun set.'

A short while later the three girls meandered through the garden and onto the headland. The sea was as calm and flat as a pond.

A warm breeze tugged at Pearl's hair. She peered into the cove, shading her eyes against the evening sun. 'Come on!' She hurtled down the cliff steps.

'What's the rush?' called Nell.

Pearl glanced over her shoulder. 'Adela, Tim and Noel are waiting.' She reached the foot of the steps and flew across the sand.

Adela saw the girls coming and ran to meet them. They hugged, laughing and exclaiming with the pleasure of meeting again.

'It's been a whole year!' said Adela.

'You've done your hair differently.' Pearl patted Adela's honey-blonde bun. 'It's so sophisticated.'

Noel and Tim waved at them.

'Come and sit with us on the rocks,' said Adela. 'I'll tell you about fearsome Great Aunt Sophronia and the ancient fossils who came to play interminable games of bridge with her. There was a hideous man she wanted me to marry. He was the nephew of one of the fossils and had jug ears and hairs in his nose and was at least fifteen years older than me. Can you imagine?' She drew them towards the rocks and they laughed while she and Lily exchanged tales of her great-aunt's vanity and the ghastliness of Miss Starke's Academy for Lady Stenographers.

Pearl sat with her arms around her knees, listening to the chatter and watching Noel watching Lily, who glanced repeatedly at him with a secret smile on her lips.

At last, the conversation dwindled.

'Shall we walk?' asked Noel.

'We must be in before dark,' said Nell.

'Ten minutes,' said Noel. He and Lily strolled towards the sea.

Nell wandered off to look for seashells.

Adela, still talking, hooked her elbow through Pearl's arm.

Tim fell into step on Pearl's other side. They came to a standstill, their toes inches away from the waves lapping the shore. The indigo sky was gloriously streaked with salmon and pink and they watched in silence as the great orange sun sank into the sea, turning it the colour of molten copper.

'We'd better go in,' murmured Pearl.

Lily and Noel were further along the water's edge, silhouetted against the dying light. Lily's arms were linked around his neck, their bodies pressed together as he kissed her.

'Well, well,' Tim drawled.

Pearl caught her breath. Lily had been right. Nothing would ever be the same after this summer.

Chapter 5

June 1914

Cornwall

Pearl held up the cutting of primrose silk to the light at the studio window. She ran the lustrous softness of the material through her fingers. 'This one,' she said to Wilfred. 'The ivory damask is too heavy for Mrs Carruthers's bedroom curtains.'

'Sure?' asked Wilfred. He looked at her intently, giving no hint as to whether he approved of her decision or not.

'Yes.'

Wilfred nodded and smiled.

Pearl heard the clip-clop of Teddy's hooves on the cobbles outside. 'That must be Augustus back from collecting Mama and Pascal from the station.'

'Why don't you run along and have tea with them?' said Wilfred.

Pearl hurried outside and saw her mother and Augustus assisting Pascal in his painfully slow descent from the trap. Once he was on the ground, Edith handed him his stick and held his arm until he'd steadied himself.

'Are you unwell, Pascal?' asked Pearl.

Her mother gave her a brief smile that didn't reach her eyes. 'Hello, sweetheart. There's been a mishap and Pascal's legs are painful.'

Pearl hadn't seen him look so shaky since the

gruelling years when he'd had to learn to walk again. He turned his face towards her and she was shocked to see purple bruising on his cheekbone.

'I am fatigué,' he said. 'The train journey . . .'

Pearl glanced at her mother with a questioning expression but she simply shook her head slightly and mouthed, 'Later.' The girl trailed behind Augustus and Edith as they supported Pascal inside the house. Ever since his accident, he'd had a bedroom and an adjacent studio converted from storerooms near the kitchen.

A short while later, he was settled on his bed. He sank back against the pillows, his eyes closed.

Edith pressed one palm against his cheek. 'I'll come and see you when you're rested.' She ushered Augustus and Pearl out of the room and closed the door quietly behind them. 'Thank you for your help, Augustus.'

'Happy to be of service. Don't worry about stabling Teddy and call me if Pascal needs assistance.'

'Dear Augustus,' said Edith, after he'd left.

'Mama, you look drained,' said Pearl. 'I'll ask Daisy to bring us some tea.'

When she joined her mother in the drawing-room, the windows were open to admit the sea air and Edith was sitting in a wing chair, her eyes closed. 'You cannot imagine how relieved I am to be so far away from all the filth of London and breathing in clean Cornish air,' she murmured.

Pearl crouched down beside her. 'Did Pascal fall?'

Just then Daisy pushed open the door and placed the tea tray on the table.

Once she'd gone, Pearl poured the tea and offered a cup to Edith but her mother's eyes were closed and

34

tears seeped from beneath her eyelids. 'Mama?' she said. A sob escaped from Edith's lips and, alarmed now, Pearl gathered her into her arms and held her.

Edith drew a shuddering breath. 'I'd intended to wait until after dinner when we're all gathered together,' she said.

'Wait for what?'

'I need to make a confession. You see, a long time ago I did something very wrong and I've lived with the shame of it ever since.'

'You?' Pearl attempted a smile. 'It couldn't have been anything very bad.'

Edith fixed her gaze on her lap. 'Perhaps I'm not the person you think I am,' she whispered.

'You're frightening me,' said Pearl. 'Did you murder someone?' She gave a brittle laugh at such a ridiculous idea.

'No,' said Edith, 'but I betrayed my ideals.'

'I don't understand.'

'I hid the truth. Now, I must pay the price. The worst thing is that those I love the most may also suffer for what I did.'

Pearl stared at her mother's bowed head, foreboding tightening her chest. 'Do you remember how, when I was little and I'd done something naughty, you always told me I must tell the truth? You said, although you might be angry, nothing would ever make you stop loving me. Now, I'm telling you the same thing.'

Edith kept her face averted from her daughter's gaze. 'Will you fetch Nell and the others?'

'Now?'

'The sooner the better. And ask Daisy to take the children down to the cove for a game of rounders. I don't want them to overhear.'

Half an hour later, Clarissa, Julian, Nell, Wilfred and Augustus had gathered in the drawing-room.

Edith had remained silent while they assembled, eyes downcast and her hands gripping the arms of the chair.

Pearl cleared her throat. 'Now you're all here, except for Pascal who isn't well, Mama has something to tell us. Mama?'

'I won't keep you long,' said Edith, 'but I have a difficult confession to make.'

'How dramatic!' said Clarissa. 'I've known you a long time and don't believe you're capable of anything too dreadful.'

Edith said hesitantly, 'Something dreadful happened while Pascal and I were at Jasper's exhibition yesterday and it may impact upon all of us here at Spindrift.' She rubbed her eyes. 'Twenty-two years ago, when Benedict and I were on our honeymoon . . .'

After the first few words, Pearl couldn't bear to look at Lily while they listened to the story unfold. She squirmed with embarrassment as she pictured her mother in the grip of uncontrollable passion. And with calm and dependable Uncle Pascal at that, whom Pearl had loved and respected all her life! Suddenly she felt like a child whose world had imploded as dramatically as a tumbling tower of wooden blocks. It shook her that her mother, whose every action had always appeared to be firmly guided by an invincible moral compass, had so spectacularly fallen by the wayside and successfully deceived her friends and family for years.

'And that,' concluded Edith, 'is how it came about that Jasper is Pascal's son.'

'Oh, Edith!' Her best friend Clarissa hurried to her

36

side. 'I would never have judged you.'

Shaking, Pearl folded her arms tightly over her chest. 'I can't believe what a hypocrite you are, Mama! How could you look me in the eye and caution me about appropriate behaviour with young men when you did that?'

Edith's cheeks flamed. 'Because I wanted to ensure you'd never find yourself in a similar situation.'

'Pearl, there's always been one set of rules for men and a completely different one for women,' said Clarissa reprovingly. 'Benedict would have thrown your mother out of Spindrift and left her begging in the streets.'

'But Mama lied!'

'Edith, I remember how you adored Benedict,' said Wilfred hastily, 'but he treated you cruelly. What you and Pascal did was out of character for both of you but, frankly, it was no more than Benedict deserved. Who the hell is he to accuse you of adultery? He was already having an affair with Pascal's sister that resulted in a child. People in glass houses and all that . . .'

Pearl was outraged to hear him make excuses for her mother.

'You deceived Papa by letting him assume Jasper was his son,' she said to Edith. 'How could you live with yourself? And Pascal is no better.'

'I've never blamed Pascal for what happened between us and it wasn't only myself I had to worry about,' protested Edith. 'There was also the welfare of the baby to consider.'

In her mind's eye, Pearl recalled the miserable sight of a young woman, a babe in her arms, begging on a street corner in Wadebridge. Would Papa really have made Mama homeless or was she making excuses?

'Everyone has secrets,' said Clarissa. 'If it weren't for Benedict behaving so despicably, you wouldn't be here now covering yourself in sackcloth and ashes.'

'Nevertheless,' said Edith, 'what I did was wrong.'

'I remember how Papa used to make you cry, Mama,' said Nell in a small voice.

Edith sighed. 'Despite everything, I could never wish I hadn't given birth to Jasper.'

Augustus cleared his throat. 'Does he know?'

Edith nodded. 'Thankfully, he's forgiven me.'

'What has any of this has to do with Pascal being unwell?' asked Pearl, sure there was more to this story.

'Benedict came to Jasper's exhibition,' said Edith. 'When he saw Jasper laughing with Pascal, he guessed they were father and son. He was incandescent with rage.' Her mouth quivered. 'He kicked Pascal so frenziedly that others had to drag him away.'

Pearl gasped. Her papa might have been inadequate as a parent but she'd never thought of him as violent.

'That's shocking behaviour!' protested Julian.

'And now Benedict's hell-bent on revenge,' said Edith.

'But what can he do?' asked Wilfred. 'After all, he's fathered two illegitimate children himself.'

'Apart from exposing me as an adulteress to my clients,' said Edith, 'he threatened to deprive me of my children. And he tells me he intends to sell his share of Spindrift to someone who will push us out.'

'But he can't do that!' said Pearl. 'Can he?'

Edith looked up, her face pinched and pale. 'He owns the greater part of Spindrift House. Our security here would depend entirely on who bought his share. And he could take you children away from me until you're twenty-one.'

'He doesn't really want us, though, does he?' said Nell.

Pearl's mouth was dry. Papa had loved her once. 'Surely he wouldn't make us homeless?' she said.

'Who knows what he'll do next?' said Edith, her voice shaky.

Pearl stood up, her fists clenched. 'Whatever happens, it will be your fault, Mama!' She ran from the room, ignoring her mother's cry of distress.

★ ★ ★

Dusk was falling and the lawn was beaded with dew when Lily and Pearl went to sit in the gazebo. They watched the bats flitting overhead while they reflected upon Edith's confession.

'You never guessed Jasper was Pascal's son?' asked Lily.

'Why would I?' said Pearl. 'I suppose there are some physical likenesses and, now I think about it, the timbre of their voices and some of their expressions are similar.'

'I assumed Jasper learned his mannerisms from Pascal because they were so often in each other's company.'

Pearl reached out to pluck a rose from the trelliswork. 'I'm horribly upset and embarrassed to think of Mama acting like that. Everything I believed about her natural goodness was a lie.' She picked at the rose and crimson petals drifted to the floor. 'Do you think she and Pascal still . . .'

'It's obvious they love each other. They may not share a bed but in other respects they behave like an old married couple. Mother and Julian do share a bed

39

and . . .' Lily pulled a face. 'Suffice it to say that the walls are thin in the coach house and my room is next to theirs. I have to put the pillow over my head if I hear the bed start to creak.'

Pearl stifled a giggle with her hand.

Lily smiled into the dusk. 'Better that than for them to argue. I remember how awful it was when your father brought Roland's mother Tamsyn to live here. Mother said he only did it to spite Edith. You're being too hard on her, Pearl. Your father caused so much unhappiness.'

'I haven't seen him for seven years now but, to me, he was like a prince in a fairy tale. When he made a fuss of me, it was as if I were basking in sunshine.' Pearl bowed her head. 'But he didn't keep his promises. I was utterly miserable when he left Spindrift. I hoped for years that he'd come back.'

She sounded so woebegone that Lily hugged her. 'Perhaps you ought to visit him? Lay the ghost, if you can. But it's Jasper you should be thinking about,' she said. 'I wonder, once it's sunk in, how he'll feel about his illegitimacy? I was horribly bullied about that at school.'

'Did Clarissa ever tell you about your real father? No one ever mentions him.'

Lily pictured her mother's forbidding expression when she'd asked that question. 'Only that he was married and she'd made a dreadful mistake when she was unhappy and confused.'

'The same excuse my mother made, then.' Pearl sighed. 'It's painful to discover the people you love and respect aren't as highly principled as you imagined.'

'I'll make jolly sure I never have a baby outside marriage,' said Lily. 'Perhaps Hugh Penrose and his wife have been right all along in their opinion of the morals of the Spindrift community? After all, Jasper, Roland and myself are illegitimate. And Gabrielle, too.' The hollow ache of shame and dread that Lily had carried inside her heart for as long as she could remember, stirred within her again.

'It never felt to me as if we were growing up in a hotbed of sin,' said Pearl, 'except perhaps when Papa brought Roland's mother to live here.' She gave Lily a sideways glance. 'Still, whatever Hugh Penrose says, I don't think Noel minds at all that you're a love child. I saw him kissing you the other night.'

Warmth flooded Lily's cheeks at the memory. 'Oh, Pearl, I do like him so much! He kissed me a few times before I went to Truro and we corresponded almost every day while I was there. Somehow, you can write things to each other you might not be brave enough to say face to face.'

'Does he have the same feelings for you?'

Lily nodded, remembering the warmth of his lips on hers last time and how he'd whispered she was the most beautiful girl he'd ever met. She'd trembled for quite an hour afterwards and had relived the thrill of it over and over again since then.

'It feels as if a whole new chapter is opening in our lives, doesn't it?' said Pearl.

Lily laughed. 'And I can't wait to read on to reach the happy-ever-after ending!'

Chapter 6

Pearl sat at her desk in Wilfred's studio and stared out of the window, thinking. She was still struggling to come to terms with her mother's confession and there was the vicious attack her father had inflicted upon Pascal... Perhaps he'd deserved her father's wrath but was infidelity justification for such a savage attack on a crippled man?

'Pearl, is there any post today?'

Wilfred's voice broke into her reverie.

'There's an enquiry for you from a Mrs Edwardes,' she said, 'about redecorating her mansion flat in Marloes Road, Kensington. She'd like to meet you next week.'

Wilfred tapped a finger against his pursed lips while he thought. 'Yes, I remember now. I redecorated another flat in that block two years ago. It's likely to be a nice little project and it's most fortuitous that it's come my way now. I've almost finished that commission for poster illustrations for the Garrick Theatre. It would suit me to go up to town and kill two birds with one stone. Write back to Mrs Edwardes, will you, Pearl?'

'May I come with you, Wilfred? I could take notes during your meeting, but really I'd like to see Jasper. What happened at his exhibition has been preying on my mind. I could stay in Bedford Gardens with Grandfather and travel back with Jasper and Lucien when they return to Spindrift for the holidays.'

'Yes, you'll enjoy seeing the bright lights for a

change,' said Wilfred. 'You'd better ask your mother, though.'

'I doubt she'd mind. She's working hard finishing a series of watercolours. And besides,' Pearl hesitated before continuing, 'I'd prefer to be apart from her for a while.'

* * *

The following week, Wilfred and Pearl left their meeting with Mrs Edwardes, discussing the project as they walked along the street. Pearl was pleased by how much attention Wilfred paid to her suggestions.

'I'll escort you to Cromwell Road,' he said. 'We'll find you a cab there.'

Horse-drawn carriages hurtled by and Pearl noticed three youths lounging against a lamp post, giving her the eye. She was relieved Wilfred was there to guide her past them.

Cromwell Road was noisy, teeming with horses and carriages, motorcars, omnibuses and crowds of men and women striding purposefully along the pavements.

'Careful!' Wilfred pulled her away from the kerb as a dray lurched past with a piano tied precariously on top.

'How does anyone ever become used to such hustle and bustle?' said Pearl.

Wilfred smiled at her. 'Necessity.'

A newspaper boy approached, shouting over the traffic noise: 'Archduke assassinated!'

Wilfred bought a paper and, frowning, scanned the headlines. 'Good God! The heir to the Austrian throne has been murdered in Sarajevo.'

43

Pearl wondered why he sounded so worried about something that had happened so far away.

He came to a standstill on the pavement, ignoring the pedestrians who side-stepped around him. ''The Archduke and his wife were in a motor cavalcade on a state visit,'' he read aloud, ''inspecting the imperial troops in Bosnia and Herzegovina, previously annexed by Austria-Hungary in 1908. The streets were lined by Serbian Nationalists protesting against the annex-ation. A student shot the royal couple at point-blank range and mortally wounded them.'' Sighing, he rolled up the paper. 'The warmongers are going to make a fine meal out of this!'

'I'm not sure I understand?'

'Austria-Hungary will want revenge on Serbia and may join forces with Germany to seek it. In which case, it's possible Germany will declare war on Russia because it's Serbia's ally. That part of the world is like a tinderbox waiting for a single spark to send it up in flames.'

He reached into his waistcoat pocket for his pocket watch. 'I must hurry to my meeting at the Garrick. It's in the opposite direction from where you're going but wouldn't you prefer to come with me?'

Pearl shook her head.

He held up his hand to a passing cab and it drew up by the kerb. Pearl clambered inside while he gave instructions to the driver. 'You're quite sure you want to see your father?' There was a hint of anxiety in Wil-fred's grey eyes.

'Absolutely.'

He gave her a handful of loose change. 'Promise me you'll take a cab back to your grandfather's house after you've seen Benedict? I don't want you walking through the streets on your own. And, Heaven forfend, don't even think of setting foot on the Underground!'

'I promise,' said Pearl.

He closed the cab door and tipped his boater to her as she sped away. Despite her protestations to the contrary, she admitted to herself that she was apprehensive and not only because she'd never been on her own before in such a big and noisy city. The cab threaded its way through the traffic and finally drew up in Berkeley Square.

Pearl walked up the front steps of the townhouse with an imposing façade and rang the bell.

A butler admitted her into a marble-floored hall and asked her to wait while he went to see if the master was at home.

Pearl stared up at the ornate cornicing of the lofty ceiling and attempted to ignore her queasy stomach. A few moments later a parlour-maid carrying a tea tray hurried through the hall and stopped in front of one of the closed doors. She balanced the heavy tray on her hip while she fumbled with the door-knob.

Fearing a disaster, Pearl hurried to assist. Through the open door, she caught a glimpse of several elderly ladies sitting in an ornate drawing-room. The maid gave her a nervous smile and scuttled inside.

Then Pearl was hauled smartly backwards by a pair of strong hands.

'What are you doing here?' hissed a familiar voice in her ear.

Shaking herself free, she spun around. 'That's a fine way to greet me after so long, Papa,' she said. Trying not to stare, she noticed that his eyes were puffy and his hair thinning. She blinked, the tarnished reality of his appearance settling like a veil over her memory of her handsome papa with thick, wavy hair and laughing eyes.

Benedict scowled at her. 'Why have you come, Pearl?'

She'd imagined he'd be pleased to see her. Hurt, she gave him a falsely bright smile. 'I'm staying in London and, since you haven't come to see me in several years, I thought I'd pay you a visit.'

Benedict looked her up and down, a crease between his eyebrows. 'You've grown up into a presentable young lady,' he said. 'Who'd have believed it? Well, we can't stay here; the Dragon will hear us and start asking questions and generally interfering.'

'The Dragon?'

'Your grandmother. Look sharp now!' He gripped his daughter's arm and hurried her out through the front door. 'We'll go into the square.'

A few minutes later they found a bench beneath the shade of a plane tree in the garden square. It was a restful scene with a fountain and spacious lawns intersected by wide gravel paths. Nearby, two little girls in frilly white dresses played with skipping ropes under the watchful eye of their nursemaid.

Benedict eyed Pearl warily. 'Did your mother send you?'

'I doubt she'd approve if she knew I were here.'

'Then why are you?'

Pearl swallowed back disappointment that he wasn't more pleased to see her and then decided she had nothing to lose. 'As I said, I wanted to see you. Besides, I'm still angry with you.'

'With me? But we haven't spoken for years!'

'Exactly. Seven years ago, you broke your promise and didn't come home for my thirteenth birthday party. Instead, we had your letter saying you weren't returning and telling Mama to send Roly to an orphanage. His mother had already deserted him and he'd been asking for you for weeks. When we had to tell him you weren't coming home, he was distraught. I'll never forget how he screamed and screamed until he was purple in the face. I thought he might die from grief. How could you, Papa?'

'It was all your mother's fault,' said Benedict. His gaze slid away from hers. 'I wanted Edith and you children to come and live here with me.' He pressed his lips together. 'But she refused. I couldn't understand it then.' He gave a scornful laugh. 'Well, now I know why. The Frenchman, that snake in the grass, had always been there, right from the early days of our marriage, whispering honeyed words of poison in her ear! And Jasper, his bastard, is the living proof of it.'

'It wasn't like that!' protested Pearl.

'And what would you know about it? You weren't even born when your mother betrayed me.'

'Mama told me what happened. She was heartbroken when she saw you, like that, with Delphine.'

'Oh, yes,' said Benedict with a curl of his lip, 'so heartbroken she jumped straight into bed with the Frenchman and subsequently bore his child.'

'But you'd already been unfaithful to her with Delphine! And you'd fathered Gabrielle.'

Her father pressed his knuckles against his eyes. 'Pearl, you're young and unaware of the ways of the world. Not all marriages are happy and, in that case, 'until death do us part' is a very long time indeed. In the eyes of society, it's accepted that a man will have affairs and a dutiful wife is understanding about such

47

things. Your mother wasn't.'

Pearl stared at him. 'Why should she be? You condemn her but what you did was no different. It's not fair!'

'The rules of society are absolute, unwritten or not, and those who break them, like your mother, must suffer the consequences.'

A shiver of unease rippled down her spine. 'What consequences?'

Benedict shrugged. 'One way or the other, I shall evict her and the rest of her henchmen from Spindrift.'

'But you can't!'

'Oh, yes, I can. There's the trifling inconvenience of the community's ownership of a small proportion of my house, but an interested party is prepared to deal with them if I sell him my share.'

'You really intend to make your own children homeless?' There was an unpleasant, fluttery feeling in Pearl's stomach.

'I'm perfectly within my rights to remove you and the twins from your mother's malign influence until you reach your majority.'

'To live here in Berkeley Square with you?' For a split second, she imagined a thrilling round of parties and theatre outings, beautiful clothes and fascinating company.

He didn't answer but studied her through half-closed eyes for a moment. Then he smiled. 'Wouldn't Edith just hate that?' He pinched Pearl's cheek. 'You really have grown up into an extremely pretty young lady. And you're still as spirited as you were when you were a little girl.' He whistled out his breath. 'By Jove, you had some tempestuous moods. But you amused me with the way you followed me about everywhere I went, even into the Golden Lion.' He chuckled. 'You demanded a port and lemon once, and then you were sick on my shoes.'

Pearl smiled faintly. 'I remember that.' She'd adored him and had suffered torments of jealousy when he'd turned his attention to Roland.

'Tell you what,' said Benedict, 'why don't I take you to tea at the Ritz? We can catch up on old times and you can tell me all about Roland. I miss the little chap.' He rose to his feet and offered her his arm.

Pearl looked up at him, silhouetted against the dazzling sun that filtered through the leaves of the plane tree. Haloed with a blaze of golden light, his features were blurred and once more he appeared the dazzling figure she adored.

'Well?' he said.

She hesitated and then slipped her arm under his.

Chapter 7

July 1914

Cornwall

The murmuring sea lapped around Edith's bare feet and the breeze cooled the scorching heat of the sun on her arms. She was alone in the cove, alone under the hot cobalt sky with the turquoise sea fading into infinity before her. This timeless seascape was where she always sought serenity when beset by anxiety.

Another wave retreated into the sea and she curled her toes into the gritty sand against the ebb of the tide. Sighing, she collected her shoes from the water's edge and trudged over the sand towards the cliff steps.

Up on the headland, she unlatched the gate and entered the garden where the air was still and heavy in the shimmering heat. A bee drifted lazily by. Ahead, the massive stone walls of Spindrift House were bathed in golden light and the windowpanes reflected the afternoon sun as if on fire.

Pascal, sitting before his easel on the terrace, waved. Blue and Star, stretched out on the flagstones beside him, twitched their paws as if they dreamed of chasing rabbits.

'Are you feeling more tranquil now, mon amour?' asked Pascal.

'I'm still worried about Benedict plotting to cause us trouble,' said Edith. 'And, of course, I'm looking forward to the children returning from London. I hope Pearl won't still be so cold towards me.'

Pascal sighed. 'She is angry with me, too.'

Blue and Star scrambled to their feet, their tails wagging, and then Edith saw Jasper hurrying towards them from the house and ran to greet him. 'Welcome home, my love!'

He enfolded her in a bear hug. 'I seem to have been away forever,' he said. He smiled at Pascal who limped towards them. 'But now I'm home for good.' He hugged Pascal. 'My father and I have some catching up to do, haven't we?'

'We certainly do.' Pascal beamed. 'And within the bounds of Spindrift House at least, there is no longer any need for me to conceal my great pride in my son.'

'Where are Pearl and Lucien?' Edith asked Jasper.

'Pearl appears to have bought a whole new wardrobe in London and Lucien is helping her to carry the parcels inside,' he said.

A short while later, the French doors burst open and Lucien sprinted across the terrace, Pearl lagging behind him.

'Dear Mama!' Once a stocky boy, Lucien had grown into a broad-shouldered young man. The dogs whined and wagged around him, desperate for attention from their favourite. He made a comic face at his mother and kneeled down to fuss them. 'Where's Nell, Mama?'

'At Polcarrow Farm with Roland, helping with the haymaking.'

'I'll walk over there after tea,' said Lucien.

Pearl hung back but then greeted Pascal and her mother quietly.

'Welcome home, Pearl.' Edith kissed her cheek, then stepped back to study her daughter's narrow skirt, lace blouse and fitted tunic jacket. 'How elegant you are!'

'Thank you.' Pearl turned away, her expression remote.

'I heard you all arrive,' called a voice as Lily appeared from the house. 'I've asked Daisy to bring us tea,' she said. 'I want to hear all about your adventures in the Big Smoke. Lucien, I swear you've grown another inch! You're looking very chic, Pearl.'

She laughed, all dimples and glossy dark hair. 'Grandfather insisted on buying me new clothes. He says I must look the part now I'm a working woman. I can't wait to show you my divine blouse. It's violet silk with pearl buttons.'

Daisy arrived with the tea tray and they gathered around the table on the terrace.

Edith poured the tea and Pearl handed around slices of seed cake while they chatted about the train journey.

'Do you all have special plans for the summer?' asked Pascal.

'I wrote to the veterinarian in Wadebridge,' said Lucien, 'and asked if I might shadow him during the summer holidays.'

'How enterprising of you!' said Edith.

'I start on Monday morning.'

'Bravo!' said Pascal.

Roland came running across the lawn. 'Nell said you'd be here by now.' He gave Lucien a playful punch on the arm.

'Did she now?' Lucien wrestled his half-brother to the ground and tickled him. 'You don't get away with punching me, you little hellion!'

'Ow, ow!' shrieked Roland.

Lucien let him go and hurried to hug Nell.

'We'll not see hide nor hair of those two now Lucien's back,' said Pearl, handing Roland a slab of cake.

'We're going down to the cove,' said Lucien a moment later. 'Roland, do you want to come with us?'

'Mama, may I get down?' Edith nodded and Roland stuffed the rest of the cake into his mouth and ran after the twins.

'I'll be back in time to pull some carrots for dinner,' called Nell, over her shoulder.

Edith refilled teacups for the others. 'Nell's worked very hard, managing the kitchen garden almost single-handedly while Dora and Ursula are in Germany.' She frowned. 'We haven't had so much as a postcard from them for ages.'

'I remember,' said Pascal, 'when Lucien was away at school, how Nell found solace in helping them grow vegetables.'

'This hot weather means there's a lot of watering to do,' said Lily. 'I'll give her a hand. I've written letters applying for two situations but I'm in no hurry to receive a reply.' She turned to Jasper. 'How did you enjoy your student years in London?'

'It was wonderful to have all the galleries and museums close at hand,' he said. 'I've learned a great deal at the Slade and my exhibition was very, shall we say, interesting. I daresay Mama has told you about that?'

'She did,' said Lily.

'I hope no one thinks any the less of her for what happened in the past.' He laughed. 'I certainly don't. I couldn't be happier to have a father I respect.'

Pascal looked fondly at his son.

'Something else good came out of my exhibition,' continued Jasper. 'A man commissioned me to paint

53

his wife's portrait. She's travelling down to Cornwall to stay with her sister in Wadebridge for the summer. I'll visit her there for the sittings.'

'That's marvellous, Jasper!' said Edith.

'It's my first commission and now I'll be able to make a proper contribution towards my board and lodging.'

'Oh, but I couldn't ask you —'

Pascal touched Edith's arm. 'Allow the boy to be a man, Edith.'

She glanced at Jasper's expression and nodded. 'Then, thank you. A contribution towards your keep will be most welcome.'

'How did you like London, Pearl?' said Lily. 'Was it exciting?'

'It's been splendid to visit the theatre and the shops. And, when I could prise him away from his sketch-book, Jasper's been a very dutiful brother and squired me about. Lucien, of course, had end-of-term exam-inations so his nose was in his textbooks most of the time.'

'Grandfather thought it was his duty to find Pearl a husband,' said Jasper. 'He called on all his acquaint-ances to invite us to their dinners and balls.' He shrugged, a gleam of amusement in his brown eyes. 'Complete waste of time. Pearl is a terrible flirt but she refused to allow any of them to capture her heart.'

'I'm not a flirt!' said his sister, in a voice full of indignation.

'Then I wonder why, on the morning after a ball, Grandfather's house was like a florist's shop and the doorbell never stopped ringing?'

'All those young men could talk about was the kerfuffle going on in Serbia and the threat of Britain becoming involved in a war,' said Pearl. 'Honestly, you'd think they actually hope it will happen so they can give the Germans a jolly good trouncing.'

She sighed. 'Anyhow, I'm determined to make a success of earning my own living before I even think of marriage. Wilfred's so busy with his illustration work, he's said I can put together the fabric samples for Mrs Edwardes's flat. And, before you ask, Jasper, I may not be a gifted artist like you but it's impossible to grow up at Spindrift without learning to hold a pencil. I shall manage to draw a very creditable pair of curtains.'

Jasper laughed. 'Good for you!'

'But now, I want to unpack. Will you come and see my new clothes, Lily?'

'I'm wondering if that violet silk blouse with the pearl buttons might fit me.'

Edith watched the two lovely young women walk away together, one so dark and the other so blonde, and was reminded of herself and Clarissa over twenty years before. She experienced a sharp and powerful yearning to protect them from the heartaches of life that she and her friend had faced.

★ ★ ★

Every day after breakfast, Lily helped Nell water the kitchen garden. She enjoyed the peaceful sound of water splashing on the dusty earth as she walked slowly between rows of carrots and beans with a watering can, her mind free to daydream about Noel. Afterwards, she and Nell often cycled along the lanes to Wadebridge, where they cooled down beneath the arches of the ancient bridge over the River Camel.

By the time they returned to Spindrift, it was Pearl's lunch break from the gallery and they went down to the cove with Rose and Roland to play smugglers as if they were ten years old again.

In the afternoons, Lily took her turn to man the gallery or dozed over a book in the hammock under the copper beech, while Edith painted her portrait. Sometimes she went into the workshop to watch her mother and Augustus making jewellery. She helped with packing the orders for posting to the smart shops in London where the items were stocked. After dinner, the young people from Spindrift played croquet on the lawn or gathered in the cove with Adela, Noel and Tim.

All through the long summer days, a secret thrum of euphoria warmed Lily from inside. Something momentous had happened. She would never have believed it was possible to be so happy. Noel had told her he loved her! Whenever she could, she slipped down to the cove to snatch a kiss from him before dinner, or she'd wait for him in the village after he'd finished work in his father's office. They'd walk home hand-in-hand along the coast path, talking about their hopes and dreams, their delight in each other growing daily. Their happiness was shadowed only when they discussed the increasing likelihood of war.

One evening, Noel hooked his arm through hers as they strolled along the tideline in the cove. 'Do you remember how, when we were children, all of us . . . and Gabrielle, too, sometimes . . . used to build ships out of sand and pretend we were pirates?'

'Our adventures were even more thrilling because we had to keep our friendship a secret from our parents,' said Lily. 'At least, until Pearl and I were trapped in the cave.' She shuddered at the terrifying memory of it. 'Mother was furious when she discovered I'd been playing with you and your siblings. She forbade me ever to see any of you again.'

'But now we're old enough to choose our own friends.' Noel dropped a kiss on her nose.

Lily watched a fishing boat sailing by. What would it be like if there was a war and there were German battleships off the coast? She shuddered. 'Do you think there'll be a war, Noel?'

'The Germans have been building up to it for years and the Kaiser's power-mad. If it comes to it, we'll have to show them we're mightier than they are.'

'But are we?'

'You don't build an Empire unless you're powerful. No red-blooded Englishman will resist the call to arms if it's a question of safeguarding our country and the people we love. I'd enlist immediately.'

'You're very brave, Noel, but I'd be so worried if you went to war.' She prayed it would never happen.

He took her in his arms. 'I could never stand idly by if you were at risk,' he murmured.

Later, when Lily returned to Spindrift, her mouth bruised from his kisses, the community had already gathered around the dinner table on the terrace. Her mother and stepfather were talking quietly with Wilfred and Augustus. Edith, Jasper and Pascal were holding hands, their expressions tight and anxious.

Lily slipped into the empty place between Pearl and Nell. 'Whatever's the matter?' she asked.

'Germany,' said Wilfred, 'has declared war on Russia and sent an ultimatum to Belgium demanding safe passage through their country.'

'That's awful,' said Lily, 'but it doesn't affect us,

does it?'

'France is allied to Russia,' said Pascal, 'and is obliged to send troops to support them.'

'And Britain won't allow Belgium and France to be attacked,' said Edith. 'Our navy has already been mobilised, to protect the French coast and the North Sea from German aggressors.'

'Does that mean we'll be at war with Germany?' asked Lily.

'I'm very much afraid it does,' said Julian.

Despite the warmth of the evening, she shivered suddenly.

'Dora and Ursula are still in Germany,' said Nell. 'If there's fighting in the Channel, how will they get home?'

Edith and Pascal glanced at each other.

'That's a very good question,' said Wilfred.

★ ★ ★

The following evening, the young people gathered in the sitting-room. Lucien sang 'When Irish Eyes Are Smiling' while Nell played the piano.

Lily slipped away but not before Pearl gave her a knowing look.

After glancing over her shoulder as she left the house, to check that no one else had observed her, Lily hastened down to the cove. Now everyone was home, it was harder to meet Noel in secret. There was no sign of him yet so she wandered along the rippled sand at the water's edge.

Then she saw Adela striding towards her.

'Don't worry,' she said. 'I've come to tell you Father mentioned he'd asked Noel to work late.'

'How did you know we were meeting tonight?'

'Noel and I don't have many secrets from each other. I know he's in love with you.'

A glow of delight warmed Lily's cheeks. 'Is he?' she said.

'Don't be coy with me, Lily Stanton!' Adela tucked her arm through the crook of Lily's elbow. 'He never stops talking about you.' She smiled. 'Mother said to me the other day that he had the look of a young man in love and asked me if he'd met a suitable girl. 'He's twenty-four and has good prospects,' she said. 'It's time he thought about settling down.' Mind you, she never stops badgering me about finding a husband, either. She desperately wants grandchildren. But, Lily, just think how lovely it would be if you married Noel. Then we'd be real sisters.'

'Noel has never said anything —'

'But he will,' said Adela.

'Even if he did, your parents will never approve of me because I'm . . .' She'd been going to say, because she was illegitimate. 'They don't approve of anyone from Spindrift.'

Adela waved her hand. 'Don't worry about that. The row Father had with Benedict Fairchild about which of them should have inherited Spindrift House was long before you were born. Besides, you aren't Benedict's so I don't see why Father should object. It might be different if it was Pearl that his son had fallen in love with. And besides, Mother adores Noel so I'm sure he can persuade her he can't be happy without you. You do love him, don't you?'

'I can't think about anything but Noel,' Lily confessed. 'When we're together it feels as if we're two parts of a whole. It's almost as if I've been missing

59

him all my life and didn't know it.'

As they meandered along the shore, she imagined herself as Mrs Noel Penrose but then, giving herself a mental shake, sighed. He had never once mentioned marriage.

And then, there he was, running across the beach towards them. 'Have I kept you waiting long?' A lock of fair hair flopped across his forehead and he brushed it away impatiently. 'Father kept me in the office looking at building specifications.'

'Adela came to tell me.'

Noel smiled at her. 'Thank you, sis.'

'I expect you two have things to talk about,' Adela said. 'I shan't play gooseberry.' She waved and made her way back towards the cliff steps.

They waited until she'd disappeared over the headland and then Noel tilted up Lily's chin and kissed her. He was gentle at first but finally he crushed her to him, his hands encircling her waist. A tremor ran through her, a sharp sweet pain in her pelvis, so intense, her knees almost gave way. She nearly cried out in disappointment when he released her.

'Let's sit and watch the sun set,' he said. His voice was hoarse and he cleared his throat. He didn't lead her to their usual sitting place but to a flat area of sand nestled into a semi-circle of rocks. Once sitting down, they were in a secret world of their own in the lee of the cliffs.

Noel slid his arm around Lily's neck. His kisses were hot and urgent and she didn't resist when he pulled her down until they were lying on the sand. Her eyes closed and her mouth opened as she savoured the sensation of his lips exploring her neck and throat while his hands caressed her hip. When he cupped one of her breasts through the thin muslin of her blouse, she gave a soft moan and his fingers moved quickly to undo the buttons. Then his mouth was on her breasts, his tongue flickering over her nipple, and she nearly fainted with the ecstasy of it.

It was only when he lifted her skirt that she gasped and pulled away from him, even though she didn't want to. 'We can't!' she said.

'Lily!' he groaned. 'I want you so much.'

She buttoned her blouse with trembling fingers. 'I'm not doing that until I'm married,' she said firmly. Mother and Edith had made that mistake and she knew what could happen as a result.

Noel sat up, his hair ruffled and his face flushed. 'You do love me, don't you?'

'You know I do!'

He let a handful of sand run through his fingers. 'I want us to be together all the time, not just in snatched moments.' His grey eyes were serious as he studied her face and then he kneeled before her. 'Please, darling Lily, will you marry me?'

Her heart was thudding so loudly she was sure he must hear it over the never-ending song of the waves lapping onto the beach. 'Oh, yes, Noel,' she said. 'I would very much like to marry you.'

He shouted in delight and smothered her face in kisses. 'We must be married at once then, in case war is declared and I have to go away.'

A niggle of doubt intruded on Lily's joy. 'But will your parents be happy for us?'

'Of course they will. Let's tell them straightaway.'

Lily bit her lip. 'But . . . I have sand in my hair.' It had all happened so fast and she needed a little time to prepare herself to meet them. 'It's getting late.

61

And . . .'

'You're not having second thoughts?'

She kissed his cheek. 'Never! I want to be looking my best, that's all. It's an important meeting. Besides, we can't announce our engagement out of the blue.'

'I suppose I might say I have someone special I want them to meet.'

'I'd better go home now, before I'm missed,' said Lily.

'Then I'll meet you here tomorrow evening at six o'clock and we'll join my parents for a drink before dinner.' Noel kissed her tenderly. 'I'm the luckiest man in the world,' he said, 'and I promise I'll do everything in my power to make you happy.'

'And I shall love you forever.'

After a last lingering kiss, Lily tore herself away and hurried back to Spindrift.

Chapter 8

Edith glanced up from her easel and frowned. For the second time that afternoon, Lily had dropped her book over the side of the hammock and it was rocking wildly as she reached down to retrieve it. Edith put down her paintbrush.

'Sorry.' Lily slid out of the hammock, her fall of blonde hair shimmering in the August sunshine. 'There's something on my mind and I'm fidgety.'

'I can't concentrate to paint you when you're like this. Is there something you want to talk about?'

'Oh! Not at the moment.' Lily glanced at the house, clearly longing to escape.

'Shall we try again tomorrow?'

Lily nodded and Edith watched as she hurried away around the corner of the house. It wasn't surprising the girl was distracted. They all were. Now that Germany had declared war on France, poor Pascal was fearful for his family there. Dora and Ursula had not sent any word from Germany for three weeks. Britain was mobilising forces to support Belgium, in case Germany violated her borders, and it was almost inevitable that, before long, they too would be at war with Germany. What would that mean for Jasper and Lucien? The prospect of either of her sons enlisting made Edith's stomach churn. What if . . .

She straightened her shoulders and picked up her brush again. There was also her continuing unease over what Benedict might do. He'd been suspiciously quiet but his bitter hostility was sure to bear poisonous fruit at some point. She must concentrate on her work to take her mind off her worries. Even without Lily to pose for her, she could capture the way the afternoon sunlight filtered through the leaves of the copper beech. Perhaps tomorrow there'd be more clarity on the political situation.

A horse clip-clopped along the lane and wheels ground to a halt at the front of the house. Lifting her head, Edith heard familiar voices drifting over the wall.

Smiling, she hurried to open the gate. 'Dora, thank heavens you're back!' She hugged her old friend. 'We've been so worried about you.'

Dora clung to her for a moment. She had a smudge on one cheekbone and her sandy hair was falling out of its pins. 'Oh, Edith! I can't tell you how relieved we are to be home.'

They both turned to look at Ursula, who was involved in a heated discussion with the driver.

'Please will you pay Mr Jarvis?' said Dora, who looked close to tears. 'Our money was stolen and he won't let us have our luggage until we've paid him.'

'I'll fetch my purse.' Edith ran inside and returned a few moments later. Mr Jarvis pocketed the tip, without a thank you, before driving away.

'Why was he so surly?' asked Edith. 'He's usually perfectly polite.'

Ursula shrugged, her face ashen and her expression closed. 'Because he knows my surname is German.' She lifted a suitcase in each hand.

Edith watched her stride away towards the house. Ursula was so cheerful and optimistic usually, but today had barely greeted her.

'Mr Jarvis didn't want to take us. I had to plead

64

with him,' said Dora. 'He spent the entire journey from the station ranting at Ursula about Germany's war-mongering.'

'I barely think of her as German,' said Edith. 'Did you tell him her father came to England before she was born and that her mother is English?'

'He wasn't interested in that; only in Ursula's 'tainted' blood. I said, in that case, our Royal Family has tainted blood too. Then he swore at me.'

'How very impolite,' said Edith. She picked up the remaining bags and they followed Ursula into the hall.

Roland came thundering down the stairs and ran to hug the new arrivals. 'I was looking out of my bed-room window and saw you arrive. I thought you were never coming home!'

'We did write,' said Dora, 'but there's so much con-fusion on the other side of the Channel, I daresay the post is delayed.'

'There's going to be a war. Did you see soldiers?' His eyes dark eyes gleamed with excitement. 'But our King is stronger than the German Kaiser. We'll send him packing, won't we?'

Ursula patted his shoulder and gave him a wan smile. 'Would you ask Daisy to bring us some tea?'

'Roly,' called Edith as he disappeared down the corridor, 'will you also tell Uncle Pascal that Dora and Ursula are home?'

In the sitting-room, Dora slumped onto the sofa.

Ursula stifled a yawn and sat down beside her. 'Sorry,' she said. 'We slept on a platform at Padding-ton Station last night.'

Edith stared at her. 'Why on earth . . .'

'There were dreadful delays. We didn't arrive until midnight.'

65

'We'd have gone to stay with my sister,' said Dora, 'but we hadn't any money and were too exhausted to walk to Kennington at that time of night.'

The door opened and Pascal came to kiss Dora and Ursula. 'How happy we are to see you safely home! We were concerned you might find it difficult, travelling through Germany.'

'We knew trouble was brewing there,' said Dora, 'so we left and went to stay on Lake Lucerne in Switzerland. We travelled to Basel on Friday night but weren't allowed to travel onwards to Ostend.'

'Crowds of passengers were milling around, wringing their hands,' said Ursula. 'Suddenly there was a great rush to catch a train that was leaving for Paris. The throng was so great that half the people were left behind. We managed to squeeze into a compartment, but after we'd crossed the frontier to France there were three deafening explosions, one after another.'

'It was awful,' said Dora. 'The last one blew out the windows and the train screeched to a halt.' She pressed her fist to her mouth at the memory. 'A poor old lady died on the spot; a heart attack, I suppose.'

'After several hours we were herded onto another train,' said Ursula. 'It was crammed with soldiers, smoking and singing the Marseillaise. There were no seats and we had to huddle in the crowded corridors, taking it in turns to sit on our cases. The heat was unbearable and we had no water or food. All the way to Paris, the countryside was full of camps and soldiers.'

'But you reached it without further incident?' asked Pascal.

Dora nodded. 'Then we discovered there were far too many people for the train accommodation available. We found a little hotel and that was when we noticed our money had been stolen. I kept it in a bag I wore across my body under my jacket but, in the press of people in the train corridor, someone must have cut the strap without me noticing.'

'And that wasn't all,' said Ursula. 'I'd changed a cheque at Basel but the Swiss paper money we received wasn't accepted once we'd left the country. Our tickets via Ostend were worthless and we had only one English sovereign between us.'

'However did you manage?' asked Edith.

'We couldn't stay at the hotel so we returned to the station and begged for help from other English passengers. They lent us some money and we waited a day until we could purchase tickets for Calais.'

'Eventually we reached the coast and boarded a passenger steamer,' said Dora. 'It was so overcrowded I was fearful it might sink. Setting aside the money for our train fare to Cornwall, we had just enough left to buy a bottle of soda water to share.' She smiled wearily. 'Ambrosia of the gods could never taste half as delicious as that lukewarm soda water.'

Daisy clattered into the drawing-room with the tea tray. Roland followed, carrying a fruit cake.

'On the other hand,' said Dora, 'there's nothing quite like a proper British cuppa.'

Edith was pouring their third cup when Lily put her head around the drawing-room door.

'I thought I heard your voices,' she said, hurrying to hug Dora and Ursula.

'My, don't you look pretty today,' said Dora. 'Are you going somewhere special?'

Lily's cheeks were flushed and her eyes bright.

'Dora and Ursula had a dreadful journey,' said

Edith. 'They're going upstairs for a nap but you'll be able to catch up on their news at dinner.'

Edith couldn't help noticing the look of relief on Lily's face as she escaped. What was the girl up to?

* * *

Lily raced down the cliff steps to the cove. She'd made herself late by borrowing Pearl's blouse at the last minute. There'd been no time to ask her permission but she was sure, for such an important event, Pearl wouldn't mind.

Noel was on the beach, looking at his watch.

She waved as he came to meet her.

'I was worried you weren't coming,' he said.

'Nothing would keep me away.' Still out of breath, she held up her face for his kiss.

'Nervous?'

She nodded. 'You?'

He grinned. 'Of course, but how could my parents not love a kind and beautiful girl like you? I know they want me to be happy. Adela has challenged Tim to a game of tennis so we won't be interrupted.'

Hand-in-hand, they made their way up the steps towards Cliff House, chattering excitedly about where and when they would be married.

Lily fell silent as they walked into the immaculately tended garden, the herbaceous borders packed with brightly coloured flowers.

On the terrace outside the French doors, Noel tightened his grip on her hand. 'Ready?'

She nodded, though her heart was hammering.

He pressed a quick kiss on her mouth, then opened the French doors.

Lily had never been inside Cliff House before. The drawing-room was painted a pale green and she gained the impression of fine furniture and pretty chintz upholstery. But her gaze was fixed on Hugh and Jenifry Penrose, her future parents-in-law, sitting sideby-side with a pre-dinner glass of sherry. She'd seen them in the village: Hugh with greying hair and shirt buttons straining across his abdomen, and Jenifry with eyes like currants in her fleshy face.

'Mother, Father,' said Noel, 'may I introduce you to my fiancée, Miss Lily Stanton?'

Lily wondered if he should have broken the news less abruptly but, nevertheless, still wasn't prepared for Hugh Penrose's reaction. As she waited, smiling in nervous anticipation, she saw his face flood beetroot red. Then, despite his corpulence, he erupted from his seat and shot across the room to grasp Noel by his collar. 'What have you done?' he roared. 'Is she in the family way?'

Lily gasped. 'No! I wouldn't —'

'Shut up, you!' yelled Hugh.

'Father . . .'

Hugh shoved Noel against the wall, one arm across his throat. 'If I ever find you with that little tart again, you'll be out on your ear.' He pushed his son aside and glared at Lily. 'Get out!'

'But . . .' she stammered.

Jenifry Penrose came to stand before her. 'I can't imagine why you might think we'd allow anyone from the Spindrift community to defile our family. Depraved, the lot of you!' She pointed her finger at Lily. 'Don't come near our son again. You heard my husband. Go!'

Stunned, Lily looked at Noel for support but he

69

was rubbing his bruised neck, his bewildered gaze still fixed on his father. Letting out a sob, Lily fled.

When she ran into Spindrift's courtyard, Clarissa was at the front of the coach house, humming to herself as she watered the pelargoniums. She looked up with a smile that quickly faded. 'Sweetheart, what is it?'

'He proposed and I was so happy,' Lily sobbed, 'but his father went berserk. He called me a tart.'

'What! Take a deep breath and tell me again. Who proposed to you?'

'Noel,' said Lily. 'We've been in love for ages and we want to marry.' Her mother's hands gripped her wrists so hard that Lily winced. 'You're hurting me!'

Clarissa's face blanched. 'Not Noel Penrose?' she whispered.

Lily dashed tears from her eyes and nodded. Clarissa swayed and her lips turned so bloodless that Lily caught hold of her in case she fainted. Guiding her mother to the bench beside the porch, she sat her down with her head between her knees.

After a while, Clarissa sat up, her complexion still milk-white and sheened with perspiration. 'You aren't in trouble, are you?'

'I'm not that kind of girl! I'm never going to make the same mistake as you and Edith.'

Her mother flinched. 'Lily, you must never even think of marriage to Noel Penrose. Never!'

'But why are you against it? Noel's kind and clever and he's going to be a partner in his father's architectural practice.' Lily swallowed another sob. 'And I love him. If I can't marry him with your blessing, then we'll elope!'

Clarissa caressed her daughter's cheek. 'My dearest

girl,' she said, her voice cracking, eyes deep wells of pain, 'you can never marry Noel. It's forbidden.'

Lily stared at her, uncomprehending.

Clarissa dropped her gaze, her mouth quivering. 'Hugh Penrose is your father,' she whispered.

'That's not true!'

'I wish it weren't. You can't marry Noel because he's your half-brother.'

The ground seemed to tilt and Lily gripped the porch post until the blackness around the edges of her vision faded. Anguish gave way to a great rage that built up inside her until she thought she might split open with the heat of her bitterness. It was all her mother's fault! She clenched her fists and her mouth twisted with loathing. 'I hate you with every ounce of my being,' she said, her voice low and shaking. 'You've ruined my entire life.'

Clarissa reached out to her but Lily shoved her away and stalked off.

Chapter 9

Pearl was tidying her hair ready to go down to dinner when Lily stumbled into the bedroom. 'Lily! That's a bit rich, you've borrowed my new blouse without asking.'

'I'm sorry.' Lily's voice cracked. 'You weren't here and there was something special—' She sank onto the bed and curled into a ball. 'My life is ruined!' she wept. 'I love him so much, I can't bear it.'

Pearl stroked Lily's hair until her tears subsided. It upset her to see her friend so distressed. 'Did you quarrel with Noel?' she asked.

'He asked me to marry him,' Lily sobbed.

Pearl couldn't imagine anything worse than having Hugh and Jenifry Penrose as her parents-in-law, but each to her own. 'That's wonderful!'

'No, it isn't. We went to tell his ghastly parents and Hugh Penrose flew into a rage. I thought he was going to kill Noel. He accused him of getting me in the family way and called me a tart — and it's not true,' Lily wailed.

'How insulting! Perhaps he'll look at it differently tomorrow?'

'Noel's mother said she'd never allow anyone from Spindrift to marry her son and defile the Penrose family. She called us depraved.'

'In the light of certain facts that have come to our notice recently,' said Pearl, 'perhaps she isn't wrong.' She handed Lily a handkerchief. 'Come to think of it, though, she can't know about that.'

72

Lily blew her nose. 'I can never marry Noel now.'

'You could elope.'

'It's not only that . . .' Lily twisted the sodden handkerchief between her fingers.

'What, then?'

'Mother said . . .' She chewed at her lower lip. 'I can't . . . It was such a shock. It's too awful to talk about.' She covered her face with her hands. 'Noel didn't stand up for me when his father was so rude. He didn't even follow me when I ran away, though he knew I was terribly upset.'

Pearl wondered if Lily was telling her the whole story.

'Mother absolutely forbade me to marry him and I told her I hated her.' Lily gazed out of the window. 'I can't bear to be near her. May I sleep here with you and Nell, like in the old days?'

Pearl patted the bedspread. 'Your bed is still here.'

Downstairs, the dinner gong boomed.

'Will you tell the others I have a headache?'

Pearl closed the bedroom door quietly behind her.

★ ★ ★

After dinner, which was notable by Lily, Clarissa and Julian's absence, despite Dora and Ursula's return, Pearl hurried down to the cove.

Adela was waiting for her there. 'Did Lily tell you what happened?'

Pearl nodded.

'Father has a terrible temper,' said Adela. Her eyes were wide with the drama of it all. 'When they were young, he used to take his belt to the boys whenever they disobeyed him. Noel still turns to stone when

73

Father has one of his shouting fits.'

Pearl stopped herself from saying that perhaps it was time Noel learned to stand up to such bullying tactics.

'My parents always expected him to marry someone from a good family with money to put into the business.' Adela shrugged. 'But no one knows who Lily's father is.'

'That isn't her fault!'

'No, and I'm sure, if Mother and Father got to know Lily, they'd see she'd make Noel happy,' said Adela. 'Tell her not to give up because I still want her for my sister-in-law.'

As Pearl returned to Spindrift, she couldn't help wondering if a short period of heartache now might not save Lily from future misery.

* * *

In the morning, Lily was hollow-eyed after a sleepless night. She refused to come downstairs for breakfast and Pearl and Nell left her lying on the bed, staring at the ceiling.

Wilfred returned from the village, carrying a newspaper. He spread it out over the dining table. 'Bad news.'

All the talk at breakfast was about the ultimatum the British Government had sent Germany, saying they must withdraw their troops from Belgium. If they refused to comply by eleven o'clock tonight, Britain would declare war on Germany.

Pascal's forehead wrinkled with worry. 'After Dora and Ursula's experiences on their journey home, I hope Gabrielle managed to travel back to France safely.'

74

Edith clutched his hand and Pearl noted sourly that they were no longer making any pretence that they were only friends.

'I'm not a violent man,' said Augustus, 'but we must put an end to the Kaiser's posturing. If the German menace doesn't withdraw, we have no choice but to go in hard and fast with our troops and show them we're the stronger power.'

'If we do,' said Wilfred, 'it'll be over by Christmas.'

Ursula rose abruptly to her feet.

'Oh, Lord!' said Augustus. 'I apologise, Ursula. I quite forgot you're half-German. My comment wasn't personal.'

Edith went to Ursula and made her sit down. 'You're among friends,' she said gently. 'None of us blames you for what's happening on the other side of the Channel.'

'Certainly not!' said Wilfred.

Dora gripped Ursula's hand. 'You're safe here.'

It gave Pearl a sick feeling to realise that they might be at war with Germany this very night. She prayed for something miraculous to prevent it.

After breakfast, Edith drew Pearl into the sitting-room. 'Has something happened between Lily and Clarissa?' she asked.

Pearl still hadn't forgiven her mother and didn't care to confide in her now. 'They quarrelled,' she said.

'But they rarely have a cross word!'

'Well, they have now.'

'Why?'

'You'll have to ask them yourself.' Pearl turned to leave.

'Wait!' Her mother's voice was sharp. 'Sweetheart, I know you're angry with me but I want to bridge the gap between us.'

'You can't.' Pearl shrugged. 'Perhaps, in time, I'll grow used to the fact that you deceived Papa in such a dreadful way and then lied to us all for years.'

Edith folded her arms over her chest. 'You've no idea what it was like, living with him.'

'I lived with him too, remember? He was such fun.' Pearl smiled. 'He still is. I went to see him when I was in London and he took me to tea at the Ritz. I'm considering whether to go and live with him.' She regretted it even as she uttered the spiteful words, but didn't allow herself to look back as she fled from the room.

* * *

Lily lay on her bed in Pearl's room, still staring at the ceiling. It was almost impossible to comprehend that, only the day before, she and Noel had been planning a happy future together.

The door opened and Pearl came in. 'There's some dreadful news,' she said. She looked as if she might cry. 'It's likely we'll be at war with Germany by tonight.'

Lily sat up abruptly. 'Oh, no! That's too awful. Our perfect summer is unravelling and now it's just one hideous event after another.'

'Perhaps it won't happen,' said Pearl. 'I went down to the sea earlier and met Adela. She sent you a message from Noel. He's not going to work today because of the bank holiday and he'll wait in the cove for you.'

Lily recalled his bewildered expression at his father's violent reaction and knew that, painful as it might be, she must speak to him.

'And this letter came for you from Launceston,'

said Pearl.

Lily opened it. 'It's from General Beaumont. I applied for the situation he offered. He's blind and needs someone to transcribe his memoirs of the Boer War. I can live in and start at once.' She swung her legs over the side of the bed. 'I'll pack straightaway.'

'But what about Noel?'

'I can't marry him and it hurts too much to stay here when he's nearby.'

Pearl stared at her. 'But you love him. You can't run away without speaking to him!'

'No.' Lily ran her fingers through her tangled hair. She couldn't face telling Pearl the truth. Not yet, while the pain was so raw. 'He didn't defend me while his parents spoke cruelly to me and . . . and I've realised I don't love him, after all. I'll tell him I made a mistake.'

'Lily . . .'

But she'd hurried from the room and her footsteps clattered away down the stairs.

* * *

Noel was waiting for Lily by the rocks. He rushed towards her, arms outstretched, but she put her hand on his chest to stop him coming any closer.

'Lily, I'm so desperately sorry for what happened last night,' he said. There were dark shadows under his eyes, as if he hadn't slept either. 'Father said unforgivable things and I should have taken you home. We'll elope —'

'No!'

'I won't let him ruin our lives!'

'It's too late, Noel, he already has.' Her face crumpled as she fought back tears.

'What do you mean? We still love each other.' Uncertainly, he studied her expression. 'Don't we?'

'And that's the difficulty.' She covered her eyes with her palms.

'Lily, what is it?'

'I hardly know how to tell you this.' She drew in a ragged breath. 'Last night, when I returned home, Mother told me something deeply shocking.'

'What?'

Lily couldn't look at him so fixed her gaze on her shoes. 'She told me that, years ago, she had an affair with your father.'

Noel laughed. 'Impossible! Father hates everyone from Spindrift. And even if that were true, it has nothing to do with us.'

Lily swallowed. 'It has everything to do with us,' she said, in a low voice. 'You see, Mother confessed that your father is my father too.'

'But . . . that's not possible!'

'It is. Don't you understand? You're my half-brother. We can never marry.'

His face blanched and a muscle twitched at the corner of one eye. 'Is it true?'

'Would I lie about something like that?'

Turning away from her, he paced down to the water's edge and stared out to sea.

After a few minutes, Lily followed him. It was such a beautiful day yet it felt wrong that the sea should be glinting in the sunshine when for them everything had ended. 'Noel?' she said. He turned his face towards her and she had a sudden premonition of how he might look when he was old.

'I shall never forgive Father,' he said. 'Nothing can ever undo the terrible harm he's caused us. I hate him.

One way or the other, I will have my revenge on him.'

His tone was so implacable that Lily shivered, despite the sunshine. 'I'm going away,' she said. 'It's too painful to be close to you, knowing . . .'

He lifted her hand, kissed her palm and folded her fingers over the kiss. 'That's the last time I shall touch you,' he murmured, 'but I will always love you.'

Lily let out a sob, her heart breaking.

'Don't cry,' he said. 'I can't bear it.' He left her then and walked back towards Cliff House.

★ ★ ★

The following morning, Edith walked into the village with Jasper, Dora, Wilfred and Augustus, to discover if their fears of a war with Germany had come to pass. As they descended Roscarrock Hill, they saw fishing boats were still at anchor in the harbour and pulled up on the beach, and the Platt was teeming with people. The faint strains of a brass band floated on the breeze and the Golden Lion was hung with bunting.

'Everyone's celebrating!' said Edith. 'Germany must have given way to our ultimatum.'

Wilfred grimaced. 'Let's hope so.'

'I'll find out,' said Jasper. He sprinted on ahead.

The sounds of merriment grew louder as they approached the Platt. It was a bank holiday and summer visitors were cheering as the band paraded up and down the beach, sunlight flashing off their brass instruments. A noisy gang of over-excited children and dogs followed behind.

Augustus pointed to a sheet painted with crude lettering and hung from the front of one of the cottages. The scarlet paint had bled in rivulets and the lettering read: God bless our boys! We are coming for you, Fritz!

'I'll fetch a newspaper,' said Wilfred, grim-faced, 'but it looks like war after all.'

'I don't understand,' said Edith, watching the crowd laughing and singing. 'Why is everyone so excited about such a dreadful thing?'

'Perhaps it's a relief that we're finally going to do something about the threat that's been hanging over us for so long,' said Augustus.

A group of youths marched by, broomsticks on their shoulders in lieu of rifles.

Dora clasped Edith's arm. 'I can't believe this is happening. Ursula's family are good, kind people and they don't want to be at war with us, whatever their politicians say.'

When Wilfred returned with a newspaper, they huddled around him to read it.

'So that's it then,' said Augustus. 'We're officially at war.'

Jasper pushed his way through the throng towards them. 'The army and navy are recruiting in the Temperance Hall. I met Tom Mellyn and he said several men have signed up already.'

'Surely Tom hasn't enlisted?' asked Edith. 'The Mellyns need him at Polcarrow Farm.'

Jasper shook his head. 'Besides, everyone says the war will be over in a few months.'

'What's this?' Edith plucked a leaflet from his fingers. "Your King & Country need you!" she read aloud. Her stomach lurched. 'Jasper! You're not going to enlist, are you?'

He took the paper from her. 'I can't imagine having to shoot anyone. I'm not sure I could, but . . .' He sighed. 'Not yet anyway.'

Edith felt as if there were a great lump of ice inside her. It was too dreadful to think of either of her boys going off to war. 'Let's go back to Spindrift,' she said, suddenly longing for the safety of home. 'I can't stay here and listen to the band playing jolly tunes and celebrating something so terrifying.'

★ ★ ★

Later, still feeling unsettled, Edith left the others sitting around the dining-room table with the newspapers. She hadn't seen Clarissa or Julian for a couple of days and wondered if they'd heard the news.

In the courtyard, she waved to Rose. 'Is your mother in?'

The girl nodded. 'She's got a headache.'

Edith knocked on the door of the coach house. The sitting-room curtain moved and a moment later Clarissa opened up, still in her dressing gown.

'Are you unwell?' asked Edith.

Clarissa pushed tangled hair off her face. Her eyelids were red and puffy and for the first time, she looked every one of her forty-four years. 'Lily's left Spindrift!' she said. 'She refused to give me a forwarding address.'

Edith followed her into the hall and closed the door behind her. 'What's going on?'

'It's my fault,' said Clarissa, once they were in the sitting-room. She perched on the edge of a cretonne-covered armchair. 'It was such a shock! I never imagined . . .' Her voice trailed away.

'What is it?'

Arms folded, Clarissa rocked herself back and forth

on the chair. 'Lily came home sobbing a couple of nights ago. Noel Penrose had proposed to her.'

'Oh! I didn't know Lily and Noel were friends, did you?'

'I'd have put a stop to it if I had.'

Edith frowned. 'Years ago, Hugh thrashed his boys for playing with our children. I thought they'd all kept clear of each other ever since.'

'Lily and Noel went to see his parents to announce their engagement. Hugh assumed Lily was pregnant and flew into a rage.' Clarissa closed her eyes and swallowed. 'He called her a tart.'

'That was unforgivable!'

'Not half as unforgivable as the terrible position I've put her in.'

'What do you mean?'

Clarissa looked at her with tragic eyes. 'I've told her to forget Noel forever.'

'Would a marriage between them be so bad?'

'It's not that.' Clarissa shook her head. 'You kept a terrible secret for years. Well, so did I. Lily can't marry Noel because he's her half-brother. Hugh Penrose is Lily's father.'

'What?' Edith's jaw dropped and she clapped a hand over her mouth. 'Clarissa! No wonder you refused to disclose who Lily's father was. Horrible Hugh! How could you?' She shuddered.

Clarissa looked away from her friend's horrified gaze. 'I've asked myself that question over and over ever since. He was so conceited. But I was very confused and dreadfully unhappy back then. My father . . .' She shrugged. 'Suffice it to say, I hated men. I thought it would be fun to make Hugh fall in love with me and then cast him aside. And I did. But I never expected to discover I was pregnant.' She gave a wan smile. 'The only good thing to come out of that sordid affair was Lily. But she hates me now, of course.'

'Oh, Clarissa!' Edith reached out for her friend's hand. 'Why didn't you tell me before?'

'I wanted to forget. I became a different person after Lily was born and I've tried my best to be a good mother.'

'You are a good mother and Lily will remember that, once she's over the shock.'

'Will she? Oh, Edith, what if she never comes back?'

Edith raised Clarissa's hand to her cheek, saying, 'Of course she will.' But was no more certain these hollow words of comfort were true than she was that her own daughter would forgive Edith her past sins.

Chapter 10

January 1915

Cornwall

It was cold in Wilfred's studio and Pearl wore finger-less gloves and a shawl while she sat at her desk writing out the last of the orders. A melancholy mood had settled upon her. Once the decoration of a townhouse in Chelsea was completed, there was no new project to take its place. Against all hopeful expectations, the war hadn't been over by Christmas and people weren't inclined to spend their money on luxuries in the present circumstances. She enjoyed being a working woman with money of her own and she'd have to find something else to do, like Lily.

Lily had written, saying General Beaumont was a 'dear old thing', though his memoirs were a rambling muddle of events and it was taking time to organise them into a cohesive whole. She'd made no mention of Noel, not even after Pearl wrote to tell her he'd enlisted with the Duke of Cornwall's Light Infantry straight after she'd left and was training at Bodmin Camp.

Pearl was distracted from her work by a clamorous noise outside, growing to a full-throated roar. She peered out of the window. A cream motorcar with big, brass headlamps was driving through the court-yard. Astonished, she stared at it. She'd seen motors in London but there'd never been one at Spindrift before. It pulled up before the stables with a squeal of brakes and a series of deafening bangs like rifle shots. The chickens squawked and fluttered away to a safe distance. The silence following the racket sang in Pearl's ears.

A tall figure wrapped in a duster coat, cap and a yellow muffler descended from the motor and looked around him.

Pearl pulled her shawl around her shoulders and went outside. She waited while the visitor took off his gauntlets and goggles. 'Can I help you?' she asked.

'I'm frozen solid in places I didn't even know I had,' he said, unwinding the muffler from the lower part of his face.

'It's certainly cold today.' She eyed his curly black hair and dimpled chin. She guessed he must be in his mid-twenties. There was something about him that was vaguely familiar but she couldn't place it.

'Maxwell Fforbes.' He flashed her a brilliant smile and held out his hand.

Tentatively, she shook it, trying not to simper when he fixed her with his piercing blue gaze. 'Pearl Fairchild,' she replied, wondering why such a divinely handsome man would visit Spindrift.

'Perhaps we ought to go inside?' he said.

Realisation dawned. 'Oh!' said Pearl. 'You must be the poet Mother mentioned at breakfast. The one who's going to rent the empty studio?'

'Novelist, actually.'

The door to the jewellery workshop opened and Clarissa and Augustus came out to see what was happening.

'This is Mr Fforbes who's taking the vacant studio,' said Pearl. 'I'll show him where everything is.'

85

'Then we wouldn't dream of interfering,' said Clarissa, giving her a knowing smile. 'Would we, Augustus?'

'Absolutely not. Though I should like to take a closer look at your splendid motorcar later.'

'By all means,' said Mr Fforbes. 'If you like, I'll take you for a spin once I'm settled?'

'I do like,' said Augustus. 'Meanwhile, we'll look forward to meeting you properly at dinner.'

They retreated to their workshop and Pearl took Mr Fforbes to the studio. 'It's a bit Spartan,' she said, 'but Daisy lit the stove earlier and it'll soon warm up.'

Mr Fforbes glanced around, taking in the shabby armchair beside the stove, the rag rug and deal table under the window. He picked up a small marble statuette of a young girl dancing; the lifelike drapes of her Grecian-style dress looked as if they'd be soft to the touch. 'This is delightful.'

'A master stonemason lived here for years,' said Pearl. She smiled, remembering Gilbert, a big bear of a man perpetually covered in stone dust. 'He left us a while ago to work on renovating the stonework in a Spanish cathedral.'

'I notice the adjacent studio is empty, too,' said Mr Fforbes.

'Yes, the former tenants, Mabel and Maude, were elderly spinster sisters, who died within four months of each other, poor things. They made the most beautiful textile collages. You can see one in the sitting-room and there are others in the gallery.'

Mr Fforbes looked at the staircase. 'May I go up?'

'Of course. Don't forget to close the blackout curtains tonight before you light the lamp. The privy and the well are outside at the end of the courtyard.'

He laughed. 'What a lark! Of course, it's a palace in

comparison to the trenches. by all accounts. It'll serve my needs.' He blew on his frozen fingers. 'I doubt I'll be here more than a few weeks anyway.'

'What a shame!' Spindrift had become so gloomy recently that Pearl was disappointed to hear he didn't intend to stay. 'I mean, it's glorious in the summer,' she stammered, hoping he didn't think she was flirting with him.

He smiled. 'I'm sure it's delightful.'

'Shall we go into the house? I'll introduce you to my mother and we'll have some tea to warm you up after your journey.'

Inside, Pearl heard her mother's voice coming from the kitchen. The door was ajar and Daisy was visible, facing Edith with her arms folded and a triumphant expression on her face. 'Twice the money,' she said, 'and shorter hours.'

Standing at the sink, Mrs Rowe the cook-house-keeper cast a disapproving glance over her shoulder and clattered a saucepan onto the drainer.

'Mama?' said Pearl.

Edith glanced at her and then noticed the visitor. 'Oh, Mr Fforbes?'

He stepped forward to shake her hand. 'Mrs Fairchild, delighted to meet you.' He glanced at Daisy. 'But I believe we're interrupting?'

'It's of no consequence.' Edith gave a distracted smile. 'Pearl, would you take Mr Fforbes into the drawing-room? I'll join you shortly.'

Pearl led the visitor away.

In the drawing-room, he walked over to the window. 'What a glorious view! There's something so peaceful about the sea, isn't there?'

'Unless it's stormy,' said Pearl. 'Then the waves

87

roar and batter the rocks, sending explosions of spray into the air.'

'How dramatic! I imagine there's always something of interest to see here, whatever the season.'

'The summer's best of all but this time of year is quieter, without the holiday makers thronging the lanes and visiting our gallery. I daresay there'll be fewer sightseers this year, though.'

Edith hurried into the room, followed by Daisy carrying a tray. 'I'm sorry to have kept you, Mr Fforbes. Please, do sit down.'

The maid clattered about with the cups, thumped the tea pot and milk jug onto the table and then banged the door shut behind her.

Edith sighed. 'I see Daisy's going to be impossible until she leaves at the end of next week. She's informed me she's going to work at a munitions factory with her sister.'

'My mother is despairing,' said Mr Fforbes, 'since the servants in our London house are sadly depleted for the same reason. One of the maids is now a bus conductress and the former scullery-maid is working in a tent-making factory. At our country house in Gloucestershire, the gardener and his boy have enlisted, along with the footman. Mother is appalled because my sister Daphne is doing voluntary work at St Thomas's Hospital.' He grimaced. 'Emptying bedpans, if you can believe it.'

'Very worthwhile, I'm sure,' said Edith. 'Still, Daisy's departure leaves us with a difficulty. Our only other servant is Mrs Rowe and she can't do everything. Still, enough of that. Welcome to Spindrift, Mr Fforbes.'

'Thank you.'

She frowned. 'I'm wondering if we might have met

88

somewhere before? I have a feeling that I recognize you.'

'Oh!' said Pearl. 'I thought that too.'

'You do have a good memory!' he said. 'I was touring in this part of the world last summer and called in to the gallery. I bought one of your lovely watercolours. Later, when I remembered I'd seen a notice advertising a vacant studio, I thought it would be just the place for some peace and quiet for me to write.'

'That must be why I thought I'd seen you before, then,' said Edith.

'You mentioned in your response to my letter that meals are included in your rent?' said Mr Fforbes.

She nodded. 'The community eats together and the vegetables and eggs are produced here. The food is simple and sustaining. If it isn't to your taste, there's the Golden Lion in the village. This drawing-room and dining-room are communal areas so don't feel you must stay in your studio. We're very informal here and use Christian names. Please, call me Edith.'

Footsteps clattered through the hall then the door burst open and Roland ran in, followed by the two Collies. 'Mama! Did you see the motorcar?' His hazel eyes shone and his cheeks were flushed. 'It has green leather upholstery and a folding roof!'

Edith smiled. 'Roland, remember your manners! Say good afternoon to Mr Fforbes.'

Roland turned to look at their visitor. 'Good afternoon have you seen the motorcar?' he said, all in one breath.

The dogs came over to inspect Mr Fforbes.

'I certainly have,' he said, patting Blue and Star. 'It belongs to me. It's a Sunbeam four-seater tourer. Come and shake hands and then, when I've finished my tea, I'll take you for a ride.' He fed the dogs a small piece of cake each and they settled down at his feet, staring up at him adoringly.

Pearl watched Mr Fforbes's easy manner with her younger brother and the dogs and her melancholy mood lifted. It would be fun to have him as part of the community, even if only for a month or two.

★ ★ ★

A fortnight later, Pearl and Dora huddled around the sitting-room fire. Pearl tutted under her breath as another stitch slipped off the knitting needle.

Dora took the misshapen piece of knitting out of her hands and carefully picked up the stitch. 'I pity the poor soldier who has to wear this sock,' she said. 'The tension's so tight it'll end up too small even for Roland.'

'I can't get the hang of using two pairs of needles,' said Pearl.

'Perhaps you should put your energy into a different kind of war effort?' Dora's face brightened. 'Come with me to the Red Cross meeting in Wadebridge this afternoon. They need volunteers to roll bandages and box up comforts for soldiers. There are first-aid classes, too.'

'I'd enjoy a change of scene.' Since Daisy had left for the munitions factory at Cligga Head, Pearl had made herself useful around the house but she longed to find something more interesting to keep her busy.

'I'll ask Ursula if she'll collect us from the station in the trap when we return,' said Dora. 'I'll be bringing bags of knitting wool and material to make hospital gowns.'

'How is Ursula?' asked Pearl.

Dora shrugged. 'Anxious. We're working together on an idea for another illustrated book but she's not really concentrating.'

'I know she was very upset when she discovered she's subject to a curfew.'

'Can you blame her?' Dora shook her head. 'She isn't allowed to travel more than five miles from home so she can't visit her parents in London. Although he's German, at least her father's too old to be interned so her mother hasn't been left on her own. I know there's a war on but it does seem harsh.'

★ ★ ★

When the community gathered for lunch, Pearl said, 'I'm going with Dora to the Red Cross meeting in Wadebridge this afternoon.'

'As it happens,' said Maxwell Fforbes, 'I have to drive into Wadebridge to find some petrol. Would you like me to drive you?'

Pearl's eyes lit up at the prospect. 'How exciting!'

Half an hour later they assembled in the courtyard. As instructed, Pearl and Dora had swathed their hats with scarves and knotted them firmly under their chins.

'Shall you sit in the front, Dora?' asked Maxwell.

'I'd prefer to be away from the business end, if you don't mind,' she said, her lips pressed together firmly.

Maxwell settled her on the back seat and tucked a travel rug over her knees. He opened the passenger door for Pearl and grinned at her. 'Hop in while I start her up.'

She watched with interest as he turned the starting

91

handle at the front of the motor two or three times and then stepped back smartly when the engine caught.

And then they were off! The countryside flashed past and Pearl laughed in delight as the wind snatched at the brim of her hat and whipped roses into her cheeks. 'Faster!' she cried.

Maxwell threw back his head and laughed. 'You're a girl after my own heart.' The engine noise increased as the motorcar gained speed. Then they careened around a bend in the lane, narrowly missing a man and his dog.

'Sorry!' Maxwell called out, over his shoulder.

Pearl glanced behind and saw the man shake his fist at them. Dora's eyes were shut and her complexion almost as green as the leather upholstery. 'This is the most thrilling thing I've ever experienced,' shouted Pearl over the roar of the engine. 'How I wish I could drive!'

'I'll teach you, if you like?'

Her eyes widened and she nodded her head vigorously.

Once they reached the outskirts of Wadebridge, Maxwell slowed down and soon the car drew up outside the church hall.

'I'll fuel the motor and return in two hours, as agreed,' he said, opening the passenger door with a flourish.

Pearl and Dora waved as he drove away. 'Wasn't that terrific?' enthused Pearl.

'If God had meant us to go that fast, he'd have given us wheels,' muttered Dora.

The church hall was crowded with chattering women.

Dora led Pearl to a trestle table where a grey-haired

woman with an impressively upholstered bosom pre-sided over a tea urn.

'A new volunteer?' she said. 'Splendid! Now do take a seat before Mrs Kingsley-Jones addresses the meeting.'

Pearl sipped her tea while she studied the other volunteers. Several spoke in the loud and unselfconscious tones of the well-off upper classes, but others were clearly working class.

Dora nudged her. 'Here's the organiser. She'll tell us what we're to do today.'

Mrs Kingsley-Jones clapped her hands and waited until there was silence before she began to speak. 'Good afternoon, ladies! We have a great deal to do this afternoon and I'm looking for volunteers to pack soldiers' comforts. There are also some items of news . . .'

Pearl allowed Mrs Kingsley-Jones's voice to drift away while she pictured Maxwell Fforbes throwing back his head and laughing with the sheer joy of hurtling along the Cornish lanes with the wind in his face.

* * *

Edith and Clarissa were sitting with Rose and Roland while they had their tea.

'Pascal had a letter from his sister to say Gabrielle still hasn't returned to France,' said Edith. 'He's worried she's having travel difficulties.'

'Gabrielle always looks out for herself,' said Clarissa, 'but it's hard for Pascal, not knowing where she is. Perhaps she'll write soon and set his mind at rest.' She sighed. 'I went into the village earlier. There isn't a single bag of sugar left on the shelves in the grocer's. Or any butter or cheese. I don't know if the food shortages are genuine or if it's because people are stockpiling. The price of flour has to be seen to be believed!'

'I'll call into the Mellyns' farm later on,' said Edith, 'and see if Tamara will put some butter and cheese aside for us.' She snatched hold of Roland's hand as he reached across the table. 'Sit down!' she said. 'It's impolite to stretch.'

'But you were talking to Auntie Clarissa and you always say it's rude to interrupt!' he said indignantly.

'Then you should wait until we've finished talking. And please give me that bag of toffees. You may have them back after tea.' She passed him the bread and butter and pocketed the sweets.

'Augustus and I are doing rather well for orders of the locket I designed,' said Clarissa. 'There's room inside for a lock of hair and a photograph. Soldiers are buying them to give to their wives and sweethearts.'

'And I've noticed a regular flow of newly enlisted men visiting Julian's studio to have their photo taken before they join their regiments,' said Edith.

Quick footsteps sounded in the hall and Pearl hurried into the dining-room. She took off her hat. 'Dora and I have solved our servant problem,' she said.

'You've found a girl to interview?'

'Yes. Well, not exactly. We discussed it and agreed the best thing to do was to bring her here straightaway.'

'Oh! I would have liked to see her first.'

'You said you wanted a maid and we've found one.'

Edith raised her eyebrows at Pearl's tone. 'I'd better meet her, then.'

Pearl strode down the corridor and Edith followed

behind. Try as she might to smooth things over, she and her daughter were always at odds with one another these days.

In the kitchen, Dora was talking to a young woman with her hair hidden under a cotton headscarf and a drab shawl around her shoulders. Her eyes were downcast.

'There you are!' said Dora. She cast an anxious glance at Edith. 'This is Annelies Declercq. She's a refugee from Belgium and she speaks French. The Red Cross needed to find homes urgently for a hundred displaced persons. I know we should have asked you first —'

'It's all right,' said Edith. She'd read in the newspapers of the atrocities suffered by the Belgian people when the Germans invaded. The news was dreadful but, until she saw the young woman with her possessions bundled up in a sheet here in Spindrift's kitchen, all that had seemed so far away.

'Anneliese is willing to work as our maid in return for her board and lodging,' said Pearl.

The young woman's complexion was waxen and her blue eyes shadowed and anxious. Her hands, trembling slightly, were clasped together.

Edith spoke to her in French, welcoming her and explaining that she would be paid the same as their last maid, if she'd undertake the same duties.

Anneliese let out her breath in a shuddering sigh. 'Merci, madame.'

'There's just one thing,' said Pearl.

It was then that Edith saw the child sitting motionless on the rocking chair by the range. Her heart sank. They really didn't want the complication of a servant with a child to distract her from her duties.

95

'This is Blanche,' said Pearl.

Perhaps four years old, the girl's blonde head was bowed and she clasped a rag doll to her chest as if she'd never let it go.

Edith rummaged in her pocket and brought out one of Roland's toffees. 'Hello, Blanche,' she said, proffering the sweet.

Slowly the child lifted her head.

Edith caught her breath. The little girl's eyes were curiously blank but that wasn't what had shocked Edith. The child's once pretty face bore an angry red scar from the middle of her forehead down to the top of her right cheekbone.

Chapter 11

January 1915

London

Gabrielle lay on her back, her legs entwined with her lover's under the eiderdown. The winter light that had filtered through the skimpy curtains earlier that afternoon had faded and been replaced by the glow of the streetlamp. She turned her head on the pillow and studied Lionel's profile. Lanky and pale-skinned, he was unfortunately English-looking in comparison to urbane and handsome Rafael, the French lover she'd been forced to leave. Six months ago, she'd thought Lionel's awkward compliments and lack of sophistication endearing. Then, he'd showered her with gifts and taken her to discreet little restaurants. Well, of course they'd been discreet; he'd chosen rendezvous places where none of his friends would see them, in case they told his wife, Muriel. He hadn't told Gabrielle about her for quite a while.

Lionel's sleeping breaths puffed in and out in the most annoying way. The novelty of him had worn off. It wasn't possible for Gabrielle to return to France to live with her mother and stepfather now they'd moved from Nice to Lille for his work. A mere six months after that, the Boche invaded and occupied north-east France, including Lille. In any case, Maman had told Gabrielle she wouldn't have her back — not after her friend, Rafael's wife, had made such a brouhaha over

97

the diamond earrings he'd given Gabrielle.

Carefully, she disentangled herself from Lionel and crept out of bed. Pulling on her wrapper, she helped herself to one of his cigarettes. She curled up in the armchair and tugged back the curtain to look at the stream of traffic in the Edgware Road. Reflectively, she blew a stream of smoke out through the window.

'I say,' said Lionel, his voice blurred by sleep, 'there's a fearful draught. Shut the window and come back to bed, there's a good girl.'

She drew deeply on the cigarette and felt strength coursing through her veins. 'It's growing dark. You should go home to your wife, Lionel.'

He sat up in bed and smoothed down his hair. 'Oh, Lord! I must have fallen asleep.'

Eyes narrowed against the smoke, she watched him dress. It would be the last time, she decided.

He slipped his loose change and cigarette case into his pocket and buttoned his coat. 'Three o'clock next Tuesday?'

She shrugged.

He hesitated. 'Everything all right?'

She pursed her lips and wondered if she should say she was bored by him and that she wasn't prepared to spend another Christmas in this shabby room while he was at home by the fireside, drinking champagne with Muriel.

Lionel patted her shoulder. 'Perhaps I might take you out for tea next time?'

She dropped the cigarette stub into the glass of water on the bedside table. It fizzled and went out, leaving a twist of acrid smoke behind. 'Adieu, Lionel,' she said.

He opened his mouth, as if about to speak, then turned and left.

She stood by the window and watched him hurry along the street. 'Tout change avec le temps,' she murmured.

★ ★ ★

On Tuesday morning, Gabrielle stayed in bed late. The past week spent pondering on her situation without reaching any conclusion had exhausted her. Sitting up too quickly, she was overcome with nausea and had to scrabble under the bed for the chamber pot. A few minutes later, she ceased staring at the garish pattern of red roses around its rim and wiped her mouth. Her pulse raced. Moving slowly to allow her stomach to settle, she fetched her diary from the chest of drawers. Feverishly thumbing through the pages, she counted the days. Another wave of nausea mixed with panic overcame her when she saw her monthly visitor was late. How could that be? Lionel had been careful and she always washed herself afterwards. She lay back on the bed, her fist pressed to her lips while she tried to absorb the terrifying possibility that she might be pregnant.

She'd intended to go out at the time Lionel was expected but it would be foolish to turn him away now. If she was enceinte, he had a responsibility that she would make sure he accepted. He didn't know she'd followed him home to St John's Wood one afternoon and discovered where he lived. She was sure he'd do whatever was necessary to prevent Muriel from finding out her husband kept a mistress.

Later, she made a special effort with her hair, patted

rouge on her ashen cheeks and put on her silk under-wear. At three o'clock, she sat beside the window to watch the flow of pedestrians in the street. Half an hour later, she drummed her fingers on the arm of the chair. Lionel still hadn't arrived. He'd probably had an unexpected meeting at his office. By five o'clock she was annoyed. Perhaps he'd call by to see her after he'd finished work? By eight o'clock she was anxious and at eleven, she went to bed.

The following morning, there was a rap on Gabrielle's door and her heart lifted. She felt queasy but, thankfully, it wasn't as bad as the day before. Hastily pinching colour into her cheeks, she hurried to let Lionel in. But it was her landlady, Mrs Butcher, who stood outside, clutching a note against her pinafore.

'Your gentleman friend,' she said, her lips curling in distaste, 'called by to pay your rent. He asked me to give you this note. The rent's paid until the end of the week. I don't allow arrears.' She clumped away downstairs.

Gabrielle slammed the door and tore open the envelope.

Dear Gabrielle,
  I am not an insensitive man and you do not need to tell me that you no longer hold me in regard. I have enjoyed our time together and will always remember you with fondness.
  I wish you nothing but happiness in the future.
  Yours sincerely,
  Lionel Glover

'Non!' She sank down on the bed, cursing herself for allowing him to see her boredom. After two attempts,

100

she penned a suitably contrite letter, saying that he'd entirely mistaken her feelings. She explained that she hadn't felt very well and that she needed to see him urgently. She underlined the last word. Would he visit her that evening? It pained her to write it but she signed the letter 'Avec amour pour toujours, your Gabrielle'. She sprayed the envelope with her perfume and hurried to deliver it to his office at the Ministry of Transport.

A clerk took the note from her and promised to hand it to Mr Glover.

For two days she waited, in vain, for Lionel to reply.

The following day was a Saturday and she dressed in the chic violet hat and coat she'd bought in Paris and took the omnibus to St John's Wood. She lurked outside Lionel's house for a while but no one went in or came out. She took a deep breath, walked up the garden path of the large semi-detached house and knocked on the door. The echo inside was so loud she knew at once no one was at home.

A woman opened the front door of the adjacent house.

Gabrielle leaned over the low wall that separated the gardens. 'I am looking for Mr and Mrs Glover,' she said.

'They've gone, dear,' said the woman. 'Upped and left in a hurry.'

A cold wash of fear flowed over Gabrielle. 'Gone?' she said.

'Mr Glover enlisted and then bundled his wife and children off to stay with her mother for the duration.'

'Children?'

'The poor dear was in a terrible state. Her husband had never once mentioned the prospect of going into the army and suddenly he was insistent on enlisting immediately. He was a civil servant and his job was a reserved occupation, you see, so there was no need.' She clicked her tongue against her teeth. 'Selfish, I call it, when he's got three children and a wife to support. There are plenty of unmarried men champing at the bit to see off the Germans.'

'It is necessary that I see him!'

The elderly woman looked at her curiously. 'Foreign, are you, dear? One of those Belgian refugees?'

'Not at all.' Gabrielle tossed her head. 'I am French.' She turned her back and walked away. There was one other course of action, though she didn't care for it.

An hour later, she waited in the elegant, marble-floored hall of Benedict's house. It was always difficult to think of him as her father. He wasn't at all like Papa, who had died when she was young. It had shocked her when Maman told her that her papa wasn't her father at all but an English gentleman was. She'd wondered if that meant he lived in a castle. She'd been disappointed when Maman introduced her to Benedict Fairchild. After that, she'd been sent to stay in his rambling house by the sea for the summer holidays. Maman said it was so she would learn to speak English well — she was half English, after all — but Gabrielle knew it was to remind Benedict that he'd promised to share his estate equally between his six children, legitimate and illegitimate. She hadn't seen him for many years, though she'd continued to spend holidays at Spindrift House until five years ago. There had seemed little point in enduring the countryside, where nothing ever happened, if her father was never there to be reminded of her existence.

Gabrielle studied the fine paintings and the magnificent flower arrangement on the hall table. She'd never visited Benedict's London house and it was far more chic than Spindrift House. Her interest was piqued. After all, one day, a share of this grand town-house would be hers too.

Footsteps clipped along the passage and Benedict Fairchild appeared. 'Gabrielle, what a surprise!' He didn't sound as if it was a pleasant one.

Once, she'd thought he was débonnaire but he hadn't aged well. 'I have been working in London,' she said. She stepped forward to kiss him on both cheeks, noticing the sour smell of whisky on his breath. 'You look well,' she lied, remembering how susceptible he'd always been to flattery. 'I can hardly believe you are old enough to be my father.'

Benedict's eyes gleamed. 'And you've grown into a beautiful woman. How time flies!' He glanced at his pocket watch. 'Shall we pop along to the Ritz for tea?'

'Why not here?' Gabrielle longed to see more of her future inheritance. How she would like to live in this grand house!

'No, no,' he said, 'that won't do at all. Mother is expected back very soon and, I'm sure you under-stand, she'd ask awkward questions.'

So, his mother, her grandmother, didn't know about Gabrielle. Still, it was not sensible to annoy Bene-dict when she needed him to help her. She smiled. 'I should like very much to take tea at the Ritz.'

★ ★ ★

Gabrielle discreetly blotted her mouth with the nap-kin. Thankfully, her stomach had settled and she'd eaten several tiny sandwiches, two scones with cream and a few exquisite pastries. In her current situation, she must make the most of every opportunity. The money she'd saved in the cigar box under her bed wasn't enough to keep her for long and she didn't want to be forced to sell Rafael's diamond earrings.

Benedict wolfed down the last meringue, leaving a smear of cream on his lip. 'So, tell me why you're in London, Gabrielle.'

'I arrived last summer to act as a companion to an elderly widow. I made her travel arrangements, booked tickets for the opera and so on. Then I escorted her to the Lake District, where she has a cousin who married an Englishman. When war was declared. Madame Armand was anxious about returning to France so her cousin invited her to remain with her.'

'And your employment ceased?'

Gabrielle nodded. 'I wanted to see more of London and imagined I still had time to return to France afterwards. Maman lives in Occupied Lille with my stepfather. I found some translating work for a few months and then . . .' She sighed, remembering how it had all started when she ran into Lionel in the street. 'Then I discovered it was difficult to return.' She glanced at Benedict from under her eyelashes. 'And perhaps I didn't want to. I came to England because I'd had a disagreement with Maman.'

Benedict grimaced. 'Tricky woman to disagree with, your maman.'

'Exactement!' Gabrielle heaved a sigh. 'But now I have no work and cannot pay my rent.' She allowed her lower lip to tremble and it wasn't hard for her to look tearful. 'I am so frightened — destitute and all alone in a strange country. I didn't know where to turn but then I thought of you!'

'What is it you want, Gabrielle?' Benedict's voice was cold.

'Somewhere to stay. A loan.' She held her breath.

'I can't help you,' he said. 'Under the terms of my father's will, I'm allowed to stay in Mother's house in Berkeley Square but I cannot have visitors. It's essential I don't upset Mother or I'll forfeit my inheritance. And I'm extremely short of funds.' His lips tightened. 'In fact, I'm in considerable debt.'

'But you must be able to do something to help me?' said Gabrielle, panic rising in her throat.

'My hands are tied.' He turned his palms up.

She scrabbled in her bag and opened her purse. 'Look!' she said. 'Not a single sou!'

'Sorry, there's nothing I can do.'

'I am expecting a child!' It had burst out of her before she could stop herself.

'Oh, Lord!' Benedict wiped his face with his palm. 'You have got yourself in a pickle.'

'You cannot walk away and leave me in the gutter.' She pressed her knuckles to her lips while her thoughts raced frantically. 'I will throw myself on your mother's mercy and tell her I am your love child.'

'You will not!' His face paled.

'Then help me!'

'Find yourself a husband, is my best advice. But you'd better make it pretty damn' quick.' He drummed his fingers on the table and then his scowl cleared. 'You might go to Spindrift.' He smiled with relief at having solved the problem. 'Have the child there and give it to an orphanage.'

Gabrielle licked her finger and blotted up some crumbs from her plate. There was merit in his suggestion. But she wanted him to do more. 'I don't have the train fare,' she said. 'Or enough to pay last week's rent.'

'Can't help you there.'

'I'm sure Grandmère will not be happy when I sit on the steps of her house in Berkeley Square, begging for pennies, because you have failed in your responsibility to me.'

Benedict raked his fingers through his hair. 'You really are infuriatingly like your dratted mother.'

Gabrielle waited while he huffed and muttered.

'Look,' he said, 'I'll find you enough for a train ticket to Cornwall and some pocket money, but then you'll have to get your uncle Pascal to look after you.' He grinned nastily. 'He has an overdeveloped sense of duty and is good at picking up the pieces of other people's problems. And there's another thing. Perhaps I'll send you more money if you'll let me know what's happening at Spindrift.'

'What kind of thing?'

'I want evidence that Edith and Pascal are sleeping together.'

She raised her eyebrows, wondering if it were true and, if so, why Benedict cared. After all, he'd deserted his wife years before.

Benedict crumpled his napkin and threw it down beside his plate. 'Edith told me, without a shred of shame, that she'd lied to me for years and Jasper is Pascal's bastard. But I can't prove it.'

Gabrielle blinked. Whoever would have imagined that her uncle, always so highly principled, had indulged in such a moral lapse? What a hypocrite! He'd been so angry with her mother when he'd discovered Gabrielle was Benedict's daughter. 'Why must you prove it?'

Benedict leaned forward and fixed her with the intensity of his gaze. 'Because Edith's still my wife and I need to find a way to force her, and the whole blasted community, out of Spindrift.'

Gabrielle shrugged. 'I'll see what I can do.'

Chapter 12

January 1915

Cornwall

Edith carried a cup of coffee into Pascal's studio and placed it on the worktable at his side.

He glanced up with a smile. 'Did I miss elevenses?' Catching her hand as she turned to leave, he lifted it to his lips. 'Sit with me?'

She pulled up a chair and leaned in to look at his canvas. 'Oh! This is very different from any of your other work,' she said. 'I like it.'

'It is a new challenge,' he said. 'Since the Defence of the Realm Act now forbids me to paint landscapes en plein air, I must do something different.'

'You'd think the government would have more important things to worry about than imagining every artist painting a pretty view is spying for the Germans, wouldn't you?'

'Hostility against them is growing,' said Pascal. 'Ursula hardly dares venture into the village.'

'Feelings are bound to run high, especially if you've lost a son to the war.' Edith studied Pascal's canvas again. 'What inspired you to try this style?'

'When I studied at the Académie des Beaux-Arts, I was interested by Seurat's work.'

'Pointillism?'

He nodded. 'You see how tiny dots of paint merge to make different colours when you stand back from the canvas? Seurat's work is subtle and uses soft tones, but Van Gogh occasionally employed the technique with bright pigment on small areas of his canvases. I shall experiment and find my own style.'

'I look forward to seeing how it develops,' said Edith. 'The important question though is whether our work will sell in wartime? I've completed several canvases for when the gallery opens in June but will visitors come to Port Isaac this summer? The families of enlisted men may feel it's wrong to have a holiday while their boys are at the Front.'

'And some will wish to be distracted from thoughts of war by visiting the seaside.'

Edith sighed. 'I have no new commissions. If we don't sell work through the Spindrift Gallery, how are we going to pay the bills? We have savings but it's impossible to know how long the war will last.'

'We shall visit the galleries where we've sold work before.'

'And then there must be some useful way to contribute to the war effort, apart from knitting misshapen socks.' She nibbled at her thumbnail, thinking. 'Perhaps a sale of work at the Red Cross hall in Wadebridge? Dora says there are some affluent volunteers there. I must do something.'

Pascal caressed her cheek. 'What is it, mon amour? You are agitated.'

She rested her face against his palm. 'I'm so fearful Jasper and Lucien will enlist. I'd hoped the war would be over by now.'

'Jasper is opposed to violence but he will do his duty if called upon,' said Pascal. 'All his life, Lucien has wanted to be a veterinarian. I do not imagine he will voluntarily abandon his course before he finishes it.' He shrugged. 'The war may be over by then.'

Edith stood up and kissed his forehead. 'Don't forget your coffee.'

Walking along the passage, she glimpsed Jasper crouched on the kitchen floor. Curious, she paused in the doorway. Anneliese was peeling carrots at the scrubbed pine table and her little daughter sat on the slate floor beneath. Jasper was talking in a squeaky voice and making Blanche's rag doll jump up and down so as to amuse her.

'Hello!' said Edith, smiling at Anneliese. 'How are you settling in?' She spoke in French, thinking that the maid would have to learn some more English or it would be difficult for her to understand Mrs Rowe's instructions.

The young woman rose to her feet and thanked her.

Jasper handed the doll back to Blanche and stood up. 'I was saying to Anneliese that I'll give her English lessons. It's uncomfortable not to know what everyone is saying.'

'I was thinking the same,' said Edith. 'If you can spare the time, that would be very helpful. And now, all those years Pascal taught you children to speak French will have been worthwhile.'

Anneliese's eyes were watchful as she listened to them.

Jasper and Edith walked together into the hall.

'I have no commissions at present,' he said, 'but I thought I might paint Anneliese and Blanche. There is such sadness in their faces that it moves me. We can talk a little while they sit for the portrait.'

'It wouldn't be easy for Blanche if she has no English when she goes to school. And then there's that dreadful scar. Such a tragedy.'

110

'A German cavalry officer's sabre did that to her. She hasn't spoken a word since.' A muscle clenched in Jasper's jaw. 'He'd already hacked her father to death in front of her and torched their farmhouse.'

Edith clapped a hand over her mouth, sickened at the thought of such an act of barbarity. 'There are no words . . .'

'Quite.'

'Anneliese brought so little with her. I suppose it all burned. I'll speak to Clarissa to see if some of Rose's old clothes might be cut down for Blanche and also what I can find for Anneliese. The poor woman probably isn't fit to for heavy work at present so I'd better warn Mrs Rowe.'

'Annaliese says hard work helps to make her tired enough to sleep at night,' said Jasper.

'We'll do what we can to make her feel safe,' said his mother.

★ ★ ★

'Don't hold it like a tennis raquet!' said Maxwell, laughing. 'Keep your thumb pointing forward next to your knuckles or you'll be sorry if the handle kicks back when the engine catches.'

Tentatively, Pearl turned the starter handle a few times.

'You're not churning butter! Rotate it a couple of times until you feel a slight resistance, then give it a sudden, firm swing downwards and back off sharpish.'

Pearl tried again. 'It's getting harder . . .'

'Now!' said Maxwell.

She threw her weight onto the handle and stepped

back smartly as the engine fired up.

The two dogs, sniffing about the courtyard, barked furiously at the sudden noise.

Maxwell cheered. 'Well done! Now hop in and I'll show you how the gears work.'

Pearl frowned as she concentrated on driving slowly around the courtyard. The dogs loped behind, snapping at the tyres.

'Let's go onto the open road now,' said Maxwell.

Pearl gripped the steering wheel and stared straight ahead, resisting the compulsion to close her eyes when she drove into the narrow driveway leading from the courtyard to the lane. The buildings to either side seemed too close together to allow the motorcar to pass between them. She let out her breath in relief as they emerged unscathed through the gateway.

Before long, they were tootling along the lanes and Pearl was enjoying herself. There was a frightening moment when a man on a horse trotted towards them but Maxwell caught hold of the steering wheel and guided the motorcar into a field gateway until the horseman had passed.

An hour later, Pearl drove triumphantly back into Spindrift's courtyard.

'You've done very well for a beginner,' he said, 'but you'll need more practice before you're quite safe on the road. I suggest you drive next time you and Dora attend the Red Cross meeting in Wadebridge.'

'I'd love that!' said Pearl. 'I never imagined I'd drive a motorcar.'

'You never know when such a skill may become useful.'

'I've taken up enough of your time for today,' she said. 'You must be aching to return to writing your novel.'

Maxwell rasped his fingers over his chin. 'Well,' he said, 'not exactly. The truth is . . .'

'What?'

He shrugged. 'I'm suffering from . . .' He frowned and then his brow smoothed. 'Writer's block, that's it! Can't seem to find the words to write what I want to say. That's why I came here. I needed peace and quiet to think.'

'Mama sometimes finds she can't paint. She says it's either because she's worried about something or she's made a fundamental mistake with the composition.'

'That's it exactly!' said Maxwell.

'What's your novel about?'

'Oh, it's . . .' He scratched his nose and peered into the distance as if he'd find the answer there.

'Yes?' prompted Pearl.

'Well, it's about a girl — a rather lovely girl actually. And she lives in a wonderful old house by the sea but . . .' He smiled. 'Yes, that's it. What she doesn't know is that there's a secret tunnel under the house and smugglers are storing their contraband there.'

'What happens next?'

'Ah, well, that's the bit I haven't worked out yet.' His expression brightened. 'But I've decided to base my fictional house on Spindrift. It's so atmospheric and would make a perfect setting for an adventure, don't you think?'

'Did you know there really are smugglers' tunnels under the Golden Lion in the village? And there's another leading from the cave on the beach up to the headland. Years ago, when we were children, Lily and I ran away and hid in the cave. We thought

113

our parents didn't love us and we wanted to frighten them.' Pearl shuddered. 'We did that, all right, and nearly died in the process. A landslip trapped us in the cave and half the village turned out to look for us. I had pneumonia and lost consciousness, but Lily managed to find the tunnel. She climbed the steps inside the cliff until she emerged onto the headland.'

'What an adventure!'

'It still makes me shiver to think of it.' Opening the car door, Pearl stepped onto the running board. 'Thank you for teaching me to drive. It's been absolutely thrilling.' She smiled. 'And perhaps a little terrifying, too. In return, will you let me know if there's something I can do to help you with your book?'

Maxwell thought for a moment. 'If I'm going to use Spindrift House as the inspiration for the house in my story, would you help me look around and decide where the secret tunnel and passages might be? Perhaps we might make a plan of the house so that I can keep it by me while I'm writing after I've left?'

She didn't want him to leave. 'Wilfred taught me how to draw plans,' she said, 'though I've never drawn any for a house as large and rambling as Spindrift.'

'Shall we start tomorrow morning, then?'

Pearl hummed to herself as she walked back to the house. She missed Lily and she hadn't seen much of Adela because it was too cold to meet for long in the cove. Now Wilfred no longer had any work for her, Pearl was unsettled and wanted to do more than knit comforts for soldiers. But Maxwell's arrival, bursting noisily into the deathly quiet of her life, had lightened her mood and brought some fun to Spindrift again.

Chapter 13

Gabrielle was irritated at having to wait in the cold at the station until the station master's boy fetched Jarvis with his pony and trap. She'd become used to the conveniences of London life and returning to the Cornish countryside held little appeal.

Arriving at Spindrift House, she didn't tip the driver because he didn't help with her baggage. She dragged her cases through the front gate and dumped them on the path. She lifted her chin for courage and knocked on the door.

'I am Mademoiselle Caron,' she said to the maid who opened the door. 'I have come to see Pascal Joubert.'

The maid indicated the hall chair and then disappeared down the shadowy passage towards the kitchen.

Moments later, footsteps clipped over the slate floor as Jasper strode towards her.

'Gabrielle,' he said, 'this is a surprise! Take a seat in the drawing-room. I'll find Pascal and send for some tea.'

'Coffee,' she said. 'I cannot abide English tea. And my luggage is outside, if you would fetch it?'

The fire hadn't been lit in the drawing-room and it was chilly. Until now, she'd only ever visited Spindrift House in the summer. Today, the sea pounded the rocks below and the sky was a leaden grey. She shivered. The last thing she wanted was to be here, in disgrace and in debt to Edith and Pascal for taking

115

her in, but there was nowhere else she could go.

The door opened and Pascal came to greet her. 'Gabrielle, why are you not in France?' he asked.

She kissed her uncle's cheeks and sat on the sofa beside Jasper when he returned. 'I didn't know where else to turn,' she said. 'I found translating work in London, intending to earn enough for my passage back to France, but Lille is now Occupied and it was too dangerous for me to return there. I was forced to use my savings to pay the rent,' she said. 'I have nothing left. Benedict wouldn't help and told me to ask you for shelter.'

Pascal ran his fingers through his hair. 'That is not just my decision,' he said.

Gabrielle tensed. Surely he wouldn't refuse her? She glanced at Jasper. He wasn't her half-brother after all but her cousin. Perhaps there was another way forward. 'Jasper,' she said, her voice quavering, 'I appeal to you. Please, will you ask your mother if I may stay? I have nowhere else to go!' Her voice rose on a wail, tinged with a very real edge of panic.

'I cannot imagine she'd turn you out,' he said, 'but I don't know what opportunities there are for you to find employment in Port Isaac. Everyone at Spindrift has to contribute to the upkeep of the community.'

She stared at him. She hadn't considered it before this but the chances of her finding work in this rural backwater were slight. It hadn't occurred to her she might be expected to pay to be allowed to stay. 'I . . .' She swallowed. 'I need time to find a situation.' But she knew few people in Cornwall would have any need of a translator. 'Perhaps I might find a position as a French teacher?'

Pascal looked doubtful and Gabrielle's spirits sank.

116

'Servants are needed since so many have enlisted or gone to work in the factories,' he said.

'A servant? Me?' An icy shudder rippled down Gabrielle's spine. If she were really reduced to that, she'd soon lose even a lowly position once it became obvious she was pregnant. Her only other choice was to find a husband. But she'd have to act quickly.

Pascal rose to his feet. 'I shall speak to Edith.'

There was desperation in Gabrielle's breast as he left the room. 'Jasper, I'm so frightened to think what will become of me.' She hid her face in her hands and wept.

After a moment, he awkwardly put his arm around her.

Sobbing, she nestled her face into his shoulder.

He patted her back. 'I'm sure you'll manage something,' he said.

She'd known him for years, this brother who was her brother no longer. Perhaps it wouldn't be too bad to be married to him? He was good-looking and he was dutiful, like her uncle Pascal. Drawing a deep breath, she gazed up at him, her eyelashes spangled with tears. 'Dearest Jasper,' she whispered. Sliding her hand behind his head, she pulled his face towards her. Something flickered in his brown eyes as their lips met. Desire? Surprise? She pressed herself against him and felt him begin to respond. But then he jerked away.

'Gabrielle, no!' He wiped his palm over his mouth, as if to wipe her kiss away.

'I thought you liked me?'

'You're my sister!'

'But I'm not, am I? Benedict told me you are Pascal's son.'

117

'Nevertheless . . .' Jasper stood up and moved away to look out of the window.

Gabrielle sighed. In truth, kissing him had felt wrong.

The drawing-room door opened and Edith came in, followed by Pascal. She looked strained and there was little welcome in her expression. 'I understand you find yourself in difficulties, Gabrielle?' she said. 'Unfortunately, commissions are very thin on the ground since the war began and we're all struggling to cover costs. We simply cannot afford to offer you charity. If you wish to become a temporary member of the community, you will have to pay for your board and lodging and take a share in the household duties, as we all do.'

'But I have no savings or employment!' protested Gabrielle.

'Then you may have your old bed in Pearl and Nell's room and stay here as our guest for one month,' said Edith. 'During that time, you must write to your mother for financial support or find yourself paid work.'

A flare of anger made Gabrielle tighten her lips. There was nothing to be done but to look meek, though. Temporary refuge was better than none at all, she supposed, and there was also the chance Benedict might send her money if she found evidence that Edith and Pascal were sleeping together. She would have to see what she could discover.

★ ★ ★

'If I'm going to continue to teach you to drive,' Maxwell said to Pearl, 'you must learn to change a tyre, top up the radiator and do other necessary checks under the bonnet before setting out on each trip.'

Pearl opened her mouth to say she didn't think such tasks were suited to a woman, when she saw the challenging gleam in his eye. If women wanted the vote, she supposed they had to prove themselves equal to men. 'Will you show me?' she said.

Surprisingly, it was all very interesting, especially when he explained the basic principles of how an engine worked. It was satisfying to discover she could complete these tasks as well as any man.

Afterwards, they scrubbed oil stains off their hands at the boot-room sink.

'It's astonishing what you can accomplish when you challenge yourself,' said Maxwell.

'Is that why you're writing a novel, to challenge yourself?'

He dried his hands on the roller towel, a frown on his face. 'Yesterday, I went into the village to buy a newspaper and Chegwin's baker's shop was closed. The blinds were down and draped with black crepe. A photograph of a young sailor was pinned up behind the glass in the door and a group of women, all weeping, stood outside.'

'Wilfred mentioned Jimmy Chegwin had fallen,' said Pearl.

Maxwell sighed. 'I was profoundly uncomfortable that a young sailor from a simple background had sacrificed his life whilst I, who inherited a significant investment portfolio, have done little for the good of others. It's time I demonstrated I'm better than that.'

It seemed to Pearl that a chill wind blew across the back of her neck. 'You're going to enlist?'

'We thought the conflict would be over by Christmas but it wasn't. How much longer can I ignore my duty?'

There really wasn't any answer to that, she thought.

* * *

That afternoon, Pearl held the end of a surveyor's tape measure while Maxwell unrolled it, walking backwards until he reached the drawing-room window.

'Twenty-five feet and three inches,' he said.

Pearl wrote down the measurement on her sketch plan.

'Isn't this the most superb view of the sea from here?' he said, scribbling in his notebook.

'It's even better from my mother's bedroom directly above,' said Pearl. 'We needn't measure that, though. It's the same size as this one.'

He looked up from his notebook with a winning smile. 'I want to see everything, even the kitchens. Spindrift will be the model for the house in my novel and I'll need to be able to picture it clearly in my mind's eye after I've left here.'

'Once we've measured the last of the main rooms we'll discuss where your imaginary secret passage might be sited.'

'It might be easier to locate secret storage rooms for the contraband near the kitchen,' said Maxwell, 'instead of having a passage all the way down to the sea. After all, you said there's a tunnel from the cave on the beach that comes up on the headland?'

Pearl shuddered. 'There certainly is. I'll show it to you but you can't go inside. A safety grille was fixed over the opening after Lily and I were trapped. I still hate being in confined spaces.'

120

Maxwell grimaced. 'I'm not sure I'd want to go in, anyway.'

Half an hour later, when they'd measured the first floor, they went up to the two attic rooms on the second floor, one either side of the small landing. Formerly servants' dormitories, the two long rooms stretched over the whole house and were now used as artists' studios. Each had rows of dormer windows in the low sloping ceilings.

Edith was absorbed in her work in one studio as they tiptoed in to measure the space. She glanced up briefly from her easel but didn't speak.

Pearl breathed in the familiar scent of oil paint and linseed oil that she always associated with her mother. As a child she'd spent hours lying prone on the floor, tracing the patterns made from the myriad paint drips and runs on the wooden boards, while Edith worked.

Maxwell gestured towards the door with his head and they left Edith to her work.

A murmur of voices came from the other studio and, when Pearl pushed open the door, she saw Jasper painting Anneliese and Blanche.

The Belgian maid sat in a shadowy corner on a low stool with her bundle of possessions tied up in a sheet beside her. Blanche sat on her knee, rag doll clasped against her chest. Winter sunlight angled through the window, highlighting Anneliese's shuttered expression and the threadbare condition of the refugees' shabby clothing.

The tableau of helpless suffering was inexpressibly poignant and, when the little girl glanced up to see who had entered the room, Pearl was shocked again by the livid scar on the girl's face. No child, nor her mother come to that, should have had to suffer as they had.

'I'm sorry to disturb you,' said Maxwell softly.

Jasper stood back and stretched. 'No matter,' he said. 'I was saying to Annelies that she and Blanche should take a break.'

Maxwell rolled out the tape measure again to take the dimensions and write some notes in his little black book.

Curious, Pearl watched as he measured the ceiling height at both the apex of the room and the eaves.

Jasper conversed quietly in French with Anneliese while Blanche studied them in silence.

'That's it, thank you,' said Maxwell, winding up the tape and heading for the door. He paused by Jasper's easel to glance at his canvas. 'I say,' he said, 'this is going to be very good.'

Downstairs again, Pearl and Maxwell investigated the kitchen, pantry and storerooms. When they went down to the coal cellar, Maxwell grasped her hand. 'Don't worry about being in a confined space,' he said, 'I'll make sure you're all right.'

She hesitated, knowing it was very forward of him to hold her hand but he seemed intent only upon opening the cellar door. He pulled her inside and she looked up at the sliver of light admitted by the tiny window beneath the low ceiling. Maxwell squeezed her hand and she was reassured by the warmth of his grip.

'I've seen enough,' he said, drawing her away. He released her hand and dropped a brief kiss on her forehead. 'Brave girl.'

She looked up and met his eyes. There was a navy ring around the cornflower blue of his irises. For a long moment they held each other's gaze. He moved a fraction closer to her but then looked away, breaking the spell.

He cleared his throat. 'I shall hide my imaginary smugglers' cache of contraband behind a false wall in the coal cellar,' he said.

Pearl bent over her sketch plan to disguise her flaming cheeks. 'I have all the information I need to draw up the plan.' Her tone was matter-of-fact but her heart thumped.

'You've been a great help,' said Maxwell.

'I shall expect a signed copy of your book once it's published.'

He flashed a smile at her. 'You'll be the first to see it if it's published.'

'You'd better get on with writing it then,' she said.

★ ★ ★

Later, Pearl went into the courtyard to feed the chickens and saw a young woman walking towards her. 'Lily!' Running, she caught her friend in an embrace. 'I didn't know you were coming home today!'

'I managed to arrange General Beaumont's memoirs into some kind of order,' she said, 'so now I'm out of work and had to come home.' She pulled a face. 'I'm dreading seeing Mother again after that argument we had before I left.'

'She was certainly very upset,' said Pearl. 'I'm on my way to Wilfred's studio to use his drawing board. He's out at present so I can brew you a cup of tea on the Primus stove and we'll have a good gossip.'

Soon they were huddled in the armchairs beside the cold stove.

Lily shivered and warmed her hands on her teacup.

'I daren't light the stove,' said Pearl. 'We're short of coal again.'

'Isn't everyone?' said Lily. 'It's important to keep the railways running though.'

'We have a new guest staying in one of the studios,' said Pearl, and told her all about Maxwell and how he was teaching her to drive.

'It sounds as if you're sweet on him,' said Lily.

Pearl remembered that long moment when they'd been transfixed by each other's gaze. She'd thought there might have been a flicker of regret in his expression when he'd turned away from her. 'He's great fun,' she said, 'but doesn't intend to stay for long. Besides, I think he's going to enlist.' She studied the hollows under Lily's cheekbones. Always slender, she'd grown very thin lately. 'Are you still unhappy about Noel?'

Lily stared down into her cup. 'What happened made me realise I don't want to marry.'

'Because Noel didn't support you?'

Lily hesitated. 'Hugh Penrose is very overbearing and he took an instant dislike to me. It would have been a disaster if I'd married into a family like that, even had it been possible.'

'You'll meet someone else.'

'Not while there's a war on. Can you imagine how painful it would be not to know if your husband would ever come home? Or if he'd return one day, terribly maimed. I've seen soldiers in Truro with legs or arms missing. Or half their face blown away.' Lily shuddered. 'I intend to put my training to good use for the war effort.'

'What will you do?'

'There are some paid positions for clerks in the Voluntary Aid Detachment. With my qualification, I might find work as a senior clerk.'

'I've been knitting scarves and rolling bandages,' said Pearl, 'but it's such a small contribution to make when young men are risking their lives for us. I must find paid work. Mama's had no new commissions and I don't want to be a drain on the family purse. Oh, that reminds me! Guess who turned up on our doorstep seeking shelter yesterday?'

Lily shook her head.

'Gabrielle. She was in London when war was declared. She's on her uppers and is staying until she finds a job.' Pearl grimaced. 'She's moved into the bedroom with Nell and me.'

'Oh! I was going to ask if I could share with you,' said Lily, and sighed. 'I'll have to go home to the coach house and face Mother, then.'

'I'm sure it won't be as bad as you think,' said Pearl, giving her a hug.

Chapter 14

Gabrielle nibbled a piece of dry toast, hoping it would settle her stomach, pondering over possible solutions to her difficulties.

'Gabrielle?'

Blinking, she realised Pearl was talking to her.

'Lily and I are going into the village to collect the socks. Would you like to come with us?'

'Socks?'

'I've organised volunteers to knit them and I collect them once a fortnight and deliver them to the Red Cross.'

Gabrielle considered the idea. It was cold outside but Edith had mentioned there was a pile of sheets that needed ironing if she had nothing else to do. 'Yes, I will come,' she said.

After breakfast, the three young women set off along the coast path. Clouds sailed across a battleship-grey sky and a gusty wind blew off the sea, making Gabrielle's eyes water. She was assailed by a sudden pang of homesickness for the heat of her childhood Provençal summers. If only she hadn't met Lionel, she wouldn't now be encumbered with an unwanted pregnancy and might have returned to France before the war ruined everything.

In the village, Pearl led them down the hill to Doctor Hardwicke's house where the maid invited them to wait in the hall.

A moment later the doctor's wife bustled in and handed Pearl three pairs of grey socks and a navy blue

126

scarf. 'I unravelled an old jumper,' she said, 'so there was enough wool for a scarf, too.'

'Splendid!' said Pearl, tucking the items into her basket. 'With news from the Front of a bitterly cold winter, these will be extremely welcome.'

'I'll try my hand at a pair of mittens next time,' said Mrs Hardwicke. 'I do so hate having cold hands, don't you?'

Outside again, they called upon half a dozen cottages and soon Pearl's basket was full.

'I want a newspaper,' said Gabrielle, stopping in front of the newsagent's shop.

'And I'll see if they have any pear drops,' said Lily.

'Wait here for me when you've finished,' said Pearl. 'I've one more call to make in Dolphin Street.'

The shop was crowded and Gabrielle had to queue for her newspaper.

A young soldier waited in front of her. Idly, she studied his broad shoulders and fair hair. Once he reached the counter, he bought a packet of cigarettes and then turned to leave.

'Noel?' Gabrielle hadn't seen him since her last Spindrift summer five years ago. She hadn't been particularly interested in him then; she'd always preferred the older, more sophisticated type, like Rafael. But now Noel was taller and the planes of his face had matured into those of a good-looking man.

'Gabrielle!' he said. 'It's been years!'

She looked him up and down. 'You've enlisted?'

He flushed slightly under her bold gaze. 'I'm training at Bodmin Camp but have twenty-four hours' home leave.'

Glancing over her shoulder, he caught his breath. 'Excuse me.' He smiled distractedly and moved away.

127

Gabrielle asked the shop assistant for advice on choosing a newspaper with a situations vacant column. Leaving the counter, she saw Noel speaking to Lily by the shelves of sweet jars. Lily shook her head and fumbled her way out of the door. Noel went after her.

Curious, Gabrielle followed them.

Outside, Noel caught hold of Lily's arm. She flinched and pulled herself free from his grip. Abruptly, she turned and bolted away.

Pearl, her basket over her arm, was walking towards them. She stopped Lily, catching hold of her in her headlong flight. They spoke briefly and then Pearl put her arm around Lily's waist and led her away.

Noel stood motionless in the street, watching them. 'Are you all right?' Gabrielle asked him.

'No, I'm bloody well not all right.' He ground his knuckles into his eye sockets. 'Sorry.'

She wondered if she ought to follow Pearl and Lily but sensed a situation that might be more profitable for her if she had time to consider it carefully. 'You look as if you've had a shock,' she said. 'Shall we call into the Golden Lion and share a pot of coffee? Or something stronger.' She took his arm and Noel allowed her to draw him away.

There was a blazing fire in the hearth at the Golden Lion and Gabrielle commandeered a table close enough to enjoy its heat. She ordered coffee and two brandies and pushed one of them towards Noel.

He gulped it down greedily and she raised her eyebrows. 'You'd better have some of this, too,' she said, pouring the coffee. 'What happened between you and Lily?'

He spooned sugar into his cup. 'We wanted to be

128

married. I didn't expect my parents to be completely delighted because of their long-standing dislike for the Spindrift community.' He grimaced as he burned his tongue on the coffee. 'But I had no idea Father would be utterly incandescent with rage. He even accused Lily of trapping me into marriage because she was pregnant.'

'Was she?' asked Gabrielle.

'No!' He stared into his coffee cup.

Gabrielle sucked her lower lip while she pictured the Penroses' home, imposing Cliff House up on the headland. 'Why didn't you marry her anyway, despite your father's disapproval?'

Noel clenched his jaw hard. 'Because the next day, Lily told me something profoundly shocking. And now I haven't the words to tell you how much I hate my own father.'

There was such venom in his voice that she blinked. 'Tell me,' she murmured. 'What was so shocking?'

Noel sipped his brandy. 'Lily meant everything to me and Father destroyed our hopes. You see, Lily discovered that he'd had an affair with her mother. When I found out about that, I went straight out and enlisted. I couldn't bear to be near him.'

Gabrielle raised her eyebrows. 'You may not like it but their affair doesn't stop you from marrying Lily.'

'It does when it turns out she is my father's daughter!' He drained his brandy glass.

'Mon Dieu!' Gabrielle hadn't expected that! 'No wonder you hate him,' she said. 'You must have had a terrible argument?'

Noel shook his head. 'I was so distressed at the time, I couldn't bring myself to speak to him.' He lifted the brandy glass. 'But a few more of these and I'll have it out with him this evening.'

Gabrielle pursed her lips, her thoughts racing.

Noel pressed his palms over his eyes for a moment. 'I should never have told you,' he said, 'but it's been churning round and round in my head ever since it happened until I'm nearly going mad. Can I rely on you to be discreet? Mother would be devastated if she learned of it.'

'Instead of an unpleasant quarrel with your father that your mother might overhear, there might be a better way to make him suffer,' said Gabrielle slowly. 'He hates Benedict Fairchild, doesn't he?'

'With a passion! He'll never forgive him for stealing Spindrift House.'

'Then a suitable revenge would be for you to marry Benedict's daughter and present him with the marriage as fait accompli, don't you think? He'd hate that but he'd be powerless to change it.'

'Marry Pearl?'

'No. Me.'

He stared at her. 'You're Benedict's daughter? I thought you were Pascal Joubert's niece?'

'I am that, too.'

'Why would you want such a marriage?'

She shrugged. 'I'm stranded in England until the war is over and I need somewhere to live. The Spindrift community will only let me stay for one month.'

'But we can't marry purely for me to get my own back on Father and to provide you with a place to stay! We don't love each other.'

Gabrielle refilled his brandy glass. 'We French are pragmatic about affairs of the heart. A love affair is exciting, while it lasts, but marriage is a contract with mutual benefits. In France, a wife turns a blind eye to her husband's passing fancies, while providing him with a well-ordered house, pleasant conversation and, in time, children. The home is always a tranquil and comfortable retreat from the world. And, of course,' she looked up at him from under her eyelashes, 'Frenchwomen are renowned for their skills in the bedroom.'

'Well,' stammered Noel, 'I have heard rumours . . .'

'Poor Noel!' She stroked the back of his hand. 'You've had a terrible shock. And you must be anxious about being sent to the Front? I would be terrified.'

Chewing his lip, he nodded.

She lifted his hand and pressed his palm to her cheek. 'What you need,' she said, 'is to have some fun so you can forget all your troubles. Why don't we go into Wadebridge and have luncheon?'

'Luncheon?'

She leaned closer to pick an imaginary speck of fluff off his shoulder. 'Tomorrow, you return to Bodmin Camp,' she said. 'Instead of fighting with your father, it is imperative you make your short leave memorable and pleasurable. Otherwise, you'll be sitting in a trench behind the Frontline before you know it, regretting you didn't grasp every opportunity.'

He frowned. 'That's absolutely true.' His chair scraped back as he stood up. Slightly unsteady, he offered his arm to her. 'May I have the pleasure?'

'Quite probably,' she said, and flashed him a brilliant smile.

Chapter 15

February 1915

Cornwall

Edith looked up from her canvas and watched Pascal while he worked, a crease between his eyebrows as he concentrated on the exact placement of tiny dots of bright pigment. Since it was impossible to keep the attics warm due to the shortage of coal, she had moved her easel into Pascal's ground-floor studio, adjacent to his bedroom. It was a little cramped for two people but they shared a meagre fire and took care not to disturb each other. Smiling, Edith reflected on how much contentment those quiet hours working side by side brought them.

Despite Pascal's anxiety about the war, there'd been a glow of happiness around him ever since it had come into the open that Jasper was his son. The manner in which Jasper had found out the truth had been upsetting but it warmed Edith's heart to see father and son now closer than ever. As for herself, she hadn't received the condemnation from the entire community that she'd expected. Her greatest sadness, however, was that Pearl still hadn't forgiven her, remaining frostily polite even months later. Added to that concern, Edith was still mentally looking over her shoulder, waiting to see when Benedict would exact his revenge upon her by forcing her out of Spindrift, if his intimidating remarks had been more than idle threats.

A movement outside the window caught her eye. Jasper and Anneliese were walking along the path beside the house with the dogs. The young woman was wearing a skirt and cardigan she recognised as having once belonged to Pearl. It pleased Edith that her daughter had charitably helped the refugee.

Jasper was holding hands with Blanche, swinging her arm as they walked. He'd devoted a great deal of time to teaching Anneliese to speak English but had confessed to Edith that he was worried about the child. She was still so shocked from her terrible experiences that she never uttered a word.

'I chatter away to her in French and English,' he'd said, 'hoping she'll understand, even if she won't speak. She ought to go to school soon but, as things are, it's likely to be even more distressing to her, particularly if the other children tease her about her scar.'

The refugees had really captured Jasper's attention. He'd painted their portraits, both together and separately, a few times. It hurt Edith to look at the canvases because they were so permeated with silent suffering they made her weep. Through the window, Edith saw Blanche stumble and fall. Jasper lifted her up and she clung to him, her face buried in his neck. A moment later they all disappeared around the corner.

Edith turned back to her canvas. It was entitled Waving the Boys Goodbye. Inspired by Jasper's paintings of the refugees, she'd wanted to capture another poignant moment of wartime at home. Since she wasn't allowed to sketch outside, Julian had lent her his Vest Pocket Kodak camera and taught her how to use it. She'd travelled to Bodmin and spent a morning at the railway station on the day newly trained recruits of the Duke of Cornwall's Light Infantry were being posted to France and Belgium. Some of the soldiers were barely old enough to shave, jostling and joking with each other like schoolboys as they waited to board their train. Dry-eyed fathers with poker-straight backs, sobbing mothers and sweethearts, counted the few remaining minutes before their loved ones clambered aboard. The new recruits hung out of the open carriage windows, last-minute uncertainty on their boyish faces.

When the train lurched into action, the mothers waved handkerchiefs and then collapsed into their husbands' arms as the final carriage disappeared into the distance behind a cloud of steam.

The raw emotion of that morning still had the power to move Edith to tears and she dreaded a day when she too might have to wave her sons off to war. She feared the fighting would grow more intense, especially since the Germans had declared the seas around the British Isles a war zone. U-boats now lurked beneath familiar waters, waiting to sink any Allied ships in the area. Sighing, she picked up her palette and began to mix titanium white with raw umber as a base colour for the khaki uniform. Her hand hovered over a tube of ochre but she thought better of it and picked up the cadmium yellow light.

Immersed in her task, she started when the door flew open without warning.

Gabrielle, dressed in hat and coat, stood in the doorway, a letter in her hand. Her gaze flickered from Edith to Pascal and then to the door standing open to Pascal's bedroom. The bed, as always, was neatly made.

Edith, her pulse still racing from the young wom-

134

an's abrupt entrance, felt her cheeks blaze. There was something prurient in Gabrielle's expression, almost as if she'd hoped to catch Edith in bed with Pascal. They had, in fact, resisted that temptation, agreeing it was too risky. After all, Woodland Cottage remained their love nest and, on the occasions they were free to escape there, it always felt like a honeymoon.

Pascal raised his eyebrows. 'Is there something you want, Gabrielle?'

'Are there any letters you would like me to post?'

He shook his head. 'Thank you but no.'

'Is that another job application you have there, Gabrielle?' asked Edith.

She shrugged. 'It's for a temporary vacancy as a teaching assistant in a private school in Somerset. The pay is low but it is a living-in position.'

'Have you had many responses to your other enquiries? I've noticed you've had several letters from Bodmin.'

Gabrielle's lips twitched in what might have been a brief smile. 'I hope I am nearing an understanding with someone about a permanent position.'

'Well, that is good!' Edith was relieved. The month she had allowed Gabrielle to spend as a guest at Spindrift was nearly over and this young woman was altogether too much like Benedict for Edith to want to cross swords with her. 'Where would you be working?'

'It is not yet confirmed,' said Gabrielle. She pulled on her gloves. 'I am well aware you are waiting for me to leave and you will be the first to know when I am able to do so.' She turned away and her footsteps clipped down the hallway.

Pascal sighed. 'I apologise for my niece's ungracious

135

manner. She is so like my sister when she doesn't have everything she wants. I wrote to Delphine and asked her to send financial support for Gabrielle but I'm afraid she refused.'

Edith gave a wry smile. 'And I was thinking she was like Benedict in her self-centredness. Let's hope she secures the situation she mentioned. I've been dreading a scene if I have to ask her to leave but I really don't feel I need take responsibility for another of Benedict's children.'

'Even he could not ask more of you.'

There was a tap at the door. 'Am I disturbing you?' asked Jasper.

'Not at all,' said Pascal, his face breaking into a wide smile. 'Come in, *mon fils*.'

Jasper pulled at his shirt collar as if it chafed his neck, then stepped forward to study Edith's canvas. 'You've caught the emotion of parting perfectly.'

'You don't think it's too sentimental?'

'Not at all. So many parents are waving their sons off to war that this will strike a chord with most families.' He picked up a handful of the photographs she'd taken at Bodmin station. 'You have enough material for here for several works.'

'The one I really want to paint is the joy on the mothers' faces when their boys come home to them safely.'

Jasper nodded. 'We cannot allow Germany to continue this war. If you had only heard some of the stories Anneliese has told me.' A muscle clenched in his jaw. 'Mama, Pascal, I must tell you . . .'

Edith's gripped the edge of her worktable to stop herself from swaying. She knew exactly what he was going to say next.

136

Pascal placed his hand on Jasper's shoulder. 'We understand,' he said in a low voice.

Jasper let out his breath in a long sigh. 'I cannot, in all conscience, fail to respond to the call to arms any longer. God knows, I don't want to fight.'

Edith let out a sob and Pascal and Jasper caught her in their arms. The three of them had no need of words. They remained clasped together until her tears stopped.

'When?' asked Edith, frightened to hear the answer.

'The recruitment officer will be at the Temperance Hall again at the end of this week,' said Jasper. 'I imagine I'll be sent to Bodmin Camp for training before I go overseas.'

'Then we must make the most of the time we have,' said Pascal. He stretched his mouth into a smile but Edith's heart nearly broke on seeing the fear in his eyes.

'Will you tell the others at dinner tonight?' she asked.

'I suppose so. I don't want a fuss or I shan't be able to bear it.' Jasper straightened his back. 'Mama, there's something I'd like you to do for me.'

'Anything.'

'I want people to know about the suffering of refugees like Anneliese and Blanche. Perhaps then it will make more sense to those families whose men are going to fight the Germans. I want to submit my refugee portraits to the Royal Academy for their Summer Exhibition.' He pulled at his shirt collar again. 'Perhaps it's presumptuous of me. I'm not yet a seasoned artist . . .'

'You are a gifted artist and your age is irrelevant,' said Pascal.

'You'd like me to send your canvases to the hanging committee at the appropriate time?'

'Yes, please.'

'It's the least I can do,' said Edith, forcing a smile, 'since I don't have the time or the skill to knit you a pair of ill-fitting socks before you leave.'

Chapter 16

March 1915

Cornwall

Gabrielle was late coming down for breakfast. She'd taken time over her toilette, putting on the flattering lavender dress Rafael had bought her from a chic little modiste in Lille and arranging her dark hair in a fashionable loose knot on the crown of her head.

She helped herself to coffee.

Roland, sitting on her right, filled the moat he'd made around his porridge with milk and then trailed a sticky stream of golden syrup over the top.

Gabrielle shuddered and wondered if she could manage a piece of dry toast. She decided against it when Roland sniffed and wiped his nose on his cuff.

'You're very smart this morning, Gabrielle,' said Clarissa. 'Edith mentioned you're going to Bodmin today for an interview.'

'If my meeting is successful, I may stay overnight.'

'It's a living-in situation, is it?' asked Pearl. 'What kind of work would you be doing?'

Roland sniffed and then coughed, spluttering porridge across the table.

Making a moue of distaste, Gabrielle edged her chair away from him. 'I prefer not to discuss the position until I know if I have secured it,' she said. She caught sight of Pearl nudging Lily and raising her eyebrows. No matter what they thought of her, if

139

everything went as she'd planned, she'd soon be leaving Spindrift for something better.

Roland coughed again.

'For goodness' sake, Roly!' said Edith. 'Where's your handkerchief?' She frowned and studied his face. 'You're flushed and it sounds to me as if you're starting a cold.' She placed a hand on his forehead and frowned. 'You've a slight fever.'

'My head hurts.'

She sighed. 'You'd better stay away from school today. Off to bed and I'll bring you some hot honey and lemon.'

One by one, the community finished their breakfast and left the dining-room.

Jasper stood up. 'Gabrielle, I'll meet you in the courtyard at ten o'clock to take you to the station.'

Half an hour later, they were in the trap, jogging their way along the lane.

Gabrielle clutched at her hat as they bumped over a particularly treacherous pothole. At least it wasn't raining and she wasn't risking her elegant shoes and chic Parisian coat being splattered with mud. It would never do to arrive at her destination looking anything less than her best, today of all days.

She glanced sideways at Jasper's aquiline profile. He was undeniably handsome but what he'd said was right; they still felt like half-siblings, even though they weren't related by blood after all.

They arrived at the station and Jasper handed her the overnight case she'd brought. 'Good luck,' he said.

Lifting her hand in farewell, she hurried into the ticket office.

Later, as the train steamed into Bodmin station, Gabrielle's fingers tapped a nervous tattoo on her lap. What would she do if all her efforts over the past month had failed? The thought of it made her feel sick. She looked anxiously out of the window as the train finally came to a stop. Her mouth was dry as she stepped down from the carriage.

She scanned the platform. It was seething with passengers, businessmen, soldiers, nurses, mothers with children, but she couldn't see the one person she sought. Her heart bumped in her chest as she walked towards the station entrance, tears of fear and disappointment prickling her eyes.

'Gabrielle!' A hand touched her shoulder.

She whirled around and gasped at the sight of the straight-backed young soldier before her. 'You weren't on the platform. I thought you had changed your mind!'

Noel smiled tentatively. 'I said I'd be here.' A muscle twitched at the corner of his eye.

'Have you got it?'

He nodded and fished a piece of paper from his pocket. 'I wasn't sure it would come through in time but here it is.'

She flung her arms around him and kissed him. It was going to be all right! This might not have been her first choice, or his, but it was the best that could be managed in such a short time.

Noel's shoulders relaxed and he kissed her back with enthusiasm.

She drew away and straightened her hat. 'We mustn't be late!'

Arm in arm, they hurried through the streets, both lost in thought, until they stopped outside the Register Office. A young soldier stood on the steps to the entrance, cleaning his nails with a penknife.

'That's my pal Alf, waiting for us,' said Noel. 'He's to be our witness. Let me introduce you.'

'I can see now why you were in a fret to get this wedding tied up before we go to France,' said the soldier, his admiring glance raking Gabrielle up and down.

Noel punched him on the shoulder and gave her a sheepish grin.

Inside the office, he handed the special licence to the Registrar. A few minutes later, Gabrielle and Noel stood before him, repeating the necessary words. And then, so quickly, it was done. She sighed in relief.

'Shall we drink to the health of the new Mrs Penrose?' asked Alf, rubbing his hands together.

They called into a nearby public house and Gabrielle sipped a glass of sherry while the men drank ale. It wasn't the wedding she'd imagined for herself when she was younger, and it had happened so fast she could hardly believe she was actually safely married to the near-stranger at her side, but it was largely done. There were still a few hurdles for her to overcome before she could fully relax.

Alf drained his pint pot. 'Another?' he asked, a hopeful expression on his face.

'Bit short of time,' said Noel. 'I'm sure you understand.'

His friend laughed and nudged him. 'I can tell when I'm not wanted. Can't say I blame you.' He offered his hand to Gabrielle. 'I wish you both a long and happy life together, Mrs Penrose.' After winking at Noel, Alf took himself off.

Gabrielle slid a little further along the bench and pressed her thigh against her new husband's leg. There wasn't much time left for her to secure her future.

'I thought for a minute he might hang about all

afternoon,' said Noel. He ran his thumb over the narrow gold band on her third finger. 'I've dreamed about you every night since that afternoon we . . .' He dropped his gaze, his ears turning pink.

'I've been longing for today, too,' whispered Gabrielle. And that was nothing short of the truth. On that afternoon last month, she'd used every seductive trick she knew to make Noel's sensual dreams come true. Nestling against his side, she blew gently in his ear.

He closed his eyes and shivered.

She giggled. 'It was very naughty of us, wasn't it? How lucky we were to find a room at the inn.'

'And then you wrote me all those letters,' he said, 'each one reminding me of that sublime afternoon . . . until I was so mad with desire for you that I almost went absent without leave to come and find you.'

She nibbled his neck. 'I've booked the honeymoon suite for us at the Queen's Head.'

Noel pulled her to her feet. 'Then we mustn't waste a moment more of our brief time together.'

* * *

Later that afternoon, Noel dozed beside Gabrielle in the big mahogany bed. It was growing dark and she lay with her arms folded behind her head, thinking. Rafael had been an ardent and experienced lover and had taught her so many ways to please a man. Without that knowledge, she'd never have been able to dazzle and beguile Noel into marrying her.

She slipped out of bed and gathered up her clothes from the floor. In the adjoining bathroom, she took a cigarette from the packet at the bottom of her wash bag and smoked it while leaning out of the window. She wasn't sure what Noel thought about ladies smoking and it wasn't a good time to risk annoying him. Afterwards, she washed, dressed and pinned up her hair, thankful that, unlike Spindrift, the inn had electric lighting. She opened the bathroom door and Noel stirred when the shaft of light fell across the bed.

'You're dressed!' he said, reaching out for her. 'Come back to bed, you little temptress!'

'Later,' she said, kissing his forehead and stepping smartly away. 'It's time for dinner.'

He yawned and stretched. 'I suppose I am hungry after all that exertion.' Smiling lazily at her, he said, 'Perhaps I'd better have a little something to keep my strength up for later?'

They sat opposite each other in the hotel dining-room, eating grilled sole and boiled potatoes.

'Thanks to you,' said Noel, 'I shall join my regiment tomorrow night with wonderful memories of a most satisfactory start to married life.'

Gabrielle reflected that it was astonishing how a man could vow undying love for one woman and, so soon after, appear to have entirely forgotten her, totally in thrall to another. She put down her knife and fork. 'Noel chéri, I am nervous of meeting your parents tomorrow. Our marriage will be a shock to them ...'

'I laid the groundwork with Mother by writing to tell her I had a special friend in Bodmin and that I intended to bring her home to meet them tomorrow afternoon.' Noel laughed delightedly. 'It really is the most delicious joke that I've married the natural daughter of the man my father hates most in the world! It will give me the utmost pleasure to see his

144

face when I tell him tomorrow.'

'I've been thinking about that,' she said. 'He'll be very angry.'

'Good!' said Noel with satisfaction.

'All very well for you,' said Gabrielle, 'but I shall be left behind to bear the brunt of his anger. I wonder if you could wait to tell him until after you return from the war?'

Noel hesitated. 'I suppose I might. I can see how it could be unpleasant for you, especially if you stay at Cliff House. But I want him to know about Benedict or I haven't had my revenge, have I?'

'Why don't you write a letter to him and leave it with me? Should anything happen to you, I would return to France after the war and I'd give him your letter then.' She held her breath.

Noel frowned and lined up the salt and pepper pots while he thought about this. 'I suppose I could do that.' He looked up at her. 'But you must promise to give him the letter when Mother isn't there. It would be very hurtful for her to know.'

Gabrielle let out a slow sigh of relief. 'I promise. Thank you, Noel. Anyway, I'm sure all will be well and that one day soon you will have the satisfaction of telling him yourself. The thought of it should keep you amused you while you are away.' She stroked his wrist with her forefinger. 'I hope Adela and Tim won't tell your parents who I am?'

'My sister and I are very close. I've written and asked to her to warn Tim not to mention that they know you.'

'I hope Adela won't be angry with me. She and Lily are good friends.'

'She's excited to have a new sister-in-law,' said Noel.

'It really isn't fair but she blames Lily for breaking off our engagement.'

'There's still the difficulty of whether your parents will allow me to stay with them,' said Gabrielle. 'I'm forced to leave Spindrift this week and my savings have almost gone. I've written to apply for a position as a teaching assistant at a school but I haven't had a response.'

'Gabrielle, you're my wife now,' said Noel, 'and it's my responsibility to find a home for you. You'd be more comfortable at Cliff House but, if there's any difficulty, you can rent a room. I have some savings and I'll arrange for you to receive the Separation Allowance, too. Once the war is over, I'll be working as an architect again and we'll have a little house of our own.'

She gave Noel a radiant smile. The prospect of living with him in a bourgeois house in the countryside for the rest of her life didn't fit at all with how she'd imagined her future. But these were uncertain times and there was no guarantee that he would return from the war. None at all. But at least her child would have a name and she would have a position in society as a respectable married woman.

The waiter came to clear the plates and bring them steamed treacle pudding.

Noel poured a generous helping of custard over his. 'This looks excellent,' he said.

Suddenly, Gabrielle was ravenously hungry. She picked up her spoon. 'It does, doesn't it?'

★ ★ ★

The following afternoon, Gabrielle and Noel stood in the lane outside Cliff House. He turned her to

146

face him and rested his hands on her shoulders. 'Everything will be all right.' He kissed her quickly and then opened the garden gate.

The front door was unlocked and Gabrielle looked about her as Noel led her into the hall. She was too tense to notice much beyond a highly polished parquet floor and a wide staircase.

Noel glanced at her as they stood outside the drawing-room. He looked pale and that made her anxious. So much depended upon the next few minutes. He opened the door and they stepped into a large, beautifully decorated room.

Noel's parents sat opposite each other to either side of the stone fireplace, reading newspapers. Adela was knitting in an armchair. She glanced up at Gabrielle and gave her a secretive little smile.

Gabrielle smiled back, hoping she would be an ally.

Noel's mother took off her gold-rimmed spectacles. Expensively but unflatteringly dressed in a blouse that was one size too small, she rose to her feet and kissed her son, exclaiming how handsome he looked in his uniform.

Mr Penrose shook Noel's hand. 'I'm pleased you've come to see us.' His voice was gruff. 'Do introduce us to your friend.'

Mrs Penrose smiled at Gabrielle, her watchful eyes noting every detail.

Noel took Gabrielle's hand. His palm was damp. 'Mother, Father, Adela, I'm proud to introduce you to Gabrielle. My wife.'

There was a brief silence and then Adela ran forward to hug Noel. 'How wonderful!' she cried. 'Congratulations to you both! My, you are a dark horse, Noel.'

'Wife? But why didn't you tell us before?' asked his

mother, glancing uncertainly at Gabrielle.

Noel gave his father a challenging look. 'I didn't care to allow anything to happen that might destroy my happiness. Not this time.' He drew himself up to his full height. 'If I'm old enough to fight for my country, I'm old enough to choose my own wife. Besides, there wasn't much time. I'm leaving for France tomorrow.'

Mrs Penrose let out a cry of distress. 'So soon?'

Noel's father slumped down on the sofa. 'You'd better tell us how you and your bride met. This is a . . .' he shook his head '. . . a great surprise to us.'

Noel gave a brief account of the story he and Gabrielle had concocted about meeting in Bodmin some months before. 'I hope that you'll take her under your wing and welcome her in to Cliff House while I'm away,' he said. 'Her own family lives in Occupied France and she's all alone.'

'You're French, Gabrielle?' asked Mrs Penrose, eyeing her askance.

'Take her in? But we don't know the girl,' said Mr Penrose.

'If you aren't prepared to welcome my wife into the family,' said Noel stiffly, 'then of course I shall make other arrangements. We'll leave here immediately. I'll be sorry never to see my family again but if that's what you prefer . . .'

'Of course it isn't!' said Mrs Penrose.

'I do not wish to be any trouble,' said Gabrielle, eyes modestly lowered. 'I will take a room in a lodging house.'

'Father,' said Adela, 'imagine what your clients would say about you if they found out your daughter-in-law was obliged to live in squalid digs while you have empty bedrooms in this great big house!'

148

Gabrielle glanced up at Noel's mother and gave her a wan smile. 'I've applied for a position as a teaching assistant in a school. If I'm successful, I shall live there. For a while anyway.' It was time to take a gamble. She pressed a hand to her stomach and looked anxiously at Noel. 'I hope the Separation Allowance will come through before too long, though, because I shall be obliged to give up work in the next few months.'

Mrs Penrose gasped.

Noel shook his head. 'As I said before, I don't expect my wife to have to work.'

'You haven't told him, Gabrielle, have you?' said Noel's mother.

'It's very early days and I wanted to be quite sure . . .'

Mrs Penrose turned to her husband. 'Well, that settles it, Hugh. Of course Gabrielle must come and stay here. She cannot bring up your grandchild in a boarding house.'

Open-mouthed, Noel and his father stared at Gabrielle.

'Is it true?' Noel whispered.

She nodded.

Adela squealed with excitement. 'I'm going to be an aunt!'

Mrs Penrose came forward and kissed Gabrielle's cheek. 'Welcome to the family, my dear!'

White-faced, Noel sank down into an armchair.

Gabrielle smiled at her new mother-in-law, light-headed with relief. She was safe! And she would no longer be obliged to work for her living or to have to sneak around at Spindrift, hoping to catch Edith and Pascal in bed together.

Chapter 17

Lily, sitting in the back seat of Maxwell Fforbes's motorcar with Dora, was full of admiration for Pearl as she drove into the courtyard.

She pulled on the handbrake with a flourish. 'There!' she said. 'How did I do?'

Maxwell sighed. 'I'm sorry to say . . .'

Pearl's expectant smile faded. 'What did I do wrong? I didn't run over any stray dogs or pedestrians, and I didn't veer off the road at all. I even mended the puncture without your assistance.'

Maxwell let out a shout of laughter. 'I'm teasing you! You're a natural and I can't teach you much more; you simply need to keep practising. The next time you go to a Red Cross meeting, you can take the motor out by yourself.'

Pearl's eyes shone. 'I'm flattered that you trust me.'

A stab of jealousy at the easy nature of Pearl and Maxwell's friendship made Lily's heart ache.

Dora gathered up the bags of knitting wool they'd brought home from the meeting. 'Thank you for the lift. I'm going to have a cup of tea with Ursula and then I shall sit with Roland for a while.' She clicked her tongue. 'German measles, poor chap.'

'Shall I carry your packages for you?' asked Maxwell.

'We've taken up enough of your time,' said Dora, 'and you must be wanting to get on with your writing.'

'Actually, it's not going too well but I'll look for inspiration while studying the splendid plan of Spindrift House that Pearl drew up for me.'

He headed off into his studio and Lily and Pearl lifted their parcels of old cotton sheets and discarded sweaters out of the Sunbeam and carried them into the house.

'I really can't bear the thought of cutting out fifty surgeons' gowns tonight,' said Pearl.

'We might start on the jumpers,' said Lily.

Upstairs in Pearl's bedroom, they unwrapped the ragged knitwear and unpicked the seams.

'Where's Nell?' asked Lily. 'I hardly ever see her these days.'

'If she isn't in the vegetable garden, she's usually at Polcarrow Farm. The Mellyns are shorthanded since the farmhands enlisted. There's the lambing and she mentioned something about helping Tom spread slurry over the fields today.' Pearl wrinkled her nose.

'That sounds ghastly, especially on a cold March day. Nell's certainly doing her bit for the war effort.' Lily pulled at a loose strand of wool, unravelling it until there was a heap of crinkled yarn on her lap. 'One by one all the young men are joining up.' Her eyes filled with tears as she recalled her chance meeting with Noel in the newsagent's the previous month. It was still painful to remember.

'And now Jasper's training at Bodmin Camp, too,' said Pearl. 'I wish Anneliese had never told him about the German atrocities in Belgium.'

'All we can do is to pray for our boys to come home safely.'

'But is that all we can do?' Pearl unpicked the side seam of a cardigan. 'They're risking their lives. Is it enough for us to roll bandages and knit socks? There are plenty of grandmothers who could do that. We're

151

young and ought to be filling the positions left empty by the men. Nell's already doing that.'

'She's sweet on Tom Mellyn,' said Lily. 'I imagine that has something to do with her dedication to the war effort.'

'She must be very sweet on him if she's prepared to spend her days spreading dung!'

'I thought I'd find work using my secretarial training,' said Lily. 'I haven't had any luck yet but Mrs Kingsley-Jones said the Red Cross are looking for VADs to work in Truro Hospital.'

'Maxwell's sister is a VAD in London,' said Pearl. 'She has to empty bedpans.'

The bedroom door opened and Gabrielle came in.

'You're back!' said Pearl. 'I assume you had good news about the situation you applied for, since you were away overnight?'

'I did,' said Gabrielle. 'I have come to pack my belongings. Your mother will be pleased to know I am leaving.'

'What work is it?' asked Lily.

Gabrielle laughed and held out her left hand. 'My husband doesn't wish me to work.'

'Your husband?' said Pearl.

'But who did you marry?' Lily was astonished. Gabrielle had never mentioned a man.

'We didn't even know you were courting,' said Pearl.

'I preferred to keep the matter to myself, until I was sure he would be granted leave for our wedding. We married yesterday and his regiment leaves for France tomorrow.'

'How sad for you.' said Pearl. 'Are we going to meet your new husband?'

Gabrielle opened a drawer and removed a pile of

clothing. 'You already know him.'

Pearl looked at Lily, her eyes questioning.

Gabrielle lifted her suitcase from underneath the bed and placed the folded garments inside. 'I am Mrs Noel Penrose,' she said.

An icy wave of shock ran through Lily's entire body.

'Noel?' Pearl glanced at Lily.

'I am moving to Cliff House.'

'No!' Lily rose unsteadily to her feet, the pile of yarn falling to the floor. 'Noel couldn't have married you,' she whispered.

Gabrielle preened her hair and gave a self-satisfied smile. 'But he did.'

A sob rose in Lily's throat. She pressed her knuckles against her mouth to muffle a cry of desolation and ran from the room.

★ ★ ★

Later that afternoon, Edith knocked on the door of the coach house and waited until Clarissa opened the door.

'Sorry to keep you,' said her friend, slightly out of breath. 'I should be in the workshop finishing off an order but I was upstairs with Rose. I'm afraid she's caught German measles.'

'Poor child! The doctor is calling to see Roland again so I'll ask him to look at Rose while he's here,' said Edith. 'May I come in?'

'Of course, I was distracted.' Clarissa led the way into her sitting-room.

'It's Lily,' said Edith sitting on one of the chintz-covered armchairs. 'She's had a shock. Pearl tried to comfort her but Lily sent her away. I found her wandering about in the garden, sobbing. It's bitterly cold and she wasn't wearing a coat so I brought her in. Clarissa, she's in a dreadful way.'

'But what happened?'

'Gabrielle has announced that she married Noel Penrose yesterday.'

'What!'

'It was a complete bolt from the blue to Lily. When I said I'd fetch you, she became hysterical.' Edith glanced away, unable to look at her friend's appalled expression. 'She wouldn't let me fetch you to comfort her. The thing is, I couldn't disclose that you'd already confided in me that Noel is her half-brother.'

Clarissa rubbed at her eyes. 'I've ruined my daughter's life.'

'Of course you haven't! She'll get over it in time but, in her current state of mind, I was worried for her. I've put her in the empty studio. I've lit the stove, made up a bed with plenty of blankets and Anneliese will take her some supper later on.'

'Thank you, Edith.' Clarissa's voice wavered. 'I'll see if she'll speak to me tomorrow. It's awful knowing she's so miserable because of what I did.'

'As to that,' said Edith, 'we've all made mistakes, haven't we?'

'Where's Gabrielle?'

'At Cliff House. Noel's regiment is entraining at Bodmin station tomorrow and the Penroses are taking her in their motorcar to wave him goodbye.'

'I never liked that girl,' said Clarissa. 'She always was underhand and selfish. All I can say is, I wish her joy of having Hugh and Jenifry Penrose for her parents-in-law.'

★ ★ ★

Two days later, Pearl hung up a pillowslip at her bed-room window and, within half an hour, saw Adela had acknowledged her signal by half-closing her curtains. Pearl put aside the wool she'd been winding into balls and went downstairs.

In the boot-room, she donned her Wellingtons and mackintosh before going outside. The grass was sodden as she hurried through the soft rain to the gate at the end of the garden. On the cliff top, she looked over to the other side of the cove and saw Adela was already descending the steps from Cliff House.

The sea boomed. When Pearl reached the foot of the cliff steps, she kept well away from the foam-topped breakers that crashed onto the sand. She picked her way through clusters of bladderwrack and driftwood washed up onto the tideline.

A few minutes later, she and Adela huddled out of the rain in the lee of the cliffs.

'I've been trying to speak to you for two days,' said Pearl. 'Did you know Gabrielle and Noel were getting married?' she demanded.

'Not until I received Noel's letter on the morning of the day they turned up together at Cliff House,' said Adela. 'He wrote to beg me not to tell Father and Mother that his bride is your father's daughter.'

'Did you tell them?' Rain dripped from the rock-face down the back of Pearl's collar. She shivered and wrapped her scarf more tightly around her neck.

'Of course not! Father might have murdered Noel.' Adela made a face. 'I was shocked, though. Noel was beside himself when it all went wrong with Lily and I'd never in a million years have imagined he'd fall in

155

love again so quickly.'

Pearl stared at the churning sea under the grey canopy of the sky. 'I wasn't even aware Gabrielle and Noel had seen each other in over five years,' she said. 'She never seemed particularly interested in him before.'

'Well, he's besotted with her now. But that's not all of it.'

'What do you mean?'

Adela's eyes gleamed with suppressed excitement. 'It seems they've been rather naughty and anticipated their wedding.' She paused for effect. 'Gabrielle is expecting.'

Pearl pressed a hand to her mouth. 'But how . . .'

Adela giggled. 'In the usual way, I expect.'

'You know that's not what I meant.'

'Don't sound so cross! Anyway, I expected Father to be absolutely apoplectic and I nearly took refuge behind the sofa, but he simply blinked and went very quiet. Mother is thrilled that she's to have the grandchild she's been longing for.'

'I don't understand,' said Pearl. 'Why was your father so horrible to Lily, accusing her of being pregnant and throwing her out of the house, when he's prepared to accept the same situation with Gabrielle?'

'Probably because he has no idea of Gabrielle's connection with Spindrift. I shan't tell him, either.' Adela rolled her eyes. 'It'd make life unbearable.'

'Lily's been desperately upset since Gabrielle made her announcement. She's made a hermit of herself in one of the empty studios and refuses to speak. All she does is cry.'

Adela lifted her chin. 'Then she shouldn't have told Noel she didn't love him.'

'If your father hadn't been so rude to her,' retorted

156

Pearl, 'she'd probably be married to Noel by now.'

'I wish it were Lily,' Adela sighed. 'The three of us have been friends forever. Still, for Noel's sake, I shall be a good sister-in law to Gabrielle.'

'She's certainly fallen on her feet now she's found a home at Cliff House,' said Pearl. 'When Mama told her she'd have to find work and pay her own way if she was to stay at Spindrift, she was so annoyed.'

'I hope she really does love Noel.' There was uncertainty in Adela's voice. 'We went to see him off at the station. All the other mothers and sweethearts were crying but Gabrielle didn't shed a single tear.'

'Well, she and Noel are married now and there's no going back,' said Pearl. She stamped her feet to dispel the cold that seeped into her boots from the wet sand.

'Tim is talking about enlisting,' said Adela. 'A woman came up to him yesterday as he was leaving work and tucked a white feather into the breast pocket of his suit. She called him a coward for not being in uniform. He hates working in Father's office. He has absolutely no ambition to be an architect and I think he'll use the white feather as a reason to enlist. No man wants to be called a coward.' She gripped Pearl's hand. 'All our boys are joining up. What will we do if they don't come back?'

'We mustn't think of that,' said Pearl. She couldn't bear to think of Jasper wounded or dead in a muddy trench in a country she'd never even visited. 'We have to concentrate on what we can do to contribute to the war effort. And I don't mean knitting socks.'

'I can't see Mother letting me work in a factory, can you?'

'There must be other opportunities.' Pearl blew on her icy fingers. 'You could come with me to the Red

Cross meeting. Maxwell's given me permission to use his motorcar.'

'I'd like that.'

'Then I'll pick you up in the lane outside your house so your parents don't know you're going with me.'

Adela pouted. 'Father will be at work anyway and Mother's too busy cosseting Gabrielle as the sacred vessel that houses her grandchild, to bother with me.'

'Tuesday at one, then.' Pearl lifted her hand and trudged towards the cliff steps.

Back at Spindrift, she went into the kitchen, where Anneliese and Mrs Rowe were busy turning out the larder. She held her hands over the range to warm them.

'There's tea still warm in the pot,' said Mrs Rowe.

Pearl took a cup from the dresser and settled herself at the pine table. Blanche sat at one end, busy with watercolours and a sketchpad. 'What are you painting, Blanche?' Pearl asked. The little girl pulled a curtain of hair over her face and then glanced up at her through the narrow gap. Pearl was saddened that, at such a tender age, Blanche had learned to be ashamed of her scarred face. 'What lovely cheerful colours! May I see?'

Slowly, Blanche turned the pad so that Pearl could view her painting.

Pearl stared at it, unable to speak. The bright red, orange and yellow paint depicted flames engulfing a crude pencil drawing of a house. A girl with her hair in spiky plaits and her mouth open in a scream stood beside the stick figure of a man lying on the ground. Scarlet blood pooled around his head and one severed arm, its hand and fingers drawn like a bunch of twigs, lay on the ground. Another figure, wearing a pointed helmet, loomed over them, holding a sabre above his head.

Tears welled up in Pearl's eyes. Gently, she stroked the little girl's hand. 'Le méchant est parti maintenant. The bad man has gone now,' she said.

Blanche sat very still for a moment and then snatched her hand away. She tore the painting off the sketchpad and dropped it on the floor. Silently, she began another.

Chapter 18

Pearl let herself into the studio with the spare key and carried the tray upstairs to the bedroom. She sighed at the sight of the figure huddled under the blankets in the fusty atmosphere. 'I've brought you a sandwich, Lily.' There was no answer. Irritated, she thumped the tray down on the chest of drawers. 'Come on now, sit up or I'll pull the bedclothes off you!'

A groan came from under the blankets.

Pearl grasped a corner of the sheet and twitched it.

'All right!' snapped Lily. She sat up in bed, her usually silky blonde hair in tangles.

'You can't go on moping forever!' Pearl put her hands on her hips. 'It's time you stopped being so selfish and thought of others for a change.'

'Selfish? I haven't done anything.'

'Exactly. Your poor mother hardly knows what to do with herself. Your sister has been very unwell with German measles and you've made no attempt to help with the nursing. Dora and I have taken it in turns to sit with Rose during the past few nights.'

Lily rubbed her eyes. 'I didn't know.'

'No wonder you didn't! You've been so mired in self-pity, you've no idea what's going on in the world outside. I don't understand you at all, Lily. You changed your mind about marrying Noel but now he's chosen someone else, you've gone into a decline.'

Lily sniffed.

'You're like a sister to me,' said Pearl. She brushed a matted lock of hair off Lily's cheek. 'I've never thought of you as careless of other people's feelings. If you saw Clarissa's distress, I'm sure you'd give her a hug.'

'I can't! You don't know . . .' Lily turned her face away.

'I don't know what?'

'I didn't stop loving Noel but I discovered the most awful thing that made it impossible for me to marry him.'

'Another girl?'

'No!'

'What, then?' said Pearl.

'We've always told each other our secrets,' said Lily, 'but this one was too painful for me to talk about. If I tell you, will you promise never to tell another soul?'

'Of course I won't tell.'

Lily wrapped her arms around her knees. 'After Hugh Penrose flew into a rage when Noel told him we wanted to marry, I ran home to Mother, seeking comfort. Instead, she told me something shocking. She said I could never marry Noel because . . .'

'What?'

'Because he's my half-brother. Mother had an affair with Noel's father.'

Pearl's mouth fell open. 'No! With Hugh Penrose? How could she? She's so beautiful, she could have had anyone.'

'If only I'd known from when I was a child that Noel was my brother, I'd never have fallen in love with him.' Lily started to weep again and pulled the bedclothes up to her chin.

'It's a hideous shock but no use crying over spilled milk, Lily. You can never be with Noel and you must stop thinking about him. It's time you got out of bed and did something useful. All those soldiers in the trenches, including Jasper and Noel, are relying on us to provide them with warm clothing, clean bandages, tobacco and sweets. Men are dying out there while you mope over a lost love.

'Maxwell has lent me his car to drive to the Red Cross meeting this afternoon. Dora is staying here to sit with Rose while your mother is working, and I'm picking Adela up at one o'clock this afternoon. You,' Pearl fixed her with a stern look, 'are coming with us.'

'Oh, I don't think . . .'

'You don't have to think. Get up and dress.' Pearl pulled back the bedclothes smartly. 'Now!'

* * *

It was dusk by the time Pearl drove Maxwell's Sunbeam back into the courtyard. She glanced at Lily as she braked to a halt. 'You're very quiet. Are you all right?'

'Yes, I am. Surprisingly so.' She hoisted a bag of old knitwear up onto her knee. 'I was talking to a woman on the First Aid course, whose injured son returned from Flanders a couple of months ago. He couldn't stop shaking when he told her how the shelling never stopped and the ground under his feet had shuddered. His wounds hadn't even healed properly before he was sent back to face it all again. His poor mother was convulsed with tears all the time she was telling me about it.'

'And Mama and Pascal are drifting about Spindrift looking like ghosts from worrying about Jasper,' said Pearl.

'I'll sit with Rose for a while and, later, try to build some bridges with Mother,' said Lily. 'Perhaps you should do the same with Edith? Family disagreements pale into insignificance beside what's happening to soldiers overseas.'

Pearl watched Lily cross the courtyard to the coach house, hesitate outside and then go in.

Maxwell opened his studio door to Pearl's knock. 'I've brought your motor home safely,' she said.

'Come in,' he said. 'I was hoping to catch you. I've just boiled the kettle and I bought saffron buns this morning.'

She took off her gloves and warmed her hands by the stove while he made the tea. 'How's the book coming on?'

'That's really what I wanted to talk about.' He waved to one of the armchairs beside the stove and handed her a saffron bun on a plate.

She sat down. There was something about his manner that was ill-at-ease and she noticed the usual mischievous glint was missing from his eyes. 'What is it, Maxwell?' she asked.

'I must return to London.' He ran his fingers distractedly through his dark hair.

Pearl, forcing herself to resist the temptation to smooth down his curls, took a moment to comprehend what he'd said. 'You're leaving Spindrift?' She heard the dismay in her voice. 'But when will you come back?'

'Not for a considerable while.'

Disappointment made her bow her head. She didn't want him to see how much she'd miss him.

'My father wrote to me to say I must hurry up and do my duty.' Maxwell sighed. 'He's right, of course. I joined the Officer Training Corps when I was at Cambridge so I daresay I'll be able to get a commission.

Naturally, my exemplary elder brother has already made Father proud by joining our grandfather's regiment.'

'When will you leave us?'

'In the next day or two. I hadn't meant to stay for so long but,' he glanced at her with a half-smile, 'I found myself in such enchanting company, I couldn't tear myself away.'

Pearl glanced down at the plate on her lap and realised she'd crumbled her saffron bun into pieces. 'It's been such fun learning to drive and helping to plan your novel.' What she wanted to say was that she'd miss him, but she didn't quite dare. Already there was a hollow feeling inside her at the prospect of Spindrift without him.

'I didn't know what to expect when I came here,' he said. 'The community is like a family and it's been a revelation to see how you support each other.'

'I've never known anything else,' said Pearl.

'You're very lucky.'

She reflected for a moment on how her mother had worked so hard to provide for her and her siblings. Family life hadn't always been sweetness and light, especially when Papa had returned to Spindrift and brought his mistress to live with them. With hindsight, that must have been unbearable for her mother. Lily was right; Pearl must repair their relationship.

'I tell you what,' said Maxwell, 'why don't we take the motor out tomorrow and drive up the coast? We'll find an inn for a farewell lunch. Bring stout shoes and we can walk out to King Arthur's Castle at Tintagel.'

She forced herself to smile and resolved to be cheerful company for the rest of their time together. After all, there'd be plenty of opportunity to miss him after he'd gone.

★ ★ ★

The following morning, Pearl pulled up the blackout blind and spring sunshine flooded the bedroom. It was going to be a lovely day, even if it was tinged with melancholy by Maxwell's imminent departure.

The door opened and Nell, wearing her dressing gown and carrying her sponge bag, said, 'The bathroom's free, if you're quick.'

A little while later, the girls went downstairs for breakfast, chatting about their plans for the day.

'The soil's warm enough for sowing vegetable seeds this morning,' said Nell, 'and then I've promised to go to Polcarrow Farm. Poor Mrs Mellyn is struggling to find time to bottle-feed the lambs. There are two orphans and several sets of triplets. The ewes can't cope with them all.'

'I'll come and help with the kitchen garden tomorrow,' said Pearl, 'but I'm going out for lunch with Maxwell today.'

Nell smiled knowingly.

Pearl blushed. 'Don't look at me like that! After all, you're spending half your time with Tom. Anyway, it's a farewell lunch. Maxwell is going to enlist.'

The smile disappeared from Nell's lips. 'You'll miss him.'

In the dining-room, Edith and Pascal, together with Dora and Ursula, were already eating their breakfast and chatting to Maxwell.

It was good to see Ursula laughing at something he'd said, thought Pearl. She'd been so subdued since

165

the war began, almost as if she were frightened of drawing attention to herself.

Maxwell smiled at Pearl and Nell. 'Good morning! And a lovely sunny one it is for a drive along the coast, isn't it, Pearl?'

'I'm looking forward to it.'

'I trust that's acceptable to you, Edith?' asked Maxwell.

'As long as you bring her back safely.'

Pearl met Edith's gaze. Tentatively, she smiled and felt her heart warmed by the answering glow of love in her mother's eyes.

'We'll visit the ruins of King Arthur's Castle,' said Maxwell. 'I promised myself I'd see them before I left Cornwall. And, sadly, I'm afraid I must return to London in the next few days. I apologise that I haven't given you much notice, Edith, but of course I'll pay a month's rent in lieu.'

'We'll be sorry to see you go,' said Ursula. 'Did you finish your novel?'

'Alas, it's a work in progress and I doubt I'll have time for writing once I've enlisted.'

'Oh, no, not you, too!' said Dora.

'Some would say I've delayed too long already.'

'We're in such strange and difficult times,' said Ursula.

Edith turned to Nell and Pearl. 'Do you remember our day trip to Tintagel in the pony and trap when you were children?'

'We had a wonderful picnic,' said Nell, 'and Dora told us stories about King Arthur and Sir Lancelot.'

'I was too frightened to go into Merlin's cavern,' said Pearl.

'That's hardly surprising,' said Maxwell, 'after your

166

previous experience in a cave. I promise I shan't make you visit Merlin and we'll be home in time for tea.'

After breakfast, Pearl settled herself in the front seat of the Sunbeam and Maxwell tucked the tartan rug over her knees.

'Would you mind if I fold the top down?' he asked. 'It may be a bit chilly but it's such a lovely day.'

'I hoped you would,' she said, pulling on her gloves.

Pearl turned her face up to the pale sun as Maxwell drove along the lanes, enjoying the fresh breeze that teased wisps of hair out from under her hat. The hedgerows were decorated in their spring finery: drifts of ragged robin and cow parsley with bright patches of celandine and sweet-scented dog violets.

Maxwell, a motoring cap jammed onto his head and his silk scarf fluttering in the wind, turned to look at her. 'Not too cold?' he shouted over the noise of the engine. She shook her head and he rested his gloved hand on her wrist for a moment.

They passed through Delabole and finally came to Tintagel. Maxwell drove slowly along Fore Street and then pointed to a substantial coaching inn.

'Here's the Wharncliffe Hotel where we'll have our lunch,' he said. He drove to the rear of the inn and parked the motor in the stable courtyard. Some of the loose boxes had been converted to garages. 'If you wait here a moment, I'll talk to that fellow over there. He'll refill the petrol tank while we're having lunch.'

Pearl remained in the car, watching the comings and goings of smart motorcars and passengers descending from a horse-drawn coach on the other side of the courtyard. Ostlers hurried out of the stables to water the horses and porters lifted suitcases down from the coach.

Maxwell returned. 'Shall we have a spot of lunch now?'

Before long, they were studying the menu in an elegant dining-room.

'What a treat to have lunch in a hotel!' said Pearl. She glanced around, studying the smartly dressed guests. 'I'm surprised it's so busy. The summer season hasn't begun.'

'Tintagel may be a small village but there are three hotels here,' said Maxwell, 'and several amenities to attract guests. King Arthur's Castle is only five minutes away by motorcar and there are golf links nearby. The sea air is recommended by doctors as a health cure, all year round. The rich can stable their horses or garage their motors here and others can be conveyed by coach from Camelford station. To be financially successful, a hotel must have special attractions to offer.'

'Goodness!' said Pearl. 'You sound like a holiday advertisement.'

His gaze slid away from her and he smiled uneasily. 'My portfolio of investments includes a hotel.' He frowned at the menu.

'The pea soup was good last time. Very warming before a bracing walk, don't you think?'

Later, replete after the hearty soup, a beef pie and apricot Charlotte, they rounded off their lunch with coffee before returning to the motorcar to change into walking shoes.

Meandering through the village, they climbed a steep path to a medieval gateway. The remains of a courtyard could be discerned on the rocky promontory beyond and they admired the dramatic clifftop views over the sea. The main castle ruins were on an island of grey rock, joined to the mainland by an isthmus. They descended precipitously steep steps down to the narrow land bridge and were soon out of breath as they climbed up the island.

Laughing, Maxwell took Pearl's hand and pulled her up the last few steps to the top, where they explored the remains of the Great Hall of the thirteenth-century castle.

It wasn't only the physical exertion that caused Pearl's pulse to race as they imagined ancient scenes of feasting and chivalric acts. The gentle pressure of Maxwell's fingers entwined with her own made her tremble.

'The climb was worth it for the view, wasn't it?' he said.

Pearl breathed deeply of the sea air. She didn't want this day to end and wished she had her mother's talent for painting so she could capture the moment forever. 'It is extraordinarily beautiful.'

Gently, he turned her to face him. 'You are extraordinarily beautiful. The most beautiful girl I've ever met.'

His lips were warm as he pressed them softly to hers and she knew, as she returned his kiss, that, whatever happened, she would never forget the sweetness of that moment.

Chapter 19

Cornwall

Gabrielle was tired. The fever and slight rash she'd suffered the week before had gone but today she had backache. Stifling a yawn, she put down her cup. Her extremely dull mother-in-law had invited her equally dull friends, Mrs Lewis and Mrs Enys, to tea to meet her son's wife. It had been a while since Gabrielle had been so bored but she supposed it was the price she had to pay for respectability and a comfortable home.

Mrs Lewis eyed her speculatively. 'My dear, do tell us how you came to meet Noel. We hadn't heard a whisper of your impending nuptials until now.'

Jenifry Penrose didn't give Gabrielle a chance to answer. 'It was quite a whirlwind romance,' she said with a high, artificial laugh. 'War changes everything, doesn't it? The wedding was very quiet.'

Adela gave Gabrielle a conspiratorial glance. 'Love at first sight, I believe?'

'Noel wanted us to be married before he was posted overseas,' said Gabrielle. 'I travelled to England as a companion to a family acquaintance.' The pain in her back had intensified and she shifted in her seat to ease it. 'We stayed in Bodmin and I met Noel there.' Gabrielle smiled blandly and wondered why so many Englishwomen wore ugly clothes that didn't flatter them.

170

'How did you learn to speak such excellent English?' asked Mrs Enys.

'My great-aunt married an Englishman. Her grandchildren used to stay with my family for the summer holidays. While they learned French, I learned English.'

'How convenient!'

Gabrielle saw Adela pretending to blow her nose to conceal her sniggering. It was time to put an end to this inquisition. 'Do you have sons in the armed forces, Mrs Enys?'

'Kenwyn enlisted last September and Ruan this January, a week after his eighteenth birthday.'

'And you, Mrs Lewis?'

'Robert is training to be a signaller. He isn't eighteen until September so he won't be posted overseas yet.'

'And what about Timothy, Mrs Penrose?' asked Mrs Enys. 'Is he intending to take up arms? Let me see.' She tapped her cheek with her forefinger. 'I believe he's a year older than Kenwyn so he must be twenty-four?'

Gabrielle noticed the flicker of unease on her mother-in-law's face.

'Naturally, he's champing at the bit to enlist,' said Mrs Penrose, 'but Hugh won't have it. He says one son has abandoned his architectural practice already and he's determined Timothy should remain to assist him.'

Adela glanced at Gabrielle again, her eyes wide in feigned shock at her mother's lie. Tim's intention to enlist had been the subject of heated debate at the breakfast table that morning. Mrs Penrose had burst into hysterical tears and vowed that she simply

171

wouldn't allow him to take the King's shilling. Tim had flung down his napkin and stormed off, leaving his eggs and bacon untouched.

'At twenty-four,' said Mrs Enys, 'Timothy hardly needs his father's permission. You don't want him to be accused of cowardice, do you?'

Mrs Penrose's cheeks flushed an unbecoming shade of magenta. 'Of course not,' she murmured. 'It's the business, you see.'

'We all have to make sacrifices.'

'Mary Pascoe's boy had his leg blown off,' said Mrs Lewis, 'but at least they won't send him back to Flanders.'

Adela, acting the dutiful daughter, offered the platter of dainty cakes and biscuits to the guests again.

Gabrielle winced at the growing pain in her back. She allowed the women's gossip to flow over her without attempting to join in.

At last, the guests said their goodbyes.

The maid brought their coats and her mother-in-law accompanied the visitors to the door.

Adela waited until she'd left the room before picking up the last slice of fruit cake. 'I say,' she said, 'you're looking a bit peaky. Are you all right?'

'I am not quite recovered from my fever,' said Gabrielle.

Mrs Penrose returned. 'My guests thought you were charming, Gabrielle. Naturally, I didn't mention your happy news.'

Adela finished her cake. 'I suppose it'd shock your friends that Gabrielle and Noel are anticipating an eight months baby.'

'I'll thank you not to mention that,' said Mrs Penrose tartly. 'It would be disastrous if it became known that Noel's bride was in an interesting condition before the wedding.' She pinched her lips together.

Gabrielle stood up. 'I am fatiguée. I shall rest for the afternoon.' She started towards the door but came to an abrupt halt at the sound of her mother-in-law's shriek.

'Your skirt,' said Adela. 'There's blood all over the back.'

Gabrielle twisted around and caught her breath at the sight of the scarlet stain.

'Noel's baby!' Mrs Penrose pressed her palms to her cheeks. 'Go upstairs at once, Gabrielle, and lie down. Put a towel underneath you and I'll send for the doctor. Adela, go with her and make sure she stays still.'

By the time Gabrielle reached her bedroom, blood had trickled down her thighs and streaked her stockings. Was she losing the baby? The possibility of a reprieve made her heart skip in jubilation.

Adela laid towels over the bed. Gabrielle wadded up another and pushed it between her thighs.

'Aren't you frightened?' asked Adela.

'I don't know.'

Adela gave her a curious look. 'Why don't you close your eyes until the doctor arrives?'

She nodded. There was a deep grinding pain in her pelvis that ebbed and flowed and she gritted her teeth through the worst of it.

Jenifry returned. 'Adela, go downstairs and look out for the doctor.'

Gabrielle clutched at the bedclothes as the pain intensified. Silently, her lips moved in prayer. It had been a very long time since she'd prayed for anything because, in her experience, God never gave her what

173

she asked for. But perhaps this time would be different and he would rid her of this unwanted child.

A trembling hand rested on her forehead. 'I shall pray for Noel's baby, too,' whispered her mother-in-law.

Gabrielle turned her head away as the pain gripped her again. She wasn't sure how much time had passed before she heard the doctor arrive. Jenifry went to greet the doctor and a subdued conversation ensued on the landing.

A moment later he stood beside the bed. 'Good afternoon,' he said. 'I'm Dr Hardwicke.'

Jenifry hovered in the edge of Gabrielle's vision. 'I shall need to examine you.' He folded back the sheet and pursed his lips.

She stared out of the window, avoiding her mother-in-law's gaze as he probed and prodded her in the most intimate way.

'I understand you had a fever and a rash.' He palpated her lower stomach. 'Did you ever have German measles?'

'No.' She groaned at another spasm.

'Hmm.' He sighed and wiped his hands on the towel proffered by Jenifry. 'Sometimes a threatened miscarriage is avoided with bed rest but I'm afraid this amount of blood loss is too great for us to hope for that.'

'My grandchild!' moaned Jenifry.

Gabrielle sighed in relief.

'It's fairly common in early pregnancies,' continued Dr Chadwick, 'and, in this case, it may be a blessing. There were several cases of German measles in the village and it seems to me that you may have caught it. The disease frequently causes severe impairment

174

to the child at this early stage and sometimes sponta-
neous abortion.'

'What kind of impairment?' asked Jenifry.

'Deafness, blindness and mental defects.' He patted her hand as she began to weep. 'It's best to allow
nature to take its course. It may take some hours so
I'll return later.'

Gabrielle closed her eyes and sent up a prayer of
thanks.

It wasn't until the following morning, when it was
all over and a covered basin had been removed from
the sickroom, it struck her that she had, unnecessarily, tied herself by marriage to a man and a family she
barely knew and didn't particularly care for.

★ ★ ★

'That's enough for today,' said Pearl. She smiled at
Blanche, who sat beside her at the kitchen table cop-
ying her name. 'That's very good. Will you show it to
Maman?'

The little girl, her expression serious as always,
picked up the exercise book and took it to her mother.

Anneliese put down the pot she was washing and
dried her hands before taking it from her. She bent
down and spoke quietly before kissing the top of her
daughter's head.

Blanche closed the book and placed it in the dresser
drawer ready for the next morning.

'Thank you, mam'selle,' said Anneliese.

'She's a clever child,' said Pearl. 'Very quick. She
knows her letters now but she still doesn't speak to
me.'

Anneliese twisted a corner of her apron, her eyes

glistening. 'Or to me. I do not know how to help. One time, she speak all day, morning to night.'

'It's clear she understands quite a lot of English.'

'I, too,' said the maid. 'The words are here,' she pointed at her temple, 'but I cannot always say.'

'You're learning quickly,' said Pearl, 'and I rarely have to say anything to you in French now. I'll continue Blanche's lessons tomorrow.'

'Thank you.' Anneliese bobbed a curtsey. She dropped her gaze. 'Is Monsieur Jasper well?'

'Mama had a letter from him a few days ago,' said Pearl. 'He expects to be sent on active service next month.'

Anneliese nodded. 'He is so kind to us. He teach me English. And now you, too . . .'

'Everyone at Spindrift wants to help you and Blanche until you can return home.'

'I have no home,' the young woman murmured, 'but, for now, we are safe here.' She turned away to finish the washing up.

Troubled, Pearl left the kitchen. It was sickening that the Belgian civilians had been treated so cruelly and, the more she came to know Anneliese and Blanche, the more she understood why Jasper wanted to take up arms to protect others like them.

In the hall, she scanned the post laid out on the console table and saw an envelope addressed to her. She slit it open and her stomach turned a somersault. Maxwell's bold signature in black ink was underlined with a flourish. The morning after that wonderful day together at King Arthur's Castle, she'd gone to his studio, only to find he'd already left Spindrift without saying goodbye. She'd pressed her fingers to her mouth, remembering his kiss and wondering if he'd ever come back. She tore open the envelope.

Dear Pearl,

Well, I've done it and there's no turning back. I've enlisted with the Gloucestershire regiment and I'm on officer training for the next few months. Having been used to spending my time as I pleased, being forced to rise before the sparrows and then cursed and shouted at on the parade ground is rather a shock. Furthermore, I've been subjected to a savage military haircut — my tousled curls now lie on the barber's floor and the back of my head feels like a boot brush! That aside, I believe I have made the right decision to do my patriotic duty. After all, if my dear sister Daphne is prepared to scrub bedpans in support of the war effort, then I must not be found wanting.

I hope you do not mind my taking the liberty of writing to you? Knowing I shall be at the battlefront before long concentrates my mind on what really matters and the usual etiquette seems irrelevant. If you think I am impertinent, please tear up this letter and pretend it never arrived. On the other hand, I would be more than delighted should you care to drop me a line now and again.

Several times, you mentioned that you wished to find something more useful to do than knitting socks for soldiers and I had a thought that might appeal to you. It would be a waste not to use your new-found skill. Daphne told me that, increasingly, lady drivers are needed to convey

the injured from Victoria Station to the surrounding hospitals and convalescent homes and
so I thought of you.

In truth, I often think of you. I carry a picture of you in my mind, laughing and out of
breath, with your black curls blowing around
your lovely face when we climbed the hill to
King Arthur's Castle. In that moment, I believe
I experienced true happiness. I apologise for
leaving Spindrift so abruptly. I hate goodbyes
and thought that, if I came to see you, I might
change my mind. A large part of me wishes I
had.

Yours,
Maxwell

Pearl read the letter twice and then carefully folded
it away in her cardigan pocket. It had been a month
since he'd left Spindrift but he hadn't forgotten her.
She'd cried herself to sleep for a couple of nights after
he'd gone, feeling as if something wonderful had been
snatched away from her. But his letter had changed
all that. A tiny bubble of happiness began to grow
inside her.

★

The Red Cross in Wadebridge became swamped with
volunteers so, now that they didn't have the use of
Maxwell's motor, Pearl and Lily had been pleased to
find meetings being held at the Temperance Hall in
the village. They'd signed up for classes in First Aid,
Home Nursing and Invalid Cookery.

After lunch, the two young women set off together

to attend another class.

'I've made a decision,' said Lily. 'Once I've passed the First Aid examination, I'm going to apply for a position in a hospital as a VAD.'

Pearl glanced at her in surprise. 'Won't it be awfully hard work?'

'I'm perfectly capable of stroking a few fevered brows!' snapped Lily. She sighed. 'Besides, I must get away from Port Isaac. Relations are still strained between Mother and myself and I really couldn't bear to run into Gabrielle.'

'I had a letter from Maxwell,' said Pearl. She wanted to tell Lily how much she'd come to care for him but that would be cruel while her friend was so unhappy about Noel and Gabrielle's marriage. 'He suggested I might apply to be a volunteer driver.'

Lily eyed her speculatively. 'I didn't know you were writing to Maxwell.'

'I wasn't.' Pearl felt warmth flame her cheeks. 'But he's asked me if I would.'

Footsteps came running along the lane behind them and Adela called out to them to wait.

'I'm coming to the meeting.' She bent over to relieve a stitch in her side. 'Besides, I have some news.'

'What's that?' asked Lily.

'Gabrielle lost her baby.'

Lily's face paled.

'Is she all right?' asked Pearl.

Adela nodded. 'She had German measles and the doctor said the child might have been deaf and blind. Apparently, it's Nature's way of preventing a damaged baby from being born.'

Pearl glanced at Lily. 'Both Roland and Rose had German measles. I hope Gabrielle didn't catch it from them.'

'There've been several cases in the village. Mother's distraught at the loss of her grandchild but Gabrielle . . .' Adela hesitated. 'She says how tragic it is and it was obviously a painful experience.' Shuddering, she said, 'It certainly put me off having babies, but I saw her expression afterwards and . . .'

'What?' said Pearl.

'She was smiling. Oh, she put on a sad expression fast enough when she saw me looking at her but I'd say she was relieved.'

'How could she be!' Lily shook her head. 'She ought to be devastated.'

'Well, she wasn't,' said Adela. 'I wish Noel hadn't married her. If only you hadn't changed your mind, Lily, then you'd have been my sister-in-law. I'm not sure I'll ever forgive you for that.'

Pearl noted Lily's anguished expression and linked arms with her.

'And I don't like the way she's wrapped Mother around her little finger.' Adela scowled. 'Nothing's too much trouble. 'Are you quite comfortable, dear? Shall I fetch you a cushion? What would you fancy for your lunch?' Honestly, I think she's forgotten I'm her real daughter.'

'Perhaps she'll stop now Gabrielle isn't pregnant?'

Adela shrugged. 'I don't want to remain at home to find out. I'm going ask at the meeting today about becoming a VAD. I fancy myself as an angel of mercy. Who knows? It might be a good way to find a husband. I'm never going to find a suitable man while I'm living in Port Isaac. I want to go to London.'

'I was just telling Pearl that I want to try nursing!' said Lily.

'It'd be much more fun if we did it together, wouldn't it? What about you, Pearl?'

'Maxwell wondered if I'd be interested in transporting wounded soldiers to the hospitals.'

Adela raised her eyebrows. 'In an ambulance?'

'I'm not sure,' said Pearl, 'but I'm going to find out.'

Chapter 20

May 1915

Cornwall

The platform was crowded with soldiers and their relatives. For a nightmarish moment, it felt to Edith as if she'd wandered into one of her own paintings. The station reverberated to the sounds of young men's bravado, the shrill tones of their mothers' fear and the gruffness of fathers maintaining a stiff upper lip.

The whole family, except for Lucien who couldn't leave London until the end of term, had come to the station to see Jasper off with his regiment. They surrounded him in a protective circle, none of them quite knowing what to say. Everything important had been said already and now they were simply waiting for the moment he would leave them for the unknown.

Pascal, lines of anxiety etched around his eyes, kept glancing up the platform to see if the train was coming. Pearl and Nell stood shoulder to shoulder, united in concern for their brother.

Edith swallowed back nausea and forced herself to smile at Jasper. 'You look so handsome in your uniform,' she said.

'And you've put on your best hat to see me off.' He reached for her hand. 'I'll write to let you know I've arrived safely. I'm told the military post is very efficient.'

She wanted to say it wasn't him arriving safely that

182

concerned her but how long it would be before he returned safely to her. Any other option was unthinkable.

'Nell and I will write, too,' said Pearl.

Edith clung to Jasper's hand. 'I wish you could be there to see your painting in the Royal Academy's Summer Exhibition.'

'It is very special that you and your mother are both exhibiting at the same time,' said Pascal. 'Refugees is a very great achievement.'

'I couldn't have painted it without Anneliese and Blanche,' he said. 'Mama, you will look after them, won't you?'

'I promise they'll have a home at Spindrift for as long as they need it.'

Pascal's hand tightened on Edith's wrist. 'The train is arriving,' he said.

They looked up the tracks and Edith's stomach lurched when she saw the billowing plume of steam in the distance, gradually growing larger. She turned away from the approaching train to study Jasper's face, memorising the curve of his cheek and the unease in his dark eyes.

He gave her a wobbly smile.

'I'm so proud of you,' she said, hearing the quiver in her voice.

Pearl and Nell both hugged him, their three dark heads close together, until Pearl broke away to hide her tears in her handkerchief.

'Give Lucien my love, won't you?' Jasper said to Nell and she nodded wordlessly.

The train thundered into the station and squealed to a halt with a hiss of steam and slamming doors.

Pascal embraced Jasper, holding him tightly for a

moment and then kissing his cheeks in the French fashion. 'You mean everything to us, mon fils,' he said. 'Every day we shall pray that God keeps you safe.'

All around, soldiers were picking up their kit bags and kissing their loved ones. One by one they boarded the train.

Edith held open her arms and Jasper came to her. She buried her face against his shoulder, the rough fabric of his army greatcoat prickling her cheek. He was so tall now, no longer a boy but a man going to fight for his country.

He kissed her forehead. 'I love you, Mama,' he murmured. Then he freed himself from her arms and shouldered his kitbag.

Pascal saw Edith falter and gripped her hand. 'There will be time for tears later,' he murmured. 'Let his last memory of us be of our smiling faces.' They stood pressed close together, watching their son as he climbed aboard the train.

Carriage doors slammed a tattoo and a woman wailed.

The guard blew his whistle in a shriek that set Edith's teeth on edge.

'I don't want him to go,' Pearl wept. She slid her hand into her mother's.

Edith caught her breath on a sob. It was the first time Pearl had voluntarily touched her since she'd discovered the secret of Jasper's birth. Although one of her sons was leaving, perhaps her eldest daughter was returning to her? She slipped her arm around Pearl's waist and Nell stood close by her sister's other side.

The soldiers squeezed together behind the open windows of the carriages, joking and waving. Most of them seemed too young for war, their smooth-skinned faces shining as they set off on their big adventure.

Bolstered by those she loved, Edith took a deep breath and smiled at Jasper through her tears.

The train let out a blast of steam and lurched forwards.

There were shouted goodbyes and cries of 'Good luck!' Handkerchiefs fluttered and women sobbed. The train picked up speed. The boys hung out of the carriage windows, waving.

Edith kept her gaze fixed on Jasper's face until it disappeared from view. Then all that was left was a platform full of weeping families and a pall of steam reeking with the sulphurous odour of the underworld.

* * *

Julian had taken photographs of Jasper in his uniform before he left and one hung on the wall of Pascal's studio. Edith's painting was forgotten as she studied the resolute outline of her son's jaw and the hint of a smile in his eyes that belied the serious set of his mouth. Her gaze blurred while she wondered if he'd been engaged in any fighting yet. The thought of Jasper shooting at another man seemed preposterous but, if ordered to do so, he'd have no choice.

Pascal put down his paintbrush and stood behind her, his arms around her waist and his chin resting on the top of her head. 'I miss him, too,' he murmured.

'The worst thing is not knowing where he is and what he's doing,' she said.

'He will write to us when he is settled.' He turned Edith to face him. 'Shall we take a break from our work and walk in the garden for a while? The sun is shining.'

Outside, they passed the open door of the walled kitchen garden and saw that Dora, Ursula and Pearl were hoeing and weeding the neat rows of vegetables. Dora waved and they went to say hello.

'You've been working hard,' said Edith.

Ursula tucked a strand of fair hair behind her ears. 'It's a good time of year. The seeds are sprouting promisingly but haven't yet grown unruly.' She smiled. 'I like to see the kitchen garden looking tidy and ordered.'

'I've been planting marrow seeds,' said Pearl. 'And look at these little feathery fronds of the carrots that Roland planted.'

'I was wondering if we should cut some new vegetable beds at the end of the lawn,' said Ursula. 'Not everyone in the village has a garden big enough to grow potatoes and we could help them.'

'Julian suggested the same thing yesterday and offered to dig up some of the turf,' said Edith. 'I'm happy to do more sowing and weeding.'

'We are taking a walk now,' said Pascal, 'but I will do the watering this evening.'

'May I walk with you?' asked Pearl.

'Of course you may!' Edith's spirits lifted. Perhaps the anger her daughter had felt towards her really was beginning to lift.

Pearl laid down her hoe. 'I won't be long, Dora.'

They meandered down the garden path, drawn as always towards the sea. Sun glittered on the water and gulls wheeled and cried overhead.

'It looks so peaceful,' said Pascal, leaning on the fence at the end of the garden, 'it is hard to imagine German U-boats lurk beneath the waves.'

'The sinking of the Lusitania by the Germans upset

186

Ursula a great deal,' said Edith. 'She feels a misplaced sense of guilt.'

'I don't think of her as German,' said Pearl.

'The British are always suspicious of foreigners,' said Pascal. 'If we lived in a city, Ursula might receive unwelcome attention. I read in the newspapers that even Germans who have lived here for years have been attacked and their businesses threatened.'

'Ursula wanted to change her name from Hoffman to Hobson,' said Pearl. 'She was anxious that keeping her surname might make it difficult for us at Spindrift. She asked about that when she went to sign in at the police station but was told it was forbidden. Apparently, it might make her look as if she was a spy, trying to conceal her identity.'

'A spy!' Edith laughed. 'Surely no one could imagine that?'

Pascal shrugged. 'People do not make rational decisions when they are afraid.'

They returned along the garden path and Edith noticed that her daughter kept glancing at her. 'Are you troubled about something, Pearl?'

'There's something I want to ask. Mama, may I come to London with you and Pascal next week?'

'You'd like to visit the Royal Academy with us?'

'I'd love to see your painting hanging there — and Jasper's, too, of course. But . . .' She chewed at her bottom lip.

'What is it?' Edith wondered if she wasn't really interested in the paintings but perhaps hoped to shop for new clothes.

'The thing is, I want to meet Daphne, Maxwell's sister.'

'Surely you can find friends closer to home?' Edith

frowned. 'You're pulling that shifty expression I used to see on your face when you were little, after you'd taken biscuits from the larder without asking.'

'Mama! I'm twenty-one now.'

'Then tell me what this is really about.' Edith heard Pascal give a snort of laughter and didn't dare look at him.

Pearl sighed. 'Daphne's a volunteer nurse and she mentioned to Maxwell that, since so many men have enlisted, there's a shortage of people to convey wounded soldiers from the stations in London to the various hospitals. I wondered if I could find out more about that. Now that I can drive —'

'Good heavens! You're not thinking of becoming an ambulance driver, are you?'

'I'm not old enough to do that overseas but I want to do more for the war effort than rolling bandages. I feel as if I'm marking time, while young men of my age are risking their lives to defend us.'

'I, too, think that there must be something I could do,' said Pascal. 'Edith, perhaps you should allow Pearl to discover more about this work?'

'I never said she couldn't! You should know me better than that, Pascal.'

'Then you'll let me meet Daphne?' said Pearl.

'Of course.'

'I haven't been driving long so I may not be suitable,' Pearl continued. 'Jasper has enlisted, Nell is labouring at Polcarrow Farm and now Lily's going to be a VAD nurse . . .'

'When was that decided?' asked Edith.

'She's passed her First Aid course and her application letter went off yesterday. She hasn't told Clarissa yet so you mustn't say anything. You can see why I

188

can't be the only one not assisting the war effort?'

'I shan't stand in your way,' said Edith. 'Work gives meaning to my life and I won't deny you the same opportunity. Besides, I've decided to join the Red Cross, too. If Jasper is a soldier, the least I can do is to assist on the home front.' She held out her arms to Pearl and hugged her tightly. 'The only thing I beg of you is that you don't put yourself in any danger. I'm anxious enough about your brother without having to worry about you, too.'

'I can't imagine there's anything very dangerous about collecting a few wounded men and driving them to hospital, can you?'

'I suppose not,' said Edith.

★ ★ ★

The afternoon was warm and sunny so Pearl followed her grandfather's directions and walked from his house in Bedford Gardens to the statue of Achilles in Hyde Park. She glanced at her watch. It was already past three but there was no sign of any young woman who might be Maxwell's sister.

She watched a nursemaid pushing a perambulator along the path with a small boy toddling beside her, and two elderly ladies gossiping on a bench. After a while, she opened her bag and took out Daphne's letter. It definitely said three o'clock. She was on the point of asking the old ladies if she'd come to the right statue when she saw a young, dark-haired woman hurrying along the path towards her.

'Hello! Pearl Fairchild?'

Pearl smiled. She knew this must be Maxwell's sister because she had the same dimpled chin and piercing blue eyes as her brother.

'So sorry I'm late. Matron caught me just as I was leaving the ward and asked me to change a patient's dressing. She's a devil; she knew it was my afternoon off and I'd have to run to catch the tram.' She held out her work-roughened hand. 'Daphne Fforbes.'

Pearl smiled and shook it.

'Shall we walk while we talk? I can't tell you how lovely it is to be in the fresh air and to rid my nose of the stench of carbolic.'

'Is nursing dreadfully hard work?' asked Pearl. 'Two of my friends are now enrolled as fully fledged members of the Red Cross. They're waiting to hear from Devonshire House if they've been accepted to work at one of the London military hospitals.'

Daphne laughed. 'It's hideously hard work. My feet are covered in blisters and Matron and the trained nurses despise us volunteers. They make our lives miserable by giving us all the most menial jobs.'

'But why don't you leave?'

'Because of the patients, of course. They've been to hell and back. Some of them have been blinded or lost a limb and most of them are so young.' She glanced at Pearl, her eyes brimming. 'Last night, I sat with a boy called Peter as he lay dying. He was crying out for his mother. I stroked his hair until he was calm. At the end, he whispered, 'Goodnight, Ma,' and then slipped away.' Daphne briefly pressed a handkerchief to her eyes. 'If I can help even one of those poor boys, I shall feel it was worth every stinking bandage and basin of vomit.'

'My brother went to the battlefront two weeks ago,' said Pearl. 'If he were to be wounded, I pray he'd be comforted by someone such as you.'

'I worry about Max, too,' said Daphne. 'He'll find it tough to buckle under to army discipline. Mother's horrified I'm volunteering in a hospital. She says I'll never find a husband after the 'indelicate' things I've seen.' Daphne suppressed a giggle. 'I haven't dared to tell her about giving the soldiers bed baths. She'd be sure to fall into a swoon and say I've been ruined.'

'Isn't that a terribly embarrassing thing to have to do?'

'It was, the first time. Now I sing hymns under my breath and make sure never to meet the patient's eye.'

'I'll pass that advice on to Lily and Adela.'

They strolled along the path beside the Serpentine and paused to watch children feeding the ducks.

'Everything looks so normal. It's hard to believe what's happening on the other side of the Channel.' Pearl was thinking of Jasper, and of her mother and Pascal's mute fears for his safety.

'Do you mind if we sit down? The blisters on my feet are killing me,' said Daphne.

They found a bench in the sunshine and she sighed in relief before smiling at Pearl. 'Max said you were extraordinarily pretty. You've made quite an impression on him. He's had the pick of society's beauties but has always held them at arm's length.'

Pearl looked down in embarrassment, remembering the moment he'd kissed her. 'I like him very much. He makes everything seem such fun. What a shame he's unlikely to finish writing his novel now.'

Daphne laughed. 'Novel? He's such a tease! But he taught you to drive?'

'He mentioned you thought volunteers might be needed to convey wounded soldiers from Victoria Station?'

'Incoming casualties are increasing every day. Sometimes they're left to lie on the station platforms until transport and a hospital bed can be found for them.' Daphne rubbed at her eyes. 'There's a new voluntary service called the Women's Reserve Ambulance Corps or the Green Cross Corps. It's funded through donations and subscriptions from the public. Evelina Haverfield is the name of the organiser, if you'd like to contact her? You'd have to be living in London, though.'

'I'm meant to be returning to Cornwall in a few days' time but I've invited myself to lodge with my grandfather in Kensington,' said Pearl, 'just in case.'

Daphne opened her bag and brought out a notebook and a silver pencil. She jotted down an address, tore out the page and handed it to Pearl. 'Normally, I'd suggest you write to Mrs Haverfield but, since you're returning to Cornwall, you might call on her and see if she'll interview you immediately.'

'I'll do that.' Pearl shrugged. 'If she refuses me, I expect I can volunteer with Lily and Adela.'

'I haven't put you off?'

'Not at all,' said Pearl.

Daphne smiled. 'Max said I'd get on with you like a house on fire. I hope you do stay in London so we can see each other from time to time.' She stood up. 'Come on, let's go to the Lyons Corner House at Marble Arch and I'll treat you to a cup of tea and a Chelsea bun.'

Chapter 21

May 1915

London

Over the years, Edith and Pascal had both been delighted to have their work regularly hung in the Royal Academy's Summer Exhibitions but, this year, they were even more thrilled that their son's first submission had been selected by the hanging committee. Lucien had lectures and was unable to view the exhibition until the following day but Edith, her father, Pascal and Pearl took a taxicab to Burlington House. The party chattered animatedly together on the pavement while Pascal paid the driver.

'Shall we find Jasper's painting first?' asked Edith's father.

'By all means,' said Pascal. 'Although I know the canvas, I am eager to see it hung in such illustrious surroundings.'

The exhibition was less crowded and more subdued than on the other occasions Edith had attended. Due to the war, the entrance fee had been waived for men in uniform. Tommies were as much in evidence as officers and there were naval men present too. The remainder of the gathering consisted of groups of ladies and gentlemen who were above service age. Edith scanned the visitors carefully as they walked through the exhibition rooms. She couldn't help recalling the terrible scene Benedict had made at

Jasper's graduation show at the Slade. Almost every day still she wondered if he might fulfil his threat to evict the community from Spindrift.

Pascal led the way to where Jasper's canvas, Refugees, was hung.

Edith's father stood silently before the painting for some time before blowing his nose and discreetly dabbing his eyes. 'No one could fail to be moved by it,' he declared. 'It's a tremendous feather in the dear boy's cap. He should have been here to enjoy his moment in the limelight, but I'll write to tell him how proud of him I am.'

'I've always admired Jasper for his certainty about what he wanted to do in life,' said Pearl.

Pascal, standing close by Edith's side, brushed his hand against hers. 'To see our beloved son's work hanging here means more to me than any of my own achievements,' he murmured. 'I knew from his early years that he had a special gift. Even his letters from the Western Front are embellished with little vignettes of his surroundings.'

'He's worked hard and it's sad the wretched war means he can't be here to celebrate his success,' said Edith. Covertly, she eyed a small group of visitors beside them who were gazing at Refugees. 'Shall we move on to allow others to study the canvas more closely?' she said to her father.

An elegantly dressed woman in a smart hat smiled at Edith as she stepped back. 'This painting breaks your heart, doesn't it?' she said. 'The artist has captured the grief of the whole Belgian nation in this portrait.'

'The artist is my son,' said Edith, so proud she thought her heart might burst.

'Do congratulate him,' said the woman. 'Tell him I shall never forget this portrait.'

Mr Hammond offered Edith his arm. 'Lead on, my dear. I wish to see my talented daughter's work next.'

They walked through the exhibition until they came to Waving the Boys Goodbye. It was hanging in a good position at eye level and Edith tried to study it objectively. She thought it was pleasing to the eye and it certainly pulled on the heartstrings.

Pearl stared at the canvas for some time and then turned to her mother. 'When I was small, I was jealous of the time you spent painting and wanted your attention for myself. I'm relieved now that you didn't let a selfish child stop you.' She kissed Edith's cheek. 'The world would be a lesser place without your work.'

Tears started to Edith's eyes. 'Thank you, Pearl. That means a great deal to me. Finding the balance between being an artist and a mother was the hardest thing I ever had to do.' She sighed. 'I'm still not sure it's possible to be good at both at the same time.'

'You were, you are, a good mother.' Pearl squeezed her mother's wrist. 'I'd like it if you'd show me some of the other paintings and tell me what you like best about them.' She glanced at her watch. 'But I shall have to leave in about an hour if I'm to catch Mrs Haverfield.'

Later, after Pearl and her grandfather had left, Edith and Pascal stood before a large oil painting by John Lavery, The First Wounded, London Hospital, depicting a ward filled with warm light. A Union Jack hung proudly from the window and sunlight pooled in bright patterns on the floor. In the foreground, a nurse tended to an injured soldier.

'Look at the details of the nurse's trolley: the gleam-

195

ing glass bowls, cotton wool and bandages,' said Pascal.

'Do you see the man on crutches behind the nurse?' said Edith. 'There's a patient in a wheelchair and another reading his newspaper. There's something so peaceful about the atmosphere of calm efficiency evoked by the artist, isn't there?'

Behind her, Edith heard someone clear his throat. A well-built man with iron-grey hair and shrewd dark eyes under bushy eyebrows was smiling at her. 'Marvellous, isn't it?' he said.

'Mr Rosenberg, how delightful to see you!'

'I saw your exhibit, Waving the Boys Goodbye, Mrs Fairchild, and I hoped I might find you here to congratulate you.'

'Thank you. May I present my friend Mr Joubert, also a member of the Spindrift artists' community?' she said. 'Pascal, Mr Rosenberg gave me my very first commission, when I graduated from the Slade School of Art.'

'I remember,' said Pascal, shaking Mr Rosenberg's hand. 'Exploring the Ruins was the canvas, I believe?'

'Indeed it was!' He smiled broadly. 'It hangs on the wall of my dining-room and still gives me pleasure every time I look at it. Talking of dining-rooms, would you care to join me for luncheon? There's something I'd like to discuss with you, Mrs Fairchild. We could try the Grill Room at the new Regent Palace Hotel on Piccadilly.'

A short while later Edith caught Pascal's eye when they found themselves in an immense and luxurious restaurant with marbled columns and a deeply coffered ceiling. Silver and glassware gleamed on crisply starched tablecloths and thick carpet underfoot muffled the diners' conversations and muted the chink

196

of bone china. Waiters moved silently amongst the guests, replacing bottles of wine in silver ice buckets. The maître d' came in person to take their order, then hurried away.

'What did you think of the exhibition, Mr Rosenberg?' asked Pascal.

Their host sipped water from a crystal tumbler while considering his answer. 'I found it interesting that, during a time of war, there were very few paintings of battles.'

'There was one, Retreat from the Marne,' said Edith. 'A chaotic scene of injured men and terrified horses, but it struck me there was no hint of modern warfare there. It was a tableau that could easily have been painted during the Crimean War.'

'That is very true,' agreed Pascal.

'There were numerous paintings of classical gardens with ponds, fountains and statues, as if these peaceful vistas act as an antidote to the horrors of war.' Mr Rosenberg leaned his elbows on the table and steepled his fingers. 'And then there are the paintings that depict scenes away from the theatres of war that nonetheless demonstrate the conflict's effects upon those remaining at home.'

'We were very taken with John Lavery's painting of a military hospital ward,' said Edith. 'It was reassuring to see the competence of the nurses so calmly tending to the wounded.'

Mr Rosenberg nodded. 'I particularly liked your painting of the young soldiers going off to war. The faces of the mothers trying to be brave as they waved their handkerchiefs almost made me weep. My own son is in Gallipoli so I, too, have experienced the pain of sending a child into battle.' His voice cracked and he blinked rapidly.

The waiter brought their food and Edith's eyes widened at the sight of her magnificent mixed grill. It was becoming more and more difficult to purchase any meat at all in Port Isaac, never mind a tender steak and a plump sausage.

'These portrayals of humanity and heroism on the home front strike a deeply emotional and patriotic chord in the onlooker,' said Mr Rosenberg, 'and that gave me an idea.' Frowning, he sliced into a kidney. 'I've made my fortune by buying up unsuccessful businesses, finding out what causes them to fail and then turning them around to make a profit. Sometimes I sell the businesses afterwards and sometimes I keep them and employ a good manager. I'm now in a position where I own several factories that I'm putting to good use for the war effort.'

'How interesting,' said Edith politely.

There was a glint of amusement in his eyes. 'Hear me out because this may concern you.'

Edith put down her knife and fork.

'My factories are making buttons and dyeing khaki wool for soldiers' uniforms. Others produce tents and canvas water buckets, cigarettes, fruitcakes and Christmas puddings for Red Cross parcels. The thing is, so many men have enlisted, it's not always easy to find enough workers.'

'Perhaps women might fill those vacancies?' said Pascal.

Edith nodded. 'My daughter is applying for a position as a driver.'

'The sad truth,' said Mr Rosenberg, 'is that I'm sure it will be easier to fill the vacancies as the casualty figures mount and widows need to work to feed their children.'

'I'm not sure how this concerns me,' said Edith.

'I want to commission you to make a series of paintings and posters showing women at work in my factories. After all, the suffragettes have been saying for years that they're as good as men. I'm sure you can stir women's patriotic emotions to make them want to work, and to feel valued while they do it. I'd use the posters for recruiting factory hands but the oil paintings will hang in the boardroom. What do you think?'

Edith's thoughts raced. She desperately needed new commissions. Her savings were dwindling all too rapidly and there were unlikely to be many summer visitors this year to make purchases in the Spindrift Gallery.

'Well?' said Mr Rosenberg.

Edith glanced at Pascal who nodded. 'I do believe,' she said, 'that such paintings would make a far more successful contribution to the war effort than some of the socks and mittens I've knitted.'

Mr Rosenberg threw back his head and laughed.

★ ★ ★

It was late when Edith and Pascal returned to the house in Bedford Gardens. They hurried to change for dinner and came downstairs together, drawn by the sound of laughter in the drawing-room. Her father was relating an amusing anecdote about one of his friends to Pearl and Lucien.

'There you are!' said Mr Hammond. 'Sit down! Sit down! There's just time for a glass of sherry.'

'Grandfather and Pearl have been telling me about

199

their visit to the exhibition this morning,' said Lucien. 'I wish I could have been there but I couldn't miss the lecture on deworming practices in equine management.'

'Sounds fascinating!' said Pearl, grimacing.

'It was, actually. Anyway,' said Lucien, 'several of my friends are coming to the exhibition with me tomorrow and I'll be able to boast about my talented mother and brother to them. Meanwhile, Pearl has some news for you.'

'Did you see Mrs Haverfield?' asked Edith.

Pearl nodded, her eyes shining. 'I start next week, subject to a driving test and learning the quickest routes to all the hospitals. I'll have two weeks' training, then I'll be accompanied by another driver until I've passed my probationary period.'

'Congratulations!' said Edith, trying her best to look delighted. Jasper had left for the battlefront, Nell was all too often at Polcarrow Farm and now Pearl was to remain in London with Lucien. The only child to stay by her side was Roland and even he would be going to boarding school in September. 'I hope you won't find it too upsetting,' she said. 'Some of the soldiers may be badly injured.'

'I'll only be driving the sitting wounded,' said Pearl. 'Stretcher cases will travel by ambulance and, although I've done my Red Cross First Aid course, I don't expect to be called upon to give medical care. In any case, the work isn't only driving. I'll have to take my turn at Victoria Station, giving assistance to servicemen arriving from or departing to the Front, who need to find overnight accommodation.'

'I am happy for you, Pearl,' said Pascal. 'Though you will be greatly missed.'

Edith turned to her father. 'And you really don't mind if Pearl stays here with you, Papa?'

'Good Lord, no! I'll be delighted to have another young person around and Pearl will be a bit of youthful company for Lucien when he's at home. There isn't that much I can contribute to the war effort at my age but, if providing my granddaughter with a place to stay allows her to carry out useful work, then I'm delighted to help in that way.'

The butler announced that dinner was served and they went into the dining-room.

Edith waited until Pearl had run out of things to say about the Green Cross Corps before mentioning Mr Rosenberg. 'An opportunity has presented itself to me today, too,' she said, and told them about the new commission. 'I'll have to visit his factories in different parts of the country, all expenses paid, spending a few days making sketches and talking to the workers before returning to Spindrift to work on the paintings.'

'How many paintings did Mr Rosenberg commission?' asked Lucien.

'Seven, initially,' said Edith.

Lucien whistled. 'Well, that'll keep you in saffron buns for a while!'

'I certainly hope so. Commissions have been very thin on the ground.'

'There are worrying economic times ahead,' said Mr Hammond. 'But your Mr Rosenberg has cleverly turned the difficulties to his advantage by using his factories to supply the great war machine. I should hang onto his coat tails, Edith, and hope his good fortune benefits you, too.'

Rubbing her temples, she said, 'When you put it like

201

that, Papa, it makes me uncomfortable. I shouldn't like anyone to think I was profiting from the war.'

Mr Hammond shrugged. 'Your paintings will be used to help productivity, which will benefit the war effort. Providing Mr Rosenberg doesn't profit over and above what is reasonable, that's perfectly creditable.'

Edith and Pearl left the men to their glass of port and went to the drawing-room for their coffee.

'Pearl,' said Edith, 'there's something I must say to you.'

'Yes?'

Edith clasped her hands together in her lap. 'I hope you aren't leaving home purely to distance yourself from me and Pascal?'

Pearl flushed and looked away. After a moment, she said, 'If I'd been offered the opportunity of leaving home last summer, when the truth came out, I'd have grasped it without hesitation.' She placed her coffee cup carefully on a side table. 'What happened still upsets me, even though Papa treated you shamefully. I know this but the small girl inside me still loves him.'

'I've never tried to stop you loving him.'

'Some mothers might have done so. I also know how steadfast Pascal has been over the years. His love for you is clear to me every time he looks at you. The truth is, he has always been more of a father to me than Papa ever has. I wish you and Pascal could be married.'

'So do I,' said Edith. 'Ever since Jasper's exhibition, I've been living in dread that your father will destroy everything we've worked for at Spindrift. He can be very spiteful. Just because he hasn't evicted us yet doesn't mean that he won't attempt to. He's like the Sword of Damocles hanging above my head.'

Pearl hugged her. 'Perhaps I've grown up a little since last summer and have a better understanding of what you suffered.'

Edith kissed her cheek and wondered if it was Maxwell Fforbes who had encouraged this new maturity in her daughter.

Chapter 22

June 1915

London

Mr Hammond brandished his newspaper at Pearl and Lucien. 'This is enough to spoil anyone's breakfast! There's been an airship bombing raid over Stoke Newington and it's left a trail of destruction over Shoreditch and Whitechapel too. It's a pretty poor state of affairs when the German nation drops incendiaries on children, don't you think?'

'They dropped bombs on Essex and Kent, too, earlier this month,' said Lucien. 'The press call the Zeppelins 'babykillers' now.'

'It's abhorrent that they targeted civilians,' said Pearl.

'And it's what drove a well-brought-up young lady such as yourself to volunteer for what should be man's work.'

Pearl smiled. Grandfather was so old-fashioned. 'I can hardly believe I've been in London for more than a month already,' she said.

Her grandfather peered at her over the top of his newspaper. 'No regrets?'

She held out her hand. 'Only that my fingernails are permanently ingrained with motor oil. The training has been challenging but it's good to do something useful.' Once she'd passed the driving test set for her by the Women's Reserve Ambulance Corps, she'd

204

learned to drive the various motorcars and ambulances garaged in the mews behind a townhouse in Duke Street. Mr MacTavish, dour Scotsman and former chauffeur, trained new recruits in motorcar maintenance.

Lucien, sitting opposite her at breakfast, said, 'I never thought I'd see a sister of mine wearing khaki!'

'What use would a muslin dress be to me when I'm changing a wheel or filling a petrol tank?' Pearl rubbed at a smudge of dirt on the sleeve of her military-style jacket. 'I do wish the wool wasn't so itchy, though.'

'I mustn't be late for my lecture,' said her brother, standing up.

'Not more on worming horses?' asked Pearl, a hint of laughter in her voice.

He shook his head. 'Urinary problems in cats,' he said, with an answering glint of humour in his green eyes.

'Can't abide cats,' said their grandfather.

'I may be a little late for dinner today,' said Pearl. 'If I'm not here in time, please don't wait for me.'

'Not meeting a young man on the sly, are you, Pearl? I'd have your mother to answer to then.'

'Certainly not, Grandfather! And if I were, I'd hardly wish to hold an assignation in this oh-so-flattering uniform, would I?'

'Who knows what goes on in the world these days? I expect women will be wearing trousers next!' He snorted with laughter and picked up his newspaper again.

After breakfast, Lucien and Pearl walked briskly towards the Underground. Somehow, Pearl felt energised by the masculine style of her uniform. The shorter skirt, with hem raised to ten inches above the ground, gave her more freedom of movement. Sturdy laced boots and thick stockings meant she remained perfectly decent.

'So who is it you're meeting after your shift?' asked Lucien. 'Do I need to be worried about some cad threatening your virtue?'

Pearl gave him a sideways look. 'I am meeting a man but it's not what you think.'

'What then?' He took her arm to cross the busy road.

'It's Papa.'

'Good Lord! Why do you want to do that? He's never taken a blind bit of interest in us.'

She shrugged. 'I want to see if I can find out if he's still planning some dastardly act to force Mama out of Spindrift. She's worried sick about the threats he made when he discovered the truth about Jasper. At the time, I was so angry with her but, on reflection, it might never have happened if Papa hadn't behaved so dreadfully. He used to be fond of me and I want to persuade him to stop seeking revenge on Mama.'

'Is it wise to stir things up? Perhaps he's forgotten his threat.'

Pearl shrugged and they chatted about inconsequential things for the rest of the walk. Since they were travelling in opposite directions around the Circle line, they said goodbye outside the ticket office.

Waiting on the platform, Pearl considered the wisdom of asking her father about his intentions, until the rumble of an approaching train and a blast of fetid heat from the tunnel put it out of her mind.

★ ★ ★

At the end of her shift, an entire day spent at Victoria Station passing on information and advice to servicemen, Pearl hurried to the refreshment room. She scanned the crowded tables until she spied Benedict slouched over a half-eaten sandwich and a glass of brandy. Slipping into the chair opposite him, she sighed in relief at being off her feet at last. On the days she was driving she could at least sit down some of the time.

'Hello, Papa.' It dismayed her to notice his hairline had receded even further and the pouches under his bloodshot eyes were puffy and bruised-looking.

'Good God!' he said. 'What is that loathsome article on your head, Pearl?'

'That's a nice way to greet me when we haven't seen each other for a year.' She straightened her felt hat. 'It's part of my uniform. Aren't you proud of me for doing my bit for the war effort?'

'I could hardly believe it when I received your note. Driving! Wherever did you learn to drive? Surely your mother hasn't a motorcar?'

'Hardly! No, we had a charming paying guest in one of the studios at Spindrift for a while and he brought his Sunbeam tourer with him.' Absentmindedly, she picked up her father's abandoned sandwich and took a bite. There hadn't been time for any lunch and she was ravenous. 'He let Roland sit in the driving seat and then he taught me to drive.'

Benedict smiled indulgently. 'Do I detect a fondness in your tone? A touch of romance, perhaps?' He sipped his brandy.

Pearl bent her head to hide her blushes. 'I do rather like him. He's called Maxwell Fforbes and —'

'Fforbes?' Benedict started and he slopped brandy

onto the table. Irritably, he raised a hand to attract the waitress's attention. 'Another brandy for me and tea for my daughter. And mop this up, will you?'

'Do you know him, then?' asked Pearl.

'I certainly do.' He clenched and released his jaw. 'Maxwell Fforbes is a devious liar and a cheat. He swindled me at cards, forcing me into a very precarious financial position. You're to avoid that man at all costs. Do you understand?'

Dismayed, she pushed away the rest of the sandwich. 'He didn't seem like a cheat. But, in any case, he's been posted overseas.'

Benedict relaxed. 'Believe me, Fforbes is known in London as a playboy and a gambler. He'd ruin you given half a chance.'

'A playboy? He behaved like a perfect gentleman while he was at Spindrift.'

'Well, he would, wouldn't he? All confidence tricksters smile as they spout honeyed words . . . and then cut the legs from beneath you with one swipe of the sword. And what the hell was he doing at Spindrift anyway?'

'Writing a book.'

Benedict raised his eyebrows. 'Don't be absurd!' He scowled. 'I won't have him at Spindrift. D'you hear?'

The waitress returned with a tray and set a glass of brandy and the tea things onto the table.

Pearl took her time pouring the tea. Maxwell had been easygoing and entertaining but he'd never tried to take advantage of her. She couldn't believe he was a card sharp.

Benedict sighed. 'Don't go gloomy on me. Looking at the endless lists of casualties, it's highly likely he won't return from the war. Not as a whole man anyway.'

'That's a horrible thing to say!'

'You must have seen that for yourself, if you're driving the wounded to hospital?'

She didn't want to think about the condition of some of the poor boys she'd seen sent back from the Front. She drove them very slowly to avoid aggravating their injuries. At night, she dreamed of their groans of pain and didn't want to imagine Maxwell suffering like that. Shuddering, she sipped her tea. 'Did you know Gabrielle came to Spindrift?' she said.

Benedict eyed her warily. 'How is she?'

'Married.'

'Is she, by Jove?' He laughed. 'She's a wily one. Who did she lead by the nose to the altar then?'

'Noel Penrose. None of us knew anything about it until the deed was done. Not even his parents.'

'What?' Benedict snorted with laughter. 'How I would have enjoyed seeing Hugh's expression when he discovered his son had married my daughter.'

'I'm not sure he does know whose daughter she is. He was shocked enough to learn the happy couple had anticipated the wedding and that there was a baby on the way.'

'Ah, yes.' Benedict pursed his lips. 'Gabrielle mentioned the baby when she came to see me after Christmas. I advised her to find herself a husband.'

'After Christmas?' Pearl frowned. 'But . . .'

'There was nothing I could do for her.'

'She miscarried.'

'I daresay that was a relief.'

'Yes,' said Pearl slowly. 'I daresay it must have been.' She stared at the tea leaves in the bottom of her cup, thinking.

'So, what's happening at Spindrift?'

'Everyone is trying to manage on their savings until the war ends. Wilfred's given up decorating houses because there's no call for it currently. Clarissa and Augustus are still making jewellery but, apart from lockets and identity bracelets, there are very few orders coming in. Julian is fairly busy with portraits of soldiers and their families. Dora and Ursula are still writing and illustrating their books, including a new one on growing vegetables for victory, and Mama has a commission for some paintings of women working in factories.'

'And what about the Frenchman? Your mother's lover.' Benedict's lip curled. 'Did she ever confess to you what I discovered about Jasper?'

'I know he is their son if that's what you mean. As for Pascal being Mama's lover,' Pearl shrugged, 'that may have been the case when Jasper was conceived, but I've never seen any evidence of it since. You made threats to her about forcing her out of Spindrift but you haven't lived with her, or loved her, for years. Can't you put aside your grievances after all this time?'

'I'll never forgive Edith for cuckolding me. I'm determined to make her suffer for it.'

'But you'd already betrayed her with Delphine! And you went on to bring your mistress into Spindrift and have a child with her.'

'Enough!' Benedict jabbed his finger at his daughter. 'I intend to force your mother and her sycophantic coterie of friends out of Spindrift.'

'The community owns a large percentage of the house,' said Pearl, refilling her cup. 'And they pay you rent on the rest, so that's an idle threat.'

He reared to his feet, jarring the table and knocking

over Pearl's cup. 'Idle threat, is it?' He jutted out his jaw. 'I'll show the lot of you! I've already made my plans and your mother and her Frenchman will be squeezed out, along with the rest of the damned community.' He spun around and strode towards the exit, slamming the door behind him.

The refreshment room chatter ceased. Pearl's cheeks burned as disapproving faces stared at her. She'd only wanted to help but it seemed she'd made things worse. It was then that she realised her father had left her to pay for his brandies and sandwich, as well as her pot of tea.

Chapter 23

Aug 1915

Cornwall

Julian ran a hand through his greying hair. 'Several orders need to be delivered urgently' he said. 'There simply aren't enough hours in the day.' He'd been kept busy by a flurry of newly enlisted soldiers who'd had only a few days' notice to join their regiment and wanted to leave photographic portraits of themselves with their families.

'Why don't I deliver the village ones?' said Lily. 'I'll take the rest to the post office.'

Her stepfather sighed in relief. 'That would help me out of a sticky spot. Would you mind putting the prints in the envelopes and addressing them for me, too?'

Lily set off along the coast path to the village. It was a sunny, blustery day and the sea was a deep navy blue, the waves crested with white horses. Wind mischievously flapped her skirt and teased her hair. Breathing in the briny air, she realised how very much she'd miss the sea when she went to London. If she went to London. Neither she nor Adela had received confirmation from Red Cross Headquarters that their applications for nursing duties had been accepted. They had, however, both received letters to say there would be delays due to the number of applications.

'Honestly!' Adela had said. 'They appeal for volunteers to come forward immediately, to avert the staff crisis in hospitals, and then make it as difficult as possible for you actually to help.'

In the village, Lily delivered the photographs and wished the newly enlisted men good luck. After she'd delivered the final one, she called in to the post office.

The postmistress took the envelopes from her and affixed the stamps. 'There's two letters in the second post for Spindrift House,' she said. 'Would you take them with you? The postman's poorly today and it would save him a bit of a walk.'

One was a letter from Jasper to Edith and Pascal but the other, with an envelope marked Devonshire House, was addressed to her. She tore it open and took out several sheets of paper. The first page was a letter informing her that she was to report to the 1st London Military Hospital in Camberwell in two weeks' time. Included in the envelope was a Form of Agreement for her to sign, a Declaration of Loyalty and a uniform list. The annual salary was twenty shillings and volunteers had to provide their own uniform. An allowance would be made for travel, board, lodging and washing.

Her hands shook slightly as she tucked the papers back in the envelope. Although she'd been keen to leave home and do her patriotic duty, now she was nervous.

Halfway back along the coast path, she saw Blue and Star trotting towards her, their tails wagging. She bent down to tickle their ears. 'What are you two doing here?' Shading her eyes from the sun, she peered ahead. Her gaze was caught by a glint of reflected sunlight and then she saw Dora and Ursula sitting on the edge of the clifftop. Whistling to the dogs, Lily set off to join them.

Dora, her sketchbook open on her lap, looked up and waved. 'We've been watching the puffins. They've made burrows in the cliff below.' The dogs settled down beside her on the grass.

Ursula lifted a pair of binoculars from around her neck. The sunlight caught the glass, momentarily dazzling Lily. 'Take a look,' said Ursula. 'Puffins have such a comical walk but when you see them diving headfirst into the water to catch their prey, it's quite a different story.'

A fishing boat bobbed about on the water below and Lily trained the binoculars on it for a moment before watching the puffins diving into the sea. 'They're handsome birds, aren't they?' She returned the binoculars to Ursula. 'I've heard from Red Cross headquarters,' she said. 'I'm to report to the military hospital in Camberwell in a fortnight.'

Dora's hand flew to her mouth. 'Another of you to fly the nest.'

'May I borrow your sewing machine? And I might need some help with making my uniform.'

'Have you told your mother?'

Lily shook her head and stood up. 'Not yet.' She waved and continued on her way back to Spindrift.

Clarissa paled when Lily told her she was leaving. 'I don't like to think of you all alone in London.'

'I shan't be alone! I have accommodation in the hospital and there'll be other girls for company. You should be pleased I'm doing my bit for the country.' But as she walked away, Lily experienced a niggle of guilt for speaking so sharply. Perhaps some time spent working in London would allow her to put aside her anger and, eventually, forgive her mother.

Later that afternoon, when Lily went to hang a pillowcase at Nell and Pearl's bedroom window, hoping to meet Adela after dinner, she saw that her friend had already displayed her own signal. Lily smiled, hoping Adela also had received a letter from Devonshire House.

She went down to the dining-room where the community were gathering for dinner. Edith was reading out snippets from Jasper's letter and Roland and Rose played marbles at one end of the table.

After they'd finished their vegetable pie and were waiting for blancmange, there was a sharp rat-a-tat on the front door. A moment later, Anneliese came into the dining-room, followed by the police constable from the village.

Conversation ceased and Pascal stood up to greet him. 'Good evening, constable. May we help you?'

He ignored Pascal and turned to Ursula. 'Miss Hoffman, I must ask you and Miss Cox to accompany me to the station.'

Ursula pressed a hand to her chest. 'But why? I have abided by the curfew.'

'You were observed on the cliffs this afternoon with Miss Cox. I've received a serious allegation against you both and, as I said, you must accompany me to the station.'

Dora gasped and clutched Ursula's hand. 'We've done nothing wrong!'

'That's still to be decided. You'll both come with me now.'

'It must be a mistake,' said Pascal, 'but perhaps it is better to go to the station now and deal with the matter. I will accompany you and escort you home afterwards.'

Ursula rose slowly to her feet and Dora took her arm. As the small party left the room, Ursula glanced back over her shoulder, eyes wide with apprehension.

A few moments later, the echo of the front door slamming behind them reverberated down the hall.

'I cannot imagine Ursula or Dora doing anything wrong,' said Edith. 'I'm sure Pascal is right when he says it's a mistake.'

After dinner, Lily left the others drinking coffee in the drawing-room and went down to the cove.

Adela came running towards her waving an envelope. 'Did you get a letter?'

'I did! The First London Military Hospital at Camberwell?'

'Yes!' Adela caught hold of Lily's hands and spun her about in a mad dance. After a moment, breathless with laughter, they went to sit on the rocks.

Adela smiled dreamily as she gazed out to sea. 'Wounded officers will call us angels of mercy when we smooth their pillows. Perhaps they'll fall in love with us and propose?'

'Dora's going to help me sew my uniform,' said Lily.

'Mother's sending for her dressmaker to make mine. I shall insist it's cut to flatter, despite the petty rules and regulations. Don't forget to pack something pretty for when we have time off.' She clapped her hands together. 'Just imagine it, Lily, the bright lights of London! We'll meet up with Pearl and visit the shops, the music halls . . .'

It was growing dark by the time Lily returned to Spindrift. She glanced into the drawing-room and saw Dora being comforted by her mother. 'Where's Ursula?' she asked.

'In a cell at the police house for tonight,' said Pascal.

His dark eyebrows were drawn together in a frown. 'She has been accused of communicating with German submarines.'

'But that's preposterous!'

'A fisherman saw her on the cliffs this afternoon, signalling with flashes of light in Morse code. Tomorrow afternoon, both Dora and Ursula will attend court in Wadebridge to determine if they are spies.'

'There's been a dreadful misunderstanding,' said Lily. 'I was there! We were birdwatching. I saw a glint of sunlight catch the binoculars once or twice but —'

'I've already told the constable that,' sobbed Dora. She buried her face against Clarissa's shoulder. 'If they think Ursula's a German spy, signalling to U-boats, she could be shot. And if they knew I was sketching outside, it would make it even worse for her and I might be shot, too.'

'But she isn't a spy,' protested Lily. 'Neither of you is. I shall go to court tomorrow and tell the judge exactly what I saw.'

* * *

Late the following afternoon, Lily, Dora, and Pascal brought Ursula home. Her eyes were red and her hands trembled so much she couldn't hold the cup of tea Lily brought her.

'Come, my dear,' said Dora, 'you shall rest and I'll read to you until you fall asleep.'

'What happened?' asked Edith, after they'd left the drawing-room.

'Both Dora and I spoke on Ursula's behalf,' said Lily. 'The men who'd lodged the accusation were

217

fishermen, Robert and Joe Tregowan. I was shocked because they were at school with me. The judge decided there was insufficient evidence of any subversive acts, but both Ursula and Dora were cautioned. Ursula isn't allowed to travel more than two miles from home and can't use binoculars or a camera or she'll be back in court.'

'But she's done nothing wrong!'

'The British do not generally like foreigners,' said Pascal. 'Some men in the courtroom shouted threats at her and the judge was obliged to call for order. Hugh Penrose was there, cheering them on.'

'I'm sure Ursula will take particular care to do nothing that might lead to any other misunderstanding,' said Edith.

Later, Lily and Rose were searching for sea glass in the cove when the Tregowans' fishing boat sailed by. Lily watched it until it disappeared from sight. It disquieted her that Robert and Joe Tregowan, young men she'd known for most of her life, had turned against Ursula. And the rabble-rousers in court had yelled out venomous threats against the Spindrift community for harbouring a 'German spy'. Was the war being fought overseas going to infiltrate Britain and destroy the peace at home, too? Lily shivered. Perhaps it was already happening.

* * *

Edith was working in her studio. A portrait of a smiling girl filled the foreground of the canvas. In the background was a busy factory production line, piled with Christmas puddings. The worker wore a flattering mob cap and her voluminous cotton pinafore was cinched by a belt around her tiny waist. Across the top of the canvas were the words 'Doing Her Bit for Our Boys', and across the bottom, 'Enrol at Rosenberg's, now!'

Edith added another touch of pink to the apples of the girl's glowing cheeks and the tiniest highlight to her white and even teeth. Mr Rosenberg had liked her proposal sketch, even though the portrait didn't have a great deal in common with the workers she'd seen at his Sheffield factory. Though their pinafore dresses were clean, none of the women she'd spoken to there had the same healthy complexion as the girl in her portrait. Exhausted at the end of their twelve-hour shift, few of them had wanted to speak to her. She'd persisted and asked one girl, 'What do you like most about working here?'

She'd looked Edith up and down, her eyes hard. 'Going home.' Then she shrugged. 'I suppose it's better than a munitions factory.'

Mr Rosenberg had presented Edith with a Christmas pudding. 'One of our finest,' he'd said, 'made for the officers.'

She had travelled home by train the following day, with the pudding on her knee. The crowded carriage was overheated by the August sun and she received some strange looks from her fellow passengers.

Halting footsteps came up the stairs and then Pascal appeared in the doorway. 'I knew you were short of Alizarin and I found a tube when I was in Wadebridge this afternoon. And I bought coloured pencils to send to Jasper in a tin small enough to keep in his breast pocket.'

'He'll be so pleased,' said Edith. 'I love the little drawings he sends in his letters.'

219

'The portraits of his fellow soldiers give an interesting insight into their everyday lives,' said Pascal, 'but the landscapes, so barren and broken, are painful to see.' Absentmindedly, he straightened the row of brushes on her worktable. 'It is hard to know his life is in danger every day while I do nothing to help. I knew the difficulties with my legs would prevent me from active duties like fire-watching but I went to the Red Cross meeting today and they have found a purpose for me. I have been charged with assisting in the organising and collection of hospital clothing and supplies for soldiers. I will collect socks, shirts and belts and help to pack them into Red Cross parcels. We need blankets, bandages, splints and swabs, too. There are so many casualties and never enough equipment.'

'I'm sure I can find some blankets to donate, even if they're a bit threadbare,' said Edith. 'There are some worn sheets, too, perfect to tear into strips for bandages.'

'And I shall ask Wilfred to make some posters to pin up in the village, asking for contributions.'

Edith visited the kitchen to ask Mrs Rowe to make a fruitcake for Jasper, to be included in his parcel.

'We're short of dried fruit,' said Mrs Rowe. 'Supplies are scarce. But I'll use the last of what we have. I don't know how we'd manage without the produce from the kitchen garden. I couldn't get more than a poor bit of scrag end of lamb from the butcher today. I'll have to use a lot of pearl barley and plenty of herbs to give it a bit of flavour.'

'Thank you, Mrs Rowe.' Edith returned to her studio, trying not to think about how long the community would be able to continue to pay the cook her wages,

220

and how her own promise to Jasper to give Anneliese and Blanche a home for as long as necessary could be honoured.

★ ★ ★

During dinner that evening, Pascal told the community about his volunteer work.

'Since the gallery is unlikely to see many holiday-makers this year,' said Clarissa, 'perhaps you should ask the villagers to bring their donations there?'

Augustus nodded in agreement. 'We could store everything behind screens and still keep the gallery open —'

All at once, there was an explosive bang and glass shattered as a brick sailed through the window.

Clarissa screamed and Ursula clutched Dora as the missile crashed onto the table.

Edith pressed a hand to her thumping heart.

Then a bottle with a piece of flaming rag stuffed in the neck flew through the broken window and landed on the floor amongst shards of glass.

Pascal pushed Wilfred aside, snatched up the bottle and flung it back through the shattered window. A second later, it exploded into a fireball.

They watched in horrified silence as flames burned a large black patch on the lawn. Finally, the fire flickered and died away, leaving behind the smoky stench of paraffin.

Pascal picked up the brick. There was a strip of paper wrapped around it. He untied the string that held it in place and drew in his breath sharply.

'What is it?' asked Wilfred.

Wordlessly, Pascal handed him the note.

Wilfred read it and then glanced up at Ursula. 'We can't ignore this,' he said. 'We must speak to the police.'

Edith took the paper from him and let out a cry of distress. The note read: The German bitch must die!

Chapter 24

London

Lily and Adela reported for duty at the 1st London Military Hospital in Camberwell, a large red-brick building overlooking a municipal park. A flustered administration assistant ticked off their names on her clipboard and sent them out again to their hostel a mile and a half away.

'Report back for duty at three,' she said. 'Don't be late.'

Obliged to take another taxicab since their trunks were too heavy to carry, they stared out of the cab's windows at the mean, rubbish-strewn streets and the dilapidated housing.

'It's not at all what I imagined,' said Adela.

'No,' said Lily, whose infrequent forays to London had been to stay with Aunt Minnie in her luxurious mansion flat.

Their accommodation, in a solid, cheerless building of grey stone, consisted of a small room curtained off to form four cubicles, each with just enough room for a narrow bed, a bedside table and a washstand. Lily unpacked her nightdress and sponge-bag and pushed the trunk under the bed. There was nowhere to hang her clothes, save for two hooks on the wall, and no window in her cubicle. At least she wouldn't have to remember the blackout blind.

On their return to the hospital later, the ward sister sent Adela to scrub a soiled bed-mackintosh while Lily was told to change the sheets after a patient had been removed to the mortuary.

The shift passed in a flurry of bed pans, tea-making, disinfecting the sluice room, scrubbing surgical trolleys and collecting soiled dressings removed from suppurating wounds. At eight o'clock they were released from duty and given a supper of boiled potatoes and a stew notable only for its lack of any recognisable meat. Afterwards, they caught the tram back to the hostel. Any hope of soaking in a hot bath before bed was lost when they discovered twenty young women shared the only bathroom and the ancient geyser took half an hour to provide a few inches of lukewarm water.

Falling into bed at ten p.m., Lily called 'Goodnight' to Adela in the adjacent cubicle and heard a muffled reply.

Lily pictured Noel's face, as she so often did before she fell asleep. A year ago they were planning to marry and she simply wouldn't have believed it if she'd been told it wasn't to be. Instead, he'd married Gabrielle and now here Lily was, embarking upon a different life as a nurse — if she could endure it. She sighed and plunged into an exhausted sleep, not stirring until her alarm clock shattered her dreams at half-past five.

* * *

The first weeks at the hospital were hard. It seemed to Lily that she and Adela were always in the wrong place, doing the wrong thing at the wrong time. One or other of the trained nurses was always shouting at them to hurry up. Lily's hands chapped, her feet blistered and she was permanently bone-weary. For the first month, her weekly half-day and the couple of hours between the morning and afternoon shift were spent sleeping. Once she'd grown used to the physical toll of her duties, she found it infuriatingly difficult to meet Pearl and Adela at the same time because her afternoon off was rarely allocated until the morning of the same day.

One evening, the two young women waited for the tram to take them back to the hostel but, yet again, it was full.

'Despite the difficulties,' said Lily, as they set off in the drizzle to walk up the hill, 'I believe we're doing something worthwhile.'

Adela yawned. 'No one can say we're not doing our bit.'

That week, they were both called in to discover they'd passed their probationary period. Lily was assigned to the acute surgical ward situated in a long, makeshift hut in the park adjacent to the hospital. The work was exhausting and, frequently, a convoy of ambulances would arrive with wounded soldiers straight from the battlefields. There was no question then of finishing work at the end of her shift. In the whirlwind of activity punctuated by the screams and groans of the wounded, she occasionally caught a glimpse of Pearl as she unloaded injured Tommies from an ambulance, but there was rarely time for them to do more than wave at each other. Once the last broken man had been assessed by a doctor, stripped of his lice-ridden and bloodstained clothing, washed, fed and put to bed, only then was it possible for Lily to return to the hostel and sink into the sweet oblivion of sleep.

One morning she was run off her feet doing her rounds and giving blanket baths. She'd become used to displaying a brisk and impersonal face while carrying out this last task, to save embarrassment for both herself and the patient. As she pulled up a red-faced young Tommy's sheet and plumped his pillows, a nurse snatched aside the screen. 'Leave that! Come with me,' she said.

Lily followed her along the ward to where an altercation came from behind a curtained bed.

Inside the cubicle, a doctor was soothing the soldier, hardly more than a boy, who had become distressed. He was thrashing about and trying to get out of bed.

'Support his leg,' said the nurse, 'while I remove the dressing.' She lowered her voice. 'The patient's just been told they couldn't save his lower leg so you'll need to hold tight.'

Lily swallowed and gripped the boy's thigh firmly. He screamed in agony and, full of remorse, she let go.

'Such a fuss!' said the nurse, sending her a black look. 'Support the patient's leg, nurse!'

Warily, Lily did as she was told while the doctor restrained the young soldier and the nurse unwrapped the bandage. The dressing had stuck to the wound and the poor boy sobbed for his mother. Lily glanced at the swollen and bloodied stump and felt her gorge rise. She turned away and snatched up a kidney basin just in time to catch a stream of vomit.

Another nurse pulled her into the sluice room. 'Have you no consideration for the patient?' she snapped. 'I don't know why the Red Cross keep sending us such useless specimens. Why did you apply to work in a hospital if you turn sick at the sight of blood? Now clean that basin and return to the ward.'

226

Miserably, Lily scrubbed and disinfected the basin, tears rolling down her face. She heard footsteps behind her and turned to see the doctor. 'I'm sorry,' she said. 'That poor patient . . .'

'Feeling better?' He smiled sympathetically. 'Was that the first amputation wound you've seen?'

She nodded her head, afraid she'd cry if she had to speak.

'Don't worry. It affects a lot of people like that.'

His kindness made her burst into tears. 'Nurse was so angry and the patient was in enough distress without me making a fuss,' she sobbed.

Patting her shoulder, he waited until her tears subsided.

'Sorry,' she sniffed.

He handed her a folded handkerchief. 'Now dry your eyes and go back to the ward as if nothing had happened.'

'Yes, doctor. Thank you, doctor.'

'Doctor Bennett.' He smiled again.

Despite still feeling shaky, Lily couldn't help noticing the spark of interest in his brown eyes.

★ ★ ★

It was a chilly October evening at the end of Pearl's shift when she returned to the mews garage in Duke Street. All vehicles had to be made ready for the morning before the drivers went home. Kathleen, Elsie and Constance were brewing tea on the Primus and MacTavish was working under the bonnet of the Daimler ambulance. Two of the other girls, Millicent and Betty, were filling the radiator of the Sunbeam ambulance.

227

The garage was ill-lit, making it difficult for Pearl to see what she was doing. She topped up the Ford's radiator and ensured the back tyre was still holding air. The motor had developed a slow puncture and she'd had to repair it on the street before hurrying back to Victoria to collect the last of the wounded bound for the Paddington VAD hospital.

The Silver Ghost drove into the garage, braked to a stop, and Hilda, one of the other drivers, got out. 'There were searchlights on a Zeppelin over Green Park just now,' she said. 'The Zep was drifting towards Covent Garden.'

Millicent wiped her hands on an oily rag. 'That's it. I'm done for the evening.'

MacTavish peered around the corner of the bonnet. 'Refilled the tank, have you?'

'Yes, Mr MacTav —'

A deafening bang reverberated through the air.

'What on earth?' said Millicent.

'Sounded like an incendiary device dropped by that Zeppelin,' said MacTavish. 'And not far away.'

Three more explosions followed in quick succession while the girls stared at each other.

'There might be casualties,' said Pearl.

'Don't just stand there!' yelled MacTavish. 'Get in the ambulance and see what you can do!' He slammed the bonnet shut. 'I'll start her up.'

Constance leaped into the driving seat. 'I'll wager you that Zeppelin dropped its load on Covent Garden.'

The rest of the girls piled into the back of the ambulance, while MacTavish swung the starting handle. As soon as the engine growled into life, they drove off into the night. The streetlights were dimmed and

228

there was little moonlight so progress was slow.

'Look!' said Hilda, as Constance turned the ambulance into Pall Mall. 'Do you see the fire?'

Driving along the Strand, the sky to their left was lit up by an orange glow.

'I said the bombs must have fallen on Covent Garden,' said Constance. She drove into Exeter Street but slowed and opened the window to call out to some men running along the road. 'Where did the incendiaries land?'

'The Lyceum Theatre and the Old Bell public house. The streets are in chaos!'

'Seven bombs. One killed a man standing right next to me!'

Constance edged the ambulance through the darkness, avoiding the fleeing crowds, until the flames from nearby buildings illuminated a crater in the road. She braked and the girls leaped out.

Pearl glanced about to get her bearings. The road was littered with rubble and burning timber and the air was full of smoke and dust. Several people had fallen to the ground and a cluster of onlookers huddled around a screaming man with his arm blown off. Everywhere she looked, the flickering light of the fires showed people standing in shocked groups. Shrieks from the maimed and dying assailed her ears. It looked, sounded and smelled like a scene from hell.

She took a deep breath and hurried to tend to a young woman in a fur coat who lay slumped against a nearby building. Blood ran from a cut on her forehead.

'Can you sit up?' Pearl opened her satchel and found her torch and a package containing a wad of lint. She pressed the lint firmly to the wound on the woman's head. 'Hold that in place and wait over there by the ambulance.'

A strident ringing of bells heralded the arrival of a fire engine. A policeman moved the bystanders back and the firemen trained their hoses on a burning building.

Pearl saw Hilda calming a woman in a fit of hysterics and Millicent was assisting another policeman to move an unconscious sailor away from burning debris.

'I can do that,' she said to the policeman.

He passed her the dead weight of the man's legs and she and Millicent heaved him away from the flames.

'There was a doctor here a few minutes ago,' said the policeman.

Millicent felt for a pulse on the man's throat. 'We've lost him,' she said.

The policeman shook his head. 'We'd better make a temporary mortuary by that wall. I'll fetch a tarpaulin.'

Pearl stared down at the dead man, his uniform bloodstained from the savage gash across his abdomen. There was a smudge of dirt on his boyish cheek. Ironic that he'd have been braced to die at sea but, instead, perished on home ground on a night out. She swallowed the lump in her throat. This was no time for her to wallow in sadness.

The policeman returned with a doctor, who pronounced the sailor dead. 'I was attending the theatre,' he said. 'The audience poured out of the Lyceum in the interval to take refreshments in the Old Bell.'

'We're with the Green Cross Corps,' said Pearl. 'We'll ferry any wounded to the hospital in our ambulance. I'll round up the rest of my team and bring stretchers.'

Time ceased to have any meaning for Pearl while she and the other girls searched for and found seventeen dead, twenty severely wounded and countless others who were shocked but not seriously injured. Constance and Hilda conveyed the most critical cases to Charing Cross Hospital, stopping off at the garage on the return journey to collect the other ambulance.

Two more doctors, who happened to be passing, stepped up to assist and a man from a nearby building brought oil lamps for them to work by. Additional members of the police force arrived, closed the road and moved on those who'd come to gawp. Meanwhile, Pearl and Elsie stretchered dead from the wreckage to join others covered with the tarpaulin and coats. They found severed limbs and lumps of flesh, too. Pearl had to sing under her breath to stop herself from thinking about the horror of it when she picked up a foot, complete with a polished black brogue, and placed it on the stretcher. There was a job to be done, terrible though it was, and she wasn't going to be the one who let the side down.

'Pearl? Is that you?'

She turned at the sound of her name and saw her father.

'I was at the theatre and I was hurt,' Benedict said. A dark trickle of blood ran down his forehead and he held out his hand to her.

The street was mostly dark again since many of the fires had been doused. She shone her torch on Benedict's wrist. A small shard of glass protruded from a cut about an inch long and she plucked the fragment from the wound. 'Give me your handkerchief,' she said. She tied it around his hand and then examined

231

the cut on his scalp. His breath reeked of brandy. 'It's only a scratch,' she said. 'You'd better go home and wash these out properly.'

'I can't go home,' he said bitterly. 'The bloody War Office has requisitioned it. Mother and I have been turned out and we're living with my ghastly, self-righteous brother in Hampstead.' His expression brightened. 'You're a driver. You can take me back there.'

She stared at him. 'Can't you see I'm on duty? The motor vehicle isn't for my personal use. Find a taxi. Or take the Underground.'

'But I'm injured!'

'They're only flesh wounds.' Didn't he understand how many had been killed or hideously injured tonight?

'You could slip away for an hour or two to drive me home.'

'No! I'm far too busy gathering up corpses and human remains.'

'Well,' said Benedict, 'they're not going anywhere, are they? They can wait but I'm cold and tired. It wouldn't take you long —'

'Shut up, will you!' Pearl ground her knuckles against her tired eyes, trying to erase the gruesome sights they'd witnessed that evening. Terrible anger rose in her, filling her chest until it erupted in a scream.

Benedict frowned at her. 'Whatever's the matter with you?'

'You are what is the matter with me,' Pearl said. Without another word to him, she turned and walked away.

Chapter 25

January 1916

Cornwall

Edith was heavy-hearted because Lucien had written to inform her of his decision to enlist. He'd be attached to the Army Veterinary Corps, evacuating wounded horses to the veterinary hospitals behind the lines. Already anxious for Jasper, it was hard for her to accept that soon both her sons would be facing such risks.

It was a cold winter's night at the end of January and the community huddled together around a small fire in the drawing-room. Wilfred had particularly asked that everyone be present because he had an announcement to make.

Edith listened to him speaking and clutched at Pascal's hand.

'So, you see,' said Wilfred, 'it's time for me to leave Spindrift for the duration of the war. My income's plummeted now there's no decorating work and the offer of the editorship of The Artists' Review is too good to miss. I'll take up my new post next month.'

'We've been together at Spindrift for twenty-three years,' said Edith. 'The community won't be the same without you.'

'I have been privileged to share a home with you, cousin,' said Pascal to him sadly, 'but the world has changed.'

233

'Nothing is safe anymore,' said Ursula mournfully.

'There's something else,' said Augustus. He glanced at Clarissa and she nodded, her eyes bright with tears. 'Orders for the jewellery workshop have fallen to the point that it's hard for both Clarissa and myself to make a living. We've agreed that, for now, I shall accept a situation that has been offered to me, working for a jeweller in Hatton Garden.'

A hubbub of conversation broke out.

'But where will you live?' asked Dora, her chin quivering.

'Mother and my stepfather are elderly now and worried about the bombing raids in London,' said Wilfred. 'They've rented a house in Somerset until the war is over so Augustus and I will stay in their apartment.'

Later, after the others had retired to bed, Pascal encircled Edith in his arms while they gazed into the embers of the dying fire.

She rested her head on his shoulder. 'Wilfred and Augustus leaving Spindrift is a sea change for the community and I fear for its future. Already Jasper is fighting for his country and Lucien will be sent overseas in the next month or two. Pearl and Lily have flown the nest. Nell only comes home to sleep and, except for the holidays, Roland is at school.'

'But Clarissa, Rose and Julian have no intention of moving on,' said Pascal, 'and Dora and Ursula will remain.' He sighed. 'Poor Ursula. There is nowhere else safe for her at present.'

'I hope it is safe here. Although the police cautioned Robert and Joe Tregowan for smashing our window and making threats, they're such young hotheads that I worry they'll disturb us again.'

'We shall remain vigilant.'

'What is to become of Spindrift?' she said. 'With Clarissa, Julian and Rose living in the coach house, we're going to rattle about with only four of us in the main house most of the time. Apart from Julian's photography and Clarissa's workshop, the rest of the studios aren't bringing in any rent and we still need to pay Benedict for the use of his share of the house. And then there's the gallery. It was barely worth opening last summer. Once my commission for Mr Rosenberg comes to an end, I don't know where I'll find another.'

'I was lucky to sell my last canvas through the gallery in Truro,' said Pascal, 'but we must face the fact that it is necessary for us to find another source of income if the community is to survive.'

Edith massaged her temples. 'There's a leak in the attic studio roof and the paint is flaking off the window frames but there are no funds to repair anything. Should we give Mrs Rowe notice? We cooked and cleaned for ourselves in the beginning.'

'But this is her home now and she has no family.'

'And then there's Anneliese and Blanche. I promised Jasper we'd look after them.'

'It feels good to do voluntary work,' said Pascal, 'but we cannot eat air. The time may have come for us to move to a town and seek employment.'

'We've worked so hard to build the community and now it's dying,' said Edith. 'We'd planned to travel once the children were grown but his wretched war is destroying all our dreams.' Despairing, she buried her face in Pascal's shoulder and he stroked her hair while she wept.

'I don't want to sleep alone tonight,' she whispered. 'I'm tired of living under the threat of what Benedict might do to us. I'm sure Nell and our friends won't tell him if they catch me creeping out of your bedroom.'

'Benedict is not here,' said Pascal. 'Our secret afternoons at Woodland Cottage are precious to me but for years I have dreamed of holding you in my arms for a whole night again. The world has turned upside down and we must find comfort in each other whenever we can.' He rose to his feet and she took his outstretched hand.

* * *

During the night, still wrapped in Pascal's loving embrace,
Edith awoke from a dream. 'Pascal,' she whispered.
He stirred. 'Stay a little longer,' he murmured.
'Wake up!'
'What is it?'
'I have an idea.'
'Mmm?'
'Yes, listen! We don't want to leave Spindrift to find paid work, so what if we bring work here? Remember the letter Pearl sent yesterday?'
Pascal sat up, rubbing sleep from his eyes. 'You want to drive an ambulance?'
She laughed softly. 'No. She said how hard it was to vacate hospital beds until places could be found for convalescent soldiers, even though the Red Cross will pay an allowance for each one. Don't you see? Why don't we offer Spindrift House as a convalescent home? It's so peaceful here, it must be a good place to recuperate, don't you think?'
He was silent for a moment. 'I think it is possible

236

you have had a most excellent idea, Edith. We shall discuss it further in the morning but, for now, mon amour, come here and show me how much you love me!'

She snuggled into his arms and did exactly that.

★ ★ ★

Once Edith had discussed with the community the idea of opening Spindrift House as a convalescent home, events moved quickly. Mrs Watson-Talbot, a formidably aristocratic lady from the Red Cross, inspected the house and made copious notes upon her clipboard.

'You can comfortably house a dozen ambulant convalescents in the two attic rooms and another four in each of the two large bedrooms with the wash hand basins,' she'd said. 'A Matron and two VADs will be required to provide nursing care and clean the wards and rooms used by the patients. Please arrange with your local doctor for him to call by every week.'

Edith requested for herself the position of resident Lady Superintendent and asked for Pascal to be appointed Quartermaster. After a barrage of questions to both of them, Mrs Watson-Talbot agreed. The appointments carried a small stipend and allowable expenses. Mrs Rowe and Anneliese were also interviewed and accepted paid positions as cooks, which was a great relief to Edith.

★ ★ ★

Six weeks later, Edith surveyed the rows of iron bedsteads in the two attic studios. March sunshine

237

flooded through the dormer windows and she smiled when she noticed that, although she and Ursula had scrubbed the floorboards, faint traces of spattered paint remained, each a reminder of one of her paintings. She felt a pang of regret for the loss of her studio but also a sense of pride that Spindrift House would contribute to the war effort.

Downstairs, she checked the two largest bedrooms, each now containing four beds. She'd vacated the master bedroom and moved into a smaller one to give the patients more space. Lodgings for the nursing staff were to be provided in the studios in the courtyard.

Closing the bedroom door behind her, Edith stepped aside for a workman carrying a bucket of paint along the landing.

'The bathrooms'll be finished by the end of today as promised, missus,' he said.

She pushed open the doors to the bedroom that had been divided to provide two new bathrooms. A sale of work at the church hall in Wadebridge and a collection by indefatigable lady volunteers had raised the funds to instal a back boiler and hot water tank in the kitchen, to service the new sanitary arrangements. There hadn't been enough for the pipework to be extended to the attic floor. Edith pitied the VADs who'd have to traipse up two flights of stairs with buckets of hot water and traipse down again later with the slops.

Downstairs, Dora and Ursula were dusting the drawing-room. Any delicate ornaments had been removed to the small sitting-room, where the community would now congregate in the evenings while the drawing-room was made available to the patients.

'I shall pick daffodils to fill the room with good

cheer for when the patients arrive,' said Ursula.

Edith plumped up the sofa cushions. 'There's a box of books, board games and playing cards collected by the boy scouts.' She glanced at her watch. 'Julian's taking the trap to the station to collect Matron and her nurses. They should be here in an hour. I'll see if Pascal is ready.'

In the study, soon to be the hospital's administration office, he was bent over a ledger on his side of the partners desk. He glanced up at Edith. 'A moment!'

She cast her eye over the room to check all was in order. A desk, chair and filing cabinet had been placed beside the window, all ready for Matron to update patient records.

Pascal closed the ledger. 'Every item received from the Red Cross has been documented. The dry goods are locked in the storeroom near the kitchen and I will issue the items needed to Mrs Rowe on a daily basis. Anneliese has labelled the bed linen so that it doesn't go astray when it's taken to volunteers in the village for washing. Spare nightshirts, vests, socks and patients' hospital uniforms are arranged by size on shelves in the gallery, along with blankets, oil lamps, paraffin stoves and the boxes of medical supplies.'

'You've risen to the challenge superbly, Pascal,' said Edith. 'It's such a lot of work and hasn't left you much time to paint.'

He smiled. 'Nevertheless, it has given me a new sense of purpose. It was hard watching Jasper go to war while I stood uselessly by.'

'And now Lucien must serve his country, too.' Edith rubbed her eyes. 'It doesn't seem twenty years since the twins were born. Poor Nell! She was so upset when we saw Lucien off at the station.' She pushed away the stirrings of panic in her breast every time she thought of her precious sons in danger.

'We must pray the conflict ends soon.' Pascal reached over the desk and clasped her hands. 'I long for the time when we will fulfil our plan to travel. I want to paint, sitting in warm sunshine with you by my side, somewhere far away — knowing that when the sun goes down we shall sleep in the same bed without fear of retribution from Benedict.'

'I want that, too.' She bent to kiss his fingers, which were wrapped around hers.

★ ★ ★

A short while later, Edith was in the kitchen discussing menus with Mrs Rowe when she heard Teddy's hooves on the cobbles outside. 'They're here!' she said and hurried outside to greet the nursing staff.

Matron, a middle-aged woman in a starched collar, with her hair tucked firmly under a white veil, shook Edith's hand briskly. 'Margaret Coleman,' she said, 'and this is Nurse Scott and Nurse Braithwaite.'

'Would you like some tea after your journey?' said Edith, smiling at the young nurses. She led them through the back door and into the drawing-room, where Anneliese had deposited the tea tray.

'Afterwards I'll show you your quarters,' said Edith. 'Once you've unpacked, I'll introduce you to our Quartermaster and we'll make a tour of the house.'

Nurse Scott, pale-complexioned and grey-eyed, looked out of the window and her face lit up. 'The sea!'

'There are cliff steps down to the cove,' said Edith. 'You might enjoy a walk on the beach.'

'There'll be little time for that,' said Matron, 'but the sea air will be excellent for convalescing patients. On warm days, we'll sit them in the garden.'

Edith glimpsed Nurse Scott nudging red-headed Nurse Braithwaite and rolling her eyes to the ceiling.

'Tomorrow,' said Matron, 'we'll make an inventory of the medical equipment.' She fixed the VADs with a stern eye. 'I shall outline your duties and remind you of your responsibilities. The first patients will arrive from the Royal Cornwall Infirmary the day after tomorrow and we must be ready.'

★ ★ ★

Two days later, a pair of motorcars arrived, bringing the first six patients. They'd been put on the train at Truro and volunteers met them at Wadebridge and drove them to Spindrift.

Edith went into the courtyard, closely followed by Matron and the two nurses. She watched the men climb out of the vehicles and look around them. Until that moment when she saw the lame, the blind and the limbless, blinking in the sunlight, they hadn't been quite real to her. Opening her home to convalescent soldiers had been little more than a patriotic impulse. Now, she was faced with the reality of men broken by war. She must not fail them.

She pinned a smile on her face and stepped forward, saying, 'Welcome to Spindrift House!'

241

Chapter 26

April 1916

London

It was early evening when the train rolled into Paddington. Once it had squealed to a halt, Lily and Clarissa gathered their luggage and descended. Striding briskly along the platform, Lily scanned the crowd waiting at the other side of the barrier.

'Are you sure you can't find the time to come and see Aunt Minnie with me?' asked Clarissa.

Lily shook her head. 'I'm on night duty,' she lied, walking even faster. She hadn't been pleased when her mother decided to accompany her back to London; the last thing she wanted was for Clarissa to poke her nose into private affairs.

Her mother looked disappointed. 'I'll give her your love then, shall I?'

Lily glanced over Clarissa's shoulder, searching the throng. 'Tell her I'll come when I can manage an afternoon off. I'm not sure when, though.' They went through the barrier. 'I'd better hurry to catch my bus.'

'Lily . . .' Clarissa hesitated and then sighed. 'It's been lovely to have you home for a few days and I'm so proud of your determination to continue nursing.'

'We all have to do what we can, don't we? Good luck with your fundraising!' She pecked her mother's cheek.

Clarissa enfolded her in a hug but Lily submitted

for only a second before stepping away. Her mother's stricken expression made her suffer a pang of remorse. 'I'll write,' she promised, 'but I really must run now.' Hurrying away, she felt her mother's gaze on her and, to avoid it, slipped into a knot of people heading for the exit to Praed Street. She glanced back and saw Clarissa walking towards the taxi rank. And there, only a few feet away from her, was the face in the crowd she'd been searching for.

He waved and strolled towards her. 'Nurse Stanton,' he said, his brown eyes full of laughter. 'Fancy seeing you here.'

'Dr Bennett. What a surprise!' She'd almost forgotten how handsome he was.

'Who was that elegant lady I saw with you?'

'Mother's come up to town to take advantage of my greataunt's wealthy contacts. She's on a fundraising mission for the Spindrift Convalescent Home.'

'Very laudable. Now, I believe I promised you I'd find somewhere for us to have an early dinner?' He tucked his arm through hers and led her out of the station.

Lily was very conscious of Dr Bennett close by her side as they walked in the blackout. She said little as they passed through streets illuminated only by pale moonlight and the occasional sweep of the dimmed headlights of a passing motorcar or omnibus. This would be the first time he had taken her out for dinner, though they'd met several times for tea.

Half an hour later they were settled at a corner table in a dimly lit little restaurant. Lily peered at the menu, angling it towards the candle on the table. 'After a week in the country I was looking forward to having electric light again back in London,' she said.

'But candlelight is romantic, don't you think?' Dr Bennett studied his menu and Lily studied the way his hair curled over his forehead. 'The menu's not awfully inspiring,' he said. 'The damn' Germans are still causing disruption to food supplies. Pea soup and shepherdless pie for me, I think.'

'I'll have the potted cheese and the lentil loaf.' Lily smiled. 'Your shepherdless pie is bound to be made of lentils, turnips and carrots anyway, exactly the same as my lentil loaf.'

'The sooner this war's over, the sooner I shall take you out for a proper dinner of roast beef and all the trimmings,' he said.

Lily hoped that meant he was sufficiently interested to see more of her.

'So, tell me about your leave,' said Dr Bennett. 'Are you more rested now? I was worried about you.' He laid his hand over hers.

'I can't say it felt like a real rest,' she said, hoping he wouldn't see her blush in the gloom. 'It was odd to find Spindrift House reeking of carbolic and overrun with patients in hospital blues. There were only two nurses, harried half to death by a fearsome matron. Every time she barked at them, I jumped, thinking I must have forgotten to empty a sputum cup or change a dressing.'

He laughed. 'At least you won't have as many dressings to change now you're moving from the acute surgical ward.'

'I want to continue nursing but I can't get over my queasiness at the sight of blood.'

'You're a plucky little thing not to have given up before now.' He squeezed her hand. 'You've seen things in the last six months that no woman should ever have to see.'

'Women are doing many of the jobs that only men did before — and doing them very well,' said Lily, slightly irritated by his patronising tone. 'And from what I hear, the neurological ward demonstrates that not all men are able to cope with the sights they have to see on the battlefield.'

Dr Bennett raised his eyebrows. 'My goodness, she bites!' He smiled. 'I didn't realise I was in the company of a rabid suffragist.'

There was an uncomfortable silence for a moment until the waitress brought their first course.

'I wondered if you'd like to go to a matinee?' he said. 'There's a farce called A Little Bit of Fluff on at the Criterion or we might go to the music hall and see Vesta Tilley.'

'The male impersonator they call 'England's greatest recruiting sergeant'?'

'That's the one. Very amusing, I'm told.'

'I'd like that but it's hard to be certain when I'll have my afternoon off.'

'Don't worry about that.' He tapped the side of his nose. 'Thursday next week?'

Lily nodded, flattered he'd pull strings for her.

After they'd finished dinner, Lily said she'd have to go. 'The door of the nurses' hostel is locked at ten.'

Dr Bennett sighed. 'No convenient drainpipe for you to climb up, then?'

She smiled. 'I'm afraid not.'

'I'll hail a taxicab for you.'

'Oh, no! Thank you.' She didn't have the money for a taxi all the way to Camberwell. 'I'll catch the bus.'

'Certainly not! And don't worry, my dear, I'll pay your fare in advance.'

Outside in the dark, they waited until a taxi turned into the road. Dr Bennett flagged it down and paid the driver. 'There you are,' he said, 'all set.'

'Thank you for dinner, Dr Bennett.'

'My pleasure, Nurse Stanton.' He leaned forward and kissed her on the mouth, his lips warm and insistent.

A shiver of pleasure ran through her but she placed her hands against his chest. The last man to kiss her had been Noel and she wasn't sure she was ready to fall in love again.

He laughed softly and whispered in her ear, 'I think it's time you called me Edwin when we're alone, don't you, Lily?'

And then she was in the taxi, cupping her palms over her flaming cheeks.

Back at the hostel, Lily lugged her case up the stairs, all the while thinking about Edwin. He was a good ten years older than herself and charming and sophisticated. Paying for her to take a taxicab back to the hostel had made her feel he really cared for her. And there was next Thursday's outing to look forward to. A frisson of excitement ran down her spine. But she couldn't talk to Adela about it, not when her friend was still annoyed with her for not marrying Noel. And the real reason she hadn't married him was something she could never mention.

She opened the bedroom door quietly in case any of the nurses were sleeping and put her suitcase on the bed. Then she heard a sniffing sound coming from the adjacent cubicle.

'Adela?' she whispered.

The curtain was pulled back. Adela sat on her bed with her arms around her shins and her chin on her

246

knees. Her eyes were red and swollen from weeping.

'Whatever is it?' Lily sat down on the bed beside her.

'My brother's been killed in France.'

An icy wave washed over her. 'Noel?' she whispered.

Adela shook her head. 'Tim.'

Shaking, Lily wrapped her arms around her friend and held her while she sobbed. Was it completely wicked of her to be relieved that it hadn't been Noel?

Chapter 27

London

Lyons tea shop in Piccadilly was bustling and there was a queue waiting to be seated. Pearl licked her finger and swiped up the last crumbs from her Bath bun. She glanced towards the entrance, looking for her friend. Like herself, many people were in uniform but there were also groups of elderly women enjoying tea and a gossip. If she didn't come very soon, Pearl would be obliged to order something else or she'd lose the table.

Then she glimpsed Daphne weaving her way between the throng. She nipped in front of a portly gentleman in a pin-stripe suit who was approaching the vacant chair with a purposeful air and plumped herself down beside her friend.

'I'd almost given you up,' said Pearl.

A waitress stood beside them with a pencil poised over her pad. 'Yes?'

'A bloater-paste sandwich and a pot of tea for two.' Daphne waited until the waitress had gone, and then said, 'I've a surprise for you, Pearl.' She smiled like a Cheshire cat.

'What's that?'

'Close your eyes.'

Laughing, Pearl did as she was told. She felt a movement of the air and heard a chair scrape across

248

the floor.

'Open them now.'

Blinking, she wondered if she was imagining things. Sitting opposite her was Maxwell Fforbes, grinning so much she had the full benefit of his dimples. 'Maxwell?'

'As I live and breathe.'

'But . . .'

'I was granted a few days' leave just after I posted my last letter to you. There wasn't time to write again. I arrived this morning and Daphne told me she was meeting you here so I invited myself along.'

Pearl smiled at him, suddenly a little shy and wishing she was wearing a pretty dress instead of her uniform. They'd written regularly to each other and she believed she'd come to know him well. But now that he was sitting before her, she could see he'd changed. It wasn't only that he was in uniform and his hair was cropped. There was a new wariness in his eyes. He looked older and leaner, too. There was so much to talk about but she didn't know where to begin. She sat back while brother and sister bantered and demolished the sandwich between them.

Daphne finished her tea and stood up. 'I'll leave you two to chat but I'll see you later on, Max. 'Bye, Pearl.'

There was an awkward pause while they watched her go, then they both started to speak at the same time.

'Sorry!' said Pearl.

'My parents are in town,' said Maxwell, 'so I can't escape dinner with them tonight, but may I see you another time?'

'I'd like that.'

249

'Wouldn't it be wonderful if we could take a walk to King Arthur's Castle again?'

His piercingly blue eyes were fixed on hers and she had to force herself to look away. Remembering the sweetness of his kiss on that magical afternoon warmed her cheeks. 'Wasn't it a perfect day?'

'It was.' He touched her wrist with a butterfly-soft caress. 'When the sound of the shelling grows too much for me to bear, I recall that afternoon, minute by minute, until I can catch my breath again.'

'Is it very dreadful?' she asked.

He didn't answer her but stroked her wrist again. 'It's so noisy and crowded here. Shall we go to the park?'

They ambled through Green Park and stopped to look at Buckingham Palace through the gates, before continuing into St James's Park. The September sunshine was warm but the trees were already brushed with gold and amber, a harbinger of the cooler weather to come.

'You're very quiet,' said Pearl.

'I'm making sure I never forget this moment,' said Maxwell. 'No shelling or shooting, no death and destruction, only clean air, green space and a beautiful girl at my side. It's heaven after the Somme.'

'I can't begin to imagine it,' said Pearl. 'The closest I've come was during an air raid. There was a dreadful one last October and the Women's Reserve Ambulance Corps were one of the first services on the scene. I'd never seen a person blown to bits before.' She swallowed at the memory. 'We had to clear the streets before they could be opened again.'

He came to an abrupt stop. 'You didn't tell me about that in your letters.'

250

She shrugged. 'Just as I imagine you don't write to me of all the horrors you've experienced, which are sure to be far worse. I don't know about you, but I've found a way of looking but not seeing. At that first incident, the Corps acquitted itself so well that we're now officially attached to 'D' Division of the Metropolitan Police for air-raid relief.'

'Praise indeed, especially for an all women corps!'

'When I put on my uniform,' she said, 'I think of it as my armour and become a different person. There's a job to be done, people to get to hospital. I couldn't help them if I was having a fit of the vapours.' What she didn't say was that when she went home and took off her uniform, the horrors of the day became fully real to her.

He grasped her hand. 'I had no idea I was putting you at such risk when I suggested you might become a driver. I imagined you'd simply be transferring wounded soldiers from the stations to the hospitals.'

They walked in contemplative silence for a while but then Maxwell stopped and peered at the lake. 'What's happened to the water?'

'Oh, they had to drain it,' said Pearl. 'It's so close to Buckingham Palace and the water reflected in the moonlight. It was feared that Zeppelins would use it as a landmark to target the palace.'

He drew her to a bench in the sunshine and they smiled at each other when they noticed a sailor and his girl spooning on an adjacent seat.

Pearl glanced at Maxwell out of the corner of her eye, wondering how to raise the topic of something that had been bothering her.

'What is it?' he asked.

'While you were at Spindrift, you didn't tell me you

251

know my father.'

He became very still. 'What makes you think I do?'

'Because he told me so.'

'I see.' Maxwell picked at a loose thread on his sleeve. 'What exactly did he say?'

'That you were a liar and a cheat and had swindled him at cards, leaving him in a very precarious financial position.'

Grimacing, Maxwell drew in his breath sharply. 'Do you believe that?'

She gazed into his clear blue eyes while he looked steadily back at her. 'No,' she said, and saw some of the tension drain out of his face. 'But why would he say it?'

'I first met Benedict at Harper's, a gentlemen's club for those who enjoy a game of cards. I found him affable and he put himself out to be charming to me. He'd collected around him an inner circle of friends, hard-drinking, raffish types who lived for the moment.' Maxwell smiled wryly. 'Exactly the type of companion my father had always warned me against. I'm a competent card player and enjoy a bit of a flutter but, after a while, I began to lose once too often. Eventually, I caught Benedict using marked cards.'

Pearl pressed her hand to her mouth.

'He laughed it off,' said Maxwell, 'but after that, I stopped losing. Benedict, however, began to make large losses. He rarely settled his gambling debts, always finding an excuse. He told me I was so wealthy, I could afford to write them off. When I said a gentleman never quibbled over his debts, he became angry.'

'I'm mortified he's my father,' said Pearl, a hot tide of shame staining her cheeks.

'Perhaps I shouldn't have told you,' said Maxwell,

252

'but since he's accused me of his own crime, I feel obliged to defend myself.' He sighed. 'Then, one evening, he was on a winning streak and placed a large bet on the table. His eyes glittered and I suspected he'd taken some kind of stimulant besides his usual wine and brandy. He told me he intended to clear all his debts with his next hand. I said I wasn't prepared to gamble such a large amount and he accused me of being lily-livered.'

'How ill-mannered!'

'I confess, I was angry,' said Maxwell. 'Previously, I'd enjoyed his company but he'd been acting like a wasp in my hair for months, taunting me that I'd landed in clover at a young age, inheriting the sort of fortune it takes others a lifetime to accumulate. And I acknowledge, I've been very lucky.'

'When I was young and Papa lived at home, I adored him,' said Pearl. 'I trailed about after him like a puppy. When he was in a good mood, I basked in the sunshine of his casual affection. But there were times when he hurt me terribly.'

'So you can understand why I still went on seeing him? I knew from the beginning he was after my money, but when he wasn't drinking, Benedict was the archetypal lovable rogue.'

'I understand only too well.'

'He goaded me until eventually I saw red. I placed an even larger bet than his. He crowed but, before the cards were dealt, I insisted on calling for a brand new pack. When I saw the expression on his face, I knew I was right. He'd marked the cards again.'

'So he lost?' said Pearl.

'He did.'

'Has he settled his debt?'

A muscle tensed in Maxwell's jaw. 'Not yet but he will. I have a legally binding promissory note from him, to be redeemed once he comes into his inheritance.'

'But that might be years away still!' said Pearl. 'I've never met my grandmother and Papa doesn't want me to. I suspect he's told her dreadful lies about Mama to conceal his own shortcomings. Grandmother, as I understand it, is fit and well despite her age, and currently the house Papa expects to inherit in time has been requisitioned by the War Office.'

Maxwell took Pearl's hand in his. 'Please don't worry. Frankly, it's the last thing on my mind while the war is raging.' He stood up. 'Come, let's walk again.'

★ ★ ★

That night, as Pearl undressed for bed, she ruminated over her father's poisonous influence over all those with whom he came into contact, and the devastating effect he'd had upon his own family. Jasper had been overjoyed to discover Pascal was his true father and now she envied him that. Pascal had been her true father too, in every way except for a blood connection. She'd been quick to judge her mother for passing Jasper off as Benedict's child but now wondered if, on finding herself in a similar position, she'd have the strength of character to act any differently.

Chapter 28

October 1916

Cornwall

'Noel has home leave?' Jenifry Penrose clasped her hands to her chest, her face radiant. 'It's been so long since I've seen my darling boy and now that poor Timothy . . .' She fumbled for her handkerchief.

Gabrielle closed her eyes momentarily, hoping Jenifry wasn't going to start wailing again. The six months since Timothy died had been intolerable. She folded the letter and stuffed it back in the envelope.

'Oh, mayn't I read it?' begged Jenifry, sniffling.

'It is a private letter,' said Gabrielle, ignoring her mother-in-law's disappointed expression. The last thing she wanted was for Jenifry to read Noel's resentful little jabs at his wife because she hadn't written to him. But really, what was there for her to write about?

'I shall speak to Cook about Noel's favourite dishes.' Jenifry shook her head worriedly. 'Though whether we can obtain supplies is another matter altogether. Eggs are so scarce and . . .' Still talking to herself, she wandered out into the hall.

Gabrielle sighed. She despised Jenifry and missed Adela's company more than she'd thought she would since her sister-in-law had gone to London. At least while Noel was at home she might be excused her mother-in-law's tea parties with the so tiresome and middle-aged Mrs Lewis and Mrs Enys. Gabrielle shook her head in disgust that she was reduced to looking forward to her weekly visits to the Vicarage for the Comforts for Soldiers afternoon. Smiling to herself, she imagined soldiers would be far more comforted by having a pretty girl to warm their bed than the lumpy knitted mittens, scarves and waist-coats they received.

Over the following week, Jenifry made the servants' lives miserable by insisting Cliff House was scrubbed and polished from top to bottom, as if for a royal visit. Finally, it was the day of Noel's arrival and Hugh, on his way home from the office, drove to the station to collect him.

Gabrielle and her mother-in-law waited in the draw-ing-room. Jenifry hurried into the hall the moment she heard Hugh's key in the lock. Gabrielle listened to her squeals of joy and reluctantly rose to her feet to greet her husband. If it hadn't been for the photograph on the piano, she'd barely have remembered what Noel looked like. Waiting in the doorway, she watched Jeni-fry fussing over him, while his father clapped him on the shoulder. After a moment, she stepped forward and Noel turned to look at her.

He released himself from his mother's clutches. 'Gabrielle,' he said.

'Welcome home, Noel.' She kissed him on each cheek, recoiling slightly at the prickle of his unshaven face and the unwashed smell of his uniform.

He hesitated a moment and then hugged her. 'It's wonderful to be here.'

'Come into the drawing-room, my boy,' said Hugh. 'We'll have a sherry before dinner.'

The evening seemed interminable to Gabrielle. She listened to Jenifry and Hugh grill Noel about his

256

experiences and his frequent attempts to deflect the inquisition by changing the subject. Once or twice, he snapped at them.

Jenifry wept while she reminisced about Timothy. 'I shall keep his room exactly the same forever,' she said. 'That way, I can still imagine he'll walk through the door one day.'

Staring straight ahead, Noel gripped his knees. One of his eyelids began to twitch. Gabrielle felt quite sorry for him.

Abruptly, he stood up. 'The journey from France was exhausting,' he said. 'I'm going to bed.' He held out his hand to Gabrielle. Silently, she took it.

'Goodnight, my darling boy,' said Jenifry.

Noel nodded at his parents and left without another word, pulling Gabrielle along beside him. She released his hand to pick up an oil lamp from the table at the foot of the stairs.

Upstairs, they went into his old bedroom, the one Gabrielle had occupied while he was away. He picked up a cricket ball from the bookshelf and polished it against his trouser leg. 'I'm sorry you lost the baby,' he said. 'I'd imagined teaching him to play cricket.'

'You make it sound as if you think I was careless,' said Gabrielle, her voice sharp. She put down the lamp on the bedside table. 'The doctor said that since I'd had German measles, it was a blessing it didn't survive.'

'German measles. That's another bloody thing I blame on the Hun,' he said bitterly. He ran his finger along the bookshelf where serried ranks of tiny lead soldiers waited for a small boy to send them into battle. 'Everything is exactly the same,' he said, 'and yet everything is quite different.' He rubbed his eyes. 'I

257

can't believe I'll never see Tim again.'

Gabrielle sat on the bed. 'I suggested that your room be redecorated in a manner more fitting for a married couple,' she said, casting a scathing glance at the Noah's Ark frieze, 'but your mother forbade it.'

Noel slumped down on the bed beside her. 'It hardly matters. I shan't be here for long.' He caught hold of her chin and turned her face towards the light. 'Gabrielle, tell me the truth. It was my baby, wasn't it?' A muscle tightened in his jaw.

She shook his hand away. 'Of course it was!'

'You hardly ever wrote to me, apart from to inform me of your miscarriage. And that was only a brief note that didn't sound as if you cared.' He stared at her accusingly.

'There's nothing much to say,' she said, pouting.

'You're a cold fish, Gabrielle! You could have told me you missed me and wanted me at home in bed beside you. Or that you were worried for me. You wrote me wonderful letters before we were married, after that first time.'

But that was when she'd had to exert herself to catch a husband in a hurry. Now, the truth was, she didn't especially want Noel in bed with her.

He undid the buttons of his khaki jacket and shrugged it off. There were half-moon stains of perspiration under his arms.

She wrinkled her nose. 'I hope you intend to wash before you come to bed?'

'Wash?' He gave a short bark of laughter. 'I'm sorry if my smell offends your delicate sensibilities. I've been rather busy killing Germans. You have no idea of the conditions I've been living in.'

'Then you will be pleased to make use of the bathroom here.'

Wordlessly, he snatched up his old dressing gown from the hook on the door and strode out of the room.

Sighing, Gabrielle undressed. She was unpinning her hair when Noel returned.

Closing the door behind him, he watched her silently.

She shook out her dark hair until it tumbled down her back and began to brush it with slow, sensuous strokes. If she was going to have to endure Noel fumbling beneath her nightgown, at least she'd attempt to obtain some pleasure from it.

He buried his face in the silky mass for a moment. Then, lifting her in his arms, he carried her to the bed. A moment later he lay naked beside her. 'I've dreamed of this,' he whispered, pulling up her nightgown to kiss her breasts.

It was all over in five minutes. Afterwards, Gabrielle slid away from him and hurried to the bathroom, where she washed herself thoroughly. The last thing she wanted was another baby. When she returned, Noel was already asleep.

★ ★ ★

In the morning Gabrielle went down to breakfast, leaving her husband snoring under the bedclothes.

'The poor boy!' said Jenifry. 'He looked completely drained last night. I'll ask Cook to make him a fresh breakfast when he comes down.'

Hugh rustled his newspaper irritably. 'He's coming into the office with me today. There are a few things he can do to help now that Tim isn't . . .' He cleared his throat and returned to his paper.

259

Jenifry tightened her mouth into a thin line. 'My friends are coming for tea to greet the returning hero.'

'He will spend the day with me,' said her husband, in a tone that forbade argument. 'Besides, Noel won't wish to spend his leave with a coven of gossiping old biddies.'

'You always were entirely selfish, Hugh Penrose,' said his wife.

He answered her sharply and Gabrielle sipped her coffee and wished she were somewhere else.

By the time Noel appeared, dressed in civilian clothing, his parents had ceased bickering and were waiting in resentful silence.

He wolfed down a plateful of eggs and bacon with intense concentration.

'We're going into the office today, Noel,' said his father.

Noel froze in the act of lifting his cup to his mouth. 'I'm only here for three days, Father. I've better things to do.'

Gabrielle watched with interest as Hugh's face turned magenta.

'Better things to do? Better than receiving instruction about the business you'll one day own?'

'Absolutely,' said Noel. 'Who knows if I'll ever return from this damned war anyway?'

Jenifry moaned, 'Don't say that! After poor Tim . . .'

'I'm not going to waste my precious day doing your filing when I could be taking my wife out for lunch.' Noel set his face obstinately against his father's protests. 'Let's go, Gabrielle!'

He led her out of the French windows and through the garden. Unlatching the gate, they walked together onto the headland. The Atlantic was calm and the air balmy for October.

'This is the view I think about just before we go over the top,' he said. 'I've longed to be back in Cornwall. When the war's over, I'll never leave.'

'But you must!' Gabrielle clutched his sleeve. 'I hate it here. I'll die of boredom and the people are so bourgeois . . .'

He wrenched his arm free and hurried down the cliff steps.

Gabrielle trudged after him through the soft sand.

He stood watching the waves roll in for a while and then looked up at the clifftop. His gaze rested on Spindrift House and she wondered if he was thinking of Lily.

'You can't know how it tormented me,' he said, 'hunkered down in a trench, frightened witless and wondering if the baby was actually mine.'

'I told you it was . . .'

'But can I believe you?' He thrust his hands deep into his pockets. 'I don't know what possessed me to marry you.'

'You know perfectly well that we married so that you could revenge yourself upon your father.'

'And to get you out of a hole, by providing you with a home and a husband. Do you still have my letter for Father, should anything happen to me? I'd hate to think I'd married you for nothing.'

'It's perfectly safe,' she said.

He wiped his palm over his face. 'It is a mistake, our marriage, isn't it?'

Suddenly wary, she shook her head, thinking quickly. It was too soon to end things when there was no prospect of her returning to France. And she had nowhere else to go.

'No,' she said slowly, 'you don't know me and I don't know you. Not yet. A love affair is exciting — while it lasts. But your affair with Lily didn't, did it? Don't you remember what I said that day in the Golden Lion? Marriage is a contract with mutual benefits. In France, a wife turns a blind eye to her husband's passing fancies, while providing him with a well-ordered house, pleasant conversation and children.'

'Well,' said Noel bitterly, 'you've failed to provide me with any of that.'

Gabrielle lowered her eyes. 'That was cruel.'

He sighed. 'Sorry.'

'The war hasn't allowed us to get to know each other yet,' she said. 'To make our marriage successful, we need our own home.'

'Perhaps.' He sounded doubtful.

She touched her hand to his cheek and gave a tentative smile. 'Let us walk and you can tell me what it is about Cornwall that has captured your heart.' He studied her face and she gazed guilelessly into his eyes, hoping he couldn't read her mind.

'Once the war is over . . .'

Gabrielle stood on tiptoe and silenced him with a kiss. Then she held out her hand to him.

Hesitantly, Noel took it.

She breathed a silent sigh of relief.

Chapter 29

London

The doors to the neurological ward burst open with a bang and crashed against the wall. An anguished scream rent the air.

Lily's heart sank as a procession of rattling trolleys and wheelchairs, each bearing a new patient, trundled noisily down the ward. She hurried to the bed nearest the door but she was too late. The terrified patient had thrown himself underneath it and was curled up in a foetal position with his hands over his ears, rocking himself back and forth. It was useless to attempt to encourage him back into bed when he was like that so she draped a blanket over his head and shoulders, to muffle the noises that frightened him so.

Lily had been working on the neurological ward for seven months and it was intensely painful to see the suffering of these soldiers lost in living nightmares. The relentless influx of patients 'wounded in mind' and returned from the battlefronts made it increasingly difficult to find beds for the long-term cases in the county mental asylums and private institutions.

An hour later, when the patients had been arranged as tidily as possible with sheets tucked tightly across their chests, Dr Whitworth and a junior doctor arrived. Matron accompanied them on their rounds and Lily was instructed to join them.

Dr Whitworth, gold-rimmed spectacles perched on the end of his nose, peered at his clipboard of notes. 'Says here you're mute,' he said to a patient. 'What's your name, Private?'

The man opened his mouth and made a gargling sound.

Dr Whitworth turned to the junior doctor. 'Send him down for electric shock treatment to his larynx.' He frowned and walked to the adjacent bed where the patient was sobbing and shouting.

Lily caught hold of the man's hands and tried to soothe him while Matron spoke sharply to him.

'Quiet, man!' commanded Dr Whitworth. 'You should be ashamed of yourself for making such a commotion. This one had better be put into one of the solitary confinement cells, Matron, until he learns to behave himself,' said Dr Whitworth. 'Damned cowardice, I call it.'

Lily gritted her teeth. The previous week, she'd attempted to tell Dr Whitworth that his treatments often made the patients even more distressed but he'd ignored her and Matron had reprimanded her.

By the end of the morning, Lily was drained. She'd agreed to meet Edwin for tea at the Copper Kettle before her evening shift but realised she'd have preferred to return to the hostel for a nap.

Outside the hospital, a bitter wind infiltrated itself under her uniform as she walked into Myatt's Fields, the park adjacent to the hospital.

Edwin was waiting for her by the oak tree. 'I'm only free for an hour,' he said.

He never kissed her while they were anywhere near the hospital; it would be inadvisable unprofessional, he said, but the expression in his eyes made her melt.

She nodded, deciding she'd still have time to go back to the hostel afterwards.

They were walking out of the park gates when Lily heard someone call her name. She turned to see Adela running towards them, her nurse's cap askew and her face tearstained. 'What is it?' she asked, as her friend flew into her arms.

'Oh, Lily!' Incoherent with distress, she buried her face in Lily's shoulder.

'Tell me what happened!'

'Father sent me a telegram,' sobbed Adela. 'It's Noel. He's dead!'

Lily let out a cry. The shock was as sharp as if she'd been ducked unexpectedly into an ice bath. 'Not Noel!' She clung to her friend.

Edwin cleared his throat. 'You're both upset. Let's get out of this cold wind and have some tea.'

The cafe was nearly empty and Edwin found them seats by the window. 'Put sugar in your tea, Nurse Penrose,' he said. 'Doctor's orders.' He murmured to Lily, 'Who is Noel?'

'Adela . . .' Her lips found it hard to form the words. 'That is, Nurse Penrose's brother.'

'It's too awful,' said Adela. 'It's only seven months since my other brother was killed.' She began to weep again.

Lily held Adela's hand, unable to speak. Numbness crept up inside her, like frost flowers growing overnight upon a windowpane. She pictured Noel smiling at her, fair hair ruffled by the breeze in the cove, the touch of his lips on hers . . .

'Matron's given me compassionate leave and I'm going home,' sniffed Adela.

'I'll help you pack,' said Lily.

Edwin reached into his pocket and brought out his wallet. 'Take this for a taxi to the station,' he said, giving Adela some money.

She looked up at him, her mouth quivering and her blue eyes still swimming with tears. 'That's very kind, Dr Bennett.'

Edwin patted her hand. 'Not at all, my dear.' He stood up. 'I'd better get back to the ward.' He inclined his head to Lily. 'Nurse Stanton.'

Lily and Adela watched as he walked away down the road.

'Why were you meeting Dr Bennett?' Adela asked. 'You looked as if you were old friends.'

'Oh!' Lily pushed her cup away. 'We ran into each other in the park, that's all. Come on, let's go and pack.'

* * *

After Adela had returned to Cornwall, a letter arrived for her at the hostel. A small shock, like a jolt of electricity, ran through Lily when she saw that the envelope was addressed in Noel's handwriting. She lifted it to her lips with trembling fingers and kissed it. There was no compassionate leave for her, even though it felt as if her heart had been ripped out. Her grieving for the man who'd been forbidden to her must be done in private. She couldn't even claim compassionate leave on the grounds that he was her half-brother. Turning the letter over, she toyed with her conscience, wondering if she dared steam open the envelope and read his last words to Adela. Sighing, she placed the letter under her friend's pillow.

Lily survived the following week by throwing herself

266

into her work. At night she returned to the hostel too exhausted and miserable to do anything but fall into bed. Edwin asked her out to dinner but she couldn't accept while she was mourning another man.

Adela returned to the hostel, pale and tearful. 'My parents would rather I'd died instead of my brothers,' she said. 'Mother's taken to her bed and Father hides in his study and weeps because he has no son to carry on his business.'

'It's dreadful for you all.'

'Noel died a hero,' said Adela. 'He went out onto No Man's Land to bring back a wounded soldier but was shot even before he'd got through the barbed wire.'

'How's Gabrielle taking it?'

Adela shrugged. 'She rarely shows any emotion.'

'There's a letter from Noel for you under your pillow,' said Lily. Adela let out a cry and snatched at the envelope. 'He must have posted it just before . . .' Lily couldn't say the words. She watched her friend's face as she read, her grief changing to anger. 'What is it?'

'He says he made a terrible mistake in marrying Gabrielle. She seduced him into marriage when he was desperately unhappy about losing you. And all the time he was fighting for his country, he suffered agonies because he was wondering if her baby was another man's.'

'Surely she wouldn't have . . .' Lily pressed her fingers to her mouth. 'But their marriage happened so suddenly, didn't it?' she said, remembering her own shock and disbelief. 'She'd run out of money and needed somewhere to live.'

'She trapped him at a time when he wasn't thinking straight. He'd never have married her if you hadn't broken his heart!' cried Adela. 'He was distraught when you jilted him.' She shook the letter in Lily's face. 'He says here he hopes to die because living is too painful. Don't you see? That's why he played the hero and went into No Man's Land. He'd never have risked it if you hadn't deserted him!' Her voice rose. 'And while he was suffering torments of misery, you were off having secret assignations with Dr Bennett. I hope you can live with yourself, Lily Stanton, knowing it's your fault Noel died!'

★ ★ ★

Over the following month, Adela refused to speak to Lily, turning her back whenever she made a tentative overture of friendship. Lily agonised over whether she should have confessed her real reason for not marrying Noel, but for her to do that risked the remnants of Adela's family being torn apart.

Edwin Bennett called into the neurological ward and discreetly asked Lily if she'd like to go to the theatre. A flicker of annoyance crossed his face when she said it wasn't fair to expect him to put up with her company until she was more cheerful. He walked away without saying goodbye.

Eventually, Lily managed to get through the days without weeping but she was lonely. A few times she managed to meet Pearl at a cafeteria. She mentioned she'd had a quarrel with Adela but didn't want to talk about either Noel or Edwin, and Pearl was too exhausted to press her.

One morning, at the end of her shift, Lily loitered by the doors to the acute surgical ward, looking out for Edwin. She finally caught up with him as he appeared in the corridor.

'I hoped I'd see you,' she said. 'I wondered if we might meet for tea at the Copper Kettle?'

He glanced at his watch. 'I'm too busy today.'

'Perhaps tomorrow then?'

'We'll see. Excuse me, I'm in rather a rush.'

Lily watched him hurry off down the corridor and knew, with cold certainty, that he wouldn't invite her out again.

One afternoon in December, she couldn't face walking through the sleet to the hostel and decided to call in to the Copper Kettle. She'd sit in the warmth with tea and an iced bun and read the paper before her next shift.

Dusk was falling but a welcoming glow of light spilled from the tea-shop window across the damp pavement. Lily glanced through the window and came to a sudden halt. Edwin sat at their usual table, his head inclined towards the young nurse who sat opposite him. Adela! Their elbows rested on the tablecloth and their fingers were entwined. Lily stared in disbelief as Edwin lifted her friend's hand to his lips.

Adela, perhaps seeing the shadow at the window, turned her head. She gave Lily a hard stare, then leaned across the table to plant a lingering kiss on Edwin's mouth. Afterwards, she looked straight back at Lily, her lips curved in a triumphant smile.

Chapter 30

December 1916

Cornwall

The dining-room at Cliff House was quiet except for the subdued chink of cutlery and Jenifry sniffing into her handkerchief. The mirror above the fireplace was draped with black crepe and the curtains remained half-drawn as a mark of respect for the dead.

Hugh put down his soup spoon and focused his attention on Gabrielle. 'I'm sure you'll understand when I tell you it's time for you to move on,' he said.

Her stomach lurched even though she'd been expecting this conversation. 'As Noel's widow,' she said, 'I'm part of the Penrose family.'

'As Noel's widow,' said Hugh, 'you will shortly be in receipt of a pension that will allow you to be self-sufficient. Since you did not provide us with the expected grandchild, there's no reason for you to remain at Cliff House.'

'Noel would have been shocked by your heartless attitude to the woman he loved,' she said. 'Since his estate is negligible, I shall be in difficult financial circumstances until I receive the pension. I trust you will permit me to remain until then?' She looked at Jenifry. 'I imagine Mrs Lewis and Mrs Enys might be startled if I am obliged to call upon them for financial assistance since you have made me homeless only days before Christmas?'

270

Hugh snorted in disgust and tossed his crumpled napkin onto his side plate. 'You may stay until the pension is arranged. Then you'll pack your bags.'

A surge of rage made Gabrielle clench her fists under the tablecloth. The thought of having to search for lodgings was exhausting. The pension of sixteen shillings and threepence per week would barely cover the cost of a decent room and her keep. Still, immediately the war was over, she'd return to France. Thank God Noel wouldn't be around to make it difficult.

* * *

A week later, feeling out of sorts, Gabrielle sat by the fire in the morning room. She heard the key in the front door and groaned. Her mother-in-law had returned from one of her visits to her friends.

A moment later, Jenifry burst into the room.

'Close the door,' said Gabrielle. 'There's a draught.' She frowned at Jenifry, who still wore her black coat and hat. Her cheeks were pink and her eyes bright, something Gabrielle hadn't seen for a long time. 'What has happened?' she asked.

'I came straightaway to tell you,' said Jenifry. 'I've had a message from Noel.'

Gabrielle eyed her warily. 'From Noel?'

'I had an invitation to visit Mrs Hudson, an acquaintance of mine. Her boy fell at Ypres so she understands exactly what I'm going through. She told me about Mrs Lee, who has the second sight . . . Romany blood, you see . . . and invited me to join her today for the next séance.'

'You believe she talks to the dead?' It was all too ridiculous.

271

'I know it,' said Jenifry. 'She has an Indian spirit guide called Chenoa, that means White Dove, who passes on the messages through Mrs Lee.' She clasped her hands to her chest. 'Chenoa is a young girl and her voice comes out of Mrs Lee's mouth, it's incredible —'

'Absolutely,' said Gabrielle drily.

'Chenoa said Noel had a message for his dear mother. Well, you can imagine how I felt! He said to tell me that he's with Timothy now and they're working together to guide the fallen to the other side. Isn't that the most wonderful news? I can't tell you what comfort it brings me.'

Gabrielle opened her mouth to say Mrs Lee was a charlatan but thought better of it. It wasn't sensible to upset Jenifry, not while Gabrielle had nowhere else to live.

'I've asked Mrs Lee to come to Cliff House on Thursday,' said Jenifry. 'I'm sure dear Noel and Timothy will have more to say to me then. You must join hands with us, too. Mrs Lee says the vibrations will be stronger if you're there.'

'It will be beyond astonishing to hear Noel's message,' said Gabrielle, her smile bland. This was all too absurd but a séance might at least dispel her boredom.

Jenifry blinked shortsightedly at Gabrielle, as if attempting to read her expression. 'Yes, well, I shall go and take off my hat.' As she left the room, she turned back. 'I suggest you don't mention the séance to my husband. He's not remotely sympathetic to anything spiritual.'

'I wouldn't dream of saying a word,' said Gabrielle.

* * *

272

The following Thursday afternoon, Jenifry instructed her maid to move the circular table out from the bay window in the drawing-room and to place six dining chairs around it. Then she went to annoy Cook by checking that the iced fancies and slices of cake were daintily arranged on doilies.

A short while later, Mrs Lewis, Mrs Enys and Mrs Hudson arrived. Like Jenifry, Mrs Hudson wore deep mourning and a sorrowful but hopeful expression.

Gabrielle sat in a wing chair, listening to the old crows gossiping together, until a sharp rap on the door knocker silenced them.

The maid ushered into the drawing-room a small, stout figure with a felt hat jammed firmly over her black hair.

'My dear Mrs Lee!' said Jenifry. 'I believe you know everyone here, except for my son's widow?'

'How do you do?' said Mrs Lee. Her voice was surprisingly deep and mellifluous.

Gabrielle felt the woman rake her up and down with beady, dark eyes. She stared back unflinchingly. 'I shall be most interested to hear if my dead husband has any messages for me,' she said.

Mrs Lee smiled, the deep wrinkles in her olive skin deepening. 'We have an unbeliever amongst us, ladies! Perhaps we should start?' She closed the already half-drawn curtains.

Jenifry glared at Gabrielle before guiding her friends to the table in the semi-darkness.

Mrs Lee sat down, indicating that Gabrielle was to sit on her right and Jenifry on her left. 'Now we shall make a circle,' she said, reaching for their hands.

Mrs Enys took Gabrielle's other hand and Mrs Hudson whispered to Mrs Lewis as she completed

273

the circle.

'Silence!' commanded Mrs Lee. 'Close your eyes, be still and think of your loved ones. Picture their faces and allow them to come into our midst.'

Gabrielle had an itch between her eyebrows but her hands were trapped and all she could do was to wrinkle her nose. She peeped into the gloom from under her eyelashes. The others had their eyes tight shut. It was all too ridiculous! Mrs Lee gave her fingers a sharp squeeze, almost as if she sensed her thoughts and was admonishing her. Hastily, Gabrielle closed her eyes. It was peaceful sitting in the shadows, she thought a moment later. She'd been so tired lately, she could easily fall asleep.

Mrs Lee breathed slowly and regularly, as if she had fallen asleep. 'Is there anybody there?' she asked in a sonorous tone.

Gabrielle peeped again.

The medium inclined her head as if she were listening. 'Is that you, Chenoa?' She smiled. 'Welcome to our circle. We're hoping you have messages for us from Noel and Timothy Penrose and from David Hudson.' Taking a deep breath, she let it out in a long exhalation. There was a pause and then she spoke again, but this time her voice was as light and musical as that of a young girl. 'Timothy wants to tell his mother to set places for him and his brother at the table at Christmas. Although you cannot be together in the flesh, they will both be with you in spirit.'

Jenifry gave a muffled sob.

'Please, is David there?' whispered Mrs Hudson.

Gabrielle glanced at Mrs Lee, whose head was tipped back with mouth open as if in a trance.

Then the medium, with lips unmoving but speaking in Chenoa's voice, said, 'David sends a message for his dear mother. He says you must not grieve. His pain has gone and he is happy now.' There was a brief silence and then Chenoa spoke again. 'Noel has a message for his wife.'

Gabrielle gave a scornful laugh. How dare this trickster try to deceive her?

'Noel asks Gabrielle to promise that his son, the child she will bear next year, will always have a home at Cliff House.'

Jenifry let out a sobbing cry of joy.

Gabrielle gasped. 'But I'm not . . .' Mrs Lee's palm began to tingle and burn against her own like a thousand bee stings. She tried to snatch her hand away but it was as if they were fused together and she couldn't free herself. All at once, unable to move, panic blossomed inside her and she couldn't breathe. Bright spots of light danced across her vision and then she was falling, falling, into a deep, dark well.

Chapter 31

March 1917

Cornwall

Edith, seated at the desk in the office, shuffled through the morning's post. She saw one of the longed-for cream envelopes, the front divided into quarters by a green cross. The words 'Active Service' were printed across the top. A letter from Lucien! He'd been away for a whole year. Jasper had managed a week's leave the previous August but it would be another fifteen months before he'd be granted home leave again. Unfolding Lucien's letter, she smiled when she read:

> *Six of us had a rest period behind the Frontline and we went into the village of Poperinge. It's terribly battered from the shelling but there were still a few estaminets open, where we could buy beer and a few other little luxuries. There was a club there nicknamed Skindles after a famous hotel on the River Thames at Maidenhead and we went in and had an omelette and fried potatoes. Another time, since I don't smoke, I sold the cigarettes I'd had from a Red Cross parcel and bought myself a pork chop. It was the most delicious meal I had eaten in months.*
>
> *Tell Nell I am well and happy and will write to her again in a few days.*

Edith put the letter carefully in her pocket to savour later and then slit open another envelope with an official stamp. She scanned the contents and then took two new file folders from the drawer and labelled them.

Matron pushed open the door carrying two cups of coffee, as was her custom every morning.

'Two new patients for us,' said Edith. 'The letter must have been delayed because they're arriving at two o'clock this afternoon. It doesn't give us much time to prepare.'

'Nurse Scott stripped Private Holt's bed straight after he left us this morning,' said Matron, 'and the adjacent bed was changed the day before.'

'I'll speak to Mrs Rowe about two extra for dinner.' Edith's brow furrowed. 'I do hope the new patients aren't on special diets. Milk and eggs are in short supply, though Nell did say she'd see if she could bring some back from Polcarrow.'

Matron sipped her coffee. 'Who do we expect today?'

'Private Tompkins.' Edith referred to the letter. 'Chest injuries and nerves. Sergeant West has a facial disfigurement. It also says here that he tried to take his own life.'

'We'll keep a close eye on him,' said Matron. 'I'll not have any suicides on my wards.'

'That's too awful to think of,' said Edith, shuddering. 'I'd better go and see Pascal and ask him to issue nightshirts and underwear for our new patients.'

She went into the hall and heard gales of male laughter emanating from the dining- room. Peering around the door, she saw Nurse Braithwaite sitting at the table with five of the patients playing Housey-housey. 'It sounds as if you're all having fun,' Edith said.

'Nurse Braithwaite keeps us entertained, all right,' said Private Wells.

'Don't worry, Mrs Fairchild,' said the nurse, her eyes alight with mischief, 'I have four brothers so Matron knows I can keep this rabble in order.'

'I'll leave you to it then,' said Edith. The door to the drawing-room stood ajar and she could see half a dozen men inside, reading or dozing. 'Is everybody all right?' she murmured.

Sergeant Harley glanced up from his book and nodded. The empty right sleeve of his jacket was pinned neatly across his chest.

Private Stoughton let out a rumbling snore from the armchair by the window and Edith retreated.

Outside in the courtyard, she stopped to pat the dogs before opening the door to one of the vacant studios. Inside, Pascal had set up a still life arrangement of daffodils in a blue and white jug and three patients were drawing what they saw.

'Excuse me for interrupting your art class, gentlemen,' said Edith. 'Pascal, we have two new patients arriving after lunch. Will you issue the necessary supplies?'

'But of course.' He turned to the men. 'I shall return shortly.'

Edith and Pascal walked together to the gallery, now the storeroom. Inside, the display boards and cabinets had been stacked together. The walls were bare of artwork but open shelves housed dry goods, clothing, spare blankets and boxes of medical supplies.

'It makes me so despondent when I come in here,' said Edith. 'Usually, we'd be busy finishing new work

278

ready for the gallery to open in June.'

'When I suffer from those melancholy feelings,' said Pascal, 'I remind myself what useful work we are doing instead. If Jasper or Lucien had been wounded, it would give me comfort to know they were being cared for with compassion in peaceful surroundings.'

'One of the new patients, a Sergeant West, will need all our compassion. A facial disfigurement led him to attempt to end his life.'

Pascal collected nightshirts and underwear from the shelves and took them to the desk to make entries in the ledger of the items he was issuing.

'What I find most upsetting,' said Edith, 'is that, once the soldiers are better, so many of them are returned to the battlefront and risk being injured all over again.'

* * *

That afternoon, Mrs Watson-Talbot drove into the courtyard in her dark green Daimler. She helped a fair-haired young man out of the back seat of the motorcar. 'Here we are, Private Tompkins!'

Edith and Matron stepped forward to greet the new patients and Blanche, who was scattering carrot peelings on the cobbles for the chickens to peck at, stood and watched from behind the curtain of hair she always pulled over her scarred face.

'This is Matron and Mrs Fairchild, the Lady Super-intendent,' said Mrs Watson-Talbot.

'Welcome to Spindrift House,' said Edith but the new patient only stared at the ground, his body twitching.

'Come with me,' said Matron, 'and we'll book you

in. Did you bring the patients' notes, Mrs Watson-Talbot?'

The other patient climbed out of the motorcar and a gust of wind snatched away his silk scarf and whisked it across the courtyard.

Blanche ran after it and gravely handed it back to its owner, watching intently as he hastily wrapped it around his head and face again.

'Hello,' called Edith. 'I'm Mrs Fairchild. You must be Sergeant West?'

He turned and nodded. His face was swathed in the scarf, right up to his eyes, one of which was pulled downwards by an ugly, puckered scar.

'Will you come with me?'

Blanche waved to him as he followed Edith inside.

A short while later the two men sat in the office while Edith described the daily routine at Spindrift House. 'We aim to provide a family atmosphere,' she said, 'and have an excellent kitchen garden where we grow our own produce. We ask that any patient whose health permits it should assist with weeding, watering and harvesting. Almost all patients, whether they have any experience of gardening or not, have enjoyed the benefit of gentle exercise in fresh air.'

'No patient will be allowed to malinger in their bed all day,' said Matron sternly, 'although proper rest at the prescribed times is essential. Redressing of any wounds will take place before breakfast and during the day, as necessary. Smoking is not permitted inside the house since some patients suffer breathing difficulties.'

Edith glanced at Private Tompkins, whose whole body trembled all the while. 'When Matron has taken your details,' she said, 'I'll show you both the facili-

280

ties available. There's a choice of books, board games, cards and so on. You may use the piano in the dining-room or join the art class. When the weather is clement there's a spacious garden and you may play croquet on the lawn or sit in the sun. Cricket bats and balls are available in the gazebo and there are steps from the garden down to a small beach.'

'Two family members may visit you on Thursday afternoons between two and four,' said Matron. 'Now, I'd better look at your notes and then you can get settled.'

* * *

The following evening, after the second sitting for dinner, Pascal and Julian went to set up a ping-pong table that had been received as a gift from a previous patient's family.

Edith, Dora, Ursula and Clarissa congregated in the sitting-room and Anneliese brought them coffee.

'How did you get on with Sergeant West and Private Tompkins this afternoon?' Edith asked Dora and Ursula.

'Private Tompkins did no more than sit, shaking and twitching, on a bench in the kitchen garden,' said Ursula. 'I sat with him for a while and encouraged him to help. He didn't answer but I thought he'd lost some of the glazed look in his eyes so I said I was going to plant a row of carrots on his behalf. By the time I'd finished, he was watching me and he'd stopped trembling so badly.'

'From little acorns, mighty oaks grow,' said Dora. 'I'm convinced the garden helps our patients. We'll ask some of the others to encourage him to join us tomorrow. Sergeant West did some weeding. There's a dreadful scar across the top of his cheek and it pulls his eye down at the corner, poor man. He wouldn't look at me when I spoke to him but did some useful work in the far corner of the garden.'

'I noticed Blanche slip into the garden and start weeding the row next to him,' said Ursula. 'Perhaps she feels an affinity to him because of her own disfigurement. Of course, she's still mute but I saw Sergeant West talking to her and she was nodding.'

'It's a start,' said Edith. 'He's barely said a word to me. Perhaps it's easier for him to talk to a child? Matron read his notes and it seemed he was caught by machine-gun fire when he peered over the top of the trench.'

'I don't quite know how to ask him,' said Dora, 'but I wondered if he'd like me to make him a fitted fabric mask to disguise his injuries. That scarf is all very well but it keeps slipping and he's constantly fiddling with it.'

'Perhaps Matron might be the one to ask him?' said Edith. 'A mask might be considered a surgical appliance and then he wouldn't have to think you pity him.'

'Yes, I see that.' Dora nodded decisively. 'I'll speak to her about it.'

★ ★ ★

April brought mild and sunny weather and even the new patients enjoyed strolling around the garden or sitting in a deckchair with a blanket over their knees. The sound of the sea provided a continual, soothing background to conversation, and the fresh air brought colour to the patients' cheeks.

Edith sat with Private Davison in the gazebo, writing a letter to his wife. Jimmy Davison, blinded by mustard gas at Passchendaele, was still troubled with his lungs but he always endeavoured to remain cheerful.

'Tell Milly my good news,' he said. 'Say that St Dunstan's has a place for me next month. I'm going to learn to read braille and use a typewriter and I'll be trained for a new occupation. I've a fancy to take up market gardening. Working outside —'

'Just a minute,' said Edith. 'I can't write that quickly.' She finished the sentence. 'Go on now.'

'Say working in clean air will help my breathing and I've been able to give it a go in the kitchen garden here at Spindrift House.' He grinned. 'And I'll make sure, my dear wife, that you and the little ones will never go short of fresh vegetables.'

'Is that everything?' asked Edith.

'Let me think a bit.'

Edith waited, watching Nell and Tom Mellyn from Polcarrow Farm playing croquet on the lawn with a handful of patients and the two VADs. The sound of Nell's laughter drifted towards her and she smiled. She'd begun to hope Tom and her daughter might make a match. Nell was always so very close to her twin that it was only since Lucien had enlisted she'd blossomed as a person in her own right.

'Mrs Fairchild?'

'Yes, Private Davison?'

'Tell my wife I love her with all my heart, will you?' he said. He stared blindly out to sea, his mouth working. 'I just hope she can still love a blind man,' he whispered.

She squeezed his hand, tears starting to her eyes.

'I'm sure she's living for the day when she'll hold you in her arms again,' she said. 'I've written letters to both my sons so I'll take yours with them to the post office this afternoon.'

'God bless them!' said Private Davison. 'Looking on the bright side, at least the war is over for me.'

'Shall I take you back to the terrace to sit with the others?'

Private Davison stood up and gallantly offered Edith his arm.

It was as they walked past the game of croquet that Nell suddenly let out an anguished cry. She covered her face with her hands and her knees folded beneath her. Tom dropped his mallet and caught her in his arms while the nurses hurried to assist.

'Will you wait here a moment, Private Davison?' said Edith. 'Something's happened to my daughter.'

Tom gave Edith an anxious glance as he gently laid Nell, unconscious, on the grass. Tenderly, he smoothed her hair off her forehead.

Edith sank to her knees. 'What happened? Was it a croquet ball?'

Tom shook his head. 'We were laughing at Sergeant Dawkin's efforts to hit the croquet ball through the hoop when all at once she opened her eyes very wide. She drew in her breath sharply, as if she had a bad pain, and then she fainted.'

'I'll fetch Matron,' said Nurse Scott and hurried back to the house.

Nell's eyelids flickered and she opened her eyes.

'I'm here, sweetheart!' said Edith.

Nell stared at her mother for a moment as if she didn't know her and then her face crumpled and she held out her arms. 'Oh, Mama, it's Lucien. He's dead!'

'No!' Edith gripped her shoulders. 'Nell, look at me! You're anxious for him — we all are — but he isn't dead. He can't be.' She heard the desperation in her voice as she attempted to block out the black cloud that threatened all their lives.

Nell shook her head. 'Mama, he's my twin. I know.' She spoke with such certainty that it was impossible not to believe her.

Edith let out a cry of anguish and clasped Nell to her breast, burying her face in her daughter's silky hair. It had the same scent as Lucien's.

Chapter 32

June 1917

London

Supper in the hospital canteen, a watery plate of vegetable stew and a dried-up slice of jam roly-poly, did nothing to restore Lily's spirits. She couldn't rid herself of the memory of the sheer terror on a young soldier's face after Dr Whitworth passed him fit to return to the trenches. She'd protested and been severely reprimanded. Again. After the fourteen months she'd worked on the neurological ward, Lily didn't believe any of the neurasthenia cases she'd nursed were cowards. Every one of them lived in a nightmare world of never-ending explosions, machine-gun fire and the fear of being gassed or buried alive in a shell hole. Sometimes she wondered, if Noel had come home from the war, would he have been changed forever, too? Pushing aside her unfinished roly-poly, she left the canteen.

Outside the hospital, the summer evening was still warm as Lily set off for the hostel. The rubbish-strewn Camberwell streets were ripe with the reek of horse dung, rotting vegetables and omnibus fumes, and she longed for the invigorating sea air of Cornwall. She pondered again whether she could bear to renew her contract at the hospital for another six months. It wasn't that she didn't want to help the patients, but she frequently felt she was prevented from doing so by the doctors' inability to see that a little human kindness often made such a difference.

On her arrival at the hostel, there was a letter waiting in the hall for her from her mother. Upstairs, none of the other nurses had yet returned and the dormitory was stuffy and hot. She opened the window and plumped down on the bed. The letter opened with the usual pleasantries and then Clarissa wrote that she was enjoying reading to the patients after lunch every day.

We sit in a circle in the garden and it reminds me of when you and Rose were small and I read a bedtime story to you every night. I feel great affection for these damaged men and it makes me smile when they are frequently lulled to sleep by the sound of my voice, just as if they were children.

Now the Americans have joined forces with the Allies, your stepfather and I were relieved to hear that Will's poor eye sight has exempted him from active service. He will continue in his post at the university for now.

In other news, old Dr Hardwicke has taken on a new junior partner to assist him and Dr Gillespie is proving to be a great success with the patients. He accompanied us down to the cove for a picnic yesterday and the patients paddled in the sea. It did my heart good to see the men enjoying themselves after all they have suffered. One poor soul, Sergeant West, had his face severely damaged by machine-gun fire. One eye socket is badly puckered and his nose was blown off entirely. Dora made him a cotton mask to conceal the worst of his disfigurement but he is still terribly self-conscious.

Today, Edith and I made a plaster cast of his face. We used Plasticine to mould a new nose on the mask and to build up his damaged cheekbone. Once Sergeant West was happy with it — he said his real nose hadn't been so handsome — we made a fresh plaster cast. I shall bring this to London and Augustus will have it electroplated to make a thin copper mask. Edith is confident she will be able to paint it with enamel to match his skin tones and the mask will be fitted to a pair of spectacles to fix it over his face. Sergeant West will never look normal, but he says if he no longer looks grotesque, perhaps his wife will manage to look at him again.

It has been good for Edith to have this project to distract her from her grief for dear Lucien. Nell, however, remains inconsolable over the death of her twin. As with so many of the fallen, there isn't even a grave for them to visit.

Lily's mouth trembled, remembering Lucien's bright smile. None of the Spindrift children could ever have imagined that their close childhood circle might be torn apart by war. It had been three months since the dreadful letter confirming that he'd been killed had arrived at Spindrift. Edith had written her a note that must have been as painful to write as it was to receive. Lily was refused home leave, even though Lucien had been like a younger brother to her, but Pearl was granted a few days' compassionate leave. When she returned from Cornwall, pale and drawn, Lily had managed to meet her for an hour at a Lyons tea shop. Pearl had clung, weeping, to her hand until it was time for them both to return to work.

Sighing, Lily continued reading her mother's letter.

288

My dearest Lily, there is so much sadness in the world at present and knowing that my actions in the past have caused you lasting heartbreak is unbearable to me. Until you are a mother yourself, you will never know the depth of my love for you. I wish more than anything to repair the gulf between us. When I come to London later this week, I will stay with Aunt Minnie. Please, I beg you, allow me to meet you there and explain to you the truth about how Hugh Penrose came to be your father.
I will pray for your understanding.
Ever your loving,
Mother

Despite Lily's lingering bitterness, a sharp pang of homesickness engulfed her. She wondered what there could be to explain about her mother's adultery with Adela's father.

The bedroom door opened and Adela stood in the doorway. When she saw Lily, she turned her face away in an attempt to hide the fact that she'd been crying. She hid behind her cubicle curtain.

A moment later, Lily heard the muffled sound of her sobs. It was painful to hear such unhappiness. Tentatively, she said, 'Will you bite my head off if I ask if you're all right?'

There was silence for a moment and then the curtain was pulled aside to reveal Adela's woebegone face. She wiped tears off her blotched and swollen cheeks. 'Oh, Lily, I've been such a fool! I'm so sorry.'

'What do you mean?'

'It's all my stupid fault. I was so angry with you . . . Noel's death was a terrible shock and I needed someone to blame. And when I saw you with Edwin in the park, it was obvious you hadn't just run into him. Noel was dead but you'd moved on and found someone else to love.'

'It was never my intention to hurt Noel,' said Lily.

'I wanted to pay you back for abandoning him so I began an affair with Edwin. I thought he wanted to marry me.' Adela sniffed back tears. 'But today a woman and her little boy came to the ward and asked where they could find Dr Bennett. I said I'd give him a message. She smiled at me, such a nice smile, and said to tell him his wife had called by to remind him her parents were coming to dinner that night.'

'Edwin is married?' Lily pressed her fingers to her lips. 'I had no idea!'

'Neither had I,' said Adela. She twisted her sodden handkerchief between her hands. 'I was going to tell him tonight that I'm expecting his child.'

Lily stared at her. 'You're pregnant?' she whispered.

Adela nodded, her eyes tragic. 'But now he can't marry me, even if he wanted to.'

'What will you do?'

'I don't know,' said Adela. 'Matron is sure to notice soon and then I'll be sent home in disgrace. It's all right for Gabrielle — she's being cared for like a princess because she's carrying Noel's baby, but Father would never allow me to shame the family by having a child out of wedlock. He'll probably throw me out.'

Lily recalled the way Hugh Penrose had exploded when Noel had told him they were engaged and thought Adela was probably right. 'You must make Edwin support the baby. Perhaps he'll pay for you to go away somewhere and have it?'

'What will I do if he won't?'

'Blackmail him?'

'I couldn't!' Adela gave a great hiccoughing sob.

Lily put her arm around her friend. 'But perhaps I could.' The reason for her not telling Adela the truth about why she hadn't married Noel seemed less important now than keeping her friend safe. 'I have a confession to make,' said Lily. 'I've been keeping an awful secret from you.'

'A secret?'

'I didn't tell you because I knew it would make you unhappy but it's the reason why I couldn't marry Noel. Now I have to tell you because, if you know the truth, I'm sure your father will let you return to Cliff House.'

'You're making me uneasy.'

'Not half as uneasy as I am!' Lily drew a deep breath. 'I loved Noel with every part of me and when your father reacted so violently to our engagement, I thought my world had ended. I ran home to seek comfort from my mother, but I didn't find it. She nearly fainted when I said I wanted to marry Noel. She told me it was impossible because . . .'

'What?'

'Because Noel was my half-brother.'

Frowning, Adela shook her head.

'Your father is my father. He had an affair with my mother.'

Adela cupped her hands over her ears. 'She's lying!'

'I wish she had been.' Lily unfolded Clarissa's letter and read aloud from it. 'Please, I beg you, allow me to . . . explain to you the truth about how Hugh Penrose came to be your father.' She handed the letter to Adela, her finger pointing out the sentence. 'Don't you see? You can use this knowledge to persuade your father to support you. He won't want your mother to discover I'm his illegitimate child, will he? He's a sidesman at the church. The vicar and the congregation would condemn him if they knew about his hypocrisy.'

Adela sat with her head bowed, her hands clenching and unclenching. 'Poor Mother!' Then she looked up at Lily with a wavering smile. 'So all those years we called Pearl, you and me the Three Sisters, you and I really were sisters?'

Lily nodded. 'And sisters stick together when times are difficult. Together, we'll find a way to overcome this obstacle.'

★ ★ ★

Three days later, Lily knocked on the door of her Great Aunt Minnie's mansion flat. The maid led her into the drawing-room and Clarissa jumped up to greet her.

'Aunt Minnie isn't here,' she said, her powdered cheek cool against Lily's as she kissed her. 'She sent you her love but wanted to allow me to talk to you alone.'

'To tell me about your adulterous affair with Hugh Penrose?'

'It was barely an affair. I despised him.'

Lily couldn't imagine how her mother could have borne to be intimate with him. 'Did he force you?'

'No. It was my fault.' Clarissa twisted her hands together. 'Although, I think it's fair to say my father shares some of the blame.'

Lily scoffed. 'Your father made you commit adultery with Hugh Penrose?'

'Of course not!' Her mother folded her arms across

292

her chest defensively. 'I can't bear to know that you despise me,' she said quietly. 'Every day I wake up and the knowledge of your animosity is like a great boulder pressing on my chest.'

'What you did ruined my happiness!'

'And I'm sorrier for that than you'll ever know.'

Lily's curiosity was piqued and she decided to stop being confrontational. 'Go on.'

'My father was a cruel and unforgiving man.' Clarissa stared out of the window for a while, her posture rigid. 'When you were young, sometimes you asked why you never met your grandfather. Well, I made absolutely sure you never did. You see, he had an appetite for little girls, especially pretty ones.'

'I don't understand . . .'

'Then, forgive me, but I must make myself absolutely clear,' said Clarissa. 'My father enjoyed sexual relations with children. For most of my childhood, he used to come into my room at night and abuse me.'

Lily's mouth fell open. 'Your father did that terrible thing?'

'Yes. I can't bear to talk about it.'

'Why didn't you tell your mother?'

'She knew but was too frightened of the beatings he gave her to protest.'

'What kind of monster was he?' whispered Lily.

'I grew up imagining all men were the same as Father, vain and self-important, strutting around and taking whatever they wanted from a woman — or a child. I was determined to have my revenge on any man who behaved like that. Hugh Penrose was such a man.'

'But the shame of an unmarried pregnancy was hardly the way to take revenge on him.'

'My mind had been warped by Father's abuse and I didn't know how a normal family behaved. When I grew up, I set out to teach men like Hugh a lesson. Like the others, when I flattered him, he was so conceited it never occurred to him that I was lying. Once he was mad with love for me, I seduced him and then took delight in tearing him to shreds with cruel words. He was devastated but I was gleeful that I'd had my revenge on another smug and arrogant man. But my triumph soon faded once I realised I was expecting his child.'

'Surely you must have known the risk of that happening?'

'I believed the internal damage my father did to me when I was a little girl meant I couldn't have a child. I'd never have risked seducing Hugh if I'd thought there was any chance of having his baby.' She smiled at Lily, her blue eyes sparkling with tears. 'So I'm forever grateful I believed I was infertile because otherwise I wouldn't have had you. And you've brought me the greatest joy I've ever known.'

Lily rested her head in her hands, attempting to come to terms with what she had just heard. Pity mingled with abhorrence. And yet, what might she have done in her mother's shoes? 'It must have been dreadful to have parents like yours,' she murmured. 'I may not have had a father but I always felt loved. And Julian has been the best stepfather I could have wished for.'

'I'm so fortunate to be his wife. He loves you as his own and has completely restored my faith in men.'

'How did you manage, pregnant and alone?'

Clarissa shrugged. 'I went to pieces but Aunt Minnie and then Edith and Dora picked me up. Truly, I wouldn't be alive today without them. And I black-mailed Hugh into giving us financial support. He was terrified his wife would find out. I believe Jenifry holds the purse strings.'

Lily couldn't prevent herself from laughing.

'What's so funny?'

'History repeating itself.' She nearly laughed again at the look of shock on her mother's face. 'No, I'm not pregnant but a dear friend of mine is and I've already suggested we blackmail her lover, if he won't support the baby. It seems you and I are more alike than I knew.'

'Think very carefully before getting involved, Lily. It's a dangerous game.'

'It frightens me but she needs my help, just as you needed Edith and Dora's.' She hesitated. 'It may become necessary for me to leave the hospital. Would you mind if I return to Spindrift until I find a new situation?'

'Mind?' Clarissa caught hold of her daughter's hands. 'Nothing would make me happier, except to heal the breach between us.'

'I hate our estrangement, too,' said Lily. 'It's painful to imagine what a miserable childhood you must have had. Mine was so happy, despite the chip I had on my shoulder about not having a father.' She shuddered. 'But I'm glad I didn't know he was Hugh Penrose.'

'Tell me about your friend.'

'It's an old story; she discovered her lover is married. Her father is sure to send her packing to save bringing shame on the family.' Lily smiled. 'Strangely, you've given me the means to change his mind.'

'I have?'

'My friend is Adela Penrose. My half-sister.'

295

Clarissa looked at her, aghast.

'We intend to blackmail her father,' said Lily, 'just as you did all those years ago.'

Her mother rose abruptly to her feet and paced across the drawing-room. Then she squared her shoulders and faced Lily again. 'If you're set on this course of action, then you must let me help.'

Lily closed her eyes and a peaceful sensation washed over her, soothing away the misery that had invaded her soul for the last three years. She released a sob and held out her arms to her mother.

'It will be like the old days,' Clarissa murmured into her daughter's hair. 'You and me, against the world.'

Chapter 33

July 1917

London

Adela and Lily handed in their notice to the hospital, saying their families needed them at home. During the following month, Adela avoided Edwin, refusing an invitation to spend her next afternoon off at the shabby hotel where they'd held their trysts. A few days later, Lily saw him flirting with a new VAD on a bench in the park.

On their last day at the hospital before they returned to Cornwall, they finished work at noon. Lily waited by the entrance doors until Adela joined her. 'Did you speak to Edwin?' she asked.

'I lurked in the corridor until he came out of the ward.' Adela's face was pale and pinched. 'He said he was too busy to talk to me so I blurted out that I was expecting his baby.' She swallowed. 'He turned red and then white. He gripped me by the wrist and dragged me outside to the park.' She rubbed at her wrist. 'I'll have horrible bruises.'

'And?'

'He called me a stupid little girl and said I had no proof he was the father. I said I'd spoken to his wife. He gripped my throat then and forced me back against a tree trunk.' She drew a shuddering breath. 'I was so scared. I thought he was going to strangle me. I managed to say I'd only seen her in the ward and she

297

didn't know about me or the baby. He let me go but told me to leave the hospital and never to go near him or his family again or I'd be sorry for it.'

'What an absolute rotter!' All at once, Lily had an inkling of the rage her mother had experienced over men who took advantage of women. 'He's had his chance. Since he refuses to do the decent thing,' she said, 'we'll put the second part of the plan into action.'

'I'll go to the hostel and finish packing our trunks,' said Adela. She hugged Lily. 'Be careful, won't you?'

Adela hurried away and Lily walked unnoticed into the acute surgical ward. Still in uniform, she hoped no one would question her presence. She concealed herself in the linen cupboard, leaving the door slightly ajar. Covertly, she waited until Edwin went into his consulting room opposite. She slipped in after him, closed the door and sat down on the other side of his desk.

'What are you doing here?' he said.

She smiled. 'I haven't seen you in a while.'

He closed the file in front of him. 'I've been busy.'

'You certainly have! It must be very worrying for you, discovering Adela is expecting your child.'

He grew still. 'She's lying, of course. The little tart has been seeing someone else behind my back.'

'We both know that's a lie,' said Lily. 'A nurse has so little spare time it would be impossible to conduct two liaisons at once. The thing is, she'll have to go home. Her father, a man with an extremely bad temper, will demand to know who got her into trouble. He'll be on the first train up here when he does and, I can promise you, he won't be shy of making a hideously disruptive, possibly violent, scene when he seeks you out on the ward.'

298

'Are you threatening me?'

'Not at all, simply warning you about Mr Penrose's vile temper.' She noticed a little tic tugging at the corner of Edwin's eye. 'Of course, he might be placated if you'd already decided to do the decent thing. Adela asked me to give you this.' She withdrew an envelope from under her apron and pushed it across the desk.

Edwin ignored it.

'It's an agreement, drawn up by her solicitor,' said Lily. 'You're to pay a sum of money, sufficient for her keep and that of your child, into Adela's bank account monthly. You're required to take the agreement to the offices of Cole, Ashbrook and Son, by the end of the week. The address is on the agreement, and Mr Cole and Mr Ashbrook will arrange for your signature to be witnessed when they see you.'

'This is utterly preposterous!' Edwin pushed the agreement away with an expression of disgust on his face.

'There is one other thing,' said Lily, standing up. 'Letters have been passed into the safekeeping of an individual. Should this person be informed that you haven't signed the agreement or that the funds haven't arrived in Adela's account by the first day of every month, or if anything unpleasant happens to her, one letter will be handed to your wife and another sent to the hospital board of governors, to inform them of your actions. Legal process will then be set in motion to recover the debt. I hope that's perfectly clear?'

'Get out of my office!' Edwin Bennett scraped back his chair and clenched his fists.

Determined not to show fear, Lily lifted her chin and walked away from him and out of the hospital.

It was a humid September evening and Pearl's feet hurt after a long stint at Victoria Station. She'd been working every shift she could so that sheer exhaustion stopped her imagining Lucien being blown up by a shell or thinking about the risks Jasper and Maxwell took every day.

'This lot is for St Thomas's,' shouted a medical orderly over the hissing of the train and the groans of the wounded soldiers. The injured were laid side by side on the station platform, as closely packed as if they were sardines. 'Stretcher cases at the front, walking wounded in the row behind. The dead can wait so I've put 'em over there.'

Pearl looked at the sea of khaki-clad men. Every one of them would have family and friends who worried about them. She knew from bitter experience how the death or injury of a loved one devastated a whole family. She sighed. It was going to be a late night. Every night was a late night at present, due to the high number of casualties arriving daily from Ypres. She was on duty with Millicent again and they moved efficiently into the routine of assisting the orderlies to carry the wounded to the waiting ambulance.

On their fourth trip to St Thomas's Hospital, Pearl and Millicent were unloading a stretcher from the ambulance when Pearl caught sight of Daphne.

She waved and hurried to help her friend gently roll an injured man onto a trolley. He yelped in pain and she patted his shoulder. 'You're safe now,' she murmured.

'You're going to have a full house tonight,' said Millicent, casting her eye over several other ambulances also offloading their wounded.

'We're running out of beds,' said Daphne, her brow creasing. 'The operating theatre has been busy since dawn.'

Later, back at Victoria Station on the seventh or eighth trip, Pearl couldn't remember which, she and Millicent were lifting a patient onto a stretcher when he muttered something she couldn't hear.

'It's all right,' she said, soothingly. 'You'll be at the hospital soon.' The poor chap's jacket was only half-buttoned and exposed a large, blood-soaked dressing over his chest. He must have come straight from the battlefield because his uniform was crusted with mud. His head was wrapped in a bandage and what was visible of his face was splattered with blood. She tried not to think about the injuries Lucien must have sustained.

Two orderlies heaved the stretcher up off the platform.

The injured officer reached out with his good arm towards her. 'Pearl!' he said, in a hoarse whisper. And then he opened his eyes.

She caught her breath at the flash of blue. 'Maxwell?'

He nodded and closed them again, exhausted.

'It is you!' Her heart thumped in sudden, sickening fear for him. 'It's only a short ride to the hospital.' Pearl stroked his hand as she walked beside him towards the ambulance. 'I saw Daphne there earlier,' she said, keeping her voice calm. 'I'll go and find her when we arrive.'

'Hey, what's he done to deserve a girl like you holding his hand?' said a soldier being stretchered along beside them.

'You can choose from all the pretty nurses once we reach the hospital,' said Pearl.

Maxwell's mouth curved in a brief smile but his eyes remained closed.

Pearl rested her hand on his forehead. It was terribly hot and she was afraid his wounds must be infected. She watched as the two men were carefully stowed in the ambulance alongside another stretcher case before she closed the rear doors.

Millicent guided one of the walking wounded, a boy with a missing arm, to the ambulance and sat him in the middle of the front seat. 'There's room for a little one in the front,' she joked.

Pearl turned the starter handle. As soon as the engine fired up, she jumped into the passenger seat beside him.

'This is Billy,' said Millicent. 'Now he's got a Blighty, he'll be home to see his family before long.'

The boy gave a wan smile but a tear ran down his cheek.

'I know that officer in the back of the ambulance,' Pearl said.

Mllicent gave her a searching look. 'Your sweetheart?'

Pearl nodded. 'Daphne's brother.' The short drive to St Thomas's seemed interminable as she fretted about the extent of Maxwell's injuries. At last they arrived.

Nurses and male orderlies came to receive the patients, loading them onto trolleys and wheelchairs.

'Can you manage the next load without me, Millicent?' asked Pearl. 'I need to tell Daphne her brother's here.'

Millicent gave her a cheerful wave and drove off.

302

Inside the hospital, Pearl accompanied Maxwell to the crowded receiving area, where nurses were sorting the wounded into three groups, according to the urgency of their medical need. Maxwell was unconscious so she asked several nurses if they'd seen Nurse Fforbes. One nodded her head at a curtained cubicle and Pearl was about to peep inside when her friend backed out, carrying an armful of filthy khaki uniform.

Pearl caught hold of her arm. 'Maxwell's here. He's amongst the incoming wounded.'

Daphne gasped. 'But I had a letter from him last week.'

'Me, too. He has a fever and wounds to his abdomen and head.'

They hurried to the receiving area together and found Maxwell on a trolley.

Daphne spoke to him and he muttered something but didn't open his eyes. 'He's burning hot!' She caught hold of another VAD and had a brief conversation with her before turning back to Pearl. 'I have to return to my duties but my friend will bring me news as soon as we know which ward he'll be on.'

'I must get back to work, too,' said Pearl, 'but I'll come tomorrow.'

'I'll break the news to Mother and Father.' Daphne's voice shook. 'Heaven knows how I'll concentrate on my work now.'

'You will do your best, as always,' said Pearl. 'There are others who need you, too.'

After Daphne had hurried away, Pearl dampened her handkerchief with cold water in the sluice and gently wiped the blood from Maxwell's face and mouth. He sighed but didn't open his eyes. She kissed his forehead. 'I'll come back as soon as I can,' she murmured. It was painful to walk away, leaving him alone on the trolley, but she could delay no longer.

The ambulance was waiting for her outside the hospital.

'Hurry up!' said Millicent. 'We haven't finished yet.'

Pearl climbed into the passenger seat. All she could think about as they drove back to Victoria was Maxwell's flushed face under the bloodstained bandage.

Chapter 34

October 1917

Cornwall

'Must you go, Nell?' asked Edith. 'Why join the Women's Land Army when you can help out at Polcarrow?'

'They have Tom.'

'Pearl, Jasper and Roland are away, and Lucien . . .' Edith blinked furiously. Once she started to weep for the death of her son it was hard for her to stop. 'I don't know how I shall bear it if you go away, too.'

'I have to go, Mama.' Nell looked up at her with appeal in her green eyes, the very same green as Lucien's eyes had been. 'Don't you see? Everywhere I go, everything I see, everything I do here at Spindrift, brings back memories of seeing and doing those things with Lucien. Now he's gone, it feels as if half of me has been torn away.'

Edith gathered her youngest daughter into her arms and kissed her hair. 'What about Tom? I'd hoped —'

'That we'd marry? I wanted that, too.'

'What changed your mind?'

'How can I marry and be happy when Lucien is lying all alone in the cold earth? I can't even visit his grave.'

'He'd want you to be happy!'

'But I can't be; not without him.' Nell's tone was adamant. 'It's too painful. The place at Tregavethan Farm means I'll be in new surroundings to distract

305

me from my unhappy thoughts. The Women's Land Army will find me a permanent situation after my month's training. Please, Mama, let me do this.'

'You're old enough to know your own mind,' said Edith. 'Be kind to Tom, though, won't you? He loves you.'

'I don't want to hurt him,' said Nell, 'but if I married him while I'm grieving for Lucien, I couldn't be the wife he deserves.'

Edith sighed. 'Then go to Tregavethan Farm with my blessing but know how much I shall miss you.'

Nell kissed her mother's cheek and clung to her for a moment before hurrying away.

Heavy-hearted, Edith went to find Pascal and tell him the news. She didn't know how she'd have managed without his support in the dark weeks since Lucien's death. She needed him again now.

★ ★ ★

A few days later, the postwoman delivered a letter from Pearl. Edith was so eager to open it that she remained in the hall and read it standing up.

Dear Mama,

I am relieved to tell you that after a month in St Thomas's, Maxwell is now slowly recovering. Most of the shrapnel has been removed from his wounds — the rest he will have to live with — and the infection has reduced. He is still very weak as is to be expected after blood poisoning. I spent as much time visiting him as I could and his mother came every day. We spent a great deal of time chatting while he slept. I was embarrassed when I broke

306

down, telling her about Lucien and how worried it has made me for Jasper, but she was very kind to me.

Maxwell's bed in the hospital is urgently needed but, since he is not sufficiently well to return to active service, he must complete his recovery in a convalescent hospital. He said that, all the time he was deathly ill, he kept remembering what a special place Spindrift is and how much he longed for the Cornish air. His father pulled some strings in high places so you will soon receive notification that Maxwell's convalescence will take place with you. It eases my anxiety to know he will receive the best of care.

All is well with me, though the hours I work grow longer and longer due to the great numbers of wounded arriving daily. I do my best to maintain a professional demeanour but sometimes it is terribly distressing to see these poor men so shattered in mind and body. I dare not think how some of them will be able to return to any kind of normal life and cannot help wondering if the fallen are the lucky ones, since they are now at peace.

I have ten days' leave due and intend to come home and see you and Maxwell at the end of next week. I miss you all so much.

Grandfather sends his love, as do I,
Pearl

Edith felt her spirits lift a little. To have Pearl at home for a few days would be comforting and her leave would allow her to spend a couple of days with Nell before she left for Land Army training. Lily was now reconciled with Clarissa and had decided not to apply

307

for another nursing situation yet, so the Spindrift girls would have some time together. How heartening it would be to hear the sound of young people's chatter again!

She slipped the letter in her pocket and went to the office to see what needed to be done.

Nurse Braithwaite stood before Matron's desk, hands clasped behind her back.

Matron glanced at Edith as she entered the room then said, 'Nurse Braithwaite, you may go now. Remember that your contract doesn't end until next month and I expect you to continue with your duties in a diligent fashion until then.'

'Yes, Matron.' Nurse Braithwaite scurried out of the office.

'Do I gather she is leaving us?' asked Edith.

Matron sighed. 'I wondered if she'd been spending a little too much time with Private Reed and it seems I was right. They're engaged to be married.'

'He's a nice chap,' said Edith, 'though the gas attack will affect his lungs for the rest of his life.'

'Luckily, he'll have his very own nurse by his side to look after him.' Matron tapped her pen on the desk. 'I'll have to contact head office and request a new VAD.'

Edith hesitated. 'Perhaps it's against the rules,' she said, 'but I wonder if Lily might replace Nurse Braithwaite? She'll be seeking a new position soon and she's had two years' experience at the First London Military Hospital in Camberwell.'

'That would certainly be convenient,' said Matron. 'She wouldn't need training from scratch and I've noticed that, entirely of her own volition, she's been writing letters and reading to the patients.' She nodded decisively. 'I'll have a word with her.'

Edith worked through a pile of paperwork for an hour or so, writing out orders for new supplies as well as a number of fundraising letters. Once she'd finished, she took her sketchpad and pencil box from the desk drawer and went into the garden.

It was a golden October day and several patients were resting on the terrace in deckchairs. Some dozed, their faces turned up to the sunshine, while others read or chatted.

'May I make some sketches of you all?' she asked.

The men laughed and joked, giving her instructions to draw only their best side.

She made several rapid sketches of the scene, to catch the tonal values, and scribbled notes in the margin about the colours. The patients' hospital blues stood out against the backdrop of Virginia creeper that clad the house in a glorious display of scarlet and burgundy.

Nurse Scott brought out a tray of hot Bovril drinks and Edith made a lightning sketch of her as she distributed them to the men. She drew some details of the patients' faces and, when she'd finished, the men clamoured to see her drawings. They enjoyed examining the portraits and exclaimed on the excellent likenesses.

'I hope to use the sketches for an oil painting in due course,' said Edith.

'I'm no oil painting,' said Private Fields gloomily. 'Not with this great bandage round my head and my arm in a sling.'

'I disagree,' said Edith. 'I see a picture of a brave man who has been wounded fighting for his country.'

'We certainly all did that,' said Private Nye.

'One day, after the war ends, the Spindrift Gallery will open again and Mr Joubert and I will hold an exhibition of our wartime work, including the painting I'll make using these sketches,' said Edith.

Private Nye nudged Private Fields. 'There you are then, Arthur. It was worth losing half an ear and a couple of fingers to have your picture hanging in an exhibition, wasn't it?'

★ ★ ★

A car driven by a male VAD arrived one afternoon. Edith, followed by the two dogs, went out to greet Maxwell Fforbes. She knew he'd suffered from blood poisoning but was distressed to see how changed he was from the carefree young man who'd come to stay at Spindrift nearly three years before. His formerly broad frame was gaunt, his curly black hair had been replaced by half an inch of stubble and there was a purple scar across the crown of his skull. He walked with a stoop, one hand held to his abdomen as if his wounds still needed holding together. It was no wonder Pearl had been so worried about him.

He came forward to shake Edith's hand and she was relieved to see that the dimple in his chin and his dazzling smile remained the same as ever. 'Welcome back to Spindrift House, Maxwell,' she said, 'though I wish the circumstances were happier.'

'I can't tell you how pleased I am to be here.' Wagging their tails, the dogs came nosing forward to sniff his hands. 'Hello, Blue! Hello, Star! Do you remember me?'

'Come inside and we'll get you settled. Are you very tired after the journey?'

'I slept most of the way, dreaming of walking along the beach down in the cove with the music of the sea in my ears.'

Edith smiled. 'Very soon you'll be able to make that dream come true.'

Over the following days, Maxwell slept a great deal, often preferring to sit outside in the autumn sunshine wrapped in blankets. She was pleased that, despite his still being so weak, colour was creeping back into his cheeks and he was enjoying the wholesome Spindrift fare.

'Soup made from our home-grown vegetables will have you back on your feet in no time,' said Dora, smiling as he scraped the last spoonful from his bowl.

Dr Gillespie came on his weekly visit to the hospital to see how the patients were convalescing and, as usual, took the time to chat to them. Edith watched approvingly as he and Maxwell laughed together over some private joke.

At the end of the week, Pearl arrived home.

Edith was discussing menus with Mrs Rowe in the kitchen. She ran to kiss her daughter and then held her at arm's length. 'You're shockingly pale and thin, sweetheart.'

'I'm tired,' she said, 'but I've come to the best place to build up my strength, haven't I?'

Pascal came into the kitchen. 'I thought I heard your voice, Pearl.' His face was wreathed in smiles as he embraced her.

Edith linked her arm through Pearl's and, together with Pascal, they went into the sitting-room and caught up on the news.

'Nell's working her last day at Polcarrow Farm today,' said Edith.

'Is she any better?' asked Pearl.

'She still grieves, as we all do.' Edith reached for Pascal's hand. 'I don't know how I'd have managed without Pascal at my side. It saddens me that when Tom tries to comfort Nell, she pushes him away.'

'Where is everyone?' asked Pearl.

'Dora and Ursula are in the garden,' said Pascal.

'Lily's helping Julian frame photographic portraits for the patients to send to their loved ones,' said Edith, 'and Clarissa is writing letters with the men.'

'Has Maxwell settled in?' asked Pearl.

'He seems to be feeling a little better already.' Edith smiled at her. 'Go and find him on the terrace. He likes to sit where he can hear the sea.'

Chapter 35

October 1917

Cornwall

In Julian's photographic workshop, Lily held the cardboard window mount steady while her stepfather carefully positioned the steel rule.

Picking up the scalpel, he sliced away the surplus card. 'That should do it.' He lifted up the frame and placed it over Sergeant West's portrait.

'Poor man,' said Lily. 'It's sad to think his future happiness relies on his wife coming to terms with his altered appearance.'

'I don't think he'd have had a chance of that without the mask your mother and Edith made for him,' said Julian. 'It conceals the worst of his disfigurement but it's his renewed self-confidence that's pulled him back from the brink.'

'It's good to see him talking to the other patients now.' Lily smiled. 'And Blanche has become his little companion. I suppose she feels she knows what he's going through.' She helped Julian to tidy up the scraps of cardboard. 'If you don't need me anymore, I'll see if Pearl has arrived.'

She found her friend sitting on the terrace beside Maxwell, holding his hand. Lily had known they wrote to each other but hadn't appreciated they were that close.

Pearl's face lit up when she saw her.

313

'How lovely to have you home!' said Lily. 'But you look so tired.'

'Everyone needs a rest from this beastly war.'

'Spindrift House will work its magic on us all,' said Maxwell. He gave a half smile. 'I don't want to recover too soon, though, because then I'll be sent back.'

Pearl tightened her grip on his hand.

'I'm going to stay at Spindrift,' said Lily. 'I've been offered the opportunity to step into Nurse Braithwaite's shoes when she leaves.'

'Clarissa will be so happy,' said Pearl.

'So will I. Working in the neurological ward was a painful experience. I saw so many men suffering from neurasthenia, or shellshock as they're calling it now, but the treatments seemed unnecessarily harsh to me. Here, those suffering with their nerves are treated gently. I'm convinced that's the best way to help these poor souls.'

'I saw a lot of it in the trenches,' said Maxwell. 'The conditions there are unbearable; the constant bombardment . . . the stinking mud . . . seeing your companions blown to smithereens beside you. On and on it goes without ceasing.' His voice faltered. 'It's hardly cowardly to break in these circumstances. The generals have no idea what it's like, safely tucked away far behind the Frontline as they are.' He rested his head back and closed his eyes. 'If you don't mind, I'll doze for a little while.'

Pearl touched his shoulder and then she and Lily tiptoed away.

They went to sit in the gazebo, looking out at the tranquil view of the sea under a cloudless sky.

'You've surprised me,' said Pearl. 'I thought, after your quarrel with Clarissa, that you might never

314

return to Spindrift.'

'Something changed my mind,' said Lily. She picked a flake of green paint off the gazebo bench, recalling her mother's shocking confession. 'I'm not at liberty to explain but Mother had her reasons for having an affair with Noel's father. I can't be angry with her anymore.'

Pearl raised her eyebrows.

'I'm not betraying Mother's confidences.'

'Well, I'm happy for you that you've made up your differences,' said Pearl.

'That's only the first part of the story of why I'm back at Spindrift.'

'Go on.'

'Noel wrote to Adela on the day before he was killed. He said marrying Gabrielle was a terrible mistake and he didn't care if he lived or died.' Lily pressed her knuckles to her mouth and choked back a sob. 'The following day, he ran out into No Man's Land and was gunned down.'

'Oh, Lily!'

'For my own sanity, after he married Gabrielle, I tried hard to forget him.' She shrugged. 'When he died, Adela found out I'd become romantically involved with Edwin, a doctor at the hospital. In shock and grief, she blamed me for Noel's death because she assumed I'd jilted him and he'd married Gabrielle on the rebound.'

'But it wasn't your fault!'

'Adela was furious that while Noel was so miserable, I'd been happy with someone else. She sent me to Coventry for weeks and I was too upset to meet Edwin. And then I saw Adela kissing him.'

'She stole him from you? What a filthy trick!'

'But she's paid dearly for taking her revenge on me. You see, she discovered she was expecting Edwin's child. Then she found out he's married.'

Pearl's expression was horrified.

'I didn't want her to ruin her life and . . . well, we are half-sisters. So, when Mother came to London, I told her. After all, she'd once been pregnant and unmarried, too. She was wonderful. She arranged to have a legal agreement drawn up to make Edwin support Adela and the baby.'

'And he agreed to that?'

'Once I'd threatened to let his wife know if he didn't stump up, he did,' said Lily. 'Adela was too frightened to tell her father of her condition so Mother and I hatched a plan. Adela and I gave notice to the hospital and returned home to Cornwall. Adela had written to Hugh, asking him to meet her at the Golden Lion, and when he arrived, Mother and I were with her. Mother told him Adela was expecting and said that if he didn't allow her to live at Cliff House, Jenifry would be told the truth about his infidelity and that I'm his daughter.' Lily shuddered. She didn't think she'd ever come to terms with knowing Hugh Penrose was her father.

'So did Hugh allow Adela to return home?' asked Pearl.

'Once Mother showed him the way to save face. She suggested he put about the story that Adela had married a soldier who subsequently died.'

Pearl smiled wryly. 'Like Gabrielle.'

'Exactly. She has given birth to Noel's son, by the way.'

Impulsively, Pearl hugged her. 'That must be hard for you.'

Lily swallowed, not wanting to think about it. 'Adela's baby is due next month and I've arranged for us to meet in the cove tomorrow afternoon. It's been far too long since the three of were last there together.'

★ ★ ★

After supper that evening, Pearl and Maxwell joined some of the other patients in the dining-room for a sing-song. Dora bashed out a wide repertoire of music hall songs on the elderly and slightly out-of-tune piano in the drawing-room. Entirely self-taught, she missed some notes but none of the patients seemed to care as they sang along with gusto to 'Two Lovely Black Eyes' and 'Any Old Iron'.

Ursula had the men in gales of laughter when she donned a khaki jacket and strutted up and down, singing 'The Army of Today's All Right' in a passable imitation of Vesta Tilley. Then Private Reed got to his feet and serenaded a pink-faced and simpering Nurse Braithwaite with 'I Love a Lassie' until his damaged lungs became too wheezy and the other men had to take over.

Pearl glanced at Maxwell as they sang. He looked exhausted and she touched his arm. 'Somewhere quieter?' she asked.

He nodded and they slipped out of the dining-room during a resounding chorus of 'Nellie Dean'. In the drawing-room, patients played dominoes or cards, or chatted quietly together. In one corner, two patients suffering from shell shock sat in armchairs while Clarissa read to them from The Jungle Book.

Pearl and Maxwell sat down side by side on a sofa. 'What wonderful care the patients receive at Spindrift,' he said. 'Matron's a bit of a martinet but even she only wants to see us all well again.'

'As do I,' said Pearl, 'though I wish you didn't have to return to your regiment.' Her heart fluttered in panic at the very thought of it. 'I can't know what it's like for you but I went to the picture house and saw The Battle of the Somme.' She shivered at the memory. 'It was a horrible experience but I'm glad I went. I saw men falling into barbed wire and pictures of the battlefield littered with dead and dying soldiers, their faces contorted in agony. It was like living through a tragedy. When it was over, the audience left in silence, broken only by the sound of weeping.'

'It's the not knowing how long it will be before the war ends that's so awful.' He ran his thumb contemplatively over his stubbly skull, feeling for the scar. 'It would be unfair of me to make any plans but I'll keep on writing to you if I may.' He touched the back of her wrist with his forefinger. 'You must know you've captured my heart?'

She gripped his hand, her heart hammering. 'I know you have captured mine,' she murmured.

He looked at her steadily. 'I may never come back from the battlefront or I might be too damaged to offer you anything. You do see why I can't make any promises, don't you?'

She gazed into the blue depths of his eyes. 'I'm not sure I do. Isn't the most important thing to have hope? To be able to dream of a glorious day in the future when your hopes will come true? Even if that day never arrives, you will at least have been comforted while everything around you is in chaos.'

'You gave me courage in the hospital when I thought I was going to die and your letters brought me joy while the shelling raged around me. I cannot imagine anything I want more than to spend the rest of my life with you. But I cannot promise you anything until the war is over.'

'Then I will make a promise to you,' said Pearl. 'I will be here, waiting for you.'

He lifted her hand and pressed it fervently to his lips.

They sat quietly, simply happy to be together, until Nurse Scott did her rounds with the Horlicks before the patients' bedtime.

When Pearl went upstairs, Nell was already in bed with the covers pulled around her ears and the two dogs curled up on the mat beside her. Pearl undressed quietly and blew out the candle. She lay on her back with her hands behind her head, thinking about Maxwell. It hurt her to see him so diminished after his brush with death. She wished she could hold him in her arms and keep him safe forever. She tossed and turned, tormented by images of him running through a barrage of artillery fire until, at last, she fell into a fitful sleep.

Later, she awoke to the sound of weeping. 'Nell?' There was no reply, except for a muffled sob. 'What is it?'

Silence.

Pearl got out of bed and slipped underneath the eiderdown beside her sister.

'Oh, Pearl,' wept Nell, 'I miss Lucien so.' She buried her face in the knitted rabbit that had been her twin's when he was a toddler.

Tears started into Pearl's eyes and she drew her sister into her arms. 'I know,' she murmured. 'Nothing's the same without him.'

'I don't know how to bear the pain!' Nell gripped convulsively at Pearl, her whole body shuddering with sobs.

'Perhaps the best way is to keep Lucien alive in our memory?' said Pearl. 'Do you remember how you used to make villages out of your bricks when you were small? And I've never forgotten the time he brought in a family of baby mice to live in the little houses.'

'And one escaped and Mrs Rowe screamed and jumped on the kitchen table.'

'How we laughed! And then there was the time Papa came to live with us and brought us the puppies.'

'There was a terrible thunderstorm that night,' said Nell, 'and Lucien crept out to sleep in the pigsty with Blue and Star because he thought they'd be frightened.'

'But not half as frightened as Mama was when she couldn't find him in the middle of the night. She and Pascal were drenched when they went out into the storm to look for him, but Lucien and the puppies were fast asleep in a huddle together on the floor of the pigsty.'

'We always used to go into Mama's bed when we were frightened by thunder,' murmured Nell. 'She used to sing us to sleep with 'A Frog He Would A-wooing Go'.'

Softly, Pearl began to sing the song that brought back precious memories of warmth and love and security in their mother's arms.

After a moment Nell joined her in the chorus.

At the end of the sixth verse, Pearl couldn't suppress a yawn.

''Hey-ho! says Anthony Rowley',' crooned Nell, her voice drowsy. 'G'night, Pearl.'

320

'Good night, Nell.' Pearl listened to her sister's deepening breaths and felt the knot of pain constricting her own heart begin to loosen a little. At least Lucien had died knowing he was loved and that none of his family would ever forget him.

★ ★ ★

The following afternoon, Pearl found Lily in the hall, chatting to the doctor.

'Dr Gillespie has suggested we might take a few of the patients in his car for an outing to the village,' said Lily.

'What an excellent idea,' said Pearl, noting the way the doctor's hazel eyes stayed fixed on Lily's face.

'They'd benefit by having a change of scene,' he said. 'On Thursday afternoon perhaps, Nurse Stanton?'

'The patients and I will look forward to it, Dr Gillespie.' Lily smiled and opened the front door for him.

He nodded and they watched him walk briskly down the front path.

'Very personable, isn't he?' said Pearl. 'I'd say he's rather taken with you.'

'Oh! I'm sure he isn't.' Lily's face became suffused with pink. 'Besides, I'm not sure I could ever trust another apparently personable doctor.'

'Perhaps you should give him a chance?'

'It's time we went to meet Adela,' Lily said dismissively.

They ambled down to the cove and found their friend waiting for them by the rocks. Pearl's eyes widened at the sight of her.

'Don't say it!' Adela pleaded. 'I look like a whale,

321

don't I?'

'You look blooming,' said Pearl, kissing her cheek. 'Lily told me what happened. How is it for you at Cliff House?'

Adela grimaced. 'It could be worse. Mother suspects my so-called marriage is a lie but, since Father's supporting it, she's decided it's better to accept it and avoid bringing shame on the family. She wanted me to join her in one of her séances to see if my 'husband' had a message for me. I refused, of course.' She grinned. 'Imagine what fun I could have had exposing that fraud Mrs Lee if her spirit guide did bring me a message.'

They strolled along the strand, stepping over beached mounds of bladderwrack and driftwood.

'Lily mentioned Gabrielle's had a son,' said Pearl.

'Jérôme Noel,' said Adela. 'According to Mother, he's the image of Noel at that age. Mother hates the French name Gabrielle chose and always calls him Jeremy.' She kicked at a tangle of seaweed. 'Father's happy that Gabrielle's provided the requisite heir for his architectural practice. I wonder if Mother will be as besotted by my child when it arrives next month?' she said, her tone bitter.

'Will your father allow you to keep it?'

'I have Father exactly where I want him now that I know his secret so, yes, I will keep the baby.' Adela hugged her arms fiercely around her burgeoning abdomen. 'Mother and Father always doted on my brothers but I never quite fitted in. My child and I will make our own family, just the two of us.' She shrugged. 'Anyway, so many men have died in the fighting that there'll be hardly any spare ones left at the end of the war. They'll have their pick of the prettiest girls when they return. I doubt I'll ever find a husband and this might be my only chance to have a baby.'

'What a bleak picture you paint,' said Lily.

'A realistic one, I believe.'

Later, after Pearl had returned to Spindrift, she couldn't help thinking about what Adela had said. Unlike many girls, Pearl had never been desperate to find herself a husband, but now, at the age of twenty-four, she'd discovered she wanted to share her life with a man. So long as that man was Maxwell.

Chapter 36

Cornwall

The dulcet tones of the clock ticking on the drawing-room mantelpiece were echoed by the soft snores emanating from under the newspaper resting over Corporal Jones's face. Two patients played a silent game of chess at a small table by the window, while others read or worked on a crossword. Private Tompkins, his knees draped with a tartan rug, stared into space, his entire body trembling like an aspen leaf. A Christmas tree, paperchains and Chinese lanterns still decorated the room after the festivities and a wreath of holly and ivy was draped over the mantel.

Edith glanced up from her easel and added more delicate brushstrokes to the canvas. Grey winter light illuminated the room and she was pleased with the shadowy, contemplative tone of her painting.

Suddenly, the door banged open.

Startled, Edith dropped her brush.

Private Tompkins dived behind his armchair and curled into a ball as Roland staggered in carrying the coal bucket.

'Roland!' Edith caught hold of his sleeve and murmured, 'You mustn't forget our patients need peace and quiet. Some are especially sensitive to noise.'

'Sorry, Ma.' He had a smear of coal dust on his forehead as black as his hair. Halfway to becoming a

324

man, his shoulders had already begun to broaden. 'I thought you might need more coal.' Now fourteen, he'd suddenly shot up and his shirtsleeves exposed two inches of bony wrist.

'Very thoughtful of you but, another time, please don't crash into the room.' She went to soothe Private Tompkins, encouraged him back to his chair and draped the rug over his head and shoulders. Holding his hand, she perched on the arm of the chair until the convulsive jerking of his limbs abated.

Roland added coal to the fire and stirred the embers into a brisk blaze, taking exaggerated care not to make any disturbance.

The clock on the mantelpiece struck half-past three and Lily wheeled in the tea trolley. Roland helped her to hand around cups of tea and slices of bread and jam.

Once Private Tompkins had settled, Edith cleaned her brushes and put away her paints. The light was fading and she could do no more that day.

She left the drawing-room and went to Pascal's studio. He too had finished painting and was bent over the worktable, covering his palette to prevent the paint drying out. Wrapping her arms around his back, she nuzzled his neck.

He turned and kissed her. 'Did you have time to work today?' he asked.

'I did and it's going well. The patients are flattered to be included in my painting. They're such good models because they're happy to sit still for long periods of time, but it's a shame the days are so short and the light doesn't last.'

'We have the summer to look forward to.' He sighed. 'The fourth summer of war.'

Edith went to look at the canvas on his easel. 'Oh, it's Roland!' The painting depicted his back view as he stood on the cliff top, one hand shading his eyes as he stared out at the sun setting over the sea.

Pascal stood beside her. 'Even though we aren't allowed to work en plein air, I have completed so many seascapes I could create new ones in my sleep. When Roland told me he'd been helping the Scouts patrol the coast for U-boats, I thought it would make a good composition.'

'I like the way his figure is silhouetted against the silver of the sea,' said Edith. 'There's an almost dream-like quality to the canvas. I think this one should be submitted to the Royal Academy. What will you call it?'

Pascal shrugged. 'The Calm Before the Storm, perhaps.'

'Between us, we've accumulated a respectable body of work illustrating the war from the perspective of those who remained behind,' she said, lighting the lamp and drawing the curtains. 'Julian has some wonderful photographs too. When the fighting is over, we'll have plenty of work to exhibit in the gallery. I think we should call our exhibition Unsung Heroes.'

'A fitting name,' said Pascal. 'I long for us to travel abroad when the war is over. We have planned it for so long.'

'I dream of a summer in Provence,' said Edith. 'And can you imagine how wonderful it will be to visit Florence and Venice together?'

He cupped her face in his hands. 'Even that will not be as wonderful as holding you in my arms every night, all night long.'

Edith laughed and tipped up her face to be kissed.

326

'On a less romantic note, I must go and see what I can do about Roland's shirtsleeves. He's returning to school next week and he's already grown out of the shirts I bought him last September.'

★ ★ ★

It was during the second sitting for dinner that Edith saw Dora freeze in the act of passing a dish of cabbage to the patient beside her. Her gaze was fixed on a point beyond Edith's shoulder.

She turned to see what had caught Dora's attention. There was a split second when Edith forgot to breathe and then an icy coldness filled her core. She glanced at the other end of the table, where Pascal was laughing at something Roland had said. Slowly, Edith pushed back her chair and moved on leaden legs towards the door.

'Benedict,' she said.

'You have a full house tonight.'

'Come into the hall.' She didn't want a scene in front of Roland and the patients. 'What do you want?' Apprehension prickled down her back, like a column of marching ants.

He raised his eyebrows. 'That's not very welcoming.'

'You aren't welcome here, especially after you were so violent towards Pascal the last time we saw you.'

'I'm staying anyway.' He indicated the suitcase by his feet.

Her stomach lurched. How could this be happening again, after all these years?

'This is my house, remember?' There was a belligerent glint in his eye and he took a step towards her.

She stood her ground, arms folded across her chest. 'Not all of it. And, as you've probably noticed, Spindrift is a convalescent hospital now.'

'Gabrielle wrote and told me. Never mind, I only need one room.'

'There are none to spare.'

'You will find me a room.' His tone was flinty. 'Or shall I have the interlopers thrown out? You should have requested my permission.'

He was right, of course. Edith heard movement behind her and Pascal and Julian came to stand on either side of her. She glanced at Pascal and gave him the minutest shake of her head. If he challenged Benedict, it might lead to blows again.

'I hope you haven't come to cause trouble, Benedict?' said Julian.

'He wants to stay at Spindrift,' said Edith.

Pascal stiffened. 'And what do you wish, Edith?'

'I wish he'd go away. Unfortunately, as co-owner of the house, he has a right to stay. The question is, where to put him where he'll be the least inconvenience?'

Benedict glared at her. 'Don't talk about me as if I'm a piece of old baggage!'

'There's the vacant studio,' said Julian, ignoring him.

'Absolutely not!' said Benedict. 'It will be freezing cold and there's no indoor water closet. You forget, I own the greater part of the house. Edith, you can take the studio and I'll have your room. I always liked the master bedroom with the view of the sea.'

'The master bedroom is now a ward for the patients,' she said. 'You'd better have Augustus and Wilfred's room since they're in London for the dura-

328

tion. You should know that we have no servants. Mrs Rowe and Anneliese are employed by the Red Cross and have no duties here other than cooking. You'll need to take your laundry to the village and clean your own room.'

'I expect I can get a woman in to do that,' said Benedict grudgingly. 'And I haven't had any dinner yet.'

'I doubt there's much left,' said Edith. 'You'd better see what you can find before Anneliese clears the table. Oh, and you must give your ration book to Pascal since he manages the stores.'

'Ration book?'

'Surely you know sugar is rationed now? Other foods will follow before long, I'm sure. You can't have any pudding or sugar in your tea unless we have your ration book.'

'I left my brother's house in a bit of a hurry.'

'That comes as no surprise,' said Julian. 'Wore out your welcome, did you?'

'You'd better write and ask him to send the ration book on.' Edith chewed at her lip while she thought. 'On second thoughts, Benedict,' she said, 'I'll bring you some supper in your room.'

'I'll not be sent upstairs like a naughty child!'

'And I don't care to have you barge into the dining-room and upset Roland.'

'Why would I upset him? I'm his father.'

'Why?' She sighed. 'You and your mistress abandoned him when he was only four. You've never sent him even a single Christmas card. He was heartbroken for months after you left. Surely you don't imagine you can walk in the door and expect him to be delighted to see you?'

'Watch me!' Benedict shouldered her aside.

'And so it begins again,' said Pascal, massaging his forehead.

★ ★ ★

Over the following week, Edith attempted to keep out of Benedict's way but, wherever she went, there he was. During the morning meetings with Matron, he'd put his head around the door to ask for some writing paper or more fuel for the fire he insisted on lighting in his room. She went for a walk in the cove with Clarissa and he followed, watching her from the clifftop. She went to the kitchen to discuss menus with Mrs Rowe and he materialised a moment later, looking for a slice of cake.

One evening, following the sound of uproarious laughter upstairs, it became apparent Benedict was holding a party in his room. Cigarette smoke billowed out under the door and empty beer bottles littered the corridor outside. Roland lay on the floor, drunk, and Sergeant Andrews had to be carried to bed after he vomited on the landing. Matron, in full sail, marched into Benedict's room and expressed her keen displeasure before dismissing the patients to their beds.

The next day, Edith was obliged to reprimand Roland and dismayed when he was unrepentant and shouted at her, saying she was a sanctimonious killjoy.

'It's as if history is repeating itself,' Edith complained to Pascal later. 'Those were Benedict's words coming out of his son's mouth. Do you remember how Benedict used to incite Pearl to be rebellious, just to spite me?'

'I remember he bribed her to spy on us, hoping to catch us in flagrante delicto.' Pascal pulled Edith

330

closer to his side and kissed her forehead. 'Regrettably, there is little chance of any such delight while Benedict is here.'

'Thank goodness Roland is returning to school today and will be removed from his father's sphere of influence.' She gave Pascal a sideways look from under her eyelashes. 'There's still Woodland Cottage for when we want to be alone.'

'Temptress!'

Slipping her arms around his neck, she covered his face in kisses. After a while, she released him with a sigh. 'It's time for me to take Roland to the station.'

'I'll come and say goodbye to him.'

★ ★ ★

Half an hour later, Roland's trunk was stowed in the trap and he stood stiffly before Edith and Pascal, glowering.

'I hope you have a good term,' said Pascal. 'Don't forget to write to your mother.'

Roland shrugged. 'They make us write home after church every Sunday.'

Pascal held out his hand. 'I look forward to seeing you at Easter.'

Roland shook it. 'Thank you,' he said.

'Will you drive, Roland, or shall I?' asked Edith.

He didn't answer her but climbed onto the trap and gathered up the traces.

Sighing, she sat down beside him and Teddy jogged off down the lane. After a while she glanced at the boy and saw he was biting his lip and his cheeks were scarlet from the effort of holding back tears. 'What is it, Roly?'

'I'm sorry I was rude to you, Ma. I don't even like beer but Papa —'

'It's all right, Roly.' Edith patted his knee. 'I can imagine exactly how it happened.'

'And I have the most frightful headache.'

'I expect you have,' she said. 'That's what happens when you drink too much. You'll know next time.'

'Papa promised me he'd come and see me off but this morning he wouldn't get out of bed.'

It was painful to see the hurt in Roland's eyes. 'Your father can be great fun,' Edith said, choosing her words carefully, 'but I advise you to take his promises with a pinch of salt.'

The trap rolled along and Roland was silent for a while. 'It's odd,' he said finally. 'I know he's my father but really he's a stranger to me. I think of Pascal as my father because he's always been there.'

'And he loves you like his own child, Roly, as do I.'

Roland nodded. 'Look what he gave me when we shook hands.' He delved in his pocket and brought out a half-crown. 'That's a pretty decent tip, isn't it?'

'It certainly is.'

'I'll write and thank him.'

They arrived at the station and Roland ran to find a porter to help with his trunk.

On the platform, they waited until they saw the plume of smoke that heralded the arrival of the train.

Once it had screeched to a halt, Roland hugged Edith. 'Goodbye,' he said. Then he whispered in her ear, 'I love you, Ma.'

Tears started to her eyes and she could do no more than say, 'Love you, too,' before he climbed onto the train. The whistle blew and she waved her handkerchief until the train had disappeared into the distance.

Chapter 37

February 1918

Cornwall

Coal was running low again and it was bitterly cold in the jewellery workshop when Edith went to discuss the forthcoming sale of work with her friend.

'This is lovely, Clarissa.' She held up an identity bracelet to catch the light at the window. 'Is it silver?'

Clarissa, wrapped in a coat, scarf and fingerless gloves, shook her head. 'Alloy. I make silver ones with decorative chasing around the disc to sell in the department stores. These will be an affordable price and include the cost of engraving with the service-man's name, number and regiment. Of course, all servicemen wear tags around their necks but sometimes they get lost and then it's impossible to identify them amongst the fallen.'

Edith shivered. 'Will you make one for me to send to Jasper?'

'Of course I will. And look, there are these lockets, too. Mothers and sweethearts can keep a small photograph or a lock of their boy's hair inside.'

'Dora's given me some postcards illustrated with botanical drawings to add to the sale,' said Edith, 'and Pascal's painted a series of small seascapes. Some of the patients from his art class have donated work for the sale, too.'

'And Lily and I collected enough bric-à-brac to fill

a stall,' said Clarissa.

'It's so good to see you and Lily friends again.'

'I wondered if she'd ever forgive me,' confessed Clarissa. 'It was Adela's predicament that brought us together again.' She smiled. 'Adela brings baby Eileen to the coach house sometimes when Lily has time off.'

'Lily has settled well into working here, hasn't she?'

'She's happier than I've seen her for a long time.'

'I wonder if Dr Gillespie might have something to do with that?' said Edith.

Clarissa laughed. 'I do believe you may be right.'

Edith left the workshop, shivering in the icy wind as she hurried across the courtyard to the house. The afternoon's post was on the hall mat and she gathered it up to distribute to the patients.

In the drawing-room, Nurse Scott was dispensing tea and good cheer.

Edith handed out several letters and had set aside another half dozen for patients who were elsewhere when she saw one addressed to herself. Immediately she saw it, her heart began to race and she tore the envelope open. Inside was a printed form letter with handwritten insertions.

I regret to have to inform you . . .

Edith's vision wavered and she had to blink several times before she could continue reading.

. . . that a report has this day been received from the War Office to the effect that *Private J. Fairchild* was posted as '*missing*' on the *17th February 1918.*

Should any other information be received concerning him, such information will at once be communicated to you.

Her knees gave way and she slumped down on the sofa next to Sergeant Andrews.

'All right, Mrs Fairchild?'

'My son,' she whispered. 'Jasper's missing.'

Sergeant Andrews's concerned face floated in and out of view as she fought off dizziness.

Nurse Scott made her drink a cup of sweet tea, but as soon as she could stand, Edith hurried to find Pascal.

He stared at the letter, utterly motionless for several minutes.

'Is he really missing?' Edith asked. Her mouth was numb. 'Or do they call it that because they can't find his body?' Panic blossomed inside her. 'What if he was blown up . . .'

Pascal drew a deep breath and stared at her, his eyes dark pools of fear. 'No,' he said. 'Our son is not dead. I would feel it here.' He pressed his hand to his heart.

Edith let out a mew of anguish. 'We've already lost Lucien. We can't lose Jasper, too.'

Pascal crushed her into a fierce hug. 'He is missing but he isn't lost to us. He can't be! I waited half my life for a son and I will not lose him now.'

Weeping, she clung to him and felt his tears on her cheeks, mingling with her own.

★ ★ ★

The news spread through Spindrift House at the speed of wildfire. Matron came to express her support. 'Take a day or two off,' she said.

Edith shook her head. 'I must keep busy and hope for better news.'

Matron nodded and patted her hand. 'Chin up. That's the way.'

Dora, Clarissa and Ursula came to hug Edith, mute with sorrow and anxiety.

Dinner was subdued that night. Anneliese, her eyes reddened, brought in the fish pie and placed it silently on the table. Several of the patients awkwardly murmured consoling words to Edith and then ate their dinner without speaking again.

Benedict's mouth thinned when he glanced at her. He didn't offer any words of condolence but kept up a one-sided conversation with the men. 'It's like a mausoleum in here,' he complained. 'Who can play the piano? What about a cheerful song or two?' He studied the sober faces of those around him and sighed. 'A game of cards?' One by one, the patients drifted away.

Edith sat beside Pascal in the sitting-room while she wrote to Pearl and Nell. 'I'll ask Pearl to write to Maxwell in France,' she said. 'He might make some enquiries.'

'Someone must have seen Jasper,' said Pascal. He rubbed his eyes. 'Perhaps he was injured and is unconscious in a hospital somewhere? It is possible he is on a hospital train or ship on its way back to Britain. There must be something we can do to find him.'

★　★　★

336

Over the next fortnight, Edith and Pascal carried out their duties like automatons, each lost in their own pit of despair and waiting for news. Edith looked out for the postwoman every day, pouncing on the mail the moment it dropped through the letterbox. But there was no news of Jasper, only tearstained letters from Pearl, Nell, and Edith's father.

One day a parcel arrived addressed to Edith. She unwrapped it and began to weep uncontrollably when she saw it contained Jasper's possessions, returned from the trenches. Amongst the underwear, hand-knitted socks and gloves, there were the letters she and Pascal had written to him, together with several from Nell and Pearl. There was a separate bundle of envelopes tied up with a bootlace. She opened one and was surprised to find it was written in French and signed by Anneliese. Jasper had never mentioned they were writing to each other. A small tin contained a few cigarettes, a piece of shrapnel and a well-thumbed book of poetry.

Then Edith found his sketchbook, its cover dog-eared and water-stained. Inside, every inch of space had been used. Tiny sketches of his pals as they polished their buttons, dozed or smoked were crammed in side-by-side. Silhouetted against the sky, men crouched over, steel helmets on their heads and rifles in hand, as they clambered out over the top of a trench. A soldier, shrouded in mist and entangled in barbed wire, held his mouth wide in a soundless scream. A wilderness landscape from hell, ground pockmarked with shell holes and punctuated by a lone leafless tree.

Pascal found her sitting on the bottom of the stairs, hugging Jasper's sketchbook to her breast. He gathered her into his arms and carried her into the sitting-room, where he wrapped her in a rug and held her until the storm of weeping was over.

Utterly drained, Edith rested her head on his shoulder.

They were still encircled in each other's arms when Benedict entered the room. 'What in damnation?' He strode towards them, grasped Pascal's collar and pulled him to his feet. 'How dare you touch my wife?' Benedict's face was only inches away from his rival's.

'Let me go!' said Pascal.

'Not a chance, pal!'

'Can you not see Edith is grieving?'

'If anyone is going to comfort my wife, it will be me.'

'You have never in all your life had any regard for her comfort or happiness.' Pascal wrenched his collar free from Benedict's grip. 'You may not care that Jasper is missing but when Lucien, your own son, was killed, even then you did not reply to Edith's letter or show her a moment of kindness in her grief.'

'Filthy little adulterer!' Benedict punched Pascal on the shoulder, making him stagger backwards towards the fireplace.

Edith screamed and scrambled to her feet. 'Don't hurt him!'

Benedict, his teeth bared, raised his hand and slapped her cheek. 'Jezebel! Don't you dare tell me —'

Pascal roared, the outcome of years of pent-up anger against this man who had insulted him and ill-treated the woman he loved. He snatched up the poker from the hearth and, with a visible summoning of self-control, held it to his side, his arm rigid. 'If you ever touch Edith again, I'll kill you and feed you to the dogs.'

'You?' Benedict laughed, incredulous.

'This is my last warning to you.' Pascal's legs were planted wide and his nostrils flared.

Benedict took a step forward, a sneer twisting his lips. 'You really think you are man enough to —'

Pascal raised the poker aloft with both hands and yelled as he swung it in a wide arc. It connected with Benedict's knees and he crashed to the ground, moaning.

Sergeant Andrews and Dr Gillespie surged through the open doorway.

'I'll take that, if you don't mind,' said the doctor.

Pascal stared at the poker in his fist and then handed it over.

'Did I harm him?' His voice was dull.

'I wouldn't blame you if you did,' said Sergeant Andrews. 'I saw him hit Mrs Fairchild. Look at her poor cheek!'

Dr Gillespie crouched down and pulled up Benedict's trouser leg. 'A bit of bruising, Mr Fairchild, that's all. No cause to bleat about it. I suggest you take yourself somewhere quiet for the afternoon, to get over your fit of temper.'

'I'll make sure that he does,' said Sergeant Andrews. He yanked Benedict to his feet and pushed him out of the door.

'Nurse Stanton will bring you a cold compress for your cheek, Mrs Fairchild,' said Dr Gillespie. 'Are you all right, Mr Joubert?'

Pascal nodded, white-faced.

'Try and keep out of Mr Fairchild's way, won't you?' said Dr Gillespie as he left the room.

Pascal sank down on the sofa and buried his face in his hands. 'I apologise, Edith.'

339

'You have nothing to be sorry for,' she said, sitting down beside him.

'I am not a violent man,' he said, lifting his head to look at her, 'but in that moment, I wanted to kill him.'

'I've spent half my life wanting to kill him.'

'We cannot live like this,' he said. 'Something must change or either Benedict or I will be murdered and the other hanged.'

Chapter 38

April 1918

Cornwall

Lily peeled back the dressing on Private Francis's shoulder and Dr Gillespie peered at the wound. She studied the crisp auburn waves of his hair as he bent over his patient and wondered what it would be like to touch them. She ran a finger around the inside of her starched collar, suddenly rather warm.

'It's healing well, Nurse Stanton,' said Dr Gillespie. 'We'll have you on your way back to your regiment before long, Private Francis.'

'Can't be soon enough for me,' he said gloomily. 'Who'd want to stay here where there are soft beds, regular meals and pretty nurses, when I could be sitting waist-deep in muddy, freezing water, waiting to go over the top and get machine-gunned again?'

Dr Gillespie patted the soldier's good arm but Lily saw the despondent expression on his face as he turned to the next patient.

Lily redressed Private Francis's shoulder and straightened his bed while he sat in the chair. Matron was a stickler for a tidy bed.

Before she went downstairs, she peeped into the master bedroom, known as the Quiet Ward. The curtains there were half-drawn and Nurse Scott moved about like a wraith while she swept the floor. Two of the shell-shocked patients lay on their beds while the

341

other two sat on chairs.

'Private Tompkins,' whispered Lily, 'shall I bring you some tea or will you come downstairs today?'

His eyes, wide and unfocused, turned slowly towards her.

'Hold my arm,' she murmured, 'and I'll find you a chair in a nice quiet corner.'

'Th-thank you.'

She assisted him downstairs to the drawing-room and settled him in an armchair, facing the sea. As she left, she met Dr Gillespie coming downstairs.

'If you're returning to the surgery now, I wondered if you might give me a lift into the village?' she asked. 'I have some errands to run for the patients in my lunchbreak.'

'It would be my pleasure.'

Lily hurried to fetch her cloak and a minute later was sitting in the passenger seat of the doctor's Wolseley.

'How is Mrs Fairchild keeping?' asked Dr Gillespie, as he drove out of the courtyard. 'It was dreadful news for her to receive about her son.'

'Every day that passes makes it more unlikely Jasper will be found,' said Lily. 'Edith's very brave but no mother should have to face losing both her sons.' Her own heart ached at the probability of never seeing Jasper again.

'This war is a wicked business.' Dr Gillespie shook his head. 'There's hardly a person untouched by the grief it carries in its wake; you only have to see the broken men at Spindrift to know that. I worry about what will happen to them all, once the war is over.'

It was a fresh spring day and the lanes were lined with celandines and primroses. Before long, the

342

Wolseley nosed its way down the steep hill into the village. Dr Gillespie stopped the motorcar beside the harbour and walked around to open Lily's door.

'Thank you so much,' she said.

'When will you return?' His hazel eyes smiled at her.

'I must be back in an hour.'

'Then I'll drive you.'

'Oh, but —'

'Really, it's no trouble,' he said. 'I have to call at Polcarrow Farm this afternoon.' He gave a cheery wave and climbed back into the Wolseley.

Lily smiled as she watched him drive away. Five minutes later, as she called into the tobacconist's for Private Francis's smokes, she realised she was still smiling. Really, Dr Gillespie was nothing at all like Dr Bennett.

★ ★ ★

The fundraising tea party and sale of work held in the Spindrift Gallery was a great success. The patients who'd been well enough to mingle with the guests enjoyed themselves, but Edith longed to escape to a darkened room by the time the last visitor had left. Many of the ladies had expressed their condolences, which was kind of them, but each time it felt like another nail in Jasper's coffin, intensifying her anguish. She survived each day by keeping busy and refusing to believe he wasn't coming home, but during her sleepless nights she was forced to accept that awful probability. She longed to find comfort in Pascal's arms but Benedict's glowering presence made that impossible.

Dora and Ursula had helped with the sale of work and now they collected the cups and saucers and returned them to the house. Pascal counted the proceeds while Julian folded down the trestle tables.

Edith and Pascal walked back to the house with the cashbox. In the courtyard, Pascal said abruptly, 'I must go to London. I have an interview at Carlton House Terrace.'

'An interview?'

'I didn't discuss it with you before,' said Pascal, 'in case it didn't happen and I upset you unnecessarily. The Red Cross has a department tasked with searching for missing soldiers. I have applied to work there, cross-checking names of the missing against the lists of newly admitted hospital patients, prisoners-of-war, and also soldiers' verbal accounts of the death or wounding of their fellows on the battlefield.'

'But what about your work here as Quartermaster?'

'If my interview is successful, Dora and Ursula are willing to take over my position. They will still have time to manage the kitchen garden, if they share the duties.' He ran his fingers through his hair. 'I shall take my portfolio to some of the galleries and return after a few days. I don't want to leave you with Benedict but you must see that I have to do this?'

Edith knew nothing she could say would deter him from his purpose. 'It's valuable work,' she said, 'and if you find even one lost boy and reunite him with his family, it will be worthwhile.'

'Jasper is out there somewhere. I know it!'

'I lie awake at night,' she said, 'wondering if it's better to know for certain that he's dead or to carry on living a half-life in the hope that one day he will return to us.'

344

Edith saw Pascal onto the train at Port Isaac Road station. They clung together for a second, mute in their shared misery, before he climbed into the carriage. She watched the train steam out of the station, taking him with it and leaving her heavy-hearted.

Arriving back at Spindrift, she found Dora in a state of consternation.

Her freckled face was pink with indignation. 'Wilfred and Augustus have received their call-up papers. Wilfred's forty-nine and Augustus is only a couple of years younger. Can you imagine anyone less likely to make good fighting men?'

'I'm sure they'll do their best,' said Edith, though it was impossible for her to envision Wilfred, always immaculately turned out, having to contend with muddy trenches, lice and a lack of freshly ironed shirts. Augustus's gentle nature rendered him entirely unsuitable to carry a rifle, never mind actually use it to harm another.

'It doesn't bode well for victory for Britain when such unlikely candidates are called up, does it?' said Dora. 'The trouble is, our backs are against the wall and we're running out of men. I read in the newspaper that General Haig says the German offensive is so intense there's no course open to us but to fight to the bitter end. Our freedom depends upon it.' Dora's mouth trembled. 'What if it goes on so long that Roland is called up?' She broke down then. 'Our beautiful boys! I loved Jasper and Lucien as much as if they were my own and now they're gone,' she sobbed.

Edith hugged her friend, their tears mingling in shared sorrow.

On the day on which Edith had anticipated Pascal's return, a letter arrived from him.

My dearest Edith

The Red Cross has accepted me and I begin work on Monday. Time is of the essence and I must make a start on discovering where to find Jasper and the other soldiers. Behind every missing man is a grieving family.

I delivered your letters to Pearl and your father. When he heard of my new position, he was so kind as to offer me a room for the duration. They are both well, although naturally still distressed about Jasper and Lucien.

Your father and I sat up with a glass of brandy tonight and it is late now. If Benedict becomes too troublesome, your father asked me to tell you that you may always seek shelter in his house.

I will do everything possible to find our son. I love you more than I can express and hope to be reunited with you before too long.

Forever yours,
Pascal

The hope that Edith had clung to that Jasper might still be alive somewhere had begun to fade by now. She'd heard enough terrible stories from the patients to know how many men were blown to pieces, leaving no trace, but Pascal would never come to terms with his grief until he had proof that their son was dead. She went to Pascal's room and made up two large parcels of his clothes and shoes. Before she set off for the village to post them, she went to the kitchen and asked if Anneliese would come with her to the sitting-room.

The maid waited for her to speak, hands clasped over her apron and eyes modestly lowered.

'Jasper's possessions have been sent to me,' said Edith. She held out the bundle of letters to her. 'I believe these are yours?'

Anneliese looked at her with alarm in her clear blue eyes. She took the letters, a blush warming her pale complexion. 'Your son was so kind as to write to me and sometimes Blanche sent him her drawings. I hope you do not mind?'

'Of course not.' Edith studied Anneliese's slender waist and fair hair. She hadn't noticed before quite how pretty she was. 'I'm happy if your letters brought him comfort.'

The young woman's eyes welled with tears. 'If only I had not told him of the atrocities in Belgium, he would not have gone to fight . . .' She wiped her eyes with a corner of her apron. 'I am sorry. It is my fault.'

'No, Anneliese,' said Edith, 'of course it isn't.' She felt a wave of pity for this girl, only a little older than her own daughters, who had experienced such tragedy. Impulsively, she reached out to touch her hand. 'My son did what he believed was right. He fights to protect England as well as Belgium. And if he hadn't volunteered, he would have been conscripted.'

'Thank you, madame.' Anneliese bowed her head and left the room.

Edith sat quietly for a moment. How could she have been so blind? Jasper had cared for Anneliese and little Blanche. In another life, perhaps the refugees might have become part of this family.

Later, after her visit to the post office with Pascal's parcels, Edith saw an old woman bent over and clinging to the school railings.

'Are you all right?' she asked. The woman straightened up and Edith suppressed a gasp of shock. 'Daisy?' She stared in dismay at the maid who'd left her employ at the beginning of the war to work in the munitions factory at Cligga Head. Her complexion was now a waxy yellow, her cheeks covered in boils and her once glossy dark hair faded to a dull ginger.

'Don't say it, Mrs Fairchild!' Daisy begged, tears starting to her eyes. 'I look a fright, don't I? Worst thing I ever did was to leave Spindrift to be a munitionette. Me and my sister have come home to die, both of us poisoned by the cordite we packed into grenades.'

Edith murmured something inadequate about her immense sacrifice for the greater good. After she'd helped the pitiful young woman home, Edith reflected bitterly that Daisy and her sister were quite as much casualties of the war as Lucien and Jasper.

★ ★ ★

Over the following weeks, Edith wanted nothing more than to pull the bedclothes over her head and hide from the world. Thankfully, Benedict remained in his bed for most of the time or took off to the Golden Lion. She disciplined herself to appear promptly every morning for her meeting with Matron and, afterwards, made it her business to speak to each patient and see if there was anything she could do to add to their comfort. By late-morning, she'd been so busy she'd usually managed to shake off her malaise. Jasper

348

and Lucien might no longer be alive but the wounded still needed her care and attention.

One morning, she noted a parcel for Clarissa on the hall table next to the post. Pouncing upon a letter from Pascal, she took it into the office, along with letters addressed to herself as Lady Superintendent. She scanned Pascal's letter first and then rested her chin on her hands while a noose of anxiety tightened inside her. He'd persuaded the authorities that, as a native French speaker, he'd be an asset if he joined the searchers behind the lines in France and Belgium. He was to visit the Allied base hospitals, army rest camps and surrounding villages, to ask the men there if they'd seen what had happened to the missing soldiers. Although he assured her he wouldn't take any unnecessary risks, she knew several of the Spindrift patients had been injured by enemy bombardments behind the lines, designed to demoralise.

She felt a flicker of anger towards Pascal because he was risking his life and leaving her when she was already grieving for her sons. But she knew that wasn't fair. Pascal had always been there to support her and, however hopeless a task it was, his way of dealing with his grief was to attempt to find Jasper. Tucking the letter in her pocket, she sent up a fervent prayer that they would both come home unscathed.

After opening the rest of her post, she began the never-ending task of writing begging letters for soldiers' comforts and funds to augment the Red Cross supplies.

Dora came to ask her if she would extend her appeal to seeds for the vegetable garden and then Clarissa joined them, delighted to be able to present a cheque and a parcel from her aunt.

349

'Aunt Minnie hosted any number of bridge parties and raffles to raise this splendid sum,' she said. 'The parcel contains tobacco, cigarettes, matches, handkerchiefs, combs, chocolate and boiled sweets for the patients.'

Then the door flew open and Benedict burst into the room, his face an angry red. 'It's monstrous!'

Edith sighed. 'What is?'

He shook a piece of paper at them. 'I've been conscripted! The age limit has been lifted to include men up to fifty-one and I've to present myself at a training camp in Salisbury next week.'

'Wilfred and Augustus received their papers last week,' said Dora.

'Good God!' Benedict shook his head. 'The army really is scraping the bottom of the barrel then.'

'They must be,' said Edith, 'if they've sent for you.' She looked him up and down. 'They'll have their work cut out to get you fit.'

'What do you mean?'

'Perhaps you haven't noticed how your stomach hangs over your waistband and that walking upstairs makes you out of breath? I expect you'll soon be doing ten-mile runs in full kit before breakfast every day.'

'When you're not cleaning the latrines, that is,' added Clarissa.

'I will not!' Benedict pulled in his stomach. 'I'll tell them I'm in a reserved occupation and am needed here.'

'And what occupation is that?' asked Edith. She pressed a finger to her chin. 'Gambler, perhaps?'

'Womaniser?' suggested Clarissa.

'Shirker, more like,' said Dora.

Benedict strode out of the room, slamming the

door behind him.

The three women looked at each other.

'Thank God he's leaving!' said Dora.

'I know it's wrong of me,' said Edith, 'since he'll soon be risking his life in battle, but I feel like jumping on the table and doing the can-can.'

Dora and Clarissa burst out laughing. Dora swished her skirt, exposing her petticoat while she hummed the can-can tune. The others joined in and, just as Clarissa gave a little shriek and Edith managed a particularly high kick, Matron opened the door.

She stood with her hands on her hips, a dour expression on her face. 'I do not expect such displays of indecorum in my hospital.'

Edith, pink-cheeked and out of breath, dropped her skirt hem, feeling exactly as if she'd been called in to see her headmistress after a schoolgirl misdemeanour. 'I apologise, Matron, but Mr Fairchild just informed me he's received call-up papers.'

Matron sat down at her desk and frowned at Clarissa and Dora. 'That will be all.'

Sheepishly, they all turned to leave but not before they heard Matron begin to hum the can-can's distinctive melody.

Chapter 39

November 1918

Cornwall

Edith and Matron were discussing arrangements for discharging three of the patients when they heard footsteps racing towards the office.

Dora rushed in. 'It's over!' she said. Laughing, she snatched Edith's hands and pulled her to her feet. 'I went to the village. Hostilities have ceased!'

And then the three of them were hugging and laughing and crying all at once, and making so much noise that Lily came to see what was happening.

'The war is over!' cried Matron.

'There's going to be an Armistice Parade this afternoon down by the harbour,' said Dora. 'The bunting's going up already.'

'We must tell the patients,' said Edith. 'Lily, will you ask all those who can to come to the drawing-room? What a shame we haven't any champagne.'

'Don't worry,' said Matron. 'I'll ask Mrs Rowe to make cocoa.'

★ ★ ★

After lunch, Julian hitched Teddy to the trap and Dora and Ursula draped it with Union Jacks and threaded scarlet ribbons through the pony's mane.

Tom Mellyn drove Polcarrow's wagon into the

courtyard, piled with hay bales covered with brightly coloured rugs.

'It's good of you to turn out,' said Edith. 'It'll lift the patients' spirits to join the village celebrations.'

'Glad to help,' said Tom. 'I wondered . . .' He shuffled his feet. 'Is there any news from Nell? She doesn't answer my letters, you see.'

'Oh, Tom!' Edith squeezed his arm. 'I know how close you were and I'm sorry she hasn't written to you. She's well but still grieving terribly for her twin.'

Tom nodded and turned back to the wagon.

The first group of patients set off with Dora, Ursula and Lily walking beside the wagon. Half an hour later, Julian and Tom returned to collect the remaining men. Edith, Nurse Scott and Clarissa accompanied them. Matron stayed with patients who were too weak to join the outing.

In the village, the houses and shops were hung with fluttering bunting and flags. A sheet hanging from the eaves of the fish cellars was painted with the words Clear Off, Kaiser! and another was draped from the windows of the Golden Lion, stating, A heroes' welcome awaits our boys! Edith bowed her head to hide her tears. Her boys wouldn't be returning to a heroes' welcome. Months had passed and Pascal was still searching for Jasper, though she no longer held out any hopes for their son's return.

The shops were closed and the Platt was thronged with villagers who'd turned out to join in the celebrations. Tom and Julian parked their vehicles side by side so that patients who weren't strong enough to mingle with the crowd had a good view. Schoolchildren had been given the afternoon off and their excited shrieks as they chased each other across the beach, waving Union Jacks and blowing toy trumpets, made Edith smile. Boats bobbed about in the harbour and a group of fishermen bellowed out sea shanties on the beach.

Then, in the distance, came the faint sound of a brass band. Villagers cheered and waved as the Band of Hope marched down the hill, followed by the boy scouts and several dogs. The band made several turns around the Platt before coming to a halt on the beach. Although their numbers were depleted since the young men had gone to war, the old men played 'Keep the Home Fires Burning' and 'It's a Long Way to Tipperary' with gusto. The crowd sang along with them, their voices rising to the heavens.

The vicar gave a short speech and a prayer of thanksgiving. 'Three cheers for the King, the sailors and the soldiers!' resounded through the crowd. The landlord of the Golden Lion and his barmaid brought a wheelbarrow laden with glasses and a barrel of ale onto the Platt and stopped beside the trap and the wagon from Spindrift.

'Free beer for our heroes!' he shouted.

The barmaid gave the convalescent soldiers a kiss along with their beer.

A chilly November wind blew in from the sea and, as the light began to fade, one by one lamps were lit inside the houses, blackout blinds left defiantly raised. Tom and Julian conveyed the most exhausted patients back to Spindrift first, while Lily and Nurse Scott rounded up the remainder and encouraged them to march on the spot to keep warm until Tom and Julian returned for them.

'What a day!' said Clarissa to Edith when they finally arrived back at Spindrift.

'It was a wonderful though bittersweet celebration,' she said. 'What will happen next? It hardly feels like victory when a generation of young men have been lost. There's a future for the survivors, I suppose, but what kind of a future?'

★ ★ ★

To Edith's great delight, Pearl and Nell arrived home in early December. Pascal, however, remained in France, searching amongst the chaos for news of the dead and wounded. There was no immediate home-coming for most of the soldiers posted there and he wrote of their frustration. Edith read out part of his letter to Pearl and Nell.

> *The army says the men are needed here until the conclusion of the peace treaties. Some soldiers are being released if they have work to go to at home while others are given mindless fatigues or kit inspections to keep them occupied. There is dissent amongst the men, made worse by a wave of influenza that has struck down those already weakened by battle.*
>
> *My work here has allowed me to send home news of many lost men, either their whereabouts or else the knowledge of where they fell. I am doing everything possible to find our son. There was a report that some men had been taken prisoners-of-war after Jasper's last battle but I have checked the lists of names issued from the enemy camps and there is no mention of him.*
>
> *There is uncertainty about when I will return but I believe I shall remain here another month or so.*

355

'I'd hoped he would return sooner,' said Edith.

'Don't look so woebegone, Mama,' said Nell, hugging her. 'You have us here now to look after you.'

'You can't know how precious that is to me.'

'At least Maxwell is safe and will come home soon,' said Pearl.

But for too many others, thought Edith, there would never be a homecoming.

★ ★ ★

The following weeks were a strange unsettled time as the Spindrift Convalescent Hospital wound down. Nurse Scott and most of the patients had already left and the attic dormitories were empty. Dora and Ursula were making an audit of the remaining supplies and arranging for the last of the bedlinen to be laundered in the village. Pearl, Nell and Lily disinfected the hospital beds before polishing the windows, scrubbing the floors and cleaning the bathrooms. The Quiet Ward was still occupied and two patients who needed nursing care for their gas-damaged lungs remained in the other large bedroom. Once they were discharged, the home would close.

'Spindrift is such a special place,' said Matron. 'It has aided the healing of mind and body of all who stayed here. I shall miss it.' Her tone was wistful.

'You'll always be welcome to visit us,' said Edith.

'I should like that.' Matron smiled. 'And then perhaps you'll call me Maggie?'

Edith, no longer fundraising or dealing with administration, found she had time to paint most of the day and set up her easel in the attic studio again.

On Christmas Eve, Edith glanced into the drawing-room where Pearl and Lily were hanging paperchains from the ceiling. Roland had returned from school, and he, Nell and Rose were decorating the Christmas tree.

'Nell,' said Edith, 'will you walk with me to Polcarrow Farm to collect the chickens for Christmas dinner?'

Nell looked up, her emerald eyes swimming. 'I can't,' she said.

'You're still avoiding Tom?'

She nodded.

'You used to be so happy together. I can't believe Lucien would want you to be miserable.'

Nell's face contorted as she tried to stem her tears. 'I'll never be happy without him.' She ran out of the room.

Edith's heart felt as if it were breaking all over again.

★ ★ ★

Later that afternoon, she went to her studio. The comforting aroma of cinnamon and orange from the Christmas puddings steaming on the range drifted up the staircase, along with Roland and Rose's laughter as they played charades. She glanced at the water stains on the attic ceiling and saw they had spread. She sighed. The leak in the roof must be worse. The windows rattled in the draughts and paint was flaking off their frames. Spindrift had grown shabby with the extra wear and tear of additional occupants during the war and there was no money to repair it. Even selling some of her paintings and finding new tenants wouldn't bring in enough. She couldn't bear to think about it now.

Arranging her canvases around the walls, Edith studied them with a critical eye to decide if they were good enough for the Unsung Heroes exhibition to be held in the summer.

Looking at Waving the Boys Goodbye, she couldn't help but remember saying farewell to Lucien and Jasper. Now, she'd never be able to paint a canvas depicting their arrival home from war as conquering heroes. She let out a sob as a wave of anguish engulfed her.

The floorboards creaked and she turned her tear-stained face to see Pascal standing in the doorway.

'Hello, mon amour,' he said, holding out his arms to her. 'I'm home for Christmas.'

Chapter 40

January 1919

Cornwall

Wind rattled the windowpanes o the day nursery and moaned down the chimney, making the flames flicker behind the fireguard.

Gabrielle handed Jérôme a red brick. He placed it with careful concentration on the top of the tower he was building. The construction wobbled then steadied and he clapped his hands and grinned up at his mother. She patted his cheek. 'Bravo, mon petit!' Now eighteen months old, he was an amusing little companion for the twenty minutes or so until he became a nuisance. God knows, there was little else to amuse her at Cliff House.

'Clever boy, Jeremy!' said Jenifry, watching her grandson with an indulgent smile.

Gabrielle gritted her teeth. 'His name is Jérôme, not Jeremy!' How often did she have to correct the stubborn old witch?

'You will make my grandson a laughing stock when he goes to school,' said Jenifry. 'Jeremy is an acceptable British name.'

The door to the adjacent night nursery opened and Adela came in, carrying her little daughter in her arms. 'Come and say hello to Grandma, Eileen.'

'Did you change her?' asked Jenifry. 'We don't want the child screeching with nappy rash again.'

'Yes, I did,' said Adela, tight-lipped.

Eileen, her round cheeks flushed from her afternoon nap, struggled in her mother's arms until she was put down on the floor, then staggered off on chubby little legs. Now she was walking, she was keen to explore. Catching sight of Jérôme's tower of bricks, she crowed and swiped at it with her hand.

It fell with a clatter and her cousin let out a shriek of fury.

Eileen burst into tears.

'Naughty Eileen,' said Jenifry. She hurried to lift up her grandson and smother his face in kisses.

Peggy the nursemaid returned to the nursery carrying a pile of clean napkins.

'Now Nurse is back,' said Gabrielle, catching Adela's eye, 'I will take a walk.'

'I'll come too,' said Adela. She closed the nursery door behind them and gave Gabrielle a conspiratorial grin.

They put on their coats and hurried outside. After a rocky start, the two young women had forged a fragile friendship out of the common bond of motherhood and their frequent irritation with Jenifry. They ran down the steps to the cove with the sea breeze in their faces, laughing with exhilaration at having escaped. The sea was in an angry mood, roaring and flinging itself against the rocks, sending up fountains of spray. Just for a moment, as Gabrielle's running feet crunched over the damp sand and pebbles, she was reminded of the joyous freedom of childhood seaside holidays at Spindrift.

Lily, bundled up against the cold in a thick scarf, waited for them below, her face turned to the fury of the sea. Adela shouted her name and Lily scrambled down the rocks, flinging her arms wide for balance. 'They're too slippery to sit on today,' she said, jumping down onto the sand. 'I thought you mightn't be coming. Anyway, I haven't long. Dr Gillespie is visiting one of the patients and I need to assist.'

'I wonder what excuse he will give to visit you once the last patient is discharged?' said Adela.

Lily smiled complacently. 'Jack no longer needs an excuse to see me,' she said. 'And Mother approves.'

Gabrielle felt a sharp stab of jealousy. It had been a long time since she'd had a man to adore her.

Heads down against the wind, they walked along the rippled sand by the water's edge.

'Have you noticed the peculiar feeling in the atmosphere?' said Lily. 'It's almost as if everybody is waiting for something to happen now the war's over.'

'Everything will be different,' said Gabrielle. 'So many men died and a whole generation of girls will grow up unable to find a husband to keep them.'

'Although it was hard work, I miss my nursing days,' said Adela. 'I had a purpose then. I've had enough of living under my parents' control and I've made a decision.'

'What's that?' asked Lily.

'While I've been living at home, I've saved up my allowance from Edwin. I'm going to move back to London and rent lodgings.'

'Will you have enough savings?' asked Gabrielle.

'I'll be pretty hard up for a while but I'll be free.' She stepped over a clump of seaweed. 'Once Eileen is at school, I'll look for work. Perhaps I'll advertise to see if I can find another young mother without a husband, with a view to sharing accommodation and childcare. The Spindrift community is what gave me the idea.'

Lily laughed. 'How that will infuriate your parents!'

'You've had more love and support from them your community than I've ever had from my parents.' A shadow passed over Adela's face. 'They aren't terribly interested in Eileen because she's a girl but Mother is besotted with Jérôme. And now Father has the grandson he wants to carry on the business.'

'I wish you luck,' said Lily. 'I'll miss nursing at the Spindrift Convalescent Home but perhaps I'll use my secretarial training.'

'What about you, Gabrielle?' asked Adela. 'You and Mother are always rubbing each other up the wrong way.'

She turned to face the sea. 'I shall return to France.'

Adela drew in her breath sharply. 'You can't take Jérôme away! It would break Mother and Father.'

Gabrielle shrugged. 'He is my son.'

Adela and Lily glanced at each other. 'I must go,' said Lily. 'Jack will be waiting for me.'

'And I'm chilled,' said Adela.

Lily waved and set off towards the cliff steps.

The others returned to Cliff House in silence.

★ ★ ★

Gabrielle spent the remainder of the afternoon in her room, looking out of the window, thinking. She'd planned to return to France immediately the war was over but, from what she'd read in the newspapers, the Western Front was still in chaos and Paris was battered. Her widow's pension was small and it wouldn't be easy to find work now she had Jérôme. But perhaps he was her means of negotiating a better future.

Drizzle pattered against the window. She glanced

362

at the mean little fire and shivered. She hadn't been properly warm since she'd left Nice. Closing her eyes, she recalled those golden summers and how the heat of the sun had soaked into her bones. The air had been perfumed with lavender and fresh coffee, and the hum of cicadas had never been far away. Perhaps she should set aside her thoughts of living in Paris and return to the South of France?

She pulled her suitcase from under the bed and slipped her hand into the slit in the lining, to withdraw her diamond earrings and Noel's letter to his father. The earrings glittered in her palm and she stood before the mirror to put them on. Turning her head from side to side, she admired her reflection. Motherhood hadn't marked her and she was confident she'd be able to find another husband, despite the unfortunate shortage of men. It was time to make a new life for herself.

★ ★ ★

After dinner, Gabrielle left Jenifry and Adela with their coffee in the drawing-room and went to knock on her father-in-law's study door. Not waiting for an invitation, she went inside.

Hugh sat in his wingchair, a glass of whisky by his side. He looked up from his newspaper and scowled.

She seated herself at his desk, pushing a pile of paperwork to one side.

'Don't touch that!'

'I have come to inform you that, now hostilities have ceased, I intend to return to France with Jérôme.' She watched with satisfaction as Hugh's face turned chalk white.

'You can't take my grandson! He's settled here and I can give him every advantage. He'll have good schooling and, in time, will inherit this house and my business.'

'I should have thought you'd be glad to see me leave. And of course I must take Jérôme.' She sighed. 'It will be hard for him at first, living in one room in a lodging house after his fine nursery here. He'll be sad to lose the nursemaid he loves, but I daresay I shall find a neighbour's child to watch him while I work.'

'You intend to leave my grandson alone with an untrained girl?'

'What other choice is there? My widow's pension will not be enough to pay a nanny and I must work if Jérôme and I are not to go hungry.'

'Then why choose to go to France and live in penury instead of staying here and living in luxury?'

'I am not welcome or happy here. Besides, Jérôme should grow up in France.'

Her father-in-law lifted his whisky glass and gave her a cold-eyed stare. 'What is it you want?'

'Perhaps it is a case of what you want?' Gabrielle smiled before she showed her hand. 'I believe you are unaware that my blood father is Benedict Fairchild?'

Hugh choked on his whisky.

'I know you detest the man. I don't care for him myself. But, the fact is, his blood runs in my veins. And therefore in Jérôme's, too.'

'I don't believe it!'

'No?' She withdrew the letter from her pocket. 'I promised Noel I'd give you this, if he was killed. He was looking forward to telling you himself and didn't want to take the risk of dying and being unable to do so.'

364

Hugh read the contents twice. Ashen-faced, he stared at her. 'He married you purely to hurt me?'

'Indeed.'

'It will kill Jenifry if she sees this. You can't take Jérôme away! She's already lost both her sons and Jérôme is our last link to Noel, no matter who his other grandfather is.' Hugh wiped one palm over his face. 'I'll pay you to stay.'

'You couldn't pay me enough to make me stay in this miserable place,' said Gabrielle. She tapped her fingers on the desk. 'But there is another option that might suit us both.'

'What?'

'Jérôme is happy here and he loves his grandmother and his nursemaid. Overcome your distaste for the fact that he is Benedict's grandson and promise to love him and give him a good life, and I might be persuaded to leave him with you when I return to France.'

Hugh's lips tightened. 'How much do you want?'

She named a sum and held her breath. It was a truly enormous amount of money.

He strode over to the window. At last, he turned to face her. 'I'll have my solicitor draw up adoption papers and you will agree to surrender all rights to your son. You will not mention this to my wife or to Adela and you will leave Cliff House before dawn the day after you sign the papers. You will never return.'

Swallowing, she nodded.

'Now get out of my sight!'

Silently, she left the room.

Chapter 41

January 1919

Cornwall

After the Christmas holidays, Roland returned to school but when an influenza epidemic swept through the boys, he was sent home again.

Dr Gillespie made his usual visit to the few remaining Spindrift patients. He looked drained and Edith invited him to join the community for lunch since it was ready. 'Sausages and mash,' she said, 'though the sausages consist mostly of bread and sawdust these days.'

He accepted gratefully and followed her into the dining-room.

'Keeping busy, Doctor?' asked Julian.

'Too busy,' said Dr Gillespie. 'I advise you to stay away from the village. Returning soldiers are bringing this dreadful Spanish influenza home with them. It's particularly cruel when they've survived the war, only to come home and die.'

'Perhaps it is preferable to breathe one's last at home instead of in some foreign field?' said Pascal.

'Except when the soldier infects his wife and children first.' Dr Gillespie sighed deeply. 'I sat up last night with young Robert Martin. He passed away at dawn, only twenty-four hours after his father.'

'How terribly sad!' said Lily. 'And you must be exhausted?'

Edith caught Clarissa's eye as her daughter clasped Dr Gillespie's hand.

Roland speared a sausage on his fork and held it aloft. 'At school,' he said, 'we call sausage and mash two Zeppelins and a cloud.'

Rose laughed. 'That's jolly funny, Roly.'

Pearl shuddered. 'If you'd ever seen a Zeppelin floating over the city and wondered when and where it was going to drop its bombs, you might not find it quite so amusing.'

Clarissa changed the subject to the June opening of the Spindrift Gallery and her hope that holidaymakers would return to Port Isaac.

After a pudding of bottled plums and custard, Pascal and other members of the community went to resume their various activities. Dr Gillespie thanked Edith for lunch and Lily went to see him on his way.

'I'm so thankful to see her happy again,' said Clarissa.

'Doctor Gillespie is a fine young man,' said Dora.

'And hard-working,' added Ursula.

Anneliese and Blanche came to clear the table. Edith smiled at the young girl and was delighted to receive a shy smile in return. All the while she'd been at Spindrift, she'd never spoken a word but Edith had recently noticed she no longer hid all the time behind her curtain of blonde hair. The scar across her face had faded to a silvery line and it was possible now to see that she was a pretty child.

'I hope you've saved some luncheon for me, Edith?'

She spun around at the sound of a familiar but unwelcome voice. A uniformed figure stood in the doorway.

'Well,' he said, holding his arms wide, 'aren't you

367

going to welcome the returning hero?'

A great weariness descended upon her. 'Why are you here again, Benedict?' His smile faded. 'Why don't you go back to your mother's house in Berkeley Square?'

'It's still in the War Office's grubby clutches and I'm certainly not going to lodge with my holier-than-thou brother again.'

'I daresay he wouldn't have you back anyway,' said Clarissa.

Benedict sighed. 'You'd think I deserve some respect for risking my life fighting off the enemy to save you from invasion.'

'You did that all by yourself?' said Dora, eyes opened wide in feigned surprise.

'Did you kill anyone?' asked Roland.

'Hundreds of 'em! The ground was littered with dead Germans by the time I left,' said Benedict.

Ursula pressed her fingers to her mouth.

Dora surged to her feet. 'Benedict, you really are the vilest man I've ever met!' She and Ursula left the room.

'Loathsome,' agreed Clarissa. 'Are you coming, Edith?'

She nodded. 'Roland, I believe you have a Latin translation for homework?'

He looked at his father, then reluctantly followed Edith and Clarissa from the room.

Edith went with lagging steps to Pascal's studio, dreading having to tell him the news. He was sitting before his easel with his brush in one hand and his palette in the other, studying his canvas.

'Benedict is back,' she said.

Pascal's shoulders drooped. 'Whenever will that

368

man leave us in peace?' he murmured.

'I expect he'll return to London when the War Office move out of his mother's house.'

'That could be months away.' He drew a deep breath. 'We must endure him as we always have. Now come and tell me what you think of this.'

She stood behind him to look at his canvas and caught her breath. The painting depicted a misty sky coloured a delicate pink by the sun peeping above the horizon. The desolate war-ravaged landscape below was scattered with the bodies of the fallen and pitted with shell holes filled with bright water, reflecting the early-morning light. A lone figure in a greatcoat and steel helmet stood outlined against the sky, his elbows raised and his hands over his ears. Edith felt as if she could hear the silent scream that emanated from his open mouth.

She swallowed. 'It's magnificent. And terrible,' she whispered.

'I shall call it The Searcher.' Jasper's precious sketchbook lay open on the table at Pascal's side and he picked it up. 'I have taken inspiration from Jasper's sketches as well as the scenes I saw in France and Flanders.'

'And you're the Searcher?'

He nodded, his dark eyes glistening.

Edith wrapped her arms around him, resting his head against her breast. 'I still can't believe he's gone from us.'

'But after all this time, I must now accept that he has.' Pascal's shoulders shuddered and she held him tight until he had wept away a little of his grief.

★ ★ ★

Edith watched in consternation as Benedict, finding little welcome from the community, turned his full charm upon Roland. At fifteen and a half, he was halfway between boy and man. Now that the war was over, he was no longer kept occupied in patrolling the coast for signs of U-boats or collecting wastepaper or metal for the war effort. Forbidden from going to the village for fear of influenza, Roland was as bored as his father.

He was often to be found sitting on Benedict's bed. laughing uproariously while his father told him lewd jokes. His most prized possession was a piece of bloodstained shrapnel Benedict had given him 'for good luck'. Nell, in some distress, told Edith she'd seen Benedict and Roland on the rocks in the cove, throwing stones at the seagulls. Edith counted the minutes until the boy could return to school.

One afternoon, she glanced into the sitting-room. The air was thick with cloying smoke from Benedict's Moroccan cigarettes and he was relating a story to Roland, whose eyes were wide with adulation. Or was it from the effects of smoke? Benedict had given him a cigarette too.

Roland, slouched in an armchair, noticed Edith and hastily concealed the evidence.

Benedict glanced up and gave her a flinty glare. 'I tell you what, Roland,' he said, 'now you're a man, I'll take you to London with me and show you the town. We'll have some fun away from this miserable place. Would you like that?' His gaze never left Edith's face as he spoke and there was a challenge in his eyes.

Roland's face shone with eagerness. 'I should like that more than anything!'

Edith knew she'd drive Roland deeper into his

father's clutches if she interfered at this point but she wouldn't allow such blatant manipulation. As she left the room, Benedict and Roland were singing a boisterous rendition of 'Mademoiselle from Armentières'.

★ ★ ★

A few days later, Matron frowned at Benedict over the breakfast table. 'You have a rash on your face, Mr Fairchild. I need to examine you.'

Benedict touched his cheek. 'It's probably a shaving rash.'

'I must be sure it isn't something infectious that might affect my patients.' Matron's tone brooked no argument and she marched him away immediately he'd finished his porridge.

Later that morning, Edith, Pearl and Nell were in the sitting-room tackling the mending when the doorbell rang.

'Would you answer it, Pearl?' said Edith. 'Anneliese is turning out the larder.'

Pearl returned a few moments later with a young soldier. 'Mama, Nell,' she said, 'this is Private Cameron. He was a pal of Lucien's.'

Nell caught her breath. 'You knew him?'

Private Cameron's face lit up in a smile. 'I see his likeness in you. We were the very best of pals and each promised the other that, if the worst happened, we'd visit our friend's relatives. I'm newly home from France.'

'Your family must have been delighted to see you?' said Edith.

He shook his head. 'I promised Lucien I'd come here first.'

'My dear,' said Edith, taken aback, 'wherever you're going, Cornwall must be very far out of your way?'

'Devon, so it's not too far.'

Pearl went to the kitchen to bring tea and soon Private Cameron was sitting on the sofa opposite Edith and Nell with a plate of Madeira cake on his knee.

'We had a letter informing us of Lucien's death,' said Edith. 'It simply said a shell landed beside him and that it would have been very quick.'

Private Cameron put his empty plate down on the table. 'Sometimes the army tells you that to spare you imagining a loved one in dreadful pain before he died.'

Nell let out a little moan and clenched her fingers together until her knuckles were as pale as a string of pearls.

'I'm so sorry,' their visitor said, glancing at her in consternation. 'It's only that I wanted you to know, in this case, it was true.'

'Will you tell me exactly what happened?' she asked. 'I can't sleep at night for wondering.'

Private Cameron looked uncomfortable. 'Oh, I don't think . . .'

'In this case,' said Edith, 'I believe it might help Nell.'

'Please!' she said.

'Well then, it happened in an instant and he really would have known nothing. We used the horses to transport goods to the combat units at the Frontline, passing through villages that had been destroyed. Sometimes there were ambushes and the Hun threw grenades or turned their machine guns on us. Sometimes houses were in flames and the horses were so frightened we had to put sacks over their heads to get them through.'

'The poor things!' said Pearl.

'The roads were full of shell holes, burned out lorries, smashed wine bottles, broken bicycles and furniture — anything the Hun could use to make it difficult for us to pass.' Private Cameron drew a deep breath. 'We were bringing the horses back to camp in the evening when it happened. I'd been shot in the thigh and was lying on a wagon. We'd fallen behind the others because it hurt my leg when we jolted over the rutted ground. Up ahead, Lucien saw a horse sink into a shell hole full of mud. The poor creature was terrified, struggling and whinnying enough to make a grown man cry. He said to me, 'Arthur, I can't leave it like that. It'll drown.''

'That's so very like Lucien,' said Edith, fumbling for her handkerchief.

'I couldn't help because of my wound,' continued Private Cameron. 'He found some timber and gradually levered the horse out of the mud until it could get its forelegs on firm ground. He wedged a beam under the horse's back end and heaved him up. As the horse scrambled free, I heard the scream of a shell and a deafening explosion. And then . . .' He pinched the bridge of his nose. 'Then Lucien wasn't there anymore.'

There was silence as they visualised the terrible scene.

'There's one more thing,' said Private Cameron. 'Lucien particularly asked me to give you a message, Nell. Twinnie or his other half, he called you.'

'What did he say?' she whispered.

'He knew it would hit you hard if he died. His message was that you mustn't grieve for him. He wanted you to grasp life with both hands and enjoy it enough for two. If you didn't, it would be as if you'd both died.'

Nell let out a sob. 'Did he really say that?'

Private Cameron nodded. 'He was most particular about it. I should be getting along now.' He stood up. 'Thank you for the tea, Mrs Fairchild.' He smiled. 'My mother's waiting for me.'

'Thank you for coming,' said Edith, 'it means a great deal to us.'

'I'll walk with you to the station, Private Cameron,' said Nell. She turned to Edith. 'And on my way home, Mama, I'll call into Polcarrow Farm and speak to Tom.'

★ ★ ★

During the afternoon, Edith was in the hall, talking to Dora, when Dr Gillespie came downstairs after visiting the patients.

'May I have a word, Mrs Fairchild?' he asked. 'Somewhere private.'

'Come into the office.' She led the way.

Dr Gillespie sat down, taking more time than necessary to adjust the trouser creases over his knees. 'I have something to say of a particularly delicate nature,' he said.

'I see,' said Edith, even though she didn't. The poor man looked apprehensive.

'I take patient confidentiality very seriously but, in this particular case, I believe I must inform you of a potentially life-threatening situation.'

'How worrying!'

'Matron asked me to examine your husband.'

'Is his rash infectious?'

'Yes, but let me reassure you that the patients and those who come into contact with him in the usual ways, in conversation or at mealtimes for example, are quite safe.' The expression in his hazel eyes was grave. 'No, it is you who may be the one at risk.'

'Me?'

'I've no intention of prying into private matters but I know Mr Fairchild recently returned from the Western Front.' Dr Gillespie scratched nervously at his neck. 'If I may speak bluntly, I cannot be sure he has your best interests at heart. I must ask if there have been conjugal relations between you since he returned from France?'

Edith felt heat flood her neck and cheeks. 'No, there have not!'

Dr Gillespie let out his breath slowly. 'Then I will say no more, except to warn you that such an event would be extremely unwise. He carries a disease that is transmitted by sexual relations.'

'I promise you, Dr Gillespie, such an event will never occur.' She shuddered at the thought.

'Mr Fairchild must be treated promptly and, as soon as I can arrange it, will spend six weeks in a designated hospital. Without specialist treatment, his life-span will be considerably shortened.'

'But what is his illness?' asked Edith.

'Shall we simply say it's self-inflicted?' He picked up his doctor's bag. 'I'll write a letter today and the hospital will inform Mr Fairchild when there's a bed available.'

After he'd gone, Edith called into Pascal's studio and found him poring over Jasper's sketchbook again. 'Am I disturbing you?'

'Not at all.' He closed the sketchbook.

'Dr Gillespie came to speak to me privately,' she said. 'It was rather an awkward conversation.' She recounted what had passed between them.

Pascal's olive complexion paled. 'I suppose I should not be surprised that Benedict should contract such a disease. When I was working behind the lines in France and Belgium, I saw crowds of soldiers drinking and singing while waiting for the brothels to open.'

'Brothels? But surely Benedict . . .' Edith covered her mouth. 'He caught the pox in a brothel?'

Pascal shrugged.

'Can he be cured?'

'Probably, but the treatment is extremely painful and humiliating.' A hint of a smile curved the corners of his lips. 'Painful enough to make the wickedest of sinners pray for forgiveness and certainly enough to make him think twice before visiting Mademoiselle from Armentières again.'

Chapter 42

February 1919

Cornwall

Pearl went to see if there was a letter from Maxwell and found Benedict muttering under his breath while he leafed through the post on the hall table.

'You'd better hurry if you want any breakfast,' she said. He gave her a baleful stare. His eyes were red-rimmed and he was unshaven. She'd heard him stumbling upstairs late the night before and guessed he'd been drinking in the Golden Lion again.

'Is this all of today's post?' he asked. The reek of stale whisky surrounded him like a cloud.

'There might be another delivery this afternoon.'

'I need to know . . .' He rubbed his eyes. 'I never thought it would come to this.'

Pearl frowned when she saw there were tears on his cheeks. 'What is it, Papa?'

'I'm frightened,' he whispered. 'I've ruined everything. Once I had my health, a wife who adored me and this handsome house. I threw it all away. I've made so many enemies that now nobody cares if I live or die.'

That was true enough but she knew she shouldn't agree with him. Awkwardly, she patted his arm. 'Why don't you go and have a lie down? You'll feel better after a nap.'

'I always had a soft spot for you, Pearl, even if I

377

wasn't the best of fathers.' Sighing heavily, he dropped the envelopes on the table before clumping up the stairs.

She watched him until he was out of sight, wondering what, apart from the drink, might have made him so maudlin. Hastily shuffling through the post, her eyes lit up at the sight of Maxwell's handwriting. She tore open the envelope, read the contents and smiled. Sprinting down the passage, she peeped into the office. 'May I come in, Mama?'

Edith looked up from her desk. 'Of course.'

'It's Maxwell,' said Pearl. 'He wrote ten days ago to say he was leaving France and was on his way home to Gloucestershire. He's staying with his family now but has asked if he might rent the studio again for a month or two after that. Perhaps he's finally going to finish writing his novel?'

Edith smiled. 'Why don't you invite him to stay as our guest?'

'Thank you!' said Pearl. She hesitated in the doorway. 'There's something I forgot to mention. I'd better tell you that he and Papa had a dreadful quarrel before the war.'

'I didn't know they knew each other?'

'Papa tried to cheat Maxwell at cards and wouldn't pay his gambling debt. Maxwell was so angry he had a lawyer draw up an agreement, making Papa promise to settle his debts once he inherited Grandmother Fairchild's house.'

Sighing, Edith rested her head in her hands.

'Do you think Papa will be horribly unpleasant to Maxwell?'

'I'm afraid he's horribly unpleasant to most people,' said Edith, 'but he's expecting an invitation at any moment to go away for a few weeks.'

'Hopefully, he'll be gone by the time Maxwell arrives.'

'He can't leave soon enough for me.' Edith's brow furrowed. 'He's a dreadful influence on Roland.'

Pearl left the office and was in the drawing-room, replying to Maxwell's letter, when Roland came in. 'Where's Papa?' he asked.

'In bed, nursing another hangover.'

His face fell. 'We were going to go down to the cove.'

'I have to go to the village,' said Pearl. 'Why don't you come with me? On the way back we'll sit on the rocks and chat for a while. You can go with Papa another time.'

They wrapped up against the February wind and, after Pearl had posted her letter, made their way back along the coast path until they came to the headland behind Spindrift House.

Roland raced off down the cliff steps and Pearl laughed and called out to him to wait for her.

They plodded over the sand towards the craggy cliffs at the end of the cove.

'Papa and I always sit over there,' said Roland, pointing.

They scrambled over the brow of the tumbled boulders and down the other side to a large, flat rock, sheltered on three sides and sloping down towards the sea in a promontory. Rock pools had formed in the troughs and undulations of the stone, eroded by the ocean over aeons.

'I don't think I've climbed over the top of these rocks for years,' said Pearl. She sat down, leaning against a boulder. 'It looks dangerously slippery by the rock pools. Come and sit by me.'

'At high tide the sea washes over here,' said Roland. 'And do you see? There's a hole where you can glimpse the waves churning underneath. Sometimes water shoots up through it like a geyser.'

'I remember Papa used to bring you down to the cove when you were a tiny tot,' she said. 'I was jealous because I'd been his favourite until you were born. I used to follow him everywhere. And then he left us.'

Roland kicked a fragment of shale and it skittered down towards the surging sea. 'I've often wondered,' he said, 'was it my fault he left?'

'Of course not! I'm afraid he's too selfish to be a good father, though.'

'I was so little when he went that I barely remember it. I like being with him now. Most of the time anyway. He tells me such stories . . . And he's promised to take me on a visit to London.' Roland's voice was full of excited anticipation. 'We're going to a music hall and to smart hotels for dinner and then on to a club . . .' He stopped, looking askance at her in case he'd said too much.

'I'm not sure what Mama would think about that.'

'We shan't tell her because she'd never let me go. But I'll leave her a note,' he said hastily when he saw his sister's disapproval.

'You must ask her permission, Roly.'

'Why?' His expression was mulish. 'I'll be with my father and Ma isn't my real mother.'

'Don't you ever say that!' snapped Pearl. 'Tamsyn had already gone before Papa walked out and left you without a backward glance. Anyone else in her place would have put you in an orphanage, but Mama picked you up and loved you and gave you a home.'

'Yes, I know. And I love Pascal too. It's only that . . .'

380

His hazel eyes were troubled. 'I need to know my real father.'

Pearl pulled him to her side in a fierce hug. 'Be careful, little brother. And another thing: I wouldn't bank on him taking you to London. He's about to go and stay with friends.'

'That can't be right. He promised!'

'Out father is very good at making promises,' said Pearl, 'it's keeping them that's his problem.'

★ ★ ★

A week later, Pearl tied her hair up in a turban and set to work dusting the studio left vacant by Nurse Scott. She hummed to herself as she put clean sheets on the bed, laid a fire in the stove and refilled the oil lamp. Tomorrow morning, before Maxwell arrived, she'd pick a posy of snowdrops for the windowsill.

Closing the door behind her, she glanced up at the gathering clouds racing across the sky. Above the noise of the wind, she heard the sound of an engine. Her heart began to race and then a cream Sunbeam tourer drove into the courtyard. It braked to a halt and Maxwell jumped out.

The next thing she knew, she was in his arms and he was covering her face with kisses. 'Maxwell!' She reached up and pulled off her turban, conscious she was in old clothes and not the pretty skirt and blouse she'd planned to wear when he arrived. 'I wasn't expecting you until tomorrow!'

'I couldn't wait,' he said. 'Mother shooed me off. She said I was like a cat on a hot tin roof and I'd better come and see you straight away. She sends her best wishes, by the way.'

'We've written to each other a few times.'

He smiled. 'It pleased me when she said you'd become friends sitting by my hospital bed.'

'We were terribly worried for you.' Pearl reached up to touch his cheek. 'But you look well now.'

'I am. After the hostilities ceased, there was nothing for me to do except fill in forms and try to keep the remaining men occupied until they were demobilised.'

'Come in out of the cold.'

'There's so much I must say to you,' said Maxwell. He took her hand as they crossed the courtyard to the house.

Pearl opened the back door and then hesitated. 'I was so pleased to see you I forgot something,' she said, a shadow blighting her happiness. 'My father's here.'

'But you wrote to say he was going to stay with friends?'

'He is, but not until tomorrow.'

Maxwell shrugged. 'I suppose I'll have to face him sometime. We've business matters to conclude but there's something I absolutely must do first. I want to tell you something. Perhaps we could make ourselves scarce and have dinner at the Golden Lion?'

'That's where Papa spends his evenings.' She didn't like to say he came home drunk every night.

Once inside, Pearl asked Anneliese to bring them tea in the drawing-room.

Maxwell went over to the window. 'I've dreamed of this view so often while I was away,' he said. 'I used to imagine you walking across the lawn, holding out your hand to me.'

Standing beside him, she looked out at the turbulent sea. 'Even when a storm is brewing, it's beautiful,

382

isn't it?'

He tipped up her chin with his thumb. 'But never as beautiful as you.' He bent his head and kissed her softly.

Anneliese, carrying a tea tray, pushed open the door, followed by Roland.

Pearl hastily drew away from Maxwell.

'Hello, young fellow!' he said.

'I heard your motor,' said Roland. 'Have you quite recovered?'

'Pretty well. I'll have to live with some shrapnel in my arm and chest but it doesn't cause me too much bother.'

Pearl poured tea and sliced the Victoria sponge. 'Will you excuse me a moment? My clothes are dusty from cleaning the studio and I'd like to change.'

She ran upstairs to wash, putting on a navy skirt and her favourite blouse with the ruffled collar before hurrying down again.

The drawing-room door stood ajar and Benedict's raised voice came from within. She halted, her heart sinking.

'What do you mean, you've come to see Pearl?' snapped her father. 'I won't have you sniffing around my daughter, Fforbes. Now clear off before I kick you out.'

'Are you threatening me?' asked Maxwell, mildly.

'Bloody right, I am! You're a liar and a cheat.'

'You're confused, Fairchild. It's you who is the liar and the cheat. Don't you remember, I caught you using marked cards? Twice.'

Pearl peered uneasily through the doorway.

Roland, wide-eyed, was watching the two men glaring at each other.

'I won't have you in my house,' yelled Benedict, his complexion an alarming shade of puce.

'Your house? There's still the matter of the large sum of money you owe me. I have your promissory note, remember? It's tied up nice and tight by my lawyer because I know you rarely honour your debts like a gentleman. You've had five years either to pay me what you owe me, with interest, or else hand over your sixty percent share of Spindrift in full and final settlement. The five years are up and I have plans drawn up and ready to convert Spindrift into a luxury hotel.'

Pearl caught her breath in confusion. Spindrift, a hotel?

'Papa?' said Roland.

'I shall contest it,' said Benedict through gritted teeth. 'I'm going away tomorrow but you'll be hearing from my lawyer.' He shouldered Maxwell out of the way and Pearl shrank back as he strode from the room.

'Papa?' Roland ran after him. 'You are taking me with you when you go, aren't you?'

'What are you talking about, you stupid boy?' Benedict ignored Roland's stricken expression and marched down the corridor with his son at his heels.

Pearl was torn between compassion for Roland and anger at Maxwell. Anger won. She stormed into the drawing-room. 'You've deceived me all this time!' she cried. 'When you very first came here and visited the gallery, it was nothing more than to spy on us, wasn't it? I should have known you were lying to me when you came here later with that stupid story about writing a novel.' She put her hands on her hips. 'How did you imagine your plans for Spindrift would go down with the community? Or don't you care about us at all?' Her voice broke as she choked back tears. 'How could you, Maxwell? I trusted you.' The words I loved you hung unspoken in the air between them.

'Pearl!' He stepped towards her.

'Don't touch me,' she hissed. She backed away and ran along the passage. The back door was open, banging in the wind. Roland must have gone out that way.

She sprinted down the garden, the damp grass soaking her best shoes. On the headland, wind buffeted her ears and whipped strands of hair against her cheeks. There, down in the cove, Benedict was striding towards the rocks, with Roland darting along beside him.

Taking the cliff steps two at a time, Pearl's palm burned as she ran it down the rope handrail. At the foot of the cliff, she ploughed over the dunes. The tide was in and the ocean was heaving and pounding the shoreline, spewing great clumps of seaweed onto the sand. Gulls screamed overhead in the lowering sky. She hurtled along on the hard, wet strip by the waterline, dodging sideways whenever a belligerent wave attempted to submerge her ankles.

Ahead, Benedict and Roland clambered over the summit of the rocks. She hurried after them and scrambled down the other side until her feet reached the rocky plateau.

Roland and Benedict were shouting and gesticulating at each other on the promontory. The wind buffeted them and the sea flung itself against the rocks, drenching them with spray.

'You promised me!' yelled Roland. 'You said we'd go to London together. Why do you always have to lie?

I'm your son. Don't you love me at all?' His cheeks were flushed and tear-stained and his black hair wild in the wind.

'I can't take you with me where I'm going,' shouted Benedict over the roar of the ocean.

'Everything's all about what you want, isn't it? You drove my real mother away and you've made our whole family unhappy. You're poisonous!' Sobbing, Roland ran at his father and battered frenziedly at his chest with his fists.

A wave gushed over the rock and a gigantic spurt of water shot up into the air like a geyser, knocking Roland over. He fell to his knees, scrabbling for a foothold amongst the slippery seaweed. Another colossal wave surged over the rock.

Pearl screamed as it engulfed her brother and swept him into the angry sea. His wet head, as dark and sleek as a seal's, appeared briefly and then disappeared below the seething foam. Keening, she scuttled to the edge of the promontory. Roland surfaced again on the rising water and stretched his hand towards her. Frantic, she reached out until their fingertips touched for a heartbeat before the wave receded and tore him way.

Benedict stood motionless beside her, frowning at the churning sea as if in a trance.

'Papa!' Pearl shook his arm violently. 'I can't reach Roly. You must save him!'

He blinked. 'Where is he?'

'There!'

Roland rose up again on the ocean swell and Benedict leaned forward to grab his hand. A wave smacked against his legs and soaked Pearl to the waist. Before her father could regain his balance, another surge

386

tossed him into the boiling sea.

Pearl gave a high-pitched cry of terror.

Benedict's head bobbed amongst the waves. Coughing, he thrashed at the swirling water, caught Roland by his hair and pulled his face clear of the water.

'Get him to me!' shouted Pearl.

A wave lifted Benedict high and he grimaced, the cords straining in his neck as he made a supreme effort to thrust his son up onto the rock.

Pearl gripped Roland's shoulders and called upon every ounce of her strength to haul his legs out of the water and drag him out of the reach of the tide. He moaned and she winced at the sight of blood oozing from his forehead and lacerated body. 'Roly, I'm coming back in a minute,' she shouted and slid herself to the tip of the promontory on hands and knees.

Benedict clung to the rocks, his fingers bone white from the effort. The sea seethed around him. She kneeled down to grab his collar, gasping as an icy jet of spray hit her in the face.

'Help me!' he gasped. He spluttered as another wave washed over him.

Pearl dragged at his clothing but the rocks were slippery and she couldn't get a firm foothold. She whimpered when she realised he was too heavy for her to pull out of the water.

Benedict was choking on a mouthful of seawater. His fingers slipped from their grip on the rocks. Panicking, he flailed at the water as he struggled for breath. His lips were blue.

'Give me your hand!' Pearl cried.

He reached out to her but he'd drifted too far away. 'Swim towards me!'

He kicked his legs, disappeared beneath a wave

then surfaced again. He looked up at Pearl with terror in his eyes as the current drew him inexorably away. And then he disappeared beneath the waves.

'Papa!' Pearl stared at the water, desperately her heart pounding as she willed him to re-emerge. Dread and anger swelled inside her until she felt as if she might split open like a rotten plum. The sea pounded endlessly against the rocks but, wherever she looked, there was no sign of her father. After what felt like a lifetime, she lost hope and turned away.

Soaked through and shivering uncontrollably, she returned to Roly. He lay exactly as she'd left him, except that blood had pooled on the rock around his head. Calling his name, she smoothed the hair off his face, but he remained motionless. Pressing her ear to his chest, she detected no movement, heard no heart-beat. Gathering him into her arms, she rocked him against her chest, willing him to breathe. He didn't stir and she turned her face up to the heavens and howled.

Chapter 43

The following morning, Edith tiptoed into her daughters' bedroom. There was just enough light creeping through the gap in the curtains for her to see that both girls were still asleep. She sat on the chair between their beds, folded her hands on her lap and waited.

It had been almost dark by the time Maxwell had staggered into the house holding Roland's dripping body in his arms. He'd laid him on the sofa in the drawing-room, then roared off in his motorcar to fetch Doctor Gillespie and the police sergeant. Pearl, her eyes unfocused and her whole body trembling violently, had collapsed on the floor beside her brother, incoherent with grief and shock. Lily had helped Edith put her to bed and Matron gave her a sleeping powder.

Edith had been too distressed to sleep after the doctor and the police sergeant had left. Pascal tried to hug her but she'd pushed him away. It felt indecent somehow, when her husband, estranged or not, was lost somewhere out there in the immense vault of the tempestuous sea. The wind had howled all night and she'd stared dry-eyed out of the window into the darkness, imagining Benedict's body battered against the rocks or dragged down to lie alone on the ocean floor.

She remembered that first day she met him and how he'd dazzled her. Handsome and as charismatic as a Greek god, he'd only to look at her with laughter in his eyes to make her melt. But it hadn't been long before the golden vision grew tarnished and Benedict became her nemesis. He'd wounded her heart and her mind innumerable times since then and his very existence had prevented her from marrying Pascal, the love of her life. She was astonished she didn't feel an enormous sense of relief at her husband's passing. Instead, she felt only sorrow for the man she'd once loved and who had fathered three of her precious children.

Pearl sighed and turned over. Then she sat bolt upright with a sudden cry.

'It's all right,' murmured Edith. 'I'm here.' She sat on the edge of the bed and put her arm around her daughter.

'Oh, Mama!' Pearl clung to her like a limpet.

Nell woke, too, and sat at her sister's other side.

After a while, Edith said gently, 'Pearl, can you tell me now what happened?'

She looked up, her eyes brimming. 'Roly was angry with Papa who'd promised to take him on a trip to London but changed his mind. They were fighting on a rocky promontory when a huge wave swept Roly into the sea. I couldn't reach him . . . I tried.'

'Oh, Pearl!' Edith hugged her tightly. 'It might have taken you, too!'

'What about Papa?' asked Nell.

Pearl explained what had happened next. 'He went into the water and hauled Roly over to me. Together, we got him onshore. Then I tried to help Papa back up but the tide was too strong. It swept him out of reach and I couldn't save him.' She gave a strangled sob. 'I watched him sink beneath the waves.'

Edith felt as if a giant hand had reached inside her and squeezed her heart.

'Then Maxwell came,' wept Pearl. 'He carried poor Roly's body back to the house.'

'His body?' said Nell. 'But Roly isn't dead!'

Pearl lifted her head. 'He wasn't breathing. Maxwell pressed on his chest and water spurted out of his mouth, but he didn't speak or move. And then Maxwell had him over his shoulder in a fireman's lift and carried him home.'

'Roly was unconscious from banging his head,' said Edith. 'He's swallowed a lot of seawater but Maxwell pushed most of it out of his lungs. Dr Gillespie says Roly's had a lucky escape.'

Pearl burst into noisy tears and Edith held her until she stopped crying. 'Peep into his bedroom and say hello, if you like.'

'He's really still alive?'

'I sat beside him all night,' said Edith, 'and when I left him an hour ago, he was snoring like a trooper.'

★ ★ ★

Later, after Pearl had reassured herself that her brother was indeed asleep and not dead, Edith insisted she breakfasted in bed and rested until eleven o'clock when the police sergeant was coming to hear her version of events.

Edith looked in on Roland and found he was awake.

He sat up and she stroked his hair, still stiff with seawater, while he wept. At last, he drew a deep breath. 'Papa died trying to save me, didn't he? So he must have loved me after all.'

'Of course he did. He loved you very much, Roly,' she said, kissing his forehead.

When the police sergeant arrived, Edith held Pearl's

391

hand while she recounted what had happened. After the policeman had written it all down in his notebook, Edith closed the front door behind him.

Maxwell was hovering in the hall, waiting to speak to her.

'How is Pearl?' he asked.

'Still shocked. She thought Roland had drowned too. The coastguard hasn't found Benedict's body yet. There'll be an inquest.'

'May I see Pearl now?'

'Of course. Would you like time alone with her?'

'I think . . .' Frowning, Maxwell jingled some coins in his pocket. 'She's angry with me.'

'Angry? But you saved her brother!'

'She overheard me arguing with Benedict before she ran after Roland. There's something important I need to explain to both of you.'

'Come into the drawing-room then,' said Edith. She led the way.

'How are you, Pearl?' asked Maxwell. Gingerly, he perched on the sofa beside her.

Recoiling from him, she folded her arms defensively. 'How do you think I am?' Her expression was stony. 'Oh, of course, I suppose I must be properly grateful to you for saving Roland.'

'Pearl!' Edith was shocked and embarrassed. 'Why so ungracious?'

'You don't know what he's done — what he's going to do to us.'

'Please,' said Maxwell, 'let me explain.'

'Explain what?' said Pearl, her eyes flashing. 'Explain that, by misrepresenting yourself, you befriended me and sweet-talked me into drawing up plans of Spindrift House for you? Plans you then used to further

392

your ambition to turn this house into a hotel.'

'Whatever do you mean?' asked Edith.

'I heard him telling Papa.' Pearl turned back to Maxwell. 'You must have planned to rid yourself of the community in some underhand way, to enable you to carry out your conniving scheme.'

'Pearl, stop!' commanded Edith. 'Maxwell, I apologise. My daughter is still shocked. In any case, you must know Spindrift House is part-owned by the community?'

'But more than half was Papa's,' said Pearl, not giving Maxwell a chance to speak.

'There's a will stating he'll leave it equally to all his children,' said Edith.

'But Papa agreed to give Spindrift to Maxwell as payment for gambling debts.'

There was an unpleasant fluttery feeling inside Edith's stomach as she stared at Maxwell. 'You're part-owner of Spindrift House now?'

He nodded. 'I came here five years ago to assure myself the house was worth as much as the debt because I intended to sell it. I visited the gallery and bought one of your lovely watercolours. I treasure it still.'

'I remember that when you rented the studio, you mentioned you'd been to visit the gallery before,' said Edith, 'but you never said anything about Benedict.'

'Of course I didn't,' said Maxwell. 'I wasn't sure then if he'd come into his inheritance and repay the debt.'

'Why didn't you tell me?' said Pearl.

'I didn't expect to fall in love with Spindrift House.' He glanced at Pearl's resentful expression. 'Or with you.'

'I won't listen to any more of your lies!'

'But you couldn't have made Spindrift into a hotel while the community inhabited it,' said Edith. Unease ran down her spine. Was Pearl right? Could he find a way to force them to leave?

'All I knew was that I passionately wanted to live here,' said Maxwell. 'I imagined it as a discreetly elegant hotel where discerning guests would be able to enjoy the tranquil atmosphere and leave feeling supremely refreshed. I intended to buy out the community for a sum it would be impossible to refuse.'

'No sum would be enough,' said Pearl. 'It's our home and you shan't push us out!'

'I have no intention of pushing you out,' said Maxwell, indignation written across his face. 'Besides, although I still believe Spindrift would make a superb hotel at some time in the future, I have a much better idea for now.'

'We don't want to hear it.'

'Pearl, please.' He turned to Edith. 'May I tell you what I have in mind?'

She pressed her palms to her burning cheeks. Reluctantly, she nodded.

'Spindrift is falling into disrepair and needs considerable investment.'

'You think I don't know that?' said Edith defensively. 'The war ate away our savings.'

'When I was wounded,' he said, 'all I could think of was that I needed to be at Spindrift so that I could heal. I was right. It's not only the sea air. The house seems to embrace you when you enter. It's a natural safe haven and those are very rare. I spent a lot of time talking to the other patients while I was convalescing here and they all felt the same. And I saw

394

how those suffering from shellshock were soothed by the wonderful care they received here.' He leaned his elbows on his knees as he continued to speak earnestly. 'I know what it feels like to be trapped in some God-forsaken trench, ears being pounded, hour after hour, day after day, by deafening explosions and continuous rounds of machine-gun fire.' He shuddered.

Pearl caught her breath.

'I've been lucky,' said Maxwell. 'Apart from the nightmares, I've put the war behind me now, but there are thousands of men whose minds remain locked in that terrifying experience. It definitely isn't over for them.'

'But the right care may help?' said Edith, sensing what he was going to say.

'Exactly!' He glanced at Pearl. 'What if Spindrift became a private nursing home for such patients?'

'But it's an artists' community,' she said.

'Pascal's art classes were very therapeutic for the patients while I was here.' Maxwell's voice was full of enthusiasm. 'Why couldn't Spindrift take a few fee-paying residents while at the same time running the gallery, the workshop and studios? Patients benefited from working in the kitchen garden too. Matron and Lily, with the assistance of Dr Gillespie, could manage any nursing care. Dora and Ursula have already proved they're excellent quartermasters. For my part, I'd invest in the buildings, pay the staff and deal with the financial side of the business.'

'But the community could remain living and working here?' asked Edith.

'The community is the beating heart of Spindrift House,' said Maxwell. 'Without it, my scheme might not work.' He looked at Pearl, her fingers twisting

395

together in her lap. 'I'm sorry I deceived you about writing a book,' he said. 'I was on the point of telling you about my plan for the hotel but then I took a commission and everything changed.'

'I wish you had told me,' she said.

'I didn't want to risk upsetting the community when there was a strong possibility I'd never return from the war. When I arrived yesterday, the first thing I said to you was that I had business matters to conclude but I had something important to tell you first. But then Benedict accosted me and set in chain the terrible events that followed. Can you ever forgive me?'

Slowly, Pearl nodded, her eyes brimming with tears.

Edith stood up. 'Stay here, both of you. I'm going to call a community meeting.' She left the room, closing the door softly behind her, but not before she saw Maxwell take Pearl in his arms.

Half an hour later, the community, very subdued, gathered in the drawing-room.

Edith stood up. 'We're all concerned that it's been impossible to maintain Spindrift properly during the war. Maxwell, however, has a proposal to put to you.'

He took the floor and explained his plan. The community bombarded him with questions but agreed there was merit in the idea. Matron was called in to see if she might remain after the Red Cross withdrew the following month.

'It's a splendid idea,' she said. 'If we take only a dozen patients at a time, they'll benefit from the family atmosphere but there'll still be plenty of space for artistic pursuits.' She smiled. 'I can't tell you how much I'd like to stay.'

'And I'd love to continue working here, too,' said Lily.

396

'Then, once the legal issues are resolved,' said Maxwell, 'I'll start the refurbishments. Apart from the roof repairs, we need more bathrooms and a generator for electric light.' He glanced at Pearl. 'I'm hoping to persuade you to advise me on the redecoration.'

The hum of excited conversation swelled and Edith smiled to herself when she noticed that Maxwell and her daughter were holding hands.

Pascal sat a few feet away from Edith. He looked up and caught her eye. She regretted pushing him away when he'd tried to comfort her last night but her thoughts were still too muddled for her to explain herself.

As soon as the community dispersed, she slipped away to the quiet haven of her studio.

Chapter 44

In the morning, the police sergeant called once more and Edith received him in the drawing-room.

'I'm sorry to tell you, ma'am, that a body was retrieved from the sea early today. I've reason to believe it's Mr Fairchild's and I must ask you to come with me to make an identification.'

Maxwell drove her to the police house where the body lay in a cell on a trestle table.

The police sergeant folded back the covering sheet.

There was a cut on Benedict's temple. Edith touched her fingers to his waxen cheek. It was deathly cold. A memory surfaced in her mind of their honeymoon in France. He was dozing on the grass in the sunshine, a hat pulled over his eyes. She'd caressed his cheek and he'd woken with a start. Laughing, he'd pulled her on top of him and kissed her, his mouth hot with sun and desire. 'I love you, Edith,' he'd whispered.

But that was in the brief time before everything went terribly wrong between them.

The police sergeant cleared his throat.

'Yes,' said Edith. 'This is my husband, Benedict Fairchild.' She turned away, a lump of grief and regret rising in her throat.

★ ★ ★

That afternoon, she called into Pascal's studio. He was leafing through Jasper's sketchbook again.

'They've found Benedict's body,' she said.

398

He took a step towards her, then came to a standstill.

'I'm sorry, Pascal,' she said. 'I was curt with you when you tried to comfort me before.'

He shrugged. 'You don't have to explain. Roland nearly died and Benedict is gone. You must have time to grieve for the man you once loved.'

'I'm so confused,' she said. 'After all the misery he caused, I never imagined I might feel sad. But I need to mourn Benedict before we . . .'

'I have waited more than half my life to make you mine,' said Pascal. 'I will wait as long as I must.'

'Thank you.'

'Perhaps it would help you to keep busy and have something to look forward to? The gallery opens in four months. We might begin to plan the Unsung Heroes exhibition?'

Edith nodded. 'I'd like that. There are Julian's photographs to exhibit and I wondered about asking Mr Rosenberg if I might borrow the portraits of the factory girls. We should include Jasper's sketchbook, too.

'And his portraits of Anneliese and Blanche.' Pascal untied the ribbons of Jasper's portfolio and they laid out his drawings on the trestle table.

'Perhaps later on we might take the exhibition to London?' she said.

Pascal smiled sadly. 'I agree. I want the world to see our son's talent.'

Heads bent over Jasper's treasured drawings, they discussed which ones they'd frame.

'This sketch of Blanche is rendered with such a delicate touch,' said Pascal, holding it up.

The door creaked open. Edith glanced up and froze, gripped by fright.

Pascal turned to see why she was staring.

A soldier stood in the doorway. His face was gaunt and his body emaciated but his dark eyes glittered with tears of joy.

The drawing drifted to the floor and Pascal let out a harsh cry. 'Mon fils!'

Jasper opened his arms wide and ran to embrace his parents.

*

Later, Edith wiped the tearstains from her face and went into the drawing-room where Pearl was reading to Private Tompkins, the last remaining patient. 'I'm sorry to interrupt,' she said. 'Pearl, would you fetch Nell and Roland and come to the sitting-room as quickly as you can?'

Her daughter looked at her curiously. 'Are you all right?'

'Never better.' Edith hurried away to the kitchen, where Blanche was making jam tarts under Mrs Rowe's watchful eye. 'Anneliese,' said Edith, 'please will you bring tea for six . . .' she hesitated '. . . no, seven, to the sitting-room? And some cake or bread and butter.'

'Yes, madame.'

'Bring Blanche with you, too.'

In the sitting-room, Pascal and Jasper were sitting side by side when she joined them.

'Mama,' said Jasper, 'Pascal told me what happened to Benedict. Despite everything, it must have been a dreadful shock to you.'

Edith nodded. 'Pearl and Roland are very upset.'

A moment later they heard footsteps in the hall.

400

Pearl opened the door and Nell and Roland followed her in.

Jasper stood up and there was silence for a heartbeat before the tears and laughter began.

'We thought you were dead!' said Nell, her voice muffled against his shoulder.

'So did I,' said Jasper. He took a flat metal box from his breast pocket and held it out. 'Do you see this?' He pointed to a dent. 'Mama and Pascal sent me this tin of pencils. I always carried it in my breast pocket and this dent is where a bullet bounced off it, instead of lodging in my heart.'

'But what happened?' asked Roland. 'Where were you?

'Sit down and he'll explain,' said Edith.

Jasper waited until they were all settled. 'It was dawn,' he said, 'and the whistle blew and we scrambled over the top of the trench into No Man's Land. Shells exploded all around, showering me with earth and . . .' He glanced at Edith. 'Men were screaming and falling to the ground. I gripped my rifle and ran, head down. It was foggy and I couldn't see far ahead but I was frightened I'd fall into a shell crater. Then there was an almighty explosion and I was thrown up in the air. Everything went dark.'

'Were you wounded?' asked Pearl.

'Not badly. I came round and found myself being dragged over the ground. My head hurt and I thought, That's lucky, the stretcher bearers are going to take me somewhere safe. Then I realised the men carrying me away were speaking German.'

Edith reached for Pascal's hand.

'Several of us were captured and herded behind enemy lines. Two soldiers with machine-guns guarded

401

us and we sat on our tin hats to keep off the mud. Eventually we were prodded into formation. We marched for two days until we came to the prisoner-of-war camp and were locked in a compound with hundreds of other men because there wasn't room for us all in the huts.' He shuddered. 'It was a bitterly cold February. Over the following week, men died every night.'

'Infamie!' said Pascal.

Jasper shrugged. 'The Germans divided us into work parties and we were marched off every day to dig gravel for roads or to lay railway tracks. Slave labour really, and our numbers dwindled daily. We never had enough to eat, only a small chunk of black bread and a spoonful of sauerkraut a day. Then a group of us were put on a train and we travelled for days. Six of us were escorted to a farm and left there. The farmer carried a rifle when we were working in the fields but we didn't see any soldiers. We had a cramped hut in the yard but at least the food was better.' He smiled. 'Mostly potatoes.'

'But I searched for your name on the lists of all the internment camps,' said Pascal.

'Some of us were never registered,' said Jasper. 'We were deep in the country, a village called Celle. One day, two of us were delivering sacks of potatoes to the station. When a train arrived there one day, an Englishman leaned out of the window. He recognised our uniforms and asked what we were doing there. I said we worked on a farm as prisoners and he told us the war had been over for more than two months.'

'And you'd not been set free!' exclaimed Nell.

Jasper shook his head. 'I gave the man our names and the name of the farm and he said he'd pass it on to the authorities. Two weeks later we got letters with a railway warrant to travel to Hamelin. There was a camp there and we were given a bath and hot soup and the next day put on another train to Holland.' He beamed at them. 'And here I am.'

'But no one thought to let us know you'd been found?' said Edith.

'I was told they'd send a telegram,' said Jasper. 'No wonder you looked as if you'd seen a ghost when I arrived!'

The door opened and Anneliese came in with the tea tray, Blanche behind her.

Jasper rose to his feet, his face lit with joy.

Anneliese faltered and the cups and saucers rattled so hard, he had to take the tray from her and put it on the table.

Blanche let out a guttural cry and launched herself at him. He lifted her up and she threw her arms around his neck.

He dropped a kiss on her blonde head. 'So, you've missed me, have you?'

'We have been waiting for you for so very long time!'

Edith stared at the little girl in astonishment. 'Today,' she said, 'I really do believe miracles can happen.'

Chapter 45

May 1920

Cornwall

On her wedding morning, Edith stood before the mirror. Slowly, she untied her dressing gown and let it fall open over her naked body. She studied her reflection impartially, as she would an artist's model. Her breasts were full and shapely still, her stomach more rounded than in her youth but her waist remained narrow. There were streaks of silver in her black hair but soon she would be fifty and they were only to be expected.

Turning away from the mirror, she put on her new crepe-de-Chine underwear. She was adjusting the seams of her stockings when there was a tap at the door and Pearl came in, followed by Nell carrying a breakfast tray.

'Good morning, Mama!' Pearl, married to Maxwell for a year, was expecting her first child.

'I've brought tea and toast,' said Nell, 'and we've come to help you dress.'

Edith slipped on her dressing gown and sat at the table with them.

'Dora and Ursula are putting the final touches to the flower arrangements,' said Pearl. 'And Clarissa, Wilfred and Augustus are making sure everything's ready in the gallery for the reception.'

'Have you seen Pascal?' asked Edith.

'He was with Jasper, talking to Grandfather,' said Pearl.

'How I wish Lucien were here for this special day,' said Nell, her expression wistful. 'He would be so happy that Jasper came home to us.'

Edith nodded, tears starting to her eyes.

'Let's dress you in your finery, Mama,' said Nell. She smiled. 'It doesn't seem two minutes since Tom and I tied the knot and you were helping me with my veil.'

There was to be no elaborate long dress with a train of Brussels lace veil for Edith's second wedding. She stepped into the simple calf-length column of eau-de-Nil silk with a cowl neck and fashionable dropped waist. Pearl did up the row of tiny satin-covered buttons down the back.

Nell fetched the long rope of pearls that Edith's father had given her and placed them around her mother's neck.

Edith tied them in a loose knot between her breasts. Pascal had forbidden her ever to cut her hair. Now she twisted it up in a thick coil and secured it with pins. 'Fetch my hat from the dresser, will you, Nell?' She placed the finely woven straw hat on her head, adjusted the angle and secured it with a pearl hatpin. The same colour as her dress, the eau-de-Nil shade intensified the green of her eyes.

Pearl fetched the ivory satin shoes and Nell kneeled to do up the buttons on the delicate ankle straps. Finally, the young women stood back to study the result.

'You look beautiful, Mama!'

'So elegant!'

Edith drew a deep breath. 'I never imagined this

day would come.'

The grandfather clock on the landing chimed the hour.

Nell handed her a bouquet of ivory roses interspersed with dark green myrtle. 'It's time,' she said.

★ ★ ★

An hour later, Edith and her father walked up the path to St Endellion's Church.

'Ready?' he asked.

She smiled. 'I've been ready for twenty-eight years.'

He kissed her forehead. 'All the best things in life are worth waiting for.'

They stepped from the sunshine into the shadowy church. Previously subdued organ music rose to a crescendo to herald the arrival of the bride. Edith processed up the aisle on her father's arm. The church was decorated with great bunches of white azaleas and their sweet perfume mingled with the musty odour of ancient hymnbooks. She smiled at her friends and family, catching glimpses of Dora's freckled face and Ursula in a new hat. Clarissa looked elegant in blue silk with Rose, Julian, Will and his wife, Cora beside her. Augustus and Wilfred nodded approvingly as she passed them. Nell and Tom, Pearl and Maxwell sat with Roland in the front pew, smiling back at her. Blanche waved at Edith and Anneliese caught her daughter's hand and hugged her to her side.

And there was Pascal, darkly handsome, waiting for her at the foot of the altar steps. Jasper, his father's best man, stood at his side. Sunlight flooded through the clear glass of the high arched window above the altar and bathed them both in its shining benediction.

Edith's heart swelled with happiness. She smiled radiantly at Pascal and stepped forward, into the light.

Historical Note

Letting in the Light explores the era that dramatically changed life for so many in Britain. The Great War was all-consuming, 'the war to end all wars', and fought on a scale that hadn't been seen in living memory. It tore families apart, forcing the men into the great maw of the war machine and spitting only some of them out at the other end. It seemed as if a large proportion of a whole generation was lost, and those who did manage to return home would never be quite the same again.

While writing this story, my focus was on what it was like for the women left alone to fight their own battles on the home front. Men had always assumed that their wives, daughters and sisters were fragile little flowers who needed protection, but these women proved to be tougher than they'd appeared. Most stepped up magnificently to the challenge of taking on the essential roles that men had vacated.

Before the war, suffragettes had been condemned as disruptive and unfeminine, never as female warriors attempting to redress the inequalities forced upon them by society. When war broke out, however, they agreed to a cease-fire on their civil disruption campaign and set to work to demonstrate what they could achieve while there were so few able-bodied men at home. And their help was very badly needed. Women workers filled shipyards, steelyards and factories. They packed gunpowder into grenades, cigarettes into packets, learned how to rivet sheet metal, became tram drivers and ticket collectors on the trains. Women worked on the farms, digging potatoes, milking cows and turning the manure pile. They were paid less than half of a man's customary wage for their efforts.

The invention of the typewriter enabled a more genteel occupation for middle-class girls, soon to replace the armies of male clerks who had enlisted. The horrific losses suffered on the battlefields meant that women were quickly allowed to take up positions as nurses, ambulance drivers and even doctors, becoming indispensable to the medical services.

Grandmothers and married women with young children who couldn't work full-time formed a vast volunteer network, knitting socks and scarves and packing them into boxes together with cigarettes, chocolate, fruitcakes and combs as 'soldiers' comforts'. They organised Red Cross and other groups to train girls how to bandage wounds and cook meals for convalescents.

Many women relished the opportunity of learning new skills and, once the war was over, few wished to return to what had often been the only choices previously: being a biddable wife and bearing children for their husbands or else accepting the poor pay and overwork that was a servant's lot.

After the war, the men who did return wanted their jobs back. Women were expected to keep to the home again, even if they were war widows who needed to support their children. However, in recognition of the wartime service women had given their country, those over thirty were awarded the vote in 1918, but it wasn't until 1928 that all women received this as of right.

* * *

To read more about the historical background of
the Spindrift Trilogy, please visit
www.charlottebetts.co.uk

Other titles published by Ulverscroft:

THE FADING OF THE LIGHT

Charlotte Betts

Cornwall, 1902. Edith Fairchild, deserted by her feckless husband Benedict eight years before, has established the thriving Spindrift artists' community by the sea and found deep and lasting love with Pascal. They have accepted that they cannot marry, but when Benedict returns unexpectedly to Spindrift House, all Edith and Pascal's secret hopes and dreams of a joyous life together are overturned. Benedict's arrival shatters the peaceful and creative atmosphere of the close-knit community. When Edith will not allow him back into her bed, the conflict escalates and he sets in motion a chain of tragic events that reverberate down the years and threatens the happiness of the community forever . . .